The
Doctor's
Lady

Books by Jody Hedlund

The Preacher's Bride
The Doctor's Lady

The
Doctor's
Lady

JODY HEDLUND

BETHANYHOUSEPUBLISHERS

Minneapolis, Minnesota

Published by Bethany House Publishers
11400 Hampshire Avenue South
Bloomington, Minnesota 55438
www.bethanyhouse.com

Cover design by Jennifer Parker
Cover photography by Kevin White Photography, Minneapolis
Author is represented by the literary agency of WordServe Literary Group.

Bethany House Publishers is a division of
Baker Publishing Group, Grand Rapids, Michigan

Printed in the United States of America

Library of Congress Cataloging-in-Publication Data
Hedlund, Jody.
    The doctor's lady / Jody Hedlund.
        p.   cm.
    ISBN 978-0-7642-0833-1 (pbk.)
        1. Missionaries—Fiction. 2. United States—History—19th century—Fiction. I. Title.
PS3608.E333D63 2011
813'.6—dc22   2011025216

Scripture quotations are from the King James Version of the Bible.

To my husband

For believing in my dream, for traveling beside me each step of the journey, and for supporting me in every way possible.

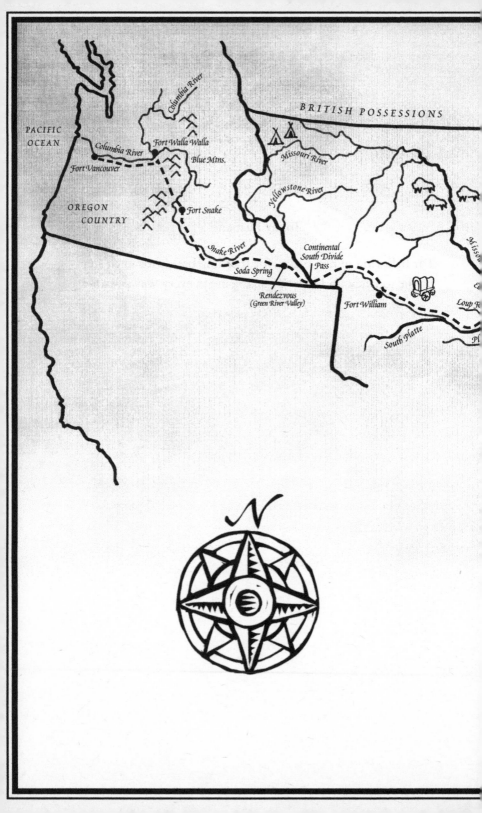

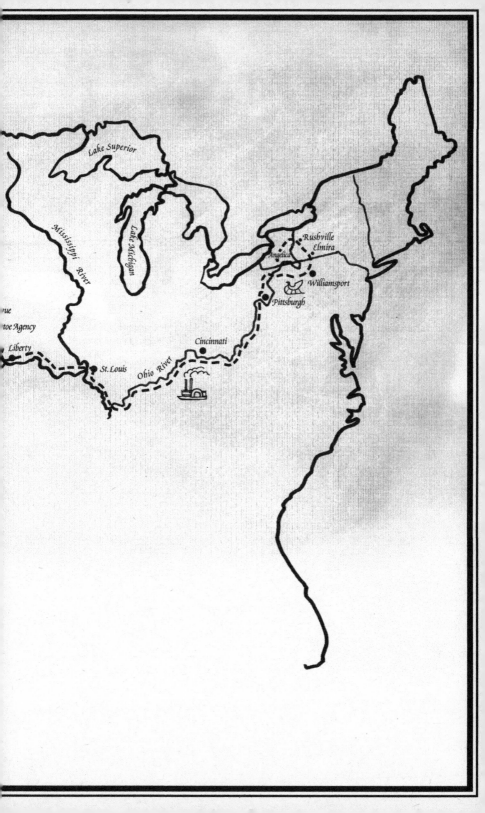

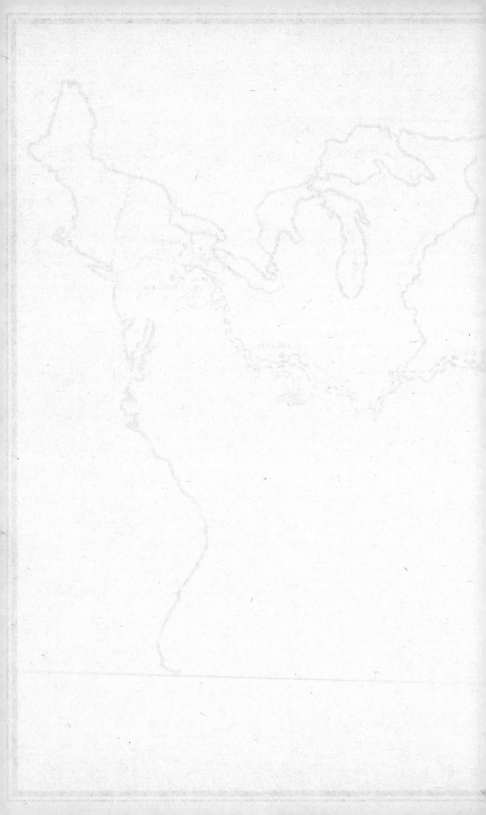

Chapter
I

*I*ndians!"

The sharp call from the back of the sanctuary jolted Priscilla White. She sucked in a breath and twisted in the pew.

"Two of them!" shouted someone else.

Additional cries of alarm erupted around her, and Priscilla strained to see the entrance of the church above the heads of the congregants behind her.

Mary Ann's fingers bit into her arm.

Priscilla patted her younger sister's hand and rose from the hard bench just enough to get a glimpse of the wide-open double doors. Sure enough, two Indian boys stalked inside.

"What shall we do?" Mary Ann tugged her. "Should we hide?"

"Oh, shush now." Priscilla squeezed her sister's hand and tried to stop the trembling of her own. "They're just boys."

The two lean youth started down the aisle with long, confident strides. Their braids dangled with beads and shells that clinked together. The fierce blackness of their eyes captivated her, and she couldn't look away, even though staring broke the rules of etiquette.

With each step they took, they drew nearer the front pew where she sat with her family, and her heart pattered harder against her chest. Why were they here? What could they possibly want?

Next to her, Mary Ann shrank into the wooden seat as much as her hugely pregnant frame would allow.

The boys' fringed leggings swished and their breechcloths flapped in cadence.

Priscilla forced herself to sit straighter, to not shrivel like her sister. The taller boy's dark eyes slid to Priscilla for the briefest instant, and she was sure he could hear the rapid thumping inside her.

The air in their wake carried the scent of melted animal fat and charred meat. She pressed a gloved hand against her nose and drew in a deep breath of the sweet mint that lingered in the satiny material.

When the Indians reached the pulpit, they spun abruptly and faced the congregation. Almost on cue, they splayed their legs and folded their arms across their chests.

A hush descended over the meetinghouse. The babbling of a baby several rows back reverberated through the eerie quietness.

Reverend Lull stood unmoving, like a wood carving, his mouth partly open and his hand raised.

For a long moment, Priscilla held her breath and, like everyone else, stared at the spectacle. There hadn't been a single Indian in Allegany County during the twenty-six years of her lifetime. Who knew how long before that?

And now there were two. What was Providence planning for them?

The decisive step of boots at the doorway echoed through the silence.

Once again, Priscilla shifted in her pew. This time she took in the tall form of a broad-shouldered man. With the brim of his battered hat pulled low, she could see nothing but the shadowed stubble on his jaw.

A twinge of trepidation wove through her stomach.

His boot heels clunked on the wooden floor, and with each step forward, the thread pulled taut until, finally, when he reached the front and turned to face them, her stomach was as tight as the stitches in her sampler.

With a flick of his finger, he tapped up his hat and gave them a clear view of his face. Blue eyes the color of a winter sky peered at them from a tanned, weathered face. "Forgive me, Reverend, for disrupting your service," he said, not bothering to look at Reverend Lull. Instead, his gaze swept across the congregation.

There was something intense and passionate in his eyes, something that spoke of adventure and of daring deeds about which Priscilla could only dream.

Mary Ann's fingers dug through Priscilla's gloves and pinched her tender skin. Priscilla absently patted her sister's hand, wishing Mary Ann's fear didn't mirror her own.

Standing next to the savage Indians, the man seemed fierce—from the pistol at his waist to the scar that cut a thin white path from the corner of his left eye to his cheek. Who was this man? And what did he want with them?

Priscilla pressed the knot in her middle. Yet even as she tried to still her quivering, she couldn't keep from trembling with the thrill of the unknown.

"I'm Dr. Eli Ernest, and I've just returned from exploring Oregon Country."

A doctor? Priscilla sat back against the hard bench. This fearsome, rugged man a doctor? She'd met with plenty of doctors over the past several years, and none had looked like this man.

And none of them had been able to offer her any hope. . . .

An ache of emptiness swelled through her middle. She slid her hand away from her barren womb and tucked it in her lap. She forced herself to not think about the pain, about the fact that she'd never be a good and fruitful wife to any man. How many times must she remind herself to embrace God's plan for her life, even if it never included marriage and children?

"John and Richard"—Dr. Ernest nodded toward the two Indian boys—"agreed to come back with me so I could show everyone just how kind and civil the Indians truly are."

The boys stared straight ahead, their expressions stoic. In their Indian attire, they looked anything but kind and civilized.

The taller boy's eyes flickered to her again, and she caught a glimpse of curiosity in their depths before he glanced away.

For an instant, she could almost picture him as one of her students. With a proper haircut and appropriate wearing apparel, perhaps he could grow to be more civilized. With the right teacher, he could quite possibly learn many things.

Her heart quickened. Soon, very soon, she would have the opportunity to change lives for the sake of the gospel. She would get to teach heathens like this boy, only in India, where the need was greater than any other place on earth.

Any day now, for she was long overdue to hear back from the Mission Board.

"They are of the Nez Perce tribe, a peaceful and generous

people," Dr. Ernest continued. "I'll be traveling back to Oregon Country in a few weeks' time, returning John and Richard to their home." His voice had a rugged quality that matched everything about him, from his oil-slicked cloak and faded trousers to his scuffed boots.

"This time I won't be coming back. The Nez Perce have asked me to set up a mission among them."

A mission? Her heart skipped forward, each beat tripping over the next, just as it did every time she thought about life on the mission field and the millions of heathen still needing the gospel.

"John and Richard's father wants to help his people. They've seen the benefit of the white man's medicine and knowledge, so they've agreed to let me buy a portion of their land and build a clinic."

A mission in the far West? Everyone knew the land in the West was unfit for civilized life. It was a place inhabited by fur trappers, wild animals, and Indians. The rugged terrain made it nearly impossible for self-sufficiency.

India, on the other hand, already had established missions and schools. They desperately needed more workers.

"I've come today on behalf of the Board of Missions," Dr. Ernest said, "to ask for your commitment of support. I've spent the winter visiting churches, raising funds necessary for our return travel and building of the mission. Now, with your support, I could raise the last of what I need."

A chorus of whispers broke the stunned silence that had prevailed since the appearance of the two Indian boys.

Reverend Lull finally moved. "Well, welcome, Dr. Ernest. You've come to the right place. We certainly are a mission-minded congregation. We already support several missionaries. The women of our congregation have formed a Female Home Missionary Society." He cleared his throat and directed his attention toward Priscilla, his face aglow with pride. "In fact, we have one of our own, my dear sister-in-law, who is planning to leave us to teach in India."

Mary Ann beamed at her husband, while Priscilla nodded and straightened her shoulders.

The doctor gave her the briefest of nods, skimming over her with obvious disinterest before turning to survey the rest of the congregation again.

She sat back in surprise and reached for the cameo pinned at her throat. Patting the twisted knot at the back of her head, she fought a strange sense of uncertainty. Had her hair come loose? Did she have something unseemly upon her face?

Dr. Ernest cocked his hat back further on his head, revealing overlong dusty brown hair with sun-bleached streaks. "As I've repeatedly told the Board, we Americans willingly pour our money and time into lands and people beyond the seas, but we neglect the need right on our back doorstep."

Did he think so highly of his *own* calling that he could dismiss *hers* so easily?

"The natives of the North American continent need our generosity just as much, if not more, than any other group in the world." Dr. Ernest rested a hand on the shoulder of the Indian boy closest to him.

"The Nez Perce are a wandering tribe and live only on the food they can hunt or scavenge, and often they go hungry. They're vulnerable to attacks by the fierce Blackfoot tribe, who kill their people or enslave them. They're being exposed to the white men's diseases through the fur trappers but don't have white men's medicine to help fight them."

His words elicited murmurs of sympathy.

He nodded at the Indian boys, and they smiled back at him, as if they knew they were getting the response they wanted.

Indignation shimmied up Priscilla's spine. Did he think being a missionary to the West was more noble and important than being one to India?

"Perhaps in holding out the hand of friendship to one tribe"— he squeezed the Indian boy's shoulder—"we'll begin to repair the damage we've done to so many others."

"Amen," called several brothers and sisters.

Priscilla pressed her lips together, wanting to speak but forcing herself to raise her hand and wait for recognition.

Dr. Ernest averted his gaze to the other side of the sanctuary.

"Miss White?" Reverend Lull held out a hand to her. "I'm sure we would love to hear your thoughts on this matter."

She stood and nodded her thanks to the reverend. Then she bestowed her sweetest smile on Dr. Ernest. "What you are telling us is all well and good, Dr. Ernest. But how can we justify focusing our attention on *one* tribe when there are *six hundred million* heathen throughout foreign lands who are perishing in sin and require our immediate help?"

Mary Ann yanked Priscilla's dress, and Mother cleared her throat. They only meant to urge her into the silence and submission that behooved a woman of her status. Yet how could she stand back without defending the place and people she would serve until the Lord called her heavenward?

"When those in foreign lands are already receptive and eager," she continued, "I don't see how we can do anything but pour our time and money into overseas missions. Especially when others have already tried to share the gospel with the Indians and have failed to see any results."

"What can we expect from the natives we've forced to relocate?" Dr. Ernest said as he slowly pivoted until he faced her. "Of course, the central plains tribes are hostile to the whites and anything they might offer."

Finally he looked at her. His eyes flickered with irritation, as if he was weary of rebuffing comments like hers. "Thankfully, most of the tribes of the Northwest are still on friendly terms with the whites. And it's my desire to keep it that way."

"Yes, but why would we want to gamble on a mission in the West with savages when the Mission Board is desperate for qualified candidates to work in the missions they've already established overseas?"

He studied her in calculated measures, starting at the tips of her soft leather boots, moving to the shiny muslin of her meeting dress, until he reached the intricately carved cameo at her throat.

She tried not to squirm under the intensity of his crystal blue eyes. Instead, she forced herself to stand taller.

He met her gaze squarely. "What would such a *fine* lady like you know of the harsh realities of mission life?"

The bold question stole away her ready answer. What did she know? Except what she'd read and heard secondhand? "I may not know everything, but I am quite prepared to give my life in service to the Lord's work."

The words of the *Missionary Herald* echoed in her mind: *A generation of heathen lives no longer than a generation of Christians.* She might be a *fine* lady, but how could she sit back in comfort and ease when so many were heading for the everlasting torments of hell?

Besides, many women of her status and background had already gone. Didn't the Mission Board continually say the most important qualities were the candidate's character, piety, and commitment?

She lifted her chin. "Fortunately, the Mission Board is quite adept in choosing their candidates. They use the utmost care to pick only the most qualified. Wouldn't you agree, Dr. Ernest?"

How could he dare to disagree without casting doubt upon himself?

His eyes narrowed, deepening the permanent crinkles at the edges. "The Mission Board needs to reevaluate its list of qualifications for women. They need to have stricter guidelines, especially for ladies like you."

"I beg your pardon?"

"Priscilla Jane White," Mother whispered, "enough."

"Every single letter of reference I obtained applauded my spiritual fervor, talent, education, and industriousness." Irritation gave liberty to her tongue, even though she knew she would suffer Mother's rebuke later. "I am physically fit, energetic, and young. I'm eager to serve the Lord and save the lost. What more is necessary?"

A shadow fell across Dr. Ernest's face, and clouds flitted through his eyes. "My friend and fellow medical student, Dr. Newell, applied for a mission in India. He took his young bride— a delicate and refined lady like you. He'd been on the foreign shore less than a month when he had to send his bride back home . . . in a coffin."

Priscilla's breath rushed in, echoing the startled gasps of those around her. She stifled a chill that threatened to crawl over her skin and shook her head, unwilling to let this stranger scare her from her calling. "I've heard similar tales. The *Missionary Herald* doesn't hide the perils of mission life from its readers."

For the first time, Dr. Ernest's lips cracked into a semblance of a smile, only it was stiff and almost contemptuous. "Ah, the glorious *Missionary Herald*. What would we do without it and all its glamorous reports of mission life?"

Her confidence faltered, and for a moment she couldn't think of a rebuttal. She grew conscious of the fact that everyone in the congregation was watching their exchange and she was making a scene unbefitting a lady.

"Sit down, Priscilla." Her mother's angry hiss pulled on her.

Priscilla lowered herself but couldn't stop from uttering one last word on the matter. "Dr. Ernest, I'm sorry your friend lost his wife. But she died in a glorious cause and surely went on to receive an unfading crown."

His eyes widened, almost as if he were seeing her for the first time. "There's a good chance any missionary—man or woman— could end up a martyr," he said slowly. "Unfortunately, the *glorious cause* seems to be partial to martyring inexperienced young ladies."

Her mother pinched her arm, and Priscilla pressed her lips together to refrain from further discourse. Let him have his morbid views of women missionaries. There was no sense arguing with a man she'd never see again—especially since they were headed to opposite ends of the earth.

Why, then, did she feel compelled to prove herself to him?

~

"My husband is giving Dr. Ernest a portion of the offering," Mary Ann whispered, peeking around the doorframe.

"I certainly didn't mean to imply that we should shun him altogether." Priscilla stacked the Sunday school materials. "Do you think everyone thought I was uncharitable toward him?"

The question had plagued her all through the children's lesson, and the satisfaction she normally drew from teaching had deserted her.

Mary Ann ducked into the small room. "Well, I'm sure if you were uncharitable, it was only because he deserved it."

Priscilla slid the bench against the wall. "You're right. It was his fault. If he hadn't been disparaging, I wouldn't have needed to rise to my defense."

Mary Ann grimaced and grasped her bulging middle.

Priscilla spun away, searching for something else to tidy, trying to ignore the sudden pang of longing in her chest.

"Don't worry about me," Mary Ann said. "This happens all the time lately. Dr. Baldwin tells me I'm just having false labor pains."

Priscilla's gaze slid involuntarily to her sister's stomach, to her fingers splayed there, to their slow circular caress.

"I guess it's pretty common." Mary Ann stuck a fist into the lower part of her back and then arched. The waist of her dress pulled tight. "Enjoy your girlish figure while you still have it. I've heard that it's gone forever after the birthing."

The sting in Priscilla's chest swelled into the base of her throat. Once again, she glanced around the room, needing something else to look at—anything besides her sister's swelling body. If she could give up her girlish figure, she certainly would.

She shook the thought from her mind and tried to muster a smile for the two young girls who'd stayed behind to help her pick up. "What would I do without my helpers?" She forced cheerfulness to her voice.

The girls smiled.

"If I could, I'd pack you in my trunks and take you to India with me."

They giggled.

"Teacher! Miss White!" A young boy's urgent call sent her heart into a dash. She rushed across the room. When she stepped into the sanctuary, she averted her eyes from the adults still meeting for their class. She pressed a finger against her lips, signaling for the boy, one of her Sunday school students, to be mindful of disturbing the question-and-answer time the congregation was having with Dr. Ernest.

"Miss White!" The breathless boy dashed toward her, wiping

his red nose across his coat sleeve. "It's my brother, Rudy. He's hurt bad."

"Oh dear." Anxiety put a hustle into her efforts to retrieve her heavy winter cloak and follow the boy outside.

Clutching fistfuls of her dress, she strode across the wide lawn, her boots squishing into the February mixture of old snow and new mud.

When she reached the boys surrounding Rudy, she was puffing. "I shouldn't have let you children out early,"

They hung their heads and moved back to let her approach the boy sprawled upon the ground.

She stepped into the circle, took one glance at Rudy's face, and gasped. She could only stare with a sickening roll of her stomach at the smears of blood.

But when his eyes opened, she read the pain in them and dropped to her knees beside him. "Rudy, what happened?"

The boy managed a groan, the white of his eyes bright against the grime. Blood oozed from a gash above his eyebrow.

She slipped her hand under her cloak to her pocket. Her fingers fumbled at the drawstring, trembling in her haste to retrieve the handkerchief she kept there. "Tell me what happened, boys." She swallowed a swell of bile.

"We were having a snowball fight," Rudy's brother offered. "I guess some of the snowballs ended up having a few rocks in them."

"Ended up?" She gripped the crisply pressed cloth with its perfectly creased edges and hesitated for only a moment before lowering it against the boy's gash.

Rudy winced.

Priscilla jerked back. "Oh, I'm sorry."

"No. Press it hard." Dr. Ernest's command was soft and accompanied a rustling next to her.

She glanced sideways, and the clear eyes of Dr. Ernest met hers.
"We need to stop the blood flow." He knelt next to her. "Once
we slow the bleeding, I'll be able to take a look at the damage."

She nodded and dabbed the handkerchief against the gash.

"Harder."

She pushed.

Rudy squirmed and clenched his teeth together.

"Keep pressing," Dr. Ernest said calmly.

At the blood, the dirt, the loose flesh on Rudy's head—her
stomach rolled, and she wanted to drop the cloth and scramble
away before she embarrassed herself. But she forced her fingers
to stay in place until a splotch of bright red seeped into the linen
and spread like the fringes of a web.

Dr. Ernest combed strands of hair away from Rudy's forehead.
"Guess you boys learned a lesson."

They nodded mutely.

Priscilla took a steadying breath, knowing she had to stay and
prove that even though she was a lady, she could withstand the
discomfort of viewing an injury. And if she could stay poised
during the situation, she could surely withstand the harsh realities of missionary life.

Dr. Ernest's long fingers wove through Rudy's hair and then
moved to his face, brushing at the mud and pebbles.

She tried not to stare at the multitude of white scars that
slashed across the tanned flesh of Dr. Ernest's hands, but the
puckered lines drew her attention. He'd certainly suffered incredible trauma to acquire so many lacerations.

"You're doing fine," he said to Rudy.

After another minute, he spoke again. "Let's have a look at
the damage now, shall we?"

She hesitated, and then lifted the bandage, making a point
of focusing on Dr. Ernest's face and not the oozing wound.

His wrinkled forehead framed tender but probing eyes. "Son, you'll need a handful of stitches, but other than that, it's safe to say you'll live."

Rudy gave the doctor a tremulous grin.

"I've got my supplies at Dr. Baldwin's house." He pushed a clean portion of the handkerchief back against the wound. "Hold this tight and head on over there so I can stitch you up."

Dr. Ernest hefted himself to his feet then reached a hand toward Priscilla. He towered over her. He'd neglected his cloak, and his shirt stretched against the hard strength of his arms and shoulders.

If she hadn't witnessed the gentleness of his hands, she wouldn't have believed a man of his magnitude capable of it. She placed her hand into his. And when his fingers closed around hers, she drew in a sharp breath. His touch was gentler than she'd imagined.

Without any effort, he drew her upward until she stood. This time when his gaze met hers, a hint of humor crinkled the corners of his eyes.

"You did a good job holding yourself together."

Was he mocking her?

The tiny crook of a grin answered her question.

"I'm a teacher, Dr. Ernest. Not a doctor's assistant." She tugged her hand out of his grip.

"Eli, you and Miss White make a good team." Dr. Baldwin clapped Dr. Ernest on the back.

"Well, you know me. I prefer working by myself."

Priscilla glanced at the crowd that had gathered, and a rush of embarrassed heat pulsed through her. She was making another spectacle with Dr. Ernest.

Taking a step away from him, she shook the folds of her cloak and brushed at the mud clinging to the embroidered edges.

Mother moved next to her and narrowed her eyes at Dr. Ernest before handing Priscilla the gloves she'd dropped in her haste to leave the building. "You're a mess." Mother tucked a strand of loose hair behind Priscilla's ear.

"I'm fine."

"And you've soiled your dress." Mother frowned at the soggy spot on her skirt.

"Hate to be the one to tell you this, ma'am—" Dr. Ernest's grin crooked higher—"but a little mud and blood is hardly the worst of what your daughter will experience when she gets to India."

Mother lifted her nose and peered at him over the top, evaluating him from his head to his boots. Then she sniffed and clutched Priscilla's arm. "Come now, dear. Let's get you home and cleaned up."

"Speaking of India," Dr. Baldwin said, stepping toward them, "I've got a letter for you, Miss White."

Priscilla froze. Even her heart floundered to a stop.

"I've just returned from a Board meeting in Prattsburgh with Dr. Ernest." The old doctor handed her an envelope. "The Board asked me to deliver this to you."

Excitement clutched her middle and twisted it. She took the letter and tried to stop the sudden shaking of her hands. Finally the Board had made its decision. She had no doubt they'd approved her for mission work. Everyone had told her she was an ideal candidate for one of the rare teaching positions they assigned to unmarried females.

The Board had made it clear they preferred sending married couples to the mission field. But she'd explained in her correspondence that she would never marry. If they wanted to use her, they would have to take her as she was.

Now, after months of waiting and raising support, she needed only to find out exactly where in India they were sending her and when she would leave. Mrs. Wilson's school for girls, perhaps? She'd just read an article in the *Missionary Herald* about how proficient the young heathen girls were becoming in their needlework.

"Thank you." She smiled at Dr. Baldwin. But instead of returning her smile, he glanced at his shoes.

She stared at the letter, and her heart lurched. Was she really ready for this? Once she read it, she might as well kiss Mother and Father good-bye.

"Go on, open it!" someone called.

Of course she was ready. Past ready. She'd wanted to go since God had laid a calling upon her heart at the revival meeting when she'd been a girl of fifteen.

She pressed her finger into the seal, broke it, and then unfolded the crisp paper. God had given her the burden and desire to use her gifts to help save depraved souls. And now it was finally time. . . .

"Read it aloud," another voice said.

Eager eyes watched her. "Very well." She lifted the paper and cleared her throat. "'Dear Miss White,'" she began, but the next words stuck in her throat. She scanned the sheet, and her chest constricted painfully until she could hardly breathe.

Quickly she folded the letter. "I think I shall wait—"

Mother snapped the sheet from her hand. "Priscilla Jane White, you'll do no such thing." Before she could think to react, Mother unfolded it. "These people are your biggest supporters. They deserve to share in your excitement."

"Mother," she murmured, "I'd rather read it in private—"

"My dear, stop being so modest." Mother stepped out of her reach and settled her spectacles upon her nose.

"Perhaps Miss White is right," Dr. Baldwin said.

"Nonsense."

"Mo-ther . . ." Priscilla's whisper contained all the agony roiling through her heart.

Mother adjusted her spectacles. "'Dear Miss White.'"

Dr. Baldwin's eyebrows drooped together over sad eyes. Even though he was on the Board, she knew their decision wasn't his fault. He was the only other person in Angelica, besides Mother and Father, who knew the truth. He'd been the one to give her the diagnosis.

He'd known how important this position was to her—one of the few positions for a single woman. He knew just how much she longed to leave Allegany County and all the friends and family who would never understand why she couldn't get married.

"'We regret to inform you that at this time we cannot accept your application . . .'" Mother's voice trailed off.

An awkward silence descended over the gathering. Mother read silently and then creased the letter back into its original fold. "Well." She pursed her lips together. "I'm sure there must be some mistake."

Each beat of Priscilla's heart spurted pain and confusion into the rest of her body. Her mother was right. The Board had made a mistake. Surely once she informed them the unmarried teacher position was her only option, they'd reconsider.

Dr. Baldwin shook his head. "They've finally made the resolution that they will not—absolutely cannot—accept unmarried candidates."

"But why?" Priscilla's confusion added a tinge of desperation to her tone. "I thought they were beginning to see the value in single female missionaries—"

"Miss White," Dr. Ernest cut in. "It won't do you any good to argue with Dr. Baldwin or the Board. Over the past few days I've talked with them until I was hoarse, and they haven't budged on their requirement."

"Oh pishposh," Mother said. "They'll make an exception for my Priscilla."

Priscilla shivered and pulled her cloak tighter.

Dr. Baldwin's eyes held hers, and the sorrow in their depths did nothing but make her shiver more.

"Now, Dr. Baldwin," Mother said, turning to leave, "you must visit us this afternoon and clear up the misunderstanding."

"Of course." Priscilla nodded, pushing aside her fears. "It's just a misunderstanding."

"You'll be wasting your breath," Dr. Ernest muttered.

Mother didn't acknowledge the young doctor's words and instead slipped her hand into the crook of Father's arm and tugged him forward.

Priscilla knew she should follow her parents, that it would do her no good to spar words with Dr. Ernest. And yet, there was something about his face—a roughened, rugged appeal that drew her attention again.

"I'm afraid you don't understand the first thing about my situation or my qualifications."

"Then go ahead and argue with the Board." His lips cocked into a half grin. "But sooner or later you'll have to accept their decision. And maybe even accept it as God's will for you to stay home."

His words dug into her, and she couldn't keep back her retort. "I find it strange that you're the only one who has questioned my qualifications. And since your opinion doesn't matter in the least, I'll continue to look to the One whose opinion matters the most. He's called me to mission work. I'll continue to trust that He'll provide a way for me to go."

She spun away from the doctor and forced herself to walk away, evenly and calmly, just as a lady should, even though her heart quavered and stumbled with each step.

Would God indeed provide a way? And if so, how?

Chapter
2

*Y*ou've turned into a good doctor, Eli," Dr. Baldwin remarked between puffs on his pipe. "Too bad you're not as good when it comes to women."

Eli pulled the silk thread up through the boy's forehead and made the last suture. His fingers flew over one another to make a tight knot. With his small scissors in hand, he squinted in the dim lighting of Dr. Baldwin's home office and snipped the loose thread.

"Oh, I'm not all that bad, Dr. Baldwin." He pressed a clean cloth against the stitches and wiped away the last traces of blood. "I've had to chase away plenty of women in my days."

The boy stared at him with wide pain-filled eyes. Traces of tears lingered on the pale face. The older brother squeezed the boy's hand.

"I've had more women hang on me than I can count." Eli winked at them.

His young patient braved a small smile.

"*Harrumph,*" Dr. Baldwin half snorted, half laughed. "Too bad you don't have any of those *countless* women hanging on you lately."

Eli forced a grin—for the sake of the boy—but it didn't reach his heart. If Dr. Baldwin's comment hadn't been so pathetically true, he could have laughed.

Truth be told, he'd never had much time for the fairer sex. He'd always counted himself too busy, too devoted to his work to pay attention to the girls who'd shown him interest.

That was before he'd begun making plans to open a clinic in the far West. When he'd approached the Mission Board with his idea, he'd had to work hard to convince them of the validity of such a post. When they'd finally agreed to support him, they'd given him one stipulation: He had to take a wife.

He'd argued long and hard about the fact that a white woman had never made a crossing overland to Oregon Country, that taking a wife along would only slow him down, perhaps even threaten the entire trip.

But the Board had insisted he go with a wife or not go at all.

"You don't need countless women." Dr. Baldwin leaned back in his chair and blew a cloud of smoke into the dusky air. "You just need one."

Eli helped the boy sit up. "I *had* one."

"Yes, *had*," Dr. Baldwin said.

Eli steadied the boy on the edge of the examining table. "And it's not my fault she married someone else while I was on my exploration trip."

His gut twisted, as it did whenever he thought about his first glance at Sarah Taylor during the Sabbath meeting the day after he'd arrived home. When she'd stood to greet him, first her eyes, then her very rounded abdomen had told him all he needed to know.

It had only confirmed the foolishness of the Board's stipulation. Sarah hadn't really wanted to go. She had deserted him at the first opportunity. And there weren't too many other women excited about the idea of traveling where no other white woman had gone.

He couldn't blame them.

"The Board knows I tried to find a willing partner. And now they need to just let me go."

Dr. Baldwin shook his head.

Eli had tried to overlook his wounded pride, tried to make excuses for Sarah. The truth was that her rejection had stung— it had hurt a lot more than he cared to admit. And he wasn't ready to face the possibility of another rejection anytime soon.

"How are you feeling?" Eli asked his young patient.

Tears pooled in the boy's eyes.

"Still hurts more than the worst whoppin', huh?"

The lad nodded.

Careful not to touch the wound, Eli wrapped a strip around the boy's head and covered the stitches. Then he nodded at the patient's brother. "You take him straight home and tell your ma to give him another dose of laudanum. It'll take the edge off the pain for a little while."

He helped the boy from the table. "And tell her to keep the wound clean."

"Thank you." The older boy slipped an arm around his brother. He hobbled with him to the door, stopped, and looked back. "Oh, Doctor, if you need a real good woman, you won't find a better lady than our teacher."

"That so?"

"Yep. Teacher . . . well, she really cares for us. And I just know she'd make a great ma someday."

"Thank you, son."

The boy nodded solemnly, as if he'd just done Eli the greatest of favors.

Dr. Baldwin coughed. And once the boys were gone, Eli turned to look at his old friend. "What?"

"Oh, nothing."

Eli dipped his hands into the basin on the bureau near the examining table. The ice cold water rushed over the calluses he'd gained during the past year and reminded him of the mountain springs he'd washed in not many months past.

He scrubbed at the blood on his fingers and glanced around at the dark paneled walls of Dr. Baldwin's office. Was this to be his fate? A tiny office? And the never-ending bumps and bruises of the neighborhood children?

Keen longing flashed through him. What he wouldn't give for a ceiling of blue skies and four walls of endless mountains. And the beautiful brown eyes of the natives who were still open to the gospel and untouched by the hate of the whites.

"You might want to take the boy up on his advice," Dr. Baldwin said.

Eli took a deep breath of the stuffy, tobacco-spiced air. What he wouldn't give for just a whiff of the fresh, wind-tossed air of the prairies.

"She's one of the best young women I know," Dr. Baldwin continued.

"Who?"

"The teacher."

Eli's stomach pinched. "I just don't want a wife."

"Eli, now, we've been over this before, and you know as well as I do that most of the single missionaries we've sent out have ended up fornicating with the native women or marrying among them."

He nodded. He couldn't fault the Board's logic. After many long months traveling with the fur trappers, he'd seen enough abuse of the native women to realize the depths to which a man could sink when he was lonely.

He shook the water off his hands and reached for the towel. But still, the Board could have given him the benefit of the doubt, especially after all the work he'd already put into planning for the mission.

Frustration contracted the muscles in his chest.

He wiped his hands and tossed the towel onto the table. He knew it would do him no good to argue about the matter any further. The American Board of Missions had made their decision. He must find a wife or he couldn't go.

The trouble was, he only had four weeks left before he needed to be in Pittsburgh, where he'd arranged to meet the missionary couple that would be joining him.

"You want some help finding a wife?" Dr. Baldwin peered at him through narrowed eyes. "Or are you going to let a little pride stand in the way of your plans?"

Eli read the kindness in the depths of the man's gaze. "Apparently you've got the perfect woman picked out for me."

He shrugged. "Of course no one is perfect. Not even you."

Eli stared at the doctor, then finally sighed. "All right. Take me to meet this teacher."

"I'm headed to her house right now." Dr. Baldwin sat forward in his chair. "Why don't you come with me?"

"It had better not be Miss White."

"And what exactly is wrong with Priscilla White?"

With a growl, Eli reached for his leather roll-up surgical case. "Come on, Doctor. If I have to take a wife, I want a strong one.

31

Not a woman who'll blow away like tumbleweed at the first hard gust." He wiped the blood from the scissors and stuffed them into the case. "I won't take a woman like her—not after what happened to Dr. Newell."

"Priscilla White is a hard worker." Dr. Baldwin tapped his pipe in the ashtray on the side table. "There's no other young woman who works the way Miss White does. Every time the church opens its door for a prayer meeting or a revival, she's the first there, helping however she can."

"Then let her stay here and do her part for missions on the home front." Eli stuffed the silk thread into his surgical case and folded it together.

Dr. Baldwin pushed himself out of his chair. "Eli Ernest, you're exasperating me."

He grinned. "I've been told that's one of my best qualities."

"You mean worst."

"That too."

Dr. Baldwin finally smiled. "Let's go, then. We'll speak to Priscilla together. The two of you can get married. And you'll both be able to fulfill your callings."

Eli stared at his friend and wished it were that easy. Even if she'd been the right type of woman to handle the rigors of missionary life, it was obvious they were worlds apart. "Her mother already turned up her nose at me. And now you expect that woman to agree to let her precious daughter marry me once she finds out I've got nothing but the hard-earned shirt on my back?"

"She'll come around."

Eli could only imagine the humiliation he'd have to suffer first. "No thanks."

"I guarantee it."

Something in the doctor's tone stopped Eli.

Dr. Baldwin lowered his voice. "Priscilla White had a severe case of mumps a few years ago."

Suddenly Eli knew what the older doctor was telling him, even before the words were out.

"She lost her monthly courses, and she's been infertile ever since." Dr. Baldwin's brows drooped. "I've done everything I can for the poor girl. But the fact of the matter is, she very likely can't—won't—ever be able to have children."

Eli stared at his friend, surprised at the weight that pressed on his chest.

"I'm telling you with the understanding you'll keep this confidential, one doctor to another."

"'Course I will."

"No one in this community knows except me. And they want to keep it that way. They don't want the disgrace of their oldest daughter becoming known as the barren wife of the community or the town's old spinster."

Eli shook his head. "There's no disgrace in not being able to have children—"

"You know as well as I do the stigma that follows women who can't conceive." Dr. Baldwin pinned him with a sharp glance.

"So she's using mission work as an escape from embarrassment?"

"See? There you go." The older doctor pursed his lips. "Exasperating me again."

"Doesn't seem like the right motivation for getting involved in missions."

"Priscilla has always had an interest in missions. Her family has encouraged her. And when she learned of her infertility, it served to strengthen her resolve toward the high calling already placed upon her heart."

"Priscilla White might have good intentions," Eli said, "but she'd never last a day on the trip west."

Dr. Baldwin heaved a rattling sigh. "I take it that means no, you won't marry her?"

Eli hesitated. He didn't want to ruin his chances of going west, but he wasn't so desperate that he'd willingly marry the wrong woman.

"Dr. Baldwin, I'm sorry to let you down. . . . I'm not partial to sending wives back in coffins. So I'll just keep praying the Almighty finds me a better option . . . and soon."

"You must go back to the Board and convince them of their mistake."

Priscilla cringed at her mother's demand.

"They won't be swayed." Dr. Baldwin squirmed in his high-backed chair by the parlor door.

"I'll go with you." Mother paced in front of the wide fireplace. The high flames crackled but couldn't bring warmth to Priscilla's fingers. "And Priscilla will come too."

"Now, Mrs. White, that's enough." Her father rubbed his mustache, circling his fingers around his chin.

"We'll leave on the morrow." Mother didn't bother to look at Father. "Once they see Priscilla and hear from her, they won't be able to say no."

"Mrs. White, I said that's enough." Father's voice boomed. Even though the room had bright green molding and vibrant gold wallpaper with pink florets, the shadows were dismal in the late winter afternoon. "Sit down and listen to what the man is saying. For once."

Priscilla plucked at the braided trim of the settee and wished she were still small enough to crawl underneath and hide.

Mother glared at Father. "Mr. White, am I to understand that you don't care what becomes of our daughter?"

"Listen to the doctor. He's told you a hundred times now that the Board won't change their decision."

"Judge White is right." Dr. Baldwin pulled at the top button of his double-breasted waistcoat. "Everyone has agreed she's an ideal candidate. And they'll willingly send her anywhere. But . . . she must get married first."

Priscilla clutched her hands in her lap. "Doctor, that's precisely the problem—"

"I have in mind a missionary who is in desperate need of a wife. If you marry him, you'll both get what you want. It's the perfect situation."

Mother stopped pacing. "Who?"

"He's an adventurous, hardworking, resourceful fellow. If I were going to the mission field, I'd want a man just like him by my side."

"And just who is this *fellow*?" Mother asked, her brow disappearing into her hairline.

Dr. Baldwin cleared his throat. "Dr. Eli Ernest."

"Absolutely not!" Priscilla's rejection came just as quickly as Mother's. "We're headed to opposite ends of the earth."

"My daughter will never marry a man like that," Mother said. "It's obvious he is of the lowest rank and would be unsuitable for her."

"There you go putting on airs again." Father rolled his eyes. "You're not the Queen of England. Your father was a chair maker. And I was only a carpenter when we got married."

Priscilla had only a vague memory of the log cabin she'd lived in as a little girl when Allegany County had been considered New York's western frontier. Father hadn't had anything but his enterprising spirit. He'd staked out a claim of eighty acres.

Over the years, he'd steadily acquired more land and wealth until he'd moved the family to a fine wood-framed house, only a half mile from the center of town, in the better part of Angelica.

Father continued. "I'm sure the doctor is about as decent a man as our daughter can find."

"He studied at the College of Physicians and Surgeons in New York, which is where I met him," Dr. Baldwin added. "He got a real degree."

"See, Mrs. White. That's more book learning than I ever got." Father smoothed a hand over his bulging stomach. His title of judge had come only after the townspeople had elected him to various local offices, certainly not because he'd earned a law degree.

Mother only shook her head. "If we are going to consider marriage for Priscilla, then we need to find a man devoted to the ministry."

"But I'm not considering—"

"I said *if*." Mother shot her a censuring glare.

Dr. Baldwin studied Mother. "Very well, Mrs. White. I understand the prestige associated with the ministry. But if you pass up this opportunity for Priscilla to marry Dr. Ernest, you will miss even greater prestige."

"How so?"

Dr. Baldwin stood and situated his black top hat onto his head. "I think the woman Dr. Ernest marries will easily become the most famous American woman of this generation."

Mother straightened. "Famous? What do you mean?"

Father snorted. "You got her attention now, Doctor."

"The woman who travels to the far West with Dr. Ernest will be the first white woman ever to make the overland trip to Oregon Country and cross the Continental Divide. I have no doubt the eyes of every single person in this country will be watching her with great interest."

A light fanned to life in Mother's eyes—a light that made Priscilla's heart thud with despair.

Dr. Baldwin sidled around his chair and exited into the front hallway. "It's too bad you aren't willing to consider him," he called. He appeared back in the doorway, having retrieved his greatcoat from the coat stand.

"Now, wait a minute, Dr. Baldwin." Mother stepped after him. "You've misunderstood me. He may not be the ideal candidate for marriage, but we are still willing to consider him."

Priscilla jumped from the settee. She couldn't sit back and listen to any more. "Dr. Baldwin, I'm sorry. But I can't possibly consider going to Oregon Country with Dr. Ernest. It's out of the question. I'm going to India."

"I realize you had your heart set on India," Dr. Baldwin said slowly, as if choosing his words carefully. "But the far West is in need of teachers too."

"Even if I agreed to go to the wilderness of Oregon Country—which I won't—I think everyone is forgetting something very important here." She took a deep breath to ease the strain in her back. "I can't get married. I'm unable to . . ."

She couldn't get the words past the tightness of her throat.

Mother was quiet for a moment. "We don't need to tell him," she finally said.

Priscilla gasped. "Mother!" They'd agreed those many years ago on that fateful day that they would never deceive a suitor, that it was their Christian duty to inform a prospective spouse of her condition before marriage.

Once they'd made their decision, they'd also resolved that she would remain single, that it was too risky to share the news with any man. They couldn't chance his spurning her and then spreading rumors about her and ruining her reputation.

Dr. Baldwin cleared his throat. "You won't need to tell Dr. Ernest anything."

Her gaze, like her parents', swung to the old man.

The sympathy in his eyes reached out to touch her. "You won't need to tell him, because . . . I already have."

"You have?" A strange tremor of anticipation rippled through her. "You told him about . . . that I can't . . . ?"

The doctor nodded.

"And what did he say?"

"Well . . ." He fidgeted with the brim of his hat. "Let's just say I got the impression your infertility was the least of his concerns."

"Then he'll marry our Priscilla, even though he knows of her condition?" The hope in Mother's voice fanned the anticipation flickering inside Priscilla.

Dr. Baldwin's brow crinkled.

His hesitation was just enough to snuff out her glimmer of hope. She rubbed her arms, suddenly cold, as if a frigid breeze had blown through the cracks in the big parlor windows.

"He didn't exactly say he would marry Priscilla," the doctor said.

This was ridiculous. She refused to marry Dr. Ernest, and she had absolutely no inclination to go west. What kind of ministry could she have there compared to what she'd have in India? She started to shake her head, but Mother's fingers dug into her shoulder and squeezed her rebuttal to the back of her throat.

"Let's not be so dramatic about it." Her mother smiled. "If God has ordained our Priscilla to become one of the first women to cross to the West in her quest to serve Him and save the heathen, then He'll most certainly protect and provide for her each step of the way."

Father shook his head. "Doctor, I'm amazed at how quickly

and smoothly you convinced this woman to marry off our daughter."

Dr. Baldwin gave a faint smile, but the light in his eyes wavered.

Priscilla tried not to squirm under her mother's grip. "He may have convinced Mother. But there's just one very major problem."

"Of course there's no problem," Mother said quickly.

"Yes, Mother, there is." She pushed aside that familiar helplessness—as if she were caught in a river current, trying to swim for the shore but never quite making it. "The problem is that Dr. Ernest hasn't agreed to marry me. And I most certainly haven't agreed to the union either."

"He'll be at the prayer meeting tonight, won't he, Dr. Baldwin?" Mother's tone was less of a question and more of a command.

"Yes," the doctor replied, stuffing his arms into his heavy coat. "I'll do my best to see that he comes."

Mother bent over and looked Priscilla in the eyes. "Then we'll dress our Priscilla up and fix her hair becomingly. All she'll need to do is be her usual charming self." The sternness in the depths of Mother's gaze warned her not to disobey.

"No man has ever been able to resist Priscilla," her mother said. "And I'm sure if she makes a little effort to win Dr. Ernest, he won't be able to resist her either."

Chapter
3

*E*li had known Priscilla was *pretty*, but he hadn't realized she was captivatingly *beautiful*.

His gaze slid across the meetinghouse to the side where she stood and attempted to converse with the Nez Perce boys, John and Richard. Her shimmering gown unfolded around her like the petals of a rose. The pink matched the bloom in her cheeks, almost as if she had planned it that way.

"Our Miss White certainly is fetching, isn't she?" Dr. Baldwin patted Eli on the back.

Elaborate golden ringlets framed her face. She'd swept the rest of her hair into a swirl at the back of her head, leaving exposed a long stretch of creamy skin from her ear to her shoulder blade.

"What? Who?" Her bodice, though modest, couldn't hide her shapely figure, one he guessed was textbook perfect.

"Miss White. She's a beautiful young woman," Dr. Baldwin repeated.

Eli dragged his attention away from her, back to Dr. Baldwin and the other gentleman who had stopped him with questions after the closing of the prayer meeting. Eli rubbed a hand across the scruff on his face, hoping to hide his embarrassment at being caught staring at the woman. He'd never made a practice of gawking at women and had always told himself that inner beauty mattered much more than outer.

Why, then, was he having such a hard time ignoring Priscilla White?

"I always said, it's too bad she decided not to get married," the gentleman said. "She'd bring some fortunate fellow a lot of pride and pleasure."

Dr. Baldwin stuck his elbow into Eli's side and cocked a brow.

Eli shook his head. "*Pretty* won't get a woman west."

"Ah." The older gentleman's eyes lit. "So you're considering asking Miss White to accompany you?"

"'Course not—"

"He can't go without a wife," Dr. Baldwin cut in. "And I've been trying my best to convince him of the merits of our wonderful Miss White."

"She's simply perfect," the gentleman added.

Eli forced a tight smile. "I won't argue with either of you. She seems like a fine woman. But as I already said, Doctor, she's not the type I need."

He was unable to resist another glance at Priscilla. She was smiling at the Indian boys, tentatively fingering the beads and feathers at the end of John's braid.

Eli had to give her some credit. She was the only one who'd made an effort after the service to put aside her fears and show kindness to the boys.

"Am I to understand you'll be traveling with another missionary couple?" the older gentleman asked.

John's dark eyes radiated excitement. Eli had no doubt Priscilla was the fairest woman the boys had ever seen, and one of the first to attempt to speak with them. Apparently she hadn't been exaggerating when she'd rattled off her qualifications—from all appearances she was every bit as pious and mission-minded as she claimed.

Too bad she was like a flower that the least heat or hardship could easily wilt or crush.

"Eli had a terrible time finding another couple willing to go," Dr. Baldwin offered. "He located a young minister and his new wife who were planning to start a mission with the Osage in Kansas. It took some arm twisting, but we finally convinced them to change their plans and travel a little further west with Eli."

"I can't imagine too many people would want to risk such a dangerous journey," the gentleman said.

Eli tore his gaze away from Priscilla, and the all-too-familiar weight of despair and irritation pressed against his sternum—irritation at the Board for their strict stipulations and frustration at the direness of his situation.

"I wasn't planning to take another couple," he said.

"Well, it's probably a relief you won't have to make the trip alone."

Dr. Baldwin raised both brows as if to caution Eli against saying too much. And Eli swallowed his rebuttal—the argument he'd already had with the old doctor and the other Board members several times.

They believed the mission would have a much greater chance of succeeding if they sent a team.

But Eli knew better. He'd never relied upon anyone but the good Lord and the sweat of his own brow. In all his thirty-one years, he'd had to overcome one obstacle after another to make something of his life. He'd scraped and slaved to save money for an education. He'd spent hour after long hour studying, pushing himself to keep at it, even though book learning had been nearly impossible for him.

But he'd done it. Earned his doctor's license. Made a new life for himself. On his own.

He didn't need anyone to help him now or in the future. He was doing just fine.

"Eli's a strong, independent man," Dr. Baldwin said, as if he knew the thoughts running through Eli's mind. "But I'm sure he'll be glad for the companionship once he's there."

"Don't forget, I'll be meeting up with Parker. He's planning to help me get the mission started." His companion from the exploratory trip had stayed west to scout out a site for the mission. Samuel Parker had decided to live with the natives through the winter and meet up with Eli at the annual fur trappers' Rendezvous in the Green River Valley. From there, Parker would lead the missionaries to their new home.

"I know Parker won't stay forever, but I'll have plenty of companionship with the natives." The Indians might have a different culture, but they would provide enough friendship to suit him.

The tinkle of Priscilla's laughter rose above the other voices and beckoned his attention once again. Richard was holding out a long feather from his braid. She took it and twisted it in her delicate fingers.

She tilted her head, and at that moment her gaze collided with Eli's. Her brows lifted in surprise, as if he was the last person she'd expected to catch staring at her.

Strangely enough, he found himself wishing he could trade places with John and Richard so he could talk with her. She'd likely be much more interesting than the men at his side. She might have a smooth, genteel exterior, but earlier he'd caught a glimpse of spark underneath, and it was a spark he wouldn't mind firing up again.

Her gaze flickered away, and the color in her cheeks blossomed.

Just then her mother grabbed her arm and whispered in her ear. Priscilla shook her head. Mrs. White's fingers tightened around Priscilla's puffy sleeve, and her expression hardened.

"You must obey me," he heard the woman say. She nodded toward him, and Priscilla hesitated but finally forced herself to look at him. This time her gray blue eyes were large and soft, like those of a kitten. And the innocence and vulnerability in the wide depths twisted his gut into a slipknot.

"We've heard rumors," the older gentleman said, "about the mountain men not wanting missionaries going west. They're saying they don't want any settlers moving there because it could interfere with their trapping. Do you think you'll be putting yourself and your traveling companions in the middle of a growing conflict?"

"They're afraid if we bring women, we'll slow down their caravan. Can't say that I blame them."

Priscilla nibbled on her bottom lip.

He couldn't imagine any woman—much less a woman of Priscilla's status and beauty—anywhere near the trappers. They were the kind of men who would eat her up and spit her out.

Her mother nudged her. "Go on."

Priscilla stumbled forward and started across the room. Her gaze locked with his, and a shy smile quivered at the corners of her mouth.

The knot in his gut pulled tighter, and he couldn't concentrate on anything but her graceful walk toward him.

"Dr. Ernest." She stopped before him, and her smile widened.

"Miss White," he managed.

She dipped her head and curtsied.

Mrs. White followed her daughter. "Dr. Ernest, we'd love to hear more about your noble plans to start the mission in the West." She pulled at Priscilla's sleeve, puffing it out. "My lovely daughter has been more excited than any of us to learn all about it."

Priscilla's smile faded into a tight circle, and she narrowed her eyes upon her mother.

"We were just talking about Miss White," Dr. Baldwin said too quickly. "And saying what a fine young woman she is."

"Wonderful." Mrs. White's voice was cheerful. "She is indeed a fine lady. I doubt there are many other missionary candidates as qualified as she."

Dr. Baldwin cleared his throat and caught Mrs. White's attention. The two exchanged a knowing glance.

Eli stared from one person to the next. What was the old doctor trying to do? Set him up with Priscilla White even though he'd made it clear she was the last woman he'd be interested in marrying?

Was Priscilla in on the scheme too?

Her eyes filled halfway with an apology before she focused on the tip of her satin slipper poking out from the folds of gauze and lace.

"Oh, I see," he said slowly, a grin working its way to his lips. They were pushing her as much as they were him. In that case, the two of them could have a little fun with her mother and Dr. Baldwin, couldn't they? "Since Miss White is so eager to learn about my trip . . ."

She gave the barest shake of her head. "I'm sure what Mother meant to say is that we'd all like to know how we can be praying for you during your travels."

45

"For starters, you can pray the trappers don't throw rotten eggs at me like they did last time."

Mrs. White gasped.

Priscilla's eyes rounded.

Eli's grin widened. "Don't worry. They learned to put up with me. Especially after I dug a Blackfoot arrow out of Jim Bridger's back."

Mrs. White's face paled.

"If you're at odds with the trappers, why are you riding with them?" the gentleman asked. "Surely you don't need them now that you've already been once and know the way."

"I'd go it alone if I could." He'd leave by himself in a heartbeat if it were possible. "But there are too many hostile tribes and too many things that could go wrong. The fur trappers might be a rough bunch, but there's safety in numbers."

"Sounds much too dangerous," the gentleman added. "And you're planning to place women—a wife—into the middle of the dispute?"

"I'd prefer not to, but it doesn't look like I've got much choice."

"And who exactly are you planning to marry?"

The gentleman's question was like salt against an open sore. "That's still in the works—"

"As a matter of fact," Mrs. White said, exchanging another look with Dr. Baldwin, "we're in the process today of working out the details of the marriage plans between my daughter and Dr. Ernest."

"You can't be serious." Eli stiffened. They were taking the matchmaking too far now.

"Marriage isn't a joking matter. We're entirely serious." Mrs. White smiled at him with a warmth he didn't trust. "When Dr. Baldwin brought up the idea, at first we weren't sure if it would work."

"'Course it won't—"

"But the more we thought about it," the woman continued, "the more we realized what a perfect match this would be, how God has completely orchestrated your meeting at just the right time."

Priscilla looked at the floor, and the crease in her smooth forehead gave evidence that she didn't consider the match nearly as perfect as her mother did.

"I can see that Miss White is as excited about the prospect as I am."

"Very good. Then since you are both excited, we shall proceed with the wedding arrangements." Mrs. White turned away and clapped her hands. "Quiet, everybody! I have an announcement to make."

Eli's heart struck against his chest with a strange mixture of apprehension and excitement. "There's no need for an announcement."

"Of course there's a need. We certainly want everyone to share in the good news." Mrs. White clapped her hands again, this time louder. "Quiet please!"

He couldn't believe how quickly the situation had spiraled out of his control. He needed to do something to stop Mrs. White before she made a fool of herself. His mind scrambled to find a suitable response, one that wouldn't cause him to lose the much-needed support he'd gained from many within the congregation.

But when Priscilla shifted her focus from her shoe to his face, a flash of longing in her eyes stopped the words of rebuttal on the tip of his tongue.

Did this woman *want* to marry him? His heart pattered to a stop.

She gave him an apologetic smile and then tugged on her mother's sleeve. "Mother, this has gone too far."

But Mrs. White brushed away her hand. "Nonsense. This is exactly what the Lord has ordained."

"But, Mother—"

"Attention everyone!" Mrs. White's strong voice carried through the meetinghouse. "My daughter, Miss White, and our missionary guest, Dr. Ernest, are getting married."

In an instant, Priscilla was surrounded by friends, with everyone talking at the same time. And those around him slapped his back and shook his hand. He couldn't find the words to formulate any semblance of an explanation that would get him out of the predicament in which he suddenly found himself.

And Dr. Baldwin had disappeared to the other side of the room, as far away from him as possible.

Over the heads of well-wishers, Priscilla managed to catch his attention and mouth the words *I'm sorry.*

He shrugged and tried to give her a reassuring grin. He wasn't planning to marry her any more than she was planning to marry him. And once they had room to breathe, he'd make sure he straightened things out.

"You'll come to our home for a late supper," Mrs. White said when the meetinghouse began to empty. "You and Dr. Baldwin both."

He wanted to refuse, but Dr. Baldwin, along with John and Richard, had already started ambling down the street in the direction of the White home.

"I'll let the two of you walk together." Mrs. White tucked Priscilla's hand into the crook of Eli's arm. "There. Now you can have a few minutes to get better acquainted."

For a moment, he stood unmoving and watched the woman stride away. She linked arms with her husband and hurried to catch up with Dr. Baldwin and the Indian boys.

Priscilla shivered and began to slide her hand away from him. "I'm sorry about this."

He locked his arm over hers and prevented her escape. "I won't ravish you. I promise."

"I didn't think you would. It's just that—"

"This turned into a pretty big mess, didn't it?" His muscles tightened.

"Why don't we put an end to it right here?" She jerked her hand, trying to free it.

But he pressed harder, holding her captive, enjoying watching her spark come to life. "We can't disappoint your mother quite yet, can we? Or you either."

In the cool evening air, the white clouds of her breath came in short bursts. "Of course you won't disappoint me."

"Are you sure?" Even though his tone teased, a chamber of his heart stopped pulsing in anticipation of her answer.

"God's called me to India." Her voice was clipped. "I've had a setback today, but He'll open a way for me yet."

"The Board isn't going to let you go by yourself."

"They might—"

"You're gonna have to get married, just like I have to."

She blew an exasperated breath. "Well, I'm not marrying you."

"That's good, because I wasn't planning to marry you either."

"I figured you wouldn't."

The soft resignation in her tone halted his breath.

"I completely understand." She tugged her hand away and headed in the direction the others had gone.

Her velvety cloak swished in finality, and she lifted her chin as if to defy him. But before she could conceal her hands within the fur of her muff, he caught a glimpse of her trembling fingers.

Surely she didn't think—

"Wait." He charged after her.

She picked up her pace.

"You misunderstood me." With his long stride, he easily caught up to her. "Yes, Dr. Baldwin did tell me about your condition."

Her boots slapped the slush on the street. "I said I understand. Why would any man want to marry a woman who can't give him a namesake?"

"Plenty of men wouldn't care."

"Well, I'd like to meet just one."

He grabbed her arm and dragged her to a stop.

"Dr. Ernest!" She glared at his hand.

He turned her until she had no choice but to meet his gaze. The shadows of the evening lurked in her eyes.

"You want to meet a man who doesn't care about a woman's fertility?"

"Yes. I do."

"Well, you're looking at one. God's given me a passion and a calling to the natives of the West. I figure that's all I need."

Her eyes widened. Framed by long lashes, they were the kind of eyes that could easily make him forget his own name if he wasn't careful.

"Listen." He glanced to where the others had stopped in front of the Whites' home, and then his gaze trailed over to the other elaborate homes that lined the street. The shack he'd lived in as a child would fit into the front parlor of some of them. "All I'm trying to say is that I can't marry you, but it's not because of your infertility."

"If that's not it, then why?"

"Children!" Mrs. White called. "Come now. You can talk more inside, where it's warm."

Priscilla waved to her mother. "We're coming." But she didn't move.

"Not that I want to marry you," she continued. "Not at all. But if not for my condition, then what reason could you have for declining my mother's offer? Certainly not because I'm a *fine* lady."

He shrugged, then cupped his hands and blew into them for warmth. "You seem to be sincere and kind and eager—but those qualities won't help you survive the challenges of living in a foreign land."

Her eyes narrowed, and she regarded him for a moment before finally speaking. "How am I to believe you when you are the only one who has ever made such a declaration? Everyone else has always encouraged me in my pursuit of missions."

"Haven't you wondered why so many women missionaries die on the field?"

"No. I haven't wondered in the least. I've only considered my sisters in Christ heroic for their willingness to joyfully sacrifice their lives."

"Priscilla Jane White," Mrs. White called. "You hurry now before you catch your death of cold."

She started forward.

He matched his pace to hers. "Maybe they're not heroic so much as they are foolish, going to places and climates that are harsh for the healthiest and facing privations that would tax even the strongest."

"It would seem your standards are too high for everyone."

"Perhaps not for everyone. Maybe just for young gals who aren't used to doing hard work."

"Oh good. Then that isn't me." Their footsteps slowed as they neared the Whites' double-storied home with its tall Greek Revival pillars set in a stately row across the front. "Because, first of all, I'm not a 'gal.' And second, I've done plenty of hard labor in my life."

"Where I come from, knitting socks isn't considered work."

She stopped and turned on him so abruptly he stumbled backward. "I am well acquainted with all varieties of work. I don't know too many other women who work as hard as I do."

The sparks in her eyes mirrored the specks of stars beginning to flicker overhead.

He grinned. "Oh, and organizing prayer meetings doesn't count either."

She clenched her fists and huffed. "You're—you're—"

"Telling the truth?"

Her eyes were even bigger and helplessly beautiful when she got her dander up. He braced himself for her claws.

But instead of spitting at him, she drew herself up, took a breath, and composed her delicate features into a mask of gentility. "You might be telling the truth, Dr. Ernest. I might not know all of the realities of mission life. But thankfully, I can trust that the One who called me will help me through the trials."

The sincerity of her words wiped away his mirth and replaced it with growing admiration. She might be foolish, but she was sincere.

Mrs. White called to them again. "Continue your conversation inside." She stood on the front porch and turned to John and Richard, who stood next to Dr. Baldwin. "Now, you two savages run along to the back of the house and use the pantry entrance."

The boys backed away from the front door.

"Wait." Unease trickled through Eli. "Why can't John and Richard come in with us?"

"They'll be taking their meal in the kitchen," Mrs. White responded. "I see no need for them to traipse through my house when they can enter and exit through the rear door."

"And why won't they be eating at the table with the rest of us?"

Mrs. White sniffed. "Well, of course they won't. They're savages."

"They're young boys, human beings—in need of your kindness and goodwill."

"And I am showing them kindness, in the kitchen."

Eli shook his head in frustration. Why were his supporters willing to throw their money at missions but not willing to truly love the people they were bent on saving? "If John and Richard are savages simply because of the color of their skin, then I must be getting close. After months of travel, I'm about as dark as they are."

"It has nothing to do with the color of their skin, Dr. Ernest."

"Then what is it? Their language? Their customs? What makes them so savage?"

Priscilla laid her hand on his arm. "I'm sure what Mother meant to say is that John and Richard are more than welcome to eat wherever they would feel most comfortable, and that we would be happy to have them join us at the dinner table."

He didn't realize how tense his body had grown until the softness of her touch penetrated his thoughts.

"Thank you, Miss White. But if John and Richard aren't welcome in your mother's home, then I don't consider myself welcome either."

"Oh, pishposh." Mrs. White opened the door and held it wide. "Priscilla's right. If you insist on having the heathen boys dine with us, I shall make an exception."

Eli backed away and nodded at John and Richard to come with him. Over the winter with him in the East, they'd learned enough English to understand Mrs. White's rudeness. Even if they didn't know what she was saying, they could recognize the snub by her tone.

"Come now," Mrs. White said.

"No thank you." The woman was too proud and controlling. He couldn't stomach the thought of sitting through a meal with her, especially if he had to endure any more of her matchmaking charade. He didn't have time to waste on those kinds of games, not when he had so little time left to finalize his plans.

For an instant he scrutinized Priscilla, the smooth skin of her cheek, the tantalizing stretch of her neck, the delicate curls by her ear. He would never see her again after tonight, so why not give himself the pleasure of a last long look at one of God's finer works of creation?

"Good-bye." His gaze traveled to her eyes.

She lifted her long lashes. "Must you really leave? Mother didn't mean to offend you."

"Why, Miss White." His insides fluttered, as though her lashes had tickled him. "I thought you'd be happy to see me go, as uncivilized as I am."

Her eyelashes came down, hiding the depths of her thoughts. When she looked at him again, her eyes shone clear. "I believe you are a good man, Dr. Ernest. And I will pray that God blesses your mission in the West."

"You're not going to beg me to stay and marry you?"

She cocked a brow as if she didn't quite know what to think of him.

It was time to go before he did something foolish. "Good-bye, Priscilla White."

Then, without waiting for a response, he turned and strode away.

Mrs. White's appeals followed him. Even Dr. Baldwin's call urged him to stop. But through it all, Priscilla's soft-spoken good-bye was the only word he heard. It was only one word, but it had all the finality and force of a slamming door.

And for some reason, the slam reverberated through him and jolted him all the way to his bones.

Chapter
4

$\mathscr{P}$riscilla sat with her pen poised above her diary, the ink nearly dry. The page of her little book was empty, reflecting the hollow ache in her chest.

She'd retired to the study after arriving home from her long day of teaching, hoping for a moment of privacy in which to capture her troubled thoughts. But Mary Ann had followed her into the dim corner of the house and settled herself into one of the room's overstuffed armchairs.

Usually she was glad for Mary Ann's mature company after a day spent in the presence of children. She'd rejoiced after her sister's marriage to Reverend Lull, when their parents had suggested the young couple live in the extra bedroom vacated by their brother, who was away at seminary training. Priscilla had been glad for the precious extra time she could spend with her sister.

But now . . . it appeared that she'd have plenty of time with Mary Ann and the rest of her family . . . likely forever.

"What do you think?" her younger sister asked. "Is it big enough for the baby, or do I need to add a few more rows?"

Priscilla shifted in the stiff chair at the massive desk. Loaded with books and ledgers for maintaining household accounts, with its honeycomb of shelves, drawers, and compartments, the desk was her favorite escape.

She swallowed her wish to tell Mary Ann to leave her be and instead glanced at the blanket her sister was knitting. The dull light from the oil lamp highlighted the even rows of soft white yarn.

"It's beautiful," Priscilla said. And so was Mary Ann, with her swelling stomach and her glowing eyes.

"Is it long enough?"

Tears pricked the back of Priscilla's eyes. "It will be absolutely perfect," she said, shifting her gaze away from the painful reminder of what she could never have.

It was at times like these when her barrenness hurt the most, when she had to work hard to remind herself that God had other plans for her. Better plans.

If only she could stop the longings, stop the desire to experience the flutter of new life in her own womb. If only God didn't surround her with constant reminders.

She blinked back the blur in her eyes and let her gaze linger on the family Bible on the round table in the center of the room. Sitting on an elegantly crocheted doily, the enormous book with its silver-edged pages reminded her that God was at the center of their home *and* her heart. He would never desert her and would yet provide a way for her to go to India.

"If only the baby's kicking didn't keep me up at night." Mary Ann's knitting needles clicked together rhythmically.

"It won't be long now. Then you'll be holding your sweet baby in your arms."

"I suppose it is just getting me used to being up at night. All my friends tell me how little sleep they get during those first few weeks after the baby is born."

"Well, don't worry. It looks like I'll be here to help you." Priscilla turned back to her blank diary page.

Some days she wished she could tell her sister the truth. Maybe then Mary Ann would show more sensitivity. But Mother had insisted they keep the subject private—even from family—not wanting to chance any disgrace that her barrenness might bring to their impeccable reputation.

"You're quiet this forenoon," Mary Ann remarked. "I realize yesterday's letter must have been quite a shock. But certainly you'll feel better about the matter in a few days."

"Perhaps. At least I hope you're correct." The pity in her sister's voice only stirred the restlessness in Priscilla's chest. She didn't want Mary Ann's pity. She didn't want pity from anyone. Especially regarding her infertility.

Mother was right. It was better to keep her condition private. The pain of her longings was burden enough. She didn't need to add embarrassment and humiliation.

"Terrible news!" Mother called from the entryway. The front door closed with a rattle that shook the walls. An instant later she appeared in the doorway of the study. "I've just returned from Dr. Baldwin's and have terrible news."

Her face was red, and Priscilla prayed it was from the cold wind and not anger.

"I intended to make amends with Dr. Ernest and invite him and his savages to join us for dinner tonight, since he stomped off so childishly last night." Mother untied the ribbon under her chin and removed her bonnet.

Priscilla didn't need to hear the rest of Mother's terrible news. She already knew.

"And what do you think Dr. Baldwin told me?" She patted her hair and smoothed the loose strands.

Priscilla stared at the elaborate bookcase next to the fireplace. It overflowed with leather-bound classics and reference books. On the bottom shelf sat the stack of yellowing issues of the *Missionary Herald* she'd collected over the years—all the numerous articles about India that had birthed in her the desire to go and help poor and depraved souls.

But what about the many obituaries that lauded the services of the women who'd given up their lives? Had Dr. Ernest been right about their foolishness? About her?

"Dr. Ernest departed from town early this morning," Mother continued, "without leaving any word of where he was going or when he would be back."

Mary Ann gasped. "Oh no!"

"I can't believe the audacity of that man." Mother slipped off her heavy woolen cloak. "How are we supposed to make the wedding arrangements now?"

Priscilla shifted her gaze away from the news articles that seemed to be mocking her. "You need to accept the fact that Dr. Ernest doesn't want to marry me. He made it quite clear I wasn't the type of woman he'd ever consider."

Mother draped her cloak over a chair. "He was attracted to you, and he'll marry you."

"Maybe I was wrong to believe Providence was leading me into missions."

"I've prayed all my life that God would have a special place for each of my children in service to Him," Mother said. "Now that Mary Ann has married a minister, she's doing her part. Edward is considering the divine calling and theological seminary. You must do your part too, Priscilla."

Mother never mentioned their younger brother anymore. None of them understood why the Lord had chosen to take him home to heaven so early. His death had only seemed to fuel Mother's need to see the rest of them in service to God, as if that would somehow save them.

"Perhaps I shall continue to serve the Lord here in Angelica, as I always have," Priscilla said hesitantly.

"Nonsense." Mother plucked at a loose thread on her sleeve. "With your academy education and your spiritual training, you're an exemplary candidate for missionary work. And if the Lord has decided not to use you in India, He can most certainly use you somewhere else. Like the West."

Priscilla shook her head, but the sternness of Mother's glare stopped her protest. "Just think how highly people will regard you for embarking on such a journey. And think of the benefit to our family's reputation."

"I'm not serving the Lord for personal recognition—"

"Of course you're not. Nevertheless, heathen *everywhere* need to hear the gospel, including those in the West," Mother continued. "And since Dr. Ernest is willing to take you as you are, we'd best take advantage of this opportunity."

Priscilla pressed her lips together. It would do no good to argue with Mother. Besides, Mother would soon see for herself that even if she wanted to go west, Dr. Ernest wasn't interested in her—not in the least.

RUSHVILLE, NEW YORK

*Y*ou're the stupidest idiot I know," Eli's stepfather said as he scraped at the hide and didn't miss a stroke.

Eli leaned against the vat of tanning liquor and kicked at the slime of loose flesh pooled at his feet. What had possessed him to think he needed to stop by home?

"Them Indians don't want no help, and you's just gonna get yourself killed."

The beaming knife grated against the bristle of the hair and meat that remained on the wet hide. His stepfather's tool scuffed with an even rhythm borne of years of experience, but the young beamers at the other benches struggled with choppy movements against the wet pigskins and cowskins.

"'Sides, you know I need you here."

"Come on, Walt." Eli held back a groan. "I'm a doctor. I won't ever take over this place, even if I wasn't heading out to the West."

How many times did he need to tell his stepfather that he didn't want to tan leather for the rest of his life? Just because he'd worked off and on at the tannery over the winter while raising funds for the mission didn't mean he was planning to continue.

"It don't take nothing to be a doctor."

Eli shook his head and clamped his jaw shut.

"Any old quack can hang out a sign and be a doctor. But this . . . ." Walt straightened and waved at the dark narrow room. Although his stepfather had recently added several large vats and hired more operators, Eli couldn't see anything but the flecks of dried blood and flesh on the walls and the puddles of putrid meat that littered the floorboards.

"This here is the business of the future." Walt puffed out his stomach, his shirt and apron coated with gristle and blood. "We been trading our boots and shoes as far away as New York City."

"I'm not here to argue with you again—"

"You're too stupid to argue with me. You think you's smart, but we all know you can't read worth spit."

The gastric juices in Eli's stomach churned, stinging as sharply as Walt's words. Even if Walt wouldn't admit it, they both knew Eli had worked himself to the bone to better himself.

He pushed away from the vat. He shouldn't have come. Walt only pestered him more with each visit, his sisters were long gone, and his ma didn't care if he lived or died. Why couldn't he just let go of his hope that she'd ever forgive him?

Tentatively, he lifted his hand and skimmed his finger down the long scar along the edge of his cheek. It was a constant reminder of how he'd failed her and Pa—a reminder he didn't need, not when his mind refused to let him forget.

"I always warned you not to waste money on school. Who needs it anyway? I never been a day in my life and look at me."

Eli looked at Walt's hands, red and raw, covered with the slime of the hides. *Yes, look at you.* Eli swallowed his sarcastic response.

"Watch what you're doing." Walt shoved the beamer next to him who'd stopped his work to watch Eli. The force sent the young man slipping backward, and he landed with a smack on the wet floor.

Walt shook his head. "Idiot."

"Guess you still think you can knock everyone around." Eli had to leave before he did or said something he'd regret. He walked over to the beamer, reached out a hand, and heaved the man up. "You all right?"

The beamer nodded and grabbed his knife, then bent his head over the hide stretched across his bench.

Eli gave him a friendly slap on the back and started toward the door. "Look, Walt, I need the wages you owe me. And I came to see if you'd donate boots for the trip. That's all."

The acrid stench of decaying flesh swirled with the bitterness of finely ground hemlock bark used in the tanning solution. Even though he'd grown up with the reek of the tannery in every pore of his skin, he didn't want to spend the next week trying to erase the odor from his clothes and hair.

"Fine. You go collect your wages and have one of the men make you a pair of boots," Walt called.

Eli was almost to the door. Something in his gut told him to leave while he could, even if it meant he had to purchase the boots out of his own money.

He elbowed aside his hesitation. "I need four pairs."

"Four?" His stepfather's voice rose on the edge of disbelief. "Why do you need four? You plannin' to trade 'em to the Indians and make a profit?"

"One pair is for me, and the others are for my traveling companions."

Walt's mouth hung open for a moment before he clamped it shut and stared.

"For the missionary couple joining me in Pittsburgh. And for . . . my wife." Even as the word slipped from his tongue, annoyance coated his salivary glands. He still hadn't found a suitable woman.

"Wife? What wife?" Walt snorted. "Someone else beat you to her bed."

"I'm not talking about Sarah Taylor." Eli's mind scrambled to find words that wouldn't invite further mockery. If Walt knew the truth—that he'd failed to find a replacement and that his whole trip was in jeopardy—he'd never hear the end of it.

"I got a girl up in Angelica," he rushed. "A pretty little thing and rich too."

For a moment, Eli wanted to knock himself over the head. What was he thinking? When he'd ridden away from Angelica, he'd vowed never to think about Priscilla again.

But after a week of hopeless leads, Priscilla White was starting to look better every day. He hadn't worked this hard to let all his plans and dreams slip away simply because he couldn't find a woman.

"You're a lyin' idiot if you think I'm gonna believe you." Walt leveled his knife against the hide in front of him.

"You just have those boots ready by next week." Eli started through the door and called over his shoulder, "You can give them to us as a wedding present."

Outside, he blew a long frustrated breath. He flexed his arms and fingers, trying to release the tension. What had he just done?

He kicked at the cord of hemlock bark stacked on one side of the doorway. Surely he hadn't just practically married himself to Priscilla White. Not when he'd promised himself that if he had to saddle himself with a wife, he'd make sure she was strong and independent.

He twisted, and this time his boot connected with a fresh bundle of hides waiting for a lime bath to loosen the hair.

"Lord Almighty, what other choice have you given me?" He lifted his face to a sky covered with a sagging dirty blanket of clouds. He wished he could wrangle them aside and get a glimpse of the wide open heavens he'd seen out west.

Why had it been so much easier for him to think and pray when he'd slept under the stars? There the Almighty's will had been as clear as a reflection in a mountain pond. He'd known without a doubt that God wanted him to be the one to establish a good relationship with the Indians of the Northwest—to reach out the hand of friendship and help before others came west and devalued and destroyed them.

But now . . . he wasn't so sure what the Almighty wanted for him.

Eli surveyed the lines of pelts, already bated and hung to dry. His gaze traveled to the log house situated too close to the tannery to escape the wretched smells. An emaciated wisp of smoke arose from the chimney, but otherwise there was no sign of his ma's presence. Even the chickens pecking among the rubbish that littered the muddy ground clucked as if their will to live had been cut from them.

His ma had never been strong, hadn't ever stood up to Walt to protect his sisters. She'd always been a weak woman. Over the years Walt had battered her down even more. Now she was all but gone, and his sisters were married off to men just like Walt.

Eli had vowed that when he married, he'd find a woman who could stand tall under the hardships of life.

With a frustrated breath, he hoisted himself up into his saddle. He'd run out of time and choices. He had no other option but to put aside his reservations about Priscilla and set his horse on the road to Angelica.

Even though Priscilla wasn't particularly interested in the West, he'd have to find a way to convince her to join him. . . .

And he'd pray she wouldn't be able to resist his charm once he laid it on her.

Chapter
5

ANGELICA, NEW YORK

*P*riscilla drew another small circle on the board to illustrate the newest planet. "Quiet, children. No more talking." She tossed the halfhearted instruction over her shoulder while she stepped back to examine her diagram.

"As you can see," she continued, "Ceres orbits between Mars and Jupiter."

The giggles grew louder.

"Children!" she chided and then stepped forward to trace her finger along the ellipse she'd drawn. If only they could know for sure whether any other planets existed beyond Uranus. What she wouldn't give to be the one to explore the far reaches of the unknown.

She chewed her bottom lip.

Sure, she could dream about exploring planets and other distant places of the universe. But was she *really* willing to go into the unknown anywhere? If she couldn't teach in India, would she be willing to go someplace else? Had she set her heart too much on one place when perhaps God had other plans for her?

A burst of laughter near the back of the narrow schoolroom finally commanded her return to earth and to her classroom.

"Now, children. You are disobeying our rule for silence." Her gaze lingered on the board for a second longer before she tore herself away and pivoted to face the class.

The younger children perched in their desks near the front of the room, and the older children sat in the back near the entrance—mostly the girls who weren't privileged enough to attend Female Academy in Troy, where she'd done a significant amount of her own schooling.

The students' wide smiles greeted her, and the afternoon sunshine pouring in the large windows lit their faces. She had only to follow their glances to the back row to see the source of their laughter.

Her fingers flew to the cameo at her neck.

With his long legs tucked awkwardly under a desk and his hand raised, Dr. Ernest was watching her with a solemn expression that didn't match the merriment in his eyes.

"Miss White." He lowered his hand. "I have a question."

She stared at him speechless, a strange mixture of excitement and apprehension stirring in her stomach.

"Some scientists say that Ceres isn't really a planet." He hunched his back to fit onto the small bench, and his knees pushed against the flimsy desktop. "After all, it's located in the asteroid belt."

What was he doing back in Angelica? And how had he managed to sneak into the school without her hearing him?

His shirt and waistcoat were crisp and clean. Without his hat, the wild, untamable waves of his hair had rebelled against his obvious attempts to smooth them down. He'd shaved the shadowy layer of stubble, but his smooth, tan skin had a scruffiness he couldn't shed. He was as well groomed as any gentleman she'd ever met. But for all his efforts, there was still something rugged about him—and something dangerously appealing.

Her hand fluttered to the wisps of hair that floated about her face. Surely he wasn't back to carry out Mother's marriage charade.

Even from the furthest row of the classroom, his winter blue eyes caught hers with their intensity. For a long moment she couldn't breathe. Nor could she look away. He was a flame, and she was the little girl who'd been warned not to touch. Only she couldn't remember why she ought to stay away, especially when every nerve in her body urged her to reach out.

"And Ceres is too small." A grin teased the corner of his mouth, almost as if he knew he was getting the reaction from her he'd intended.

She forced herself to start breathing again, calmly. If he thought he could steal into her classroom and flirt with her, then just wait until she joined in. . . . She'd had plenty of practice in her younger days, when she'd been much more carefree. He'd be no match for her ability to beguile.

"Why, Dr. Ernest." She tilted her head. "You said you had a *question*. And all I've heard are *statements*."

"Excuse me, Miss White." His grin widened. "'Course, you're right."

She lifted her lips into her sweetest, most practiced smile. "Would you like to try rephrasing your statement and show the children how to ask a proper question?"

"Certainly," he drawled. "For such a pretty lady like you, how could any man say no?"

The older girls tittered. Their flashing smiles and flushed cheeks were evidence they had already fallen prey to his winsome ways.

She braced herself. He wouldn't so easily sway her. After all, he'd made it quite clear he wasn't interested in her.

"So . . ." he started.

If he wasn't back because of her, why was he sitting in her classroom intent upon engaging her in playful banter?

"So, my question is this." A shadow filtered through his eyes and snuffed the laughter in them, making them too serious. And when he extricated his legs from the desk, instead of rising to his feet, he lowered himself into the aisle onto one knee.

She stifled a shiver.

"Miss White?" His gaze found her again.

The intensity sent her heart into a wild dash. Her fingers went back to her throat, to the delicate cameo, to the pattering of her pulse beneath.

His eyes spoke the words before he could get them out. "Will you do me the honor of becoming my wife?"

For a long moment the world crashed to a halt and ceased to exist—except for Dr. Ernest and her. The sincerity in his eyes reached across the room and wrapped around her heart, around insecurities she'd held there the past years. It was soothing balm upon the open lesions she'd tried so hard to hide.

Did he truly want to marry her? Even with the knowledge that she was incomplete as a woman and could never give him a child of his own?

She wavered and took a step back. The solidness of the blackboard met her.

"Say yes!" shouted one of the boys in the front row.

Several others chimed in until the room was alive with laughter and calls of encouragement.

Hadn't he told her he didn't want to marry her because he thought she'd be an inadequate missionary? How could he have changed his mind about her so soon?

He cocked his head and gave her a lopsided grin, the kind that tickled her stomach and made her want to ignore all the nagging questions demanding her attention.

The shouts of the children bounced off the walls. "Children!" she called, but her voice was lost in the din. She didn't know how to answer Dr. Ernest, but she did know she needed to bring order to her classroom.

She reached for the bell on her desk and swung it. The clanging rose above the voices, and silence descended over the room.

"It seems to me," she said, once she had their attention, "that we have a troublemaker in our midst today." She looked pointedly at Dr. Ernest and batted her lashes at him. She could think of no other solution to her dilemma than to continue to banter with him. At least it would buy her some time.

When his gaze wavered, she sauntered down the aisle toward him. Her boots tapped a slow rhythm with the squeak of the floorboards. "And when someone is naughty, he must suffer a penalty for his misbehavior."

His eyes widened and his brows lifted with surprise.

She let a satisfied smile curve her lips.

He watched her for a moment before his eyes took on a teasing glimmer. "Why, Miss White, I didn't know you were such a strict teacher."

Her heart faltered along with her steps. The soft giggles of the girls rang in her ears as a warning to stop, but something about his presence drew her. "Of course I am. Aren't I, class? I always issue the strictest of discipline."

He leaned onto his knee and flashed her a grin. "I'm shaking in my boots."

"As you should be." She stopped in front of him, praying he couldn't hear the wild thudding of her heart. "Just because you are a doctor doesn't mean I'll let you off easily."

She caught a whiff of his freshly groomed scent, the woodsy sweet and spice of bay rum. "I think perhaps . . ." Her gaze skimmed over the long, thin scar beneath his eye and then over the ones on his hands. How could she agree to marry a man she'd only just met—about whom she knew so little?

"So what's my punishment?" His voice was too eager for someone awaiting punishment.

She wanted to giggle with the girls but instead lowered her chin and tried to give him her most stern schoolteacher look. "You must stay after school and write one hundred times on the board, 'From now on I promise to be a good boy.'"

"Promise to be a good boy? Me?" He gave a short laugh.

"Don't tell me your wayward deeds are beyond rehabilitation, Dr. Ernest?"

He shrugged. The gleam in his eyes stoked a strange warmth in her belly. "I think you've a mind to torture me, Miss White. Staying after school with the teacher is indeed the worst punishment I could ever imagine."

The warmth swirled throughout her middle and fanned to her neck and cheeks.

Somehow she managed to dismiss the class, and when the last student had finally taken leave, Dr. Ernest made his way to the front of the room.

"So, Miss White." Now it was his turn to amble toward her, as if he made an everyday occurrence of proposing marriage to young women.

She inched behind her desk, needing to put something between them.

He stopped on the opposite side, proceeded to shove aside a stack of books, and perched half his backside on the edge. "You haven't answered my question yet." He grabbed the apple she'd forgotten to eat at lunch and rubbed it on his trousers.

"And what question was that?" She fidgeted with the astronomy pamphlet still open to the page she'd abandoned.

He crunched into the apple. "Didn't know astronomy was a standard subject in school these days," he managed between bites.

"It's not a standard subject. But I like to squeeze in science when time allows."

He ceased chewing and raised his brow.

"Is it so hard to believe a woman could like science?"

He bit off another hunk. "Not hard to believe. Just unusual."

She turned a page in the booklet. "Dr. Ernest, why do you want to marry me today, when a week ago you told me you never would?"

He chomped for a moment and then set the half-eaten apple on the desk. "In other words, you want to know what made me change my mind?"

"Yes, I do." She looked up at him, and he met her gaze straight on.

"I've had a desire to go west since I was a boy and heard the tales of Captain Meriwether Lewis and William Clark and their overland trip to the Pacific Ocean. Now, after my own exploration trip and after spending time with the Nez Perce, I can't imagine doing anything else but opening a medical clinic in Oregon Country. And I can't do it unless I get married."

"But why me? Especially after the things you said about my not being qualified."

"I've run out of time and don't have any other options."

Even though his words didn't surprise her, they still hit her chest and left a painful indentation. "So . . . you want to use me?"

The clearness of his eyes allowed her to see all the way inside—to the truth in the far reaches of his soul. "I promise I won't use you, Priscilla."

Her hands trembled, and she clasped them together within the folds of her dress.

"I'd like to think of it more like a business arrangement. We both have our hearts set on being missionaries. But we're both lacking the one thing the Mission Board requires: a spouse."

She shook her head. "I'm not sure—"

"It'll be a marriage in name, nothing more than that. Instead, we'll be business partners. You can help me achieve my dreams, and I can help you. That's it. No romantic notions, no conjugal demands, no emotional entanglements."

"That sounds so cold—"

"Look—" he blew a long sigh and then leaned toward her— "neither of us really wants to get married, but the Board is making us. We don't have to like each other, and we don't have to, well—you know—consummate . . ."

Heat rushed to her face, and she wished she could shrivel up and disappear through a crack in the floor.

"What I'm trying to say," he said, "is that we can be friends if we want. But we don't have to make a big deal about the marriage. It's just a means to get what we want."

"What *you* want."

"And you too."

"I'd planned on teaching in India."

"Does it really matter where?" The earnestness in his voice stripped away the little resistance she had left. "If God's placed a burden on our hearts to reach out to people who've yet to experience His saving love, then why would it make a difference if we reach out to the Indians of India or the Indians of the West?"

He was right. "But the West is practically uninhabitable. How would we survive?"

"I won't lie to you. It'll be rough." His eyes probed hers. "But I promise you, if it's too hard and too dangerous, I'll make provisions for you to return home. I'll find a ship to bring you around the continent—"

"Priscilla!" A call from outside the schoolhouse door made her jump. "Priscilla, hurry! Mother wants you to come home right away."

She took a step away from the desk, away from Dr. Ernest. She hadn't wanted to get married, and she'd wanted to go to India. How could she make such an enormous switch? Did she even want to?

His eyes pleaded with her to say yes.

"Exciting news!" Her sister's voice came again as the door at the back of the room swung open. "Dr. Ernest has returned to town, and he stopped by and told Mother he would come to dinner tonight."

Mary Ann stepped inside and came to an abrupt halt. She glanced from Dr. Ernest to Priscilla and back and clamped a hand over her mouth.

"I agree. It's *very* exciting." Dr. Ernest grinned.

Mary Ann blushed.

Priscilla stacked the books scattered on her desk. "Would you please tell Mother I'll be home shortly." She shot Dr. Ernest what she hoped was a censuring glare. Was he enlisting the aid of Mother in his marriage proposal? She would have no hope of resisting Mother once she discovered Dr. Ernest's intentions.

His grin widened, and he nodded, as if he could read her thoughts.

"So I ran all this distance for nothing?" Mary Ann rubbed a hand over her protruding stomach until her fingers rounded the underside of her belly and lifted it, giving aid to the weight of the baby. "I wouldn't be surprised if all this activity causes me to go into labor tonight."

"Well, if it happens at dinner, at least we won't have to run for a doctor." Priscilla's tone was sourer than she'd intended.

"True," Dr. Ernest added. "I'll be sure to bring my doctor's bag—just in case."

Mary Ann raised her brow, and her eyes wavered with uncertainty.

Remorse nagged at Priscilla. She had no reason to take out her frustrations on her sister. *Lord, help me.* When would she ever learn to control her jealousy? "I'm sorry. I didn't mean to snap at you. Forgive me."

"I should think you'd be happy," Mary Ann remarked slowly. "You've been praying all week for God to open a door for you to serve Him. And now He has."

Her sister's words made their way through the cracks in Priscilla's crumbling resolve. She had indeed prayed for God to provide a way for her to go. And here was Dr. Ernest. He'd gone down on his knee and had practically pleaded with her to marry him—even though he knew exactly what kind of woman he was getting in the bargain.

If this wasn't God's answer to her prayers, she didn't know what else could be.

Priscilla jerked her gaze away from her sister and leveled it upon Dr. Ernest.

His brows shot up.

"Yes." She slapped the astronomy pamphlet closed.

"Yes?"

"In answer to your question, my answer is yes."

A slow smile spread over his face, and the winter sunlight in his eyes began to dance. "Then it's a deal?" He held out a hand.

She slipped her hand into his. "We have a deal."

"Good." His fingers closed around hers with the softness of a caress. And when his thumb brushed against the pulse in her wrist, her heart tumbled into a dizzying spin.

She had agreed to a marriage of convenience, a marriage in name only. That's all.

And yet she couldn't prevent a tiny thrill from winding through her heart. After the past several years of convincing herself that she wanted to be single, that she'd be completely content without a husband, she didn't have to fool herself any longer.

She was finally getting the opportunity to do something every girl hoped for—she would get to have a wedding, enjoy the prestige of married life, and share the rest of her life—all her dreams and hopes—with a husband.

～

She had the voice of an angel.

Eli sat forward on his chair, and with each note of Priscilla's unaccompanied song his heart drummed louder. Tendrils of her hair floated around her face like a golden halo. With her eyes closed and her face lifted heavenward, he could almost believe she was an angel instead of the soft, genteel lady he'd agreed to marry.

"Isn't she lovely?" Mrs. White whispered.

Priscilla was indeed the loveliest creature in both heaven and earth. But he wouldn't give Mrs. White the satisfaction of a compliment. If not for her, he might have enjoyed the dinner and evening much more. But as it was, she'd prattled on about all her accomplishments as director of her missionary organization and boasted of her work with the Mite Society to help the poor.

Upon reaching the last chord, Priscilla opened her eyes. Out of all the others in the parlor, her gaze sought him. Her top teeth came down over her bottom lip, and her wide eyes waited for his reaction.

His gut twisted with sudden keenness, and he couldn't make his arms move to clap with everyone else. Instead, he nodded to her.

Her lashes came down over her flushed cheeks.

"What did you think of our Priscilla, Dr. Ernest?" Mrs. White's question nipped at him, as all her others had.

He pushed himself out of the ornately carved chair. The eyes of the other guests fastened upon him—Reverend Lull and Mary Ann, Mr. White, and Priscilla—and they waited for his answer.

The heat from the fireplace, the stuffiness of the small room, and Mrs. White's smothering had plastered his shirt to his back. He needed a breath of fresh air as much as he needed life itself.

"Miss White, thank you for the beautiful song. And I thank you, Mrs. White, for the very fine dinner."

"Must you go so soon?" the woman asked. "Surely you have time to listen to one more song?"

"I'll be back for the wedding on Sabbath eve."

"This Sabbath? That's only four days away." Mrs. White arose from the settee. "Dr. Ernest, there is absolutely no possible way we can have the wedding in *four* days. We'll need at least a month, and even then we'll have to rush to get everything ready on time."

Irritation pushed at his tongue, threatening to loosen it and make him say something he might later regret. The hassle was exactly what he'd wanted to avoid.

"Oh, Doctor, I'm sure you can allow us at least a month."

"Mrs. White, listen to Dr. Ernest." Mr. White rose from his chair and puffed out his chest.

"Now, Mr. White, you don't know anything about the enormity of planning for a wedding." Mrs. White glared at her husband. "I'll thank you to stay out of the conversation."

"Mother, we'll make do." Priscilla's voice was gentle, as if she was used to placating her mother.

"If you're going to do any planning this week," Eli said, "you'd best put your efforts into preparing Priscilla for the long journey. She'll need several plain dresses—"

"You can't possibly expect Priscilla to be ready to travel so soon either. With all the trunks to pack—"

"She gets one trunk."

Priscilla sucked in a soft breath and bumped against a round display table in the corner. Several framed portraits collapsed with a clatter.

Mary Ann made a sharp noise of protest too, but her husband, the reverend, silenced her with a touch on the arm.

"One trunk?" Mrs. White whispered, her voice laced with horror. "Impossible."

Eli's jaw tightened. "She gets one *small* trunk."

"We don't have any *small* trunks," Mrs. White replied.

"Then find one."

Priscilla stepped forward. "Are you sure there won't be room for two—one for my personal items and one for my books and school supplies?"

Was he making a mistake marrying her? How would she ever be able to handle the difficult trip and a new way of living when she was used to all this? He glanced around the lavish room with its richly papered walls, elegant furniture, and thick rugs, and then landed upon the silky layers of her dress.

"I won't send my daughter to her new home without the proper provisions—the linens, samplers, and family heirlooms she's saved all these years."

"One trunk." Eli met Priscilla's gaze.

Her eyes widened.

Was she having second thoughts about joining him? She might as well face the truth about the dangers of the journey before it was too late. "We'll be lucky to carry all the food we need for the trip, much less trunks of provisions. When we get good and hungry, we won't be able to eat linens."

For a long moment, no one spoke, as if the reality of the arrangement was finally beginning to pierce their understanding.

"I won't cover up the perils of the journey." He had no choice but to help them understand the gravity of traveling west. "We'll have about seven months of hard travel to reach Oregon Country. Any delay, even slight, means we could end up stranded in snow in the Blue Mountains, the last big range we need to cross before reaching the mission site. There's the very real possibility we could face a shortage of food; we could be attacked and killed by hostile Indian tribes; we could drown in one of the many river crossings; we—"

"That's enough, Dr. Ernest." Mrs. White's face had grown pale, revealing the blue veins in her temple. "If you are trying to scare us from allowing Priscilla to accompany you, then you are succeeding quite well."

"It's a dangerous trip, and I want you to know what you're getting yourself into. That's all."

"Thank you, Dr. Ernest." Priscilla traced the floral pattern in the plush rug with the tip of her slipper. "I had assumed I would be able to take more, similar to what I would have packed for traveling to India."

"An overland trip is different than one by ship. If you want to back out of our agreement, I'll understand. No hard feelings." He swallowed his growing disappointment. "But if you still want to marry me and come with me, then we need to get married this Sabbath."

He didn't bother to listen to more of Mrs. White's protests. Instead, he shook Reverend Lull's and Mr. White's hands and made his way into the spacious front hallway, heaviness pounding his bones with each step.

"Dr. Ernest," Priscilla called.

He grabbed his cloak from the coat stand and tossed the worn garment about his shoulders.

"Dr. Ernest, wait." She burst into the front hallway and rushed toward him.

He folded his hands across his chest and braced himself for her rejection. Sure, she was only reacting to all he'd said. But frustration clutched him anyway.

She stopped in front of him. "I'm sorry about my mother. She means well, and she only wants what's best for me. With a little time, she'll adjust to the idea of my going west and not to India. And so will I."

He hesitated. "Maybe I should have done a better job clarifying everything beforehand."

She chewed on her bottom lip for a moment and then lifted a hand to his arm. Her soft touch soaked into him. "You will come back next Sabbath?"

"Do you want me to?"

"Yes." Her answer was hardly more than a whisper.

"Are you sure?" He nodded his head to the other room where the voices of Mr. and Mrs. White had grown louder. "Maybe your mother won't let you marry me now."

"If you promise to return, then I promise to marry you."

"Even if you can't have a proper wedding?"

"If we're not having a proper marriage, why would I need a proper wedding?"

For a fraction of an instant, he thought he saw a flicker of disappointment in her eyes. "Listen, I'm sorry . . ."

Maybe they wouldn't have time for a fancy wedding, but he could still find a way to make it special for her, couldn't he? He had his wages from working at the tannery for Walt. Would he have enough time and money to have a ring made for her?

His mind flashed with a vision of her gazing up at him with the adoring eyes of a real bride as he slipped the ring on her finger. Just as quickly, he shoved aside the picture. Under normal circumstances, her family—her mother—would never have agreed to the marriage, and Priscilla wouldn't have either. Theirs was a union of convenience, and he'd do best to remember that.

"And what about all the danger?" His voice was edged with frustration at himself and the helplessness of the situation. "Didn't I scare you away?"

"When I was fifteen, I made a vow before God that I would give my life in service to Him." Her eyes lit with passion. "Don't you think God will honor that pledge and give me the strength to do whatever He's called me to? Even if I travel to the West?"

He let out a ragged breath. If he took her and she ended up dying, how could he live with himself? "The trip is just too dangerous. I shouldn't have asked you. The Mission Board shouldn't have forced me to ask *any* woman."

"I might not be the ideal candidate, but I'm much stronger than you know."

He slapped on his hat, yanked open the door, and stepped outside. The blast of cool air was a welcome relief, a reminder of the sweet air in the mountains, the beauty of the West, the freshness of a new life, the passion to help a group of people he'd grown to love—all that he would give up if he walked away from Priscilla.

She followed him onto the verandah. Her fingers circled his

forearm, and she tugged him around until he had no choice but to face her. "Remember, we are in agreement that if the rigors of life in the West are unsuitable for a woman, you shall send me home."

The muscles in his arm relaxed, and the earnestness in her eyes beckoned him to rationalize the situation. "You're right. If it's too dangerous, I'll find a way for you to return home."

If he gave the Board's foolhardy plan a try and it didn't work out, they wouldn't be able to fault him. 'Course he'd do everything he could to protect her and make sure she survived the long trip. But he wouldn't hesitate to send her back if she couldn't handle the difficulties of living in the West. He would find a ship to take her home around the continent. He could even find a way to have their marriage annulled and give her the chance to start over again with someone else.

She gave him a wavering smile. "Then it's settled. We shall get married next Sabbath eve."

"Next Sabbath eve." He could only pray that for both their sakes he wasn't making the biggest mistake of his life.

Chapter
6

*I*f she looked into anyone else's tear-filled eyes, she wouldn't be able to finish her solo.

Priscilla shifted her gaze out the meetinghouse window to the darkening Sabbath sky, to the wisps of pink cirrus clouds that reflected the setting sun.

"'Yes, my native land! I love thee,'" she sang. Her fingers dug into the satiny ripples of her black bombazine dress, her wedding dress, the most fashionable her mother could have tailored on such short notice.

> "All thy scenes I love them well;
> Friends, connections, happy country,
> Can I bid you all farewell?"

Her voice wobbled, and the ache in her heart threatened to squeeze her throat closed. When she'd picked the hymn, she hadn't realized that it would be so difficult to sing and the words would bring her friends and family to tears.

Since this was her last time to be with them before she left, she'd wanted the song to be her farewell. But she hadn't known how hard it would be to say good-bye.

She took a deep breath and lifted her voice to finish. "'Can I leave you, far in heathen lands to dwell?'"

When the strains of her song faded, the silence of the sanctuary was punctuated with sniffles.

She couldn't stop from glancing at Mother and Mary Ann in the front pew. Tears trickled down their cheeks, and they dabbed at them with handkerchiefs. She could picture herself and Mary Ann as little girls, holding hands and skipping behind their mother, always so excited whenever she allowed them to accompany her as she delivered Bibles and food to the poor. Mother had been an exemplary model and had taught all of them well what it meant to serve the Lord.

Priscilla would miss Mother and Mary Ann dreadfully.

The tightness in her throat brought a sting to her eyes. She couldn't cry here. Not now. Not during her wedding ceremony.

The soft warmth of Eli's fingers circled hers.

At the unexpected touch, her breath hitched.

He pressed gently and offered her a small smile—one that brimmed with sympathy. The gentleness of his expression and of his touch spread to her heart, wrapping it with pleasure.

A tremor of excitement threaded through her. Yes, she ached at the thought of leaving everyone and everything she held dear. But she was standing next to a strong man, pledging herself to him, and getting ready to embark on the adventure of her lifetime.

A month ago, who would have guessed she'd be getting married—a dream that had died the day Dr. Baldwin had told her she'd likely never be able to bear her own children. And who would have thought that she'd be heading into the uncivilized lands of the West to start a mission, that she'd be among the first white women to venture such a trip?

Eli arched one eyebrow at her, as if asking if she was ready to continue.

She smiled and nodded. In the deepest places of her heart, she knew she was more than ready to embark upon a new life with him.

Her life wouldn't include India, but perhaps God had provided something better for her. Eli had such resolute convictions about his mission and a desire to love the Indians. Surely she would be able to help him and do great things for the Lord.

Reverend Lull wiped the moisture from his eyes. "Time for you to exchange your vows."

Eli positioned himself so that he was facing her, and then he reached for her other hand so their fingers were meshed together between them.

Her heart dipped and resumed beating at double speed. For a man of his ruggedness, the smoothness of his touch was something she doubted she would ever get used to. It sent a shiver up her arm and down her spine.

"I, Elijah Ernest, take thee, Priscilla White, to be my wedded wife." His words were soft and his eyes sincere.

A thrill of wonder wound through her.

"And I do promise and covenant, before God and these witnesses, to be thy loving and faithful husband; in plenty and in want, in joy and in sorrow, in sickness and in health, as long as we both shall live."

He almost sounded as if he meant the words, that he wanted her as a real wife and not just a business partner. For a few minutes, it wouldn't hurt to pretend they were going to have a real marriage. Would it?

"I, Priscilla White, take thee, Elijah Ernest, to be my wedded husband."

The intensity within the depths of his blue eyes captured her and drew her in. Was he thinking the same thing—that they could be more than partners?

"I do promise and covenant, before God and these witnesses, to be thy loving and faithful wife; in plenty and in want, in joy and in sorrow, in sickness and in health, as long as we both shall live."

If she was only a business partner, what did her vows mean? What would happen if life in the West was too hard? If she had to return home, what would happen to their marriage?

"Do you have a ring?" Reverend Lull whispered to Eli.

He let go of her hands and patted his waistcoat. For a moment, he fumbled within the layers until his hand emerged with a thin silver band, a delicately engraved pattern of rose swirls covering it.

His eyes shone, and something within them told her he'd had the ring specially made for her, that he'd sacrificed of the little he had to provide this gift for her.

She lifted her hand and willed it not to shake.

Slowly he slid the ring onto her finger, his pupils growing wider with the descent of the band.

"I now pronounce you man and wife," Reverend Lull said. "Dr. Ernest, you may kiss your bride."

Eli's gaze dropped to her lips, and the blue of his eyes all but disappeared behind the darkness of obvious desire.

Her stomach fluttered. And when he inclined his face toward hers, she couldn't breathe.

Would he really dare to kiss her here in front of everyone? But how could he not? Not when it was expected of him.

The warmth of his breath hovered against her lips for only an instant before his mouth captured hers decisively.

His lips melted against hers like honey butter, devouring her startled gasp.

For an exquisite moment, she savored the sweet taste of his lips upon hers and marveled at the tenderness of his intimate touch and how it seemed to reach all the way down to her stomach and tingle there.

Then, just as quickly as he'd started the kiss, he ended it, pulling away from her and putting a firm distance between them.

She straightened and tried to restore strength to her weak knees, surprised at the wild beating of her heart.

What had it all meant? The tender passion of his kiss? And her unlikely reaction? Was it possible they would eventually develop feelings for each other?

His gaze caught hers, and the apology there reminded her of their agreement.

Inwardly she chided herself, hoping she wasn't blushing in embarrassment. She might have allowed herself to pretend they were embarking on a real marriage. But she'd do well to never forget they had agreed upon a partnership. And nothing more.

~

"You must fulfill your wifely duties." Mother's voice was as unyielding as each stroke of the brush in Priscilla's long hair.

She wanted to sneak under the bed. At least the cool darkness of the upstairs bedroom hid the flames on her face.

"I conceived on my wedding night." Mary Ann folded back the covers on the double bed Priscilla had shared with her younger sister since they were girls.

Mother glared at Mary Ann before smoothing Priscilla's hair and sliding the brush through it again. "As unpleasant as the duty may be, you must never withhold yourself from your husband."

Priscilla ducked her head. She supposed it was every mother's responsibility to prepare her daughter for the marriage bed, but Mother needn't worry. Hadn't Eli said they wouldn't consummate?

She shivered and pulled the robe tighter around the frilly nightgown Mary Ann had insisted she don. What if he changed his mind?

The taste of his kiss still lingered on her lips. It had been anything but unpleasant. If he planned on giving her more kisses like that, why would she want to withhold herself?

Of course, he hadn't looked at her since Reverend Lull had pronounced them man and wife. He'd found plenty of others to talk to and was, at that moment, locked away in the den with Father and Reverend Lull.

"Don't worry." Mary Ann rubbed her hand across the swell of her stomach. "Once you're with child, you'll get a break."

"I'm sure we'll be just fine," she murmured, wishing she could just tell them to cease speaking about the matter altogether. At least Mary Ann would never have to know the truth. She'd be far away from the questions once it was time for her to conceive and didn't.

Mother stepped in front of her and narrowed her eyes in examination. She drew a strand of Priscilla's hair around to the front and adjusted the wave so it hung down and almost touched her waist. "There. You must bear your wifely burden with both beauty and dignity."

Mary Ann leaned in and placed a kiss on Priscilla's cheek. "You look as beautiful as always."

Priscilla reached for Mary Ann's hand before she could back away and clasped it between hers. "I couldn't have gotten ready this past week without your help. Thank you."

Mary Ann just gave her a sad, tired smile.

Priscilla reached for Mother's hand and put it to her lips. "And thank you, Mother. For everything."

Mother's eyes glistened, and she quickly shook her head. "We'll have plenty of time for good-byes in the morning."

After they left the room, Priscilla sat on the edge of the bed and stared at the closed door. Her stomach clinched. What would Eli say when he opened the door and saw her waiting for him?

Should she climb under the covers and wait there? Or would that be even more presumptuous?

The glass oil lamp on the chest of drawers cast a pale light over the bedroom, over the flower print on the washbasin and the lace on the curtains.

Her gaze touched each familiar item, and her heart lingered wistfully, saying good-bye to everything she'd always known. And to her childhood.

This would be her last night. She'd overheard Eli telling others they would need to leave on the morrow to retrieve John and Richard, among other stops, before they began their journey by sleigh to Pittsburgh.

And even though Mother had once again protested the hurried departure, Priscilla had no doubt Mother and Mary Ann would be up most of the night finishing the last stitches on the serviceable dresses they'd started making that week.

Priscilla fingered the squares in the quilt. And they'd likely pack the small trunk Mary Ann had agreed to give her.

She'd wanted to help with the preparations, but they'd insisted she spend her wedding night with her husband. And now, faced with the possibility of being in the same room as Eli all night long, she was tempted to slip back into her dress.

The squeak of the steps and the distinct scuff of his boots sent her heart into a downward tumble. She smoothed her hair and folded her hands in her lap.

The door swung open.

She straightened and tried to keep breathing.

He stepped inside and kicked the door closed with his heel. He glanced around the room, taking in everything but her.

His hair was in tousled disarray, and the scruff on his face was dark in the shadows of the room. He leaned against the door and gripped the handle. He focused on his boots and said nothing.

Her stomach pinched tighter. Should she stand up and go to him? Or should she let him make the first move?

"Your mother practically forced me up the stairs. I guess, whether we want to or not, we'll have to stay in the same room."

She nodded.

Only then did he glance at her. His eyes widened. "Almighty Lord, help me," he breathed, fumbling at the door handle.

She rose from the bed. "Don't leave," she whispered.

His gaze swept over her. "Sweet, sweet Lord."

"If anyone needs to leave, let me."

"You're . . . you're absolutely . . ." The brightness of his eyes lingered over the strand of hair tumbling across her chest.

She glanced down. Her robe had fallen open, and all that shielded her body from his probing eyes was the thin linen and lace of her nightgown. Heat swirled through her, and she fumbled to pull her robe closed.

When his eyes lifted to meet hers, something in their depths sent a different kind of heat pulsing through her, the same sweet tingle in her stomach that she'd had when he'd kissed her.

"You'd better get in bed." His whisper was gruff, and he wrenched his eyes away.

With a pounding heart, she groped for the covers and somehow managed to slide under them. The coolness soothed her flushed skin.

He stepped over to the lamp, cupped his hand over the globe, and puffed out the flame.

The blackness of the night surrounded her and sent more strange tingles through her middle until she trembled.

A thunk on the hardwood floor—one discarded boot—was followed by another thunk—the other boot.

She chewed at her bottom lip. Would he undress here? Now?

At the soft slither of linen against skin, she scrunched her eyes closed. He was indeed taking off his clothes.

Of course, in the complete darkness of the room she couldn't see even his outline, but that didn't stop her from imagining the slow shed of his shirt.

His footsteps padded across the room to the opposite side of the bed.

She pulled the covers up to her neck and held her breath. She waited for the sag of the mattress.

For a long moment, his heavy breathing hovered in the air above her. Then he gave a low groan, backed away, and flopped to the floor.

Her heart picked up its pace, and she sat forward, straining through the darkness to see what he was doing.

From his hefting and the squeak of the floorboards, she had the distinct impression he was making his bed on the floor.

Slowly her breathing resumed, and her heart pattered back to normal. He would keep his bargain after all?

She stared unseeingly at the dark ceiling.

Finally he stopped squirming and silence settled over the room.

She didn't dare move. Was he peering upward at nothing too?

"Priscilla?"

His whisper made her jump. "Hmm?"

"Is there an extra blanket?"

"Certainly." She tugged on the quilt until it slid off the bed toward him.

He wriggled for a few moments, situating the blanket around his body.

She held herself rigid until he was quiet again.

Surely he wouldn't be comfortable on the floor all night. It would be much too drafty and hard. But she wouldn't dream of inviting him to share the same bed. . . . A proper lady would never do such a thing.

"I'm sorry about the floor," she whispered. "I hope you'll be able to fall asleep."

"Oh, I won't be able to sleep, and it won't be because of the floor."

Heat splashed over her, sending a fresh flush over her skin. Her mind scrambled to find an appropriate answer, but she could think of nothing except the softness of his hands.

"Good night, Priscilla," he whispered.

Would it be a *good* night? How could she sleep even a minute, knowing a man—her husband—was only a breath away?

For that matter, how would she ever sleep again?

Chapter
7

MARCH 1

"Time to go," Eli called again. He tugged on the traces already attached to the sleigh. They were as tight and ready to go as he was.

Priscilla dabbed her handkerchief at her eyes and reached to hug yet another person.

He didn't doubt that half the town had assembled outside the White home to say good-bye to her. Obviously, she felt an obligation to give each and every last person a hug.

At least Dr. Baldwin had donated his old sleigh for the first leg of the journey. And the fresh dusting of snow overnight would aid their speed to Rushville to say good-bye to his family before they retrieved John and Richard, who were staying in Ithaca with supporters while he finished his business.

"What about Priscilla's books?" Mrs. White draped another blanket across the seat of the sleigh. "She'll need her books for her teaching once you arrive."

Eli shook his head and reined in his irritation. "Whatever she needs we'll have to buy when we get there." He'd already explained to Mrs. White a dozen times that when they reached Fort Walla Walla in Oregon, they'd be able to take a canoe down the Columbia River to the British trading post of Fort Vancouver. There they'd be able to buy all the supplies they would need to start the mission.

"Miss White, we need to go. We should have left an hour ago." Would he need to physically pry her away from her family? She lifted an eyebrow.

One of the younger girls standing near Priscilla chortled. "She's no longer Miss White. She's your wife, Mrs. Ernest."

Priscilla's brow inched higher.

How could he forget? Especially after spending an entire sleepless night in the same bedroom with her, listening to her soft sighs and her shifting between the sheets. If that wasn't torture, he didn't know what was. No matter what he'd tried to think about, he hadn't been able to wipe away the image of her standing in her nightgown, the flush in her cheeks, the swirls of golden hair, and the graceful curves of her body.

From the dark circles under her eyes, he figured she hadn't gotten much sleep either.

"Mrs. Ernest." The words slipped off his tongue, and he made a slow perusal of her new traveling dress, simpler than what she'd worn previously but still fancier than she'd need in the West.

"My dearest wife." He crooked his finger at her. "If you don't make your way to the sleigh, you'll force me to pick you up and carry you here."

"There's no need for such impatience, Dr. Ernest. After all, who knows when I'll see all my beloved friends and family again." She lifted her chin. "Certainly you cannot begrudge me a few last moments with them."

With defiance in her eyes, she turned and embraced the young pregnant woman standing in front of her. "You and Reverend Lull will come west eventually and join us, won't you, Mary Ann?"

He started toward her.

Mary Ann stopped her reply midsentence and stared at him.

Priscilla glanced over her shoulder and her eyes rounded. Before she could move, he swooped her off her feet into his arms.

"What do you think you're doing—?"

He juggled her weight and hefted her against his chest. "Just speeding things up."

She sucked in a breath and wound her arms around his neck. The graceful curves of her body were every bit as soft and delicate as they looked, and he dragged in his own breath.

She peeked at the crowd. Her lashes fell and a rosy blush graced her cheeks. "Please put me down," she murmured. "You're causing a scene."

"I like causing scenes."

"Dr. Ernest, please."

He grinned and strode toward the sleigh, his boots crunching in the frozen slush. "Besides, a man has a right to hold his bride, doesn't he?"

"Not like this. Not in public. It's uncivilized."

"Who said I'm civilized?"

"I just want to say good-bye." Her lips wavered with her attempt at a smile. "This is perhaps the very last time I'll ever speak with or see many of these people."

His footsteps slowed. The sorrow in her eyes reached inside him and yanked on his heart. What would it be like to leave a home and a family that truly cared? He couldn't even begin to imagine.

"I'm sorry I have to rush you. Really I am." He reached the sleigh and lowered her onto the stack of blankets Mrs. White had assembled for the cold drive. "But dragging out the good-byes isn't going to help."

She sighed. "I know."

Mrs. White huffed and elbowed past him. "Dr. Ernest, your behavior is shocking . . . scandalous."

Priscilla settled her feet on top of the portable foot warmer. The iron box with its various shaped holes was filled with glowing coals and hopefully would help keep her feet warm until they reached their destination for the day.

Mrs. White wrapped a blanket around Priscilla's legs and feet to hold in the heat. "There is no need for you to require her to hurry this morning when you have already demanded so much."

"If we could stay longer, we would," Eli said. "But any delay could put our trip in jeopardy. Not only would I put Priscilla in danger but also Reverend Spalding and his wife."

"Reverend Spalding?" Priscilla sat up.

"The other couple traveling with us."

"There was a Reverend Spalding who proposed to Priscilla several years ago." Mrs. White folded another blanket across Priscilla's lap. "That was right after we found out—"

"Mother, please . . ."

"Well, it wasn't meant to be." Mrs. White patted Priscilla's knees. "He wasn't interested in missions the way Priscilla was, and it just wouldn't have worked out."

"I'm sure it's not the same Reverend Spalding," Priscilla rushed. "So let's cease speaking of the matter. And we shall be on our way."

Priscilla lifted her chin and set her face forward.

"Well, if you must leave . . ." Mrs. White reached for Priscilla and wrapped her arms around her daughter. "I'm proud of you."

Priscilla held herself rigid for a moment. Then she crumpled against her mother, and silent tears slid down her cheeks.

RUSHVILLE, NEW YORK

Eli tugged on the reins until the sleigh came to a halt a safe distance from the tannery.

Next to him, Priscilla stirred.

She'd remained silent on her side of the sleigh until finally she'd succumbed to sleep. It hadn't taken long for her to sidle next to him for warmth. Eventually, she'd rested her head against his shoulder, and when she'd shivered in her sleep, he'd draped his own blanket across her.

Wisps of her hair had slipped from the hood of her cloak and tickled his cheek. He watched the rise and fall of her breathing, a strange sense of pride stealing through him. His wife—this beautiful, kind lady—his wife. What would his family think of him now?

"We're here," he whispered.

With a shudder, she sat up.

She blinked several times and then swung her big eyes upon him. Wide with confusion, their softness reached out and grabbed him, twisting his lungs so he couldn't breathe.

"Where are we?" She forced the words past chattering teeth. Her stiff fingers groped at the blankets and drew them tighter.

"You're freezing." He shot to the edge of the seat, assessing her condition. He'd been an idiot. He'd wanted to make good time and hadn't bothered to check on her. But just because his big body could withstand the cold didn't mean her delicate frame would.

His heart dipped with the sudden urgency to get her inside. "I should've stopped to refill the warming box." Inwardly, he berated himself. He flicked the reins and steered the horse toward the cabin where Walt had brought them the day after he'd married Ma.

When Eli halted the sleigh in front of it, Priscilla shifted the blanket over her nose. "The scent is horrible. There must be a tannery nearby."

He nodded at the sheds across the plot. "My stepfather's."

Her gaze swept over the yard, which was littered with broken boards and rusty tools, the lifeless garden full of tall weeds, the shards of crockery cutting through the thin layer of new snow—remnants of the rages that exploded whenever Walt overindulged in his homemade liquor.

Eli could guess what she was thinking. It was a sorry sight. He wasn't proud of the place or his family. But he'd wanted to say good-bye. . . . It would be the last time. . . .

"Come on." He reached a hand to Priscilla. "I'll take you inside, and you can warm up."

She shifted among the blankets and shook violently. He half lifted her out of the sleigh, steadied her on her feet, and helped her to the door.

With one arm around her, he banged a fist against the warped planks. "Ma, it's me, Eli." His muscles tensed like the wires of a trap.

Silence greeted him.

He hesitated a moment, then shoved the door open and stepped inside.

From a rocker in front of the hearth, his ma narrowed her eyes at him through the puff of her pipe smoke. "Who are you and what do you want?" Her gruff voice stretched across the dimly lit room and socked him.

"It's me, Eli."

"Eli who?"

"Elijah, your son."

"I don't got no son named Elijah."

He slipped off his hat and gave his ma a wide view of his face. "Yep, Ma. See, it's me."

She squinted, shrugged her bony shoulders, and then took a long drag on her pipe.

His stomach caved in. Why had he come? What had ever possessed him to attempt to say good-bye to her, when she'd all but said good-bye to him twenty years ago?

"How are my sisters doing these days? Seen them lately?"

His ma only grunted, and he knew he wouldn't get any information about his siblings from her. She didn't care about them anymore either.

Behind him, Priscilla grabbed onto his arm, her shaking so intense she could hardly stand.

"Look," he said, slapping his hat back on and taking a deep breath of the tangy tobacco fumes, "Priscilla needs a place to warm up. I'm going to leave her here with you by the fire while I go get our boots."

"Who's Priscilla?" The squeak of her rocker halted, and she sat forward.

"She's my wife."

A tangle of dark hair streaked with gray dangled across the translucent skin of his ma's face. Everything about her, even her dress, was pale and colorless, like the listless smoke that hung in the air.

Priscilla stepped to his side. "I'm pleased to make your acquaintance, Mrs. Ernest."

His ma's face turned into chiseled stone. "I ain't been called Mrs. Ernest in more years than I can count."

Priscilla's eyes widened with confusion, and her fingers tightened around his bicep. "I didn't know—I'm very sorry—"

"Missy, you just take your apology and get on out of here."

"Now, Ma, settle down."

Priscilla shrank back.

"Well, look who's showed up." At Walt's voice behind them, Eli spun around.

Standing with feet straddled, Walt crossed his thick arms over his chest and leaned against the doorframe. His apron stretched taut, giving full display of streaks of blood and slimy gristle.

Priscilla shuddered and edged closer to Eli.

Walt's gaze journeyed over Priscilla and lingered too long.

Eli tugged her against his side. Without resistance, she burrowed into him and rested her trembling hand against his chest.

"And who's this little beauty?" Walt's eyes lit with a lust that Eli had seen all too often over the years, only it had been directed at his younger sisters.

"Told you I was getting married." His grip on Priscilla tightened. "This is my wife."

Walt pushed away from the doorway and ambled toward them, his attention fixed on Priscilla's generous bosom.

Eli's body tensed all the way down to the marrow of his bones. If Walt laid a hand on Priscilla, he'd beat the man to a mass of bloody pulp. Just one touch and he'd have the justification he needed to repay Walt for all those years he'd had to lie in the dark and helplessly listen to Walt's grunts and his sisters' whimpers.

Eli's fingers rounded into a fist. "We got married last night over in Angelica."

"That so?" Walt came to a halt close enough that they were enveloped by his putrid odor—a mixture of decaying animal flesh and liquor. "I think you's lying to me."

Priscilla's body turned rigid. "I beg your pardon, but Eli is telling the truth about our marriage. We were indeed married the previous eve."

She held out her hand and flashed her wedding band in front of Walt. "Eli is one of the most honest, straightforward men I've ever met. Even if he tried to lie, I doubt he's capable."

"Eli's no saint. Bet he ain't told you about his pa—"

"Time to go." Silent fury swelled through Eli's chest. Walt had no business telling Priscilla the truth about his pa. He propelled her away, past his stepfather, out the door, and toward the sleigh. "Where are the boots, Walt?"

The man guffawed and nodded toward the tannery.

Eli ushered Priscilla up onto the seat and tucked the blanket back around her legs. He'd have been better off buying the boots from a complete stranger.

And he'd have been even better off if he hadn't attempted to say good-bye to his family at all.

Chapter
8

CENTRAL PENNSYLVANIA

*P*riscilla knew she'd never be warm, truly warm, ever again. Even though Eli had stopped more frequently in the preceding days as they rode hard through Elmira, New York, and past Williamsport, Pennsylvania, the nagging chill was her constant companion.

She rubbed her hands together under the blanket. She tried to muster enthusiasm for another stop in their journey toward Pittsburgh, but she could hardly find the energy to turn her head and look through the dusk to the two-story house where they had halted.

Eli hopped out, and John and Richard reined in their horses next to the sleigh. Dressed in warm clothes that supporters had donated, the two Indian boys hardly looked like the wild savages who had walked into her church the first time she'd met Eli.

He bounded up the front steps. "If they have room, we'll stay here for the night."

So far, he had managed to find willing members of local congregations to house them and provide a meal. But now, after almost a week, Eli had moved beyond the boundaries of his supporters.

As they'd traveled he'd shared tales of the adventures he'd had with Samuel Parker, his companion from his exploratory trip, and the people they'd met, the wild animals they'd encountered, and the beauty of the land they'd traveled.

Eli's enthusiasm for the West and his excitement about returning was infectious, and Priscilla couldn't help but get more excited with every day that passed. The more he talked about the details of the clinic he planned to build and the Nez Perce who lived there, the more she wished they were already there.

According to Eli, they wouldn't arrive in Oregon Country until September. He'd explained that first they had to travel by steamboat from Pittsburgh to St. Louis. And then by steamboat up the Missouri River to the Platte River. Once they reached the Platte, they'd begin the overland portion of their journey.

It would take them six, maybe even seven, months—and that was if they didn't encounter any problems along the way.

She shivered and hugged herself.

Richard, the older of the two boys, slid from his horse. "Mrs. Doc? Cold?" His ebony eyes narrowed with concern.

She nodded and gave him a tremulous smile, hoping she could convey her gratitude for his consideration. She guessed him to be no more than twelve years old, but he had the maturity of a young man. John was a year or two younger and more spirited but had been equally attentive to her.

"I'll be very glad when spring arrives," she said. Now that they'd entered the first days of March, she hoped they'd stumble upon warm weather soon.

Richard cocked his head. "Spring?"

She really must take it upon herself to teach the boys more English. Eli spent too much time trying to converse with them in their native Nez Perce instead of helping them better themselves.

Richard reached for her hands and rubbed them between his.

She'd resisted the first time he'd done it. But she'd quickly realized how much heat the friction brought her and had set aside decorum to allow it.

John jumped from his saddle and draped another blanket around her.

"It will surely warm up once the snow melts." She gave the boys a grateful smile.

"My home not so cold," John said.

"Then I shall be pleased to live there."

The boys didn't say anything.

Did they miss their family after months of being gone? Now that they'd seen the way civilized people lived, would it be hard for them to return to their savage way of living? She bit her lip to hold back her questions. They didn't need her prying and reminding them of all they missed.

"There's room," Eli called, letting the door slam behind him. He raced down the steps, skipping every other wooden plank.

Priscilla rose on trembling legs, and Richard held her arm as she climbed out of the sleigh.

Eli rushed to her. "Let's get you inside."

He ushered her into the warmth of the building, which she soon realized was a wayside tavern. The landlord served them leftovers, a lukewarm supper of potatoes, soft carrots, and leathery beef slathered in gravy in which the fat had already started to congeal.

The evening passed in a blur of weariness, and she was grateful when Eli finally indicated that it was time for them to retire.

He led her up the stairs to the sleeping room. When he opened the door, she peered past him but recoiled into the hallway.

Eli glanced over his shoulder and jerked his head for her to follow him.

"I can't sleep in there," she whispered.

He backed out of the room and half closed the door. "Would you rather sleep in the barn with John and Richard?"

Though everywhere they'd traveled people were fascinated with the savages, they were too frightened to allow them to sleep inside their homes. John and Richard hadn't complained about bedding with the animals. She supposed they were used to it. But she was most certainly not planning to join them. Nor was she planning to sleep in a room with a dozen strangers.

She peeked through the door and examined the large room with its rows of double beds, several of which were already occupied. "Why can't we have our own room like we've had every place else?"

"It's not that bad, Priscilla. In two months when you're sleeping on the hard ground, this will seem like paradise."

She'd tried not to complain about the long hours of riding in the sleigh or the cold stiffness of her limbs. She didn't want to inconvenience him or have him regret his decision to marry her. But this—how would she possibly endure it?

She looked back into the room, swallowed hard, and nodded. What choice did she have? "You're right. I'll try to make the best of the situation."

With a sinking heart, she tiptoed behind him, past the

mismatched assortment of beds, until they reached one that was empty.

Through the rumpled blankets and sheets, she could make out the sagging mattress. "It looks like someone has already slept in it. Perhaps they'll be back?"

Eli shook his head. "This is for us."

"Us?" Surely he didn't mean for them to share a bed, not after they'd been keeping the sleeping arrangement they'd chosen the first night—where she slept in the bed and he on the floor?

"You won't get a bed to yourself here," he whispered. "If it's not me next to you, you'll end up with a complete stranger."

The man in the next bed shifted his hefty body and released a less-than-graceful bodily noise.

She shuddered.

"We can draw a line down the middle of the bed, and I'll try not to cross it." He tugged off a boot and let it drop to the floor with a clunk. "But you might want to sleep with your boots on. That way you can kick me if you need to."

The grin in his tone made her heart do a funny flip. Would she want to kick him away? "Thank you for the noble warning," she whispered back. "But I think I shall poke you with my hairpins instead."

"In that case, I'll help arm you." His whisper turned deep. "I'm sure I'd be good at playing hide-and-seek in your hair for them."

Longing curled in the pit of her stomach, and she couldn't keep from imagining his gentle fingers burrowing through her hair. Strangely, the thought was a pleasant one.

Eli tossed his other boot to the floor and fumbled at his trousers.

Heat flamed to her face. She turned her back to him and sat

down on the edge of the bed. She slipped off the sturdy leather boots Eli's stepfather had made.

The bed squeaked under Eli's weight.

She hesitated at the buttons of her dress. She'd never slept in her clothes before, but how could she possibly unclothe now, in the middle of a roomful of strangers and in the same bed as Eli? Especially if he was only half attired?

He gave a long weary sigh.

Gingerly, she leaned back. The pillowslip was greasy, and she wished she could toss it aside and sleep without it. But she was sure Eli already thought she was particular, and she didn't want to give him more justification.

With a grimace, she settled her head and pulled up the covers. The sourness of unwashed bodies assaulted her. She pinched her eyes closed and tried not to think about who had lain in the bed before her and how long it had been since the landlord had washed the sheets.

Eli stretched.

Her lungs constricted. What if he brushed against her? The full-sized bed back home had always been big enough when she'd shared it with her sister, but this one was entirely too small.

He settled on his side facing her, and the heat of his breath washed over her.

A tiny bud of warmth unfurled in her middle and spread to her limbs. She twisted the band on her finger, and the intricate grooves of the roses caressed her skin. He was her husband, after all. In the sight of God and man, they'd made a lifetime commitment to each other. And so far, everyone believed she and Eli had a real marriage—everyone except Walt.

She stared through the dark at the slanted ceiling. Why hadn't Walt believed Eli about their marriage? Moreover, why hadn't his mother acknowledged him? She'd puzzled over his strange family all week, comparing their departure from her family to his. Whereas her family had shed tears and showered her with love, his had only heaped shame upon him and shoved him away with ugliness.

"Dr. Ernest?" she whispered.

"Hmm?"

"Why was Walt so cruel to you?"

His breathing stopped then restarted faster. "That's just the way he's always been."

She shuddered to think what his life had been like as a child, and she had the urge to reach out and caress his cheek.

"What about your sisters? Where are they?"

He didn't say anything for a moment. Then the bed creaked as he turned to lie on his back. "Walt used them—took away their innocence. When they were old enough, they got away from him as fast as they could. Married the first boys who offered them a way out."

"And are they happy now?"

"I don't think they've ever known what it's like to be happy." Wistfulness tinged his voice.

She propped up on her elbow and tried to study his face through the dim light filtering through the shabby curtains. "What about your mother? Why didn't she remember you?"

The blanket shifted with his shrug, but he didn't offer an explanation.

What kind of mother could forget her own flesh and blood? For a long moment, Priscilla peered through the darkness, her heart aching for him. She wanted to know more but was afraid to ask.

Finally she took a deep breath. "What happened to your father?"

His body stiffened. "I don't want to talk about it." He flipped to his other side, turning his back to her.

"I'm sorry." She wished she could take back her question. She longed to reach out and touch him, to tell him that he could take the pins out of her hair if he wanted. But the words stuck in her throat.

He had scars from his past the same as she did. But he obviously didn't want her pity any more than she wanted his.

She'd do best to remember why she was traveling west. It wasn't about them. She was going in answer to God's calling, and she needed to remain faithful to that above all else.

Stifling a sigh, she lowered her head back to the dirty pillow. If only it were as easy as it sounded. . . .

Chapter
9

PITTSBURGH, PENNSYLVANIA

*D*o you see our boat?" Priscilla's heart banged against her chest, and she gripped the seat of the sleigh, praying, as she had the past several days, that they'd reach their steamboat in time.

More gigantic vessels than she could count bobbed in the rushing current of the Ohio River ahead of them. The murky water, swollen from recent thawing, slapped against the levy.

Eli climbed out of the sleigh and scanned the waterfront. The wharf teemed with deckhands hauling luggage and dockmen loading heavy barrels as well as the firewood that would fuel the boats. Passengers clustered in front of gangplanks, waiting to board. And on a nearby three-deck steamboat, a number of ladies disembarked.

At the sight of the crisp silk of their day dresses and the shininess of their fur cloaks, Priscilla clutched a fistful of her wrinkled and mud-splattered skirt and inwardly cringed. In the two weeks since leaving Angelica, she'd dirtied practically every dress she'd packed. How could she make an appearance among such elegance looking as she did?

They had reached Pittsburgh late last night behind schedule. The melting snow and muddy roads had slowed them down—at least that's what Eli claimed. But if Eli hadn't taken the time to stop so often to refill the warming box for her, they could have arrived sooner.

If they missed their connection, it would be because of her.

"Oh, God, help us." She stood and peered at the lines of steamboats, all shapes and sizes, their tall smokestacks belching black billows into the clear morning sky, their enormous paddlewheels churning cascades of water. "How will we ever find our boat and traveling companions in this chaos?"

Eli tipped up the brim of his hat, revealing the worried creases that cut through his forehead. "We'll find them."

A breath of spring had hovered around them the past few days. She lifted her face and relished the kiss of sunshine and the embrace of warmth. The mid-March sun dangled above the enormous cliffs on the southern side of the river valley.

She drew in lungfuls of the strange muddy scent of river water mixed with woodsmoke from the steamboats, and surveyed the enormity of the valley where the Allegheny and Monongahela Rivers met to form the Ohio. Eli had told her that Captain Meriwether Lewis launched his keelboat *Discovery* from Pittsburgh only thirty-three years earlier, and they would likely be following much of the same path the early expedition had taken, at least until they reached the central plains.

After days of traveling past small towns, rolling hills, and farmlands that varied little from her own New York home, they'd finally reached beyond the edge of all that was familiar.

The thrill of the adventure whispered through her, and she hugged her arms across her chest. This might not be what she'd planned—it likely didn't come close to the exotic wonders of India—but it was like nothing she'd ever seen before.

John and Richard's faces were alight with excitement too, and they'd made their way to the waterfront to watch the boats more closely.

"Well, it's about time," a voice called to them.

A grin spread across Eli's face. "We got here as soon as we could." She stood as Eli started toward the approaching gentleman. They shook hands, and when they stepped apart, Priscilla gasped.

With his tall black top hat, dark mustache, impeccably tailored trousers, and perfectly matching waistcoat, she found herself staring at Henry Spalding, the very man she'd considered marrying. She'd met him shortly after recovering from the mumps, during those days of wondering why she wasn't having her monthly courses anymore.

Her heart squeezed with dread. She could almost picture the scene in the parlor, not long after Dr. Baldwin had given her the devastating news. Henry had been on his knees holding her hand, begging her to reconsider his marriage proposal. And her final words were the ones Mother decided to tell everyone, the words that would hide the shame of her condition, shield her heart from rejection, and protect her family's reputation: She would never marry. Ever. Not to Henry, not to anyone.

Priscilla dropped to the seat, ducked her head, and pulled her bonnet forward. And now she was married. How would she ever explain that?

"You're several days later than you said, and I was beginning to get worried." Henry's smooth voice was the same as it had always been.

"For a while I wasn't sure if I was going to make it at all."

"Well, you're the one who told me the Fur Company won't wait for us if we're late," Henry said. "You said if we're not in St. Louis by the time their steamboat heads out for Liberty, we might as well pack up and go home until next year."

"And it's true." Eli's voice tightened. "We'll just have to get passage on the fastest steamboat—"

"Already done. When I got word of your arrival last night, I booked two cabins on the *Siam*. It's leaving in three hours."

"The supplies?"

"Being loaded even as we speak. And Mrs. Spalding is already on board."

In the ensuing silence, Priscilla had the distinct impression Henry had shifted his gaze to her and was awaiting Eli's introduction.

She shivered, not wishing to lift her head, hoping Eli would neglect propriety and forgo any formal presentations.

"Let's get the rest of our belongings on board." Eli strode back toward the sleigh and reached for Priscilla's small trunk. "Then I'll work on selling the sleigh and horses."

She didn't move.

He shimmied out the trunk and hefted it into his arms. "Where to?"

Henry cleared his throat. "Aren't you forgetting something, Dr. Ernest?"

"I may be a strong man, Henry, but this is about all I can carry at one time."

"Your wife." Henry stepped toward the sleigh. "You haven't introduced me to your wife."

She pushed herself back against the smooth seat, wishing she could disappear.

"You're right," Eli said. "Allow me to introduce you to the lovely young lady I met only a few weeks ago—"

"A few weeks ago?" Henry's tone went up a notch. "Why, Dr. Ernest, I don't understand. Is this not the young woman you were engaged to and spoke about last fall when we met?"

"No," Eli responded slowly. "Sarah Taylor decided she didn't want to go west with me after all—at least that's what I assumed when I saw her with her new husband."

Priscilla gasped and glanced sideways at Eli. She'd had no idea he'd been engaged. She searched the weathered lines of his rugged face, looking for signs of the hurt that would surely be there.

His jaw was hard and the winter blue of his eyes had turned cold.

"Then you've married a complete stranger?"

"I didn't have much of a choice. She was my last option."

She ducked her head again. He'd always been honest with her regarding the nature of their relationship. And even though she'd known she'd been his last resort—the only choice after he'd exhausted all other possibilities—his comment stung nevertheless. She couldn't understand why it would bother her— except that maybe she'd been secretly hoping he'd change his mind and see that she was a good option after all.

"Well," Henry said, his voice laced with doubt, "I'm rather surprised at your rashness regarding such a critical issue. But we'll just have to trust that you exerted wisdom."

Eli didn't say anything.

His silence stung her as much as his words had.

"You'll have to forgive my surprise, Mrs. Ernest." Henry held out a hand in front of her to help her from the sleigh. "I'm sure

Dr. Ernest has chosen wisely with his wife, just as he's chosen wisely with the rest of the decisions regarding our trip."

She squirmed, not wanting to place her hand in Henry's, yet knowing she couldn't possibly decline his offer of assistance. Tentatively, she slipped her gloved hand into his.

"Mrs. Ernest, I'm pleased to make your acquaintance—"

She lifted her head and revealed her face.

He jumped back and jerked his hand away. "Priscilla White?"

"Hello, Reverend Spalding," she whispered and clutched her hands together.

He blinked rapidly, as if trying to clear his vision. "Miss White?"

She nodded, and her stomach twisted.

His face was pale, and he took another step away. "I certainly never expected . . . that is . . . I was under the impression—"

"I'm as surprised as you," she said.

"You're married?" Henry stammered.

She looked at Eli. His eyebrows arched. "Yes. I was Dr. Ernest's *last option.*" At her clipped words, regret flashed through Eli's eyes.

Henry's slim face constricted with confusion and hurt. "But you told me you would never get married. *Ever.*"

"Whoa!" Eli cut in. "Don't tell me this is *the* Reverend Spalding who proposed to you several years ago?"

"Yes." She said the word at the same time as Henry.

Eli glanced between the two of them, his eyes narrowing with something akin to jealousy. "Then I guess I didn't marry a complete stranger after all. At least one of us knows her."

Henry's Adam's apple bobbed. "How is that you're married? Especially when you made it very clear you had no intention—"

"And I had no intention of marrying. Truly."

"Was it just *me*?" Hurt laced the threads of his strained voice. "You could have just said so."

114

"No. It had nothing to do with you." She had regarded Henry fondly enough. And of all her suitors Mother had liked him the best, particularly the fact that he'd gone to a theological seminary. "It's just that . . . at the time I wasn't . . ."

What could she say? She certainly couldn't tell him the truth about her infertility and chance the news reaching her hometown and bringing embarrassment to her family.

"I understand." Henry's face hardened into a mask of cool civility.

"It's not what you think."

He turned toward Eli and cleared his throat. "Well, Dr. Ernest, this is a most awkward situation."

Eli looked at her with raised eyebrow. "The truth is . . ."

She pleaded with him silently—hoping he'd see that she didn't want him to say anything that might reveal the painful truth of her situation.

"The truth is that Priscilla didn't want to get married. I just happened to be in Angelica the day she got a letter from the Board of Missions telling her she couldn't teach in India and that she needed to get married if she wanted to be a missionary."

Priscilla let out the breath she'd been holding and nodded at Eli gratefully.

Henry was silent. He glanced at the long line of steamboats. His Adam's apple bobbed again. Then he addressed Eli almost as if she weren't present. "I'm sure Mrs. Spalding won't be agreeable to continuing under these awkward circumstances, but since we've already come this far, we shall trust in the Lord's plans and shall attempt to put the past behind us."

When he spun and strode away, Priscilla released a long breath and let her shoulders sag.

"Of all the men we could partner with," Eli mumbled under his breath, "it would have to be an old flame."

"I'm sorry." He couldn't possibly think she liked this any more than he did, could he?

He shifted her trunk in his arms. "Was he someone special?"

She hesitated. "He was always very kind and attentive."

"And apparently you broke his heart when you told him you wouldn't marry him."

Had she broken his heart? Or simply wounded his pride?

A steam whistle blew long and shrill. Another boat drew near to the shore, water cascading through its side paddlewheel. Her heart churned with the same slapping rhythm. "I'd given him hope to believe we could marry. And he couldn't understand why I changed my mind."

Eli's muscles bulged under the weight of her trunk. "Maybe if you'd been honest with him—"

"No!"

He lifted an eyebrow.

"Please don't tell him. I don't want anyone else to know."

"What difference does it make? Won't everyone find out eventually—when we don't have a baby—"

"Maybe." Heat pricked her cheeks.

Her gaze swept over the milling crowds, and she caught a glimpse of Henry's top hat and his squared shoulders. He was a part of her past, the part she'd hoped to put behind her. "I'd prefer to keep my issues private—including the nature of our marriage."

"So now I need to lie about our marriage?"

"Not lie. Just not divulge the information."

He shook his head.

"There's no need to inform anyone that we're not truly man and wife—that we're merely partners."

Eli snorted and started off.

"It's our business and nobody else's," she called after him.

He didn't stop.

She stood, shook the wrinkles out of her dress, and did what any lady would—calm her frantic heartbeat and compose herself.

But she couldn't dispel the uneasiness. What kind of situation had she gotten herself into now?

~

The cool wind whipped at Priscilla's cloak and threatened to tug her bonnet loose. She grabbed the middle deck's promenade railing as the boat pitched her to and fro.

She'd hid in her stateroom in the stern long enough. As much as she wanted to avoid seeing Henry again and meeting his wife, she had to put aside her reservations. They would be traveling in close quarters for the next seven months and thereafter serving in a mission together.

Henry was right. They would have to put the past behind them. And she would pray that Mrs. Spalding would eventually get over her resentment and grow to like her.

By the time Priscilla stepped into the partially enclosed verandah, the wind had thrashed off her bonnet and wrested strands of hair from the neat coil at the back of her head.

She stopped beside a pillar and took a deep breath. The *Siam* wasn't the largest steamboat on the river or the fanciest, but the captain had boasted of being able to reach speeds of thirteen miles per hour. From the dizzying way the shore moved past them, she had no doubt they were making good time.

With a shaking hand, she brushed back a wisp of hair. She glanced around to the smattering of passengers seated on simple wooden deck chairs. Henry stood against a beam, his arms folded across his chest, his legs crossed at the ankles. He stared at her, admiration clear within his eyes. But when her gaze collided with his, he shifted it to the woman sitting next to him.

Priscilla lowered her lashes, sure that if her cheeks weren't already pink from the cold, they would be now.

When she chanced another glance, she caught sight of Eli watching her and Henry. Storm clouds were gathering in his eyes.

He strode across the verandah, his boots scuffing the floor. When he reached her, his fingers encircled her arm. "If we're going to pretend to be lovers," he growled against her ear, "then you'd better not flirt with all the men in the room, especially married men."

Lovers? Just the mention of the word made her insides quiver. "I'm not flirting."

"If that wasn't flirting, then I don't know what is."

"I can't help it if he looked at me. I didn't ask him to."

He tugged her forward. "Come on. I'll introduce you to his *wife*."

She wanted to protest again, but Sister Spalding was already rising. Her face was pale, but she managed a tremulous smile.

"Henry, don't you think it's time our wives met?"

The reverend glossed over her, all admiration gone, replaced instead with reserve.

Sister Spalding grasped Henry's arm. "Oh, Sister Ernest, I've been waiting to meet you."

Priscilla forced a smile.

"Mabel, this is my wife, Priscilla." Eli nudged her forward.

"I'm thrilled." Mabel extended her hand and grasped Priscilla's. The warmth of her grip matched the warmth in her eyes. And although her features were plain, almost mousey, the gentleness of her inner spirit radiated with genuineness.

"It's my pleasure." Priscilla shook the woman's hand.

"Since Mr. Spalding thought so highly of you in the past, I will count it a delight to partner with you."

Henry's face twitched, and he didn't take his narrowed glare off the passing rocky riverbank. If the news of their previous relationship had upset Mabel, as Henry had declared it would, she was certainly talented at hiding her discomfort.

"You are indeed gracious," Priscilla murmured. "And I'm sure I will find it equally delightful."

Mabel's smile widened, revealing crooked front teeth in an overbite. "You don't know how much it means to me to hear you say that."

The steamboat whistle bellowed. They were fast approaching two other riverboats.

Mabel glanced forward and blanched. She covered her mouth and swallowed. "I'm sorry, but the motion of the boat isn't helping my nausea."

"Perhaps I can give you something," Eli said. "Powdered gingerroot in hot water with a drop of honey?"

"Oh, Dr. Ernest, thank you." Her hand fluttered to her stomach, and her fingers opened into the kind of splay across the abdomen that could only mean one thing.

Priscilla's heart plummeted.

"But I'm sure I'll be just fine," Mabel continued, her eyes shining. "Especially in a month or two."

"Then you are . . ." Eli glanced at Henry, his eyebrows raised with obvious surprise.

Henry nodded. "Mrs. Spalding is in the family way."

"This isn't exactly the best timing," Eli mumbled.

"We didn't plan it," Henry said, his tone rising. "I was hoping this wouldn't happen until we were already settled. But—"

"But God is good." Mabel patted her husband's arm.

"And of course, I'll be here to help," Priscilla offered, trying to push aside twinges of jealousy.

"Oh, thank you, dear." Mabel's eyes brimmed with relief.

"Then I must remember to thank the Lord for providing not only a doctor, but a lovely new friend."

"Dr. Ernest is a charming companion when he wants to be, but I've found myself sorely missing the companionship of another woman."

Eli's brow shot up.

Priscilla flashed him a coy smile. "And of course there are the times he's quite uncivilized, which will make me all the more grateful for the presence of another lady."

Eli's eyebrow quirked higher, along with the corner of his mouth. "Some of us might be a little rough around the edges, but that just keeps us from being dull, don't you think?"

A blush crept up her neck. He was right. He was anything but dull.

Over the past days of traveling together in the sleigh, they'd been able to talk easily, almost too easily. She'd never before been able to converse with a man the way she did with Eli—almost as if he were a friend. And friendship was a good thing, wasn't it? If they weren't going to have a real marriage, then at least they could be friends.

The boat lurched and tossed her against Eli, almost as if he'd planned it. His arms captured her and steadied her against his chest.

The gasps and cries of other passengers arose around her.

The vessel jerked again.

Eli's arms tightened, and if they hadn't been in peril, she would have enjoyed the moment altogether too much.

"What's happening?" she asked against the solidness of his chest, knowing she should be afraid. After all, steamboats might be fast but they were also dangerous. Underwater snags were a constant threat, as were boilerplate blowups. Oddly, she was calm. "Are we sinking?"

"We can't be. Not so soon into our journey," his steady voice breathed against her.

She pressed her nose into his shirt and dragged in a breath of the spiciness that was uniquely him.

"I'm sure we'll be fine." He peered over her head. "Looks like we've gotten into a scuffle with one of the steamboats we're passing."

The *Siam* steadied, but the lower deck rang with shouts. "Someone's hurt!"

A chill slithered up Priscilla's spine.

Eli peered over the railing—as if he were already attempting to diagnose the problem.

"One of the deckhands," someone called, "fell against an open crate, and he's cut real bad!"

"I want you to stay here," he said, setting her aside, "where you'll be safe." His eyes cautioned her to obey, and then he pushed through the other passengers and jogged toward the steps that would take him down to the engine deck.

She crowded with the other passengers along the rail that over-looked the lower deck. Near the boiler room, a man lay sprawled among overturned crates. A crowd had gathered around him.

In less than a minute, Eli was kneeling next to the wounded man and smoothing a hand over his forehead.

A swell of pride rose within her. Eli Ernest was a brave man and a good doctor. If only she were strong enough to help him.

Suddenly she knew the one thing she could do. With trembling legs, she made her way back to her cabin. She found what she needed and then half ran, half walked to the engine deck.

By the time she approached Eli, he was already hard at work. He'd ripped off the tail of his shirt, had it bunched against the man's shoulder, and was tying a bandage with another strip of cloth.

The men around Eli stepped aside and gave her space to kneel.

The crimson had seeped through the cloth, and the man groaned. Her stomach gurgled. Maybe she should have stayed in the verandah, as Eli had instructed.

She swallowed the bile and touched his arm. "What do you need? What can I do to help?"

His gaze flicked over her. But when he saw what she was holding, his eyes widened. "My bag."

Her fingers fumbled at the leather strap. "Tell me what you need."

Surprise flitted across the blue of his eyes. The light reached out to touch her like a ray of sunshine.

It soaked inside her and spread through her heart. Maybe she could show him she wasn't a nuisance. Maybe he would eventually see that she wasn't the foolish, ill-suited woman he believed her to be.

"Find my needle holder, suturing needle, and thread."

She unrolled the long leather case, revealing an assortment of shiny metal tools in individual straps against a band of clean linen.

"Fortunately the cut isn't deep." Eli lifted the bloody scrap of cloth. "But there's a nasty surface wound."

She trailed her fingers over the handles of the instruments until she reached the needles. Which one did he need?

"This one." He pointed with bright red fingers.

At the sight of so much blood, her stomach roiled again. But she forced herself to focus on extricating the tool.

He held out his hand. She laid it across his palm, careful not to touch the blood. When he turned back to the moaning patient, she glanced up and found herself looking directly upon the mangled, oozing flesh on the man's upper arm.

Revulsion churned through her. Her stomach tumbled, and

she thrust a hand over her mouth. She scrambled backward. She was going to be sick and needed to get away before she utterly embarrassed herself in front of everyone.

She made it to the side railing before her stomach revolted. Amidst her retching, the calls and laughter of onlookers taunted her. With a last dry heave, she lifted her head, not daring to glance in the direction of the wounded man. She wiped her mouth on the edge of her cloak and shifted away from the rail with shaking legs.

She didn't want to look at Eli either, but she peeked at him anyway.

He was busy cleaning the wound and didn't bother to glance in her direction. Was he too embarrassed to acknowledge her?

If he'd thought she was incapable before, she'd most certainly proven him right.

Her chest constricted.

"Mrs. Doc?" Richard touched her elbow.

She turned, surprised to see the two boys but relieved.

Richard's dark eyes were wide with concern.

"I'm just not accustomed to so much blood." She stifled a shudder.

John held out her bonnet, which had come loose and fallen off.

"Thank you." She tried to give him a smile, but her lips only wavered.

"Mrs. Doc. Come. Sit. Rest."

The boys led her to a nearby crate and helped her sit down against one of the many barrels and boxes that lined the cargo hold. The hiss of steam and the squeak of the crank shaft hummed through the lower deck, reassurance that the engine was working as it should.

After a few minutes of taking deep breaths she began to feel better. The boys stood next to her and chatted to each other in their native language, and she was content to watch Eli from a safe distance.

He worked efficiently and confidently. It wasn't long before he finished, and friends of the wounded man carried him away. For a few moments, Eli knelt on the nearly deserted deck, wiping blood from the utensils and tucking them back into his doctor's case.

When he finally stood, Priscilla made a show of watching the passing scenery—the barren trees and brown hills with the first hints of green life struggling to break open. She tried not to notice when he ambled toward her. What would he say to her now after her dismal attempt at helping him?

He stopped directly before her. John and Richard ceased their talking. And she was left with little choice but to acknowledge Eli's presence.

She chanced a glance at him.

"Are you all right?" His blue eyes regarded her kindly, but a grin lurked in their depths and teased his lips.

"And what is so humorous? Surely not my discomfort?" She swiped at the swirls of hair the wind whipped about her face, realizing too late she'd neglected to retie her bonnet.

His grin broke free for only a moment before he brought it under control. "Of course not. Although if it makes you feel any better, I did the same thing during my first surgery."

Her breath hitched. "You did?"

He nodded, and this time when he smiled, her lips curled up into a return smile.

"You were thoughtful to get my bag for me." His voice was soft. "Thank you."

The sunshine of the day poured over her, and his kindness swirled through her, leaving her speechless. And with more admiration for her husband than she cared to admit.

Chapter
10

MISSISSIPPI RIVER

They had one day left to make it to St. Louis.

Fog shrouded the evening sky. Eli leaned over the rail and could scarcely see the water that churned in front of the boat. The Mississippi River was flooded from the spring thaw and recent rain. Danger lurked beneath the surface at every winding turn.

He kneaded his fingers into the tight muscles at the back of his neck. It wouldn't do him any good to worry, but he couldn't help it. The tension had mounted with each passing day until his prayers seemed to stick in his throat.

After traveling nearly two weeks by steamboat, they were only ninety miles from St. Louis. If they could make it through the fog, they'd get there in the morning, perhaps with time to spare.

The American Fur Company had reassured him they wouldn't

leave St. Louis until after the first of April. And they'd promised him a spot on their steamboat, the *Diana*, which would take them up the Missouri River to Liberty, Missouri, the last stop of civilization before crossing the plains.

But he didn't trust the mountain men. They hadn't wanted him along last time, and he was sure they'd be happy if he missed their meeting deadline, especially now with two women along.

The thick dampness of the fog swirled around him, heavy enough that he almost lost the sweet strains of Priscilla's song.

With a last look at the murky water, Eli returned to his spot against the wall with Richard and John just outside the doorway of the main dining salon.

"Mrs. Doc, she has voice of birds." Richard grinned.

Eli mustered as much of a smile as he could manage. The boy was right. Priscilla had a melodious voice that slipped into his blood and traveled to every part of his body, soothing him with its beauty.

She'd taken to organizing games and singing for the cabin passengers every night after dinner, following Henry's prayer meetings.

While the boys were content to watch her from the cold, windy promenade, he'd fumed that the captain hadn't allowed the Indians to dine or sleep with the other passengers, even though he'd paid their cabin fare. Instead, the captain had relegated the boys to the cramped cargo hold.

To show his protest, Eli had decided to eat and sleep with John and Richard. He figured Priscilla wouldn't mind having the tiny cabin to herself. It was better for them both if they weren't together so much. During the first couple of weeks of travel, he'd realized she was altogether too likable. But he'd promised her a business arrangement and had vowed to himself he'd give her an annulment if he needed to send her back home. It would be easier to keep his vows if he kept his distance.

She'd spent most of her time with Mabel sewing the tent they would need for the overland part of their journey. And when Priscilla wasn't sewing, she was with Richard and John, attempting to teach them more English.

Her song came to a close. The last strains wrapped around his heart, and he found himself longing for a few minutes to talk with her—more than the passing comments they'd exchanged aboard the steamboat so far.

"Night too dark for travel." Richard stalked to the rail.

"We stop," John said.

Eli shook his head. "We can't stop. We need to make it to St. Louis as fast as we can."

"Too dark," Richard repeated. He said something to John in his native tongue, and the boy snorted.

Eli didn't know enough of the language yet, but from the tone he could tell they both thought he was a fool.

Maybe he was a fool. With all the many things that could go wrong, why was he taking such risks? Especially risks to the women?

Priscilla's voice wafted to them again, rising above all the others in a poignant hymn. For just a moment, the sweetness seemed to take him to the stairway of heaven, to remind him of where his help came from. God had made him a strong man. He'd given him strength to persevere in the past. Surely God would provide—just as He always had.

A sudden jolt of the steamboat threw him to the deck with a force that took his breath away. Another screeching jerk sent him sliding against the rail. He threw out his hands to brace himself.

The screaming and crying from the dining salon penetrated his dazed mind.

Dread spilled through his stomach, causing his midsection to spasm painfully. The worst had finally happened. They'd snagged something underwater—maybe an old tree limb or sharp rock or wreckage from some other sunken steamboat. And now they would go down too.

He scrambled over to John and Richard. They spoke rapidly to each other in their native tongue. A quick glance told him they were unharmed.

Priscilla. He peered into the dining salon at the chaos of overturned chairs and tables, shattered dishes and goblets, and tangled linen tablecloths now stained with wine. Passengers were scrambling amidst the wreckage.

A rush of adrenaline pumped through his veins.

He had to get to her and save her.

With a grunt, he pushed himself to his feet. He winced at the pain in his hand, but his heart thudded with too much worry about Priscilla to glance at it.

The boat swayed back and forth, and he grabbed the door-frame to keep from toppling back over. With unsteady steps, he stumbled like a drunken man into the dining salon.

"Priscilla!" His ragged call was lost in the chaos of frightened cries and anxious shouts.

He searched the room until he caught sight of her golden head. She was kneeling next to Mabel, her arm around the woman, helping her sit up.

"Priscilla!" He staggered toward her.

Her wide eyes lifted to him. "Eli." She breathed his name with such relief, his heart snagged across the barrier he was trying to build there.

"Are you hurt?"

"Just shaken."

"And you?" he asked, turning to Mabel.

"Praise the Lord for dear Sister Ernest. She cushioned my fall."

Eli reached for Priscilla's arm and raised her to her feet.

She smoothed her dress and gasped at the crimson streaks that appeared against the muslin.

"You're bleeding." Eli's heart picked up speed, and he grabbed her hand, turning it over to inspect it.

"It's not me." Her fingers encircled his wrist, and her face grew pale. "You're cut, deeply."

Blood was oozing from a gash below his thumb. He'd need stitches, but it wouldn't be the first time in that exact spot.

Her face paled, and she swallowed hard.

"If you give me your handkerchief, I'll cover it."

She fumbled in her pocket and then shoved her handkerchief at him.

He wrapped the linen around his hand and helped Mabel to her feet. Out of the corner of his eye he could see Henry pushing his way through the crowd in an attempt to reach them.

"What shall we do?" Priscilla's eyes brimmed with trust. She slipped an arm around Mabel's waist, steadying the young woman.

"Stay by my side. Both of you." He started toward the verandah and the stairway that would take them to the lower deck. If they had to jump, he'd have to go first and catch the women. He doubted they knew how to swim. Not many did. Even though he could manage well enough, the raging spring waters would show no mercy.

The crowd surged toward the rails. Henry wove toward them from the opposite direction. "We've hit a sandbar."

"We're not sinking?" Eli asked.

"We're stuck, and it's too soon to know the damage."

Through the thick fog, they couldn't see anything and could only stand with the others and wait for news from the captain.

Word soon filtered to them that the boat hadn't sustained any damage, but any attempt to dislodge it would wait until morning. After Eli had assessed the minor cuts and scrapes of the other passengers, he and Henry shuffled back into the warmth of the dining salon.

Eli released a breath. "I'll need you to sew a few stitches."

"I'm sorry, Dr. Ernest, but I can't sew stitches." Henry reached for Mabel, and Priscilla relinquished her hold on the woman.

"If the cut was anywhere else, I'd do it myself. But I can't sew my own hand."

Henry's eyes flickered with a look of panic. "I'm quite sure you wouldn't want me to attempt it. I'd probably end up sewing two fingers together."

"You're not going to help me?" There was a spark of something that occasionally flared between Henry and himself. He wasn't sure exactly what about the man bothered him. Maybe the underlying fact that Henry still cared for Priscilla, even though he tried to not show it.

"I'm sorry, Doctor. I want to help you. But . . ." Henry's tone was apologetic, and with his free hand he brushed the dust from his vest. "I'm sure you'll find someone much more suited to the task."

"Like who?" Eli glanced around the salon to the few passengers who were speaking in anxious tones to one another.

"I really need to get Mrs. Spalding back to our cabin. After all the excitement, she's feeling sick and needs to rest."

Mabel was holding a hand over her mouth. Her eyes were weary and her face ashen.

"Looks like you're right." Eli stifled a sigh of resignation. "I'll try to come by your cabin later and check on her—see if she needs anything."

Henry nodded his thanks.

Blood was seeping through the handkerchief, and Eli pressed the cut harder and suppressed a grimace. He'd known he couldn't rely on anyone else. If he wanted something done, he'd have to do it himself, as he always had.

Priscilla touched his arm. "Let me stitch you."

He shook his head. "No. This isn't anything you need to see or handle."

"I'm stronger than you think." Her eyes pleaded with him to give her a chance.

After what had happened the last time she saw blood, he doubted she'd be able to stomach sewing his flesh. But he didn't want to tell her that.

A flush stole over her cheeks, as if she'd heard his thoughts.

"I'm very proficient with a needle and thread. And I need to learn how to see blood without—well, you know."

Who else would do it for him?

He pulled back the handkerchief and held up the gaping cut. It wouldn't heal fast enough without stitches and would end up being a pesky nuisance for the rest of the trip.

Priscilla stared at the wound and swallowed hard, but she didn't look away.

"You want to give it a try?"

She nodded.

He sighed. "All right. Then let's go."

They walked back to the cabin. As he followed her into the cubicle, his heart gave an unexpected thump at the thought of being alone with her—in her stateroom.

He kicked the door closed and surveyed the tidy bed built against the wall. What would it have been like if they had decided to have a true marriage?

She bustled about the room, retrieving papers and wearing apparel that had spilled when the boat hit the sandbar. "I'm sorry. I don't normally leave my things lying around in such disarray."

In such a narrow bed, she would have little choice but to sleep in his arms.

"Your doctor's bag is right here." When she straightened, she fumbled with the handle and refused to meet his gaze.

Was she realizing the same thing? That they were alone? Something that had rarely happened over the past weeks aboard the *Siam*.

He ambled to the edge of the bed and plopped down. "Let's get to it."

"Get to it?"

"To the stitching."

"Of course." She handed him his bag, her face flushing.

"You'll have to sit next to me so I can show you what to do." He patted the end of the bed.

She hesitated and then perched on the edge, taking care that she didn't brush against him.

"You'll have to scoot closer than that."

She inched nearer.

"A little closer."

Her body shifted a fraction, and her shoulder almost touched his.

"And just a little more."

She gave an exasperated sigh. "I suppose you think it would help if I just sat in your lap."

"Well, now that you mention it"—he unrolled his bag— "that's not such a bad idea. Hop on up."

She gasped as if scandalized. "Dr. Ernest!"

He grinned. "You wouldn't have mentioned it if you weren't secretly wishing you could."

"The thought hadn't crossed my mind. Not in the least."

His grin widened. Then he held out his hand to her.

She looked at it, and her face paled.

"Take hold of my hand."

Her smooth fingers slid around his. The unblemished ivory of her skin contrasted with the rugged tan of his. His heart did a rapid tumble. The touch of her warm skin, the nearness of her body, the heat of her breath . . .

Quickly, before he did something he might regret, he explained what she needed to do. Then he braced himself for the pain as she slipped the needle into his hand.

The sting took his breath away.

Her fingers shook, and her breath came in short bursts. "I'm so sorry. I don't think I can do this."

"Keep going." He gritted his teeth. "You can't stop now."

Her fingers trembled so fiercely she dropped the needle holder.

"You can do this, Priscilla." He tried to keep the anguish from his voice. "Just pretend you're sewing the tent."

She nodded and wiped her sleeve across her eyes. Her fingers groped for the instrument. "Oh, Lord, help me," she whispered. She pierced his skin again and again, pulling the thread taut until at last she tied the final knot.

His body swayed and he blinked back waves of dizzying pain. He mustered enough strength to hand her the scissors. Once she snipped the threads, he fell back against the bed with a groan.

"Thank you," he murmured.

"Are you in a great deal of pain?" She sniffed and swiped at a few loose tears trickling down her cheeks.

"It hurts, but it's definitely not the worst I've felt."

"What else can I do to ease your pain?"

He instructed her on a dosage of laudanum, swallowed the bitter painkiller, and then wriggled further onto the bed until his head made contact with the pillow. He laid his throbbing hand across his chest. He wanted to tell her to lie next to him and just hold him. But he bit back the words.

She hovered above him, her eyes red-rimmed and her cheeks splotchy. Even so, she was as beautiful as an angel. If he died and went to heaven, he'd have a hard time finding a prettier one.

All he needed to do was reach up and wrap his arm around her, and she would tumble down on top of him. He couldn't think of a better way to forget about his pain.

Her eyes widened, and he had no doubt she could see his desire.

"I'll find a bandage for your wound." She moved away, and disappointment swept through him. She was not only one of the most beautiful women he'd laid eyes upon, but underneath her polite reserve she was one of the most kindhearted too.

If God had given him such a woman for his wife, why had he made the business deal with her? Why hadn't he taken her their first night together when she'd been waiting for him on the bed in her nightgown?

Henry's suave, handsome face flashed to his mind, and his gut twisted. Henry Spalding was the kind of man Priscilla could have married—would have married. He was educated and cultured in a way that made Eli look like a backwoods bumpkin. After having the interest and admiration of a man like Henry, why would she ever want a man like him?

"Must be hard to be around Henry, huh?" He searched her face when she returned to his side with a bandage.

"It's awkward at times." She wrapped clean linen around his wound. "But Mabel is so sweet and does most of the talking whenever we're together."

Did she still care about Henry? The question nagged him and begged to be asked.

But he closed his eyes, refusing to give in to the question, not sure he wanted to know the answer.

Besides, it didn't matter if she liked Henry better than she liked him. His gut told him that in the long run he'd need to cut ties with her and send her back to New York, where she'd be safe.

Why waste the energy on jealousy? Why make more out of their situation than it warranted?

There were too many other more important matters—life and death matters—that needed his full attention, especially when the success or failure of the trip rested upon his shoulders.

Priscilla pressed a gloved hand against her nose to block out the putrid odors of the St. Louis waterfront—decaying fish, rotting pelts, filthy river water, maybe a mixture of it all. Whatever the cause of the stench, she breathed carefully against her glove, relishing the faint remains of the scent of home that lingered in the fabric—one that was fading all too quickly.

Eli stalked down the long landing stage onto the waterfront, which was dirty and rugged and like nothing she'd seen in any of the other places they'd stopped. In the early evening, the crowds still teemed along the banks of the Mississippi, and the number of steamboats lined up along the levee was equally staggering. As far up and down the river as she could see, smokestacks rose into the air.

She was praying that their next boat would be as clean and sturdy as the *Siam*. Thankfully, the boat hadn't sustained any damage from the crash of the previous evening.

The captain and crew had managed to loosen the steamboat from the sandbar in the morning, and they had made good time the rest of the way to St. Louis. Yet the crevices across Eli's forehead reflected his fear that they had missed their connection with the American Fur Company.

He pulled his hat low and wove through the crowd, dodging

the traffic of those both coming and going. He'd stayed in the cabin all night, and she'd slept in a chair next to the bed, wanting to watch over him and care for him. But when she'd awakened, he was gone, and she hadn't seen him all day until he'd found her just as the pilot had moored the boat at sunset along the riverfront of St. Louis. He'd told her to wait on board until he learned what they needed to do next.

She'd wanted to ask him about his hand, change the bandage, and just be near him again.

But he'd been too busy to search her out. And he certainly didn't need her feeble attempts at doctoring.

"I hope we have letters from family waiting for us." Mabel leaned against the rail next to her. She breathed heavily into her handkerchief, her face a sickly olive.

Priscilla's heart bounded. "Yes. We'll have letters." She'd instructed her family to send their correspondence to St. Louis. She'd been gone from home for a month, plenty of time for her family to have written.

"Reverend Spalding told me this would be the last place to get letters until we reach Oregon Country. And who knows how often or even *if* letters will reach us there."

An ache squeezed Priscilla's throat. Oh, what she would give for a letter from home. She'd tried to tell herself she wasn't homesick, but a longing so strong and sudden gripped her heart that she didn't know how she could stand under the pressure. She needed some word from her family, no matter how small.

Her gaze sought out the steamboat office, a dingy building on the crowded waterfront. Surely she would have letters from family and friends awaiting her there.

"I've often heard it said from other sisters in Christ," Mabel said wistfully, "that one of the hardest things about mission life is the sporadic nature of hearing from loved ones."

Priscilla swallowed the lump in her throat. "I haven't wanted to admit just how much I'm missing them, even to myself. After all, it's such a privilege to go forth in the name of the Master, and I want to cheerfully stand against the toil and privation we encounter. . . ."

"But it's only normal to miss our families."

"Then you miss yours too?"

Mabel nodded and her eyes clouded with tears. "Very much. Especially now when I'm not feeling well."

Priscilla reached for Mabel's hand and squeezed it. Determination surged through her. "Don't worry, Sister Spalding. I'll retrieve our letters this very instant." She pushed away from the rail.

"Oh, my dear, please stay. Our husbands told us not to leave the boat for any reason," Mabel called after her. "It's too dangerous."

"I'm sure I shall be just fine." Priscilla hastened along the verandah toward the stairway. "Besides, the men are occupied with other things. Someone needs to make sure we get our mail." She blocked out Mabel's protests as she made her way down the narrow flight of steps. And she didn't hesitate when she reached the top of the landing platform. Her boots clomped against the length of plank, and when her feet hit solid ground, she stumbled, her knees unsteady with their first touch of land since the previous Sabbath.

Enormous piles of logs sat near the water's edge, ready for loading and refueling the boilers that powered the steam engines. Stacks of pelts sat outside warehouses, and the stench of their bloody flesh permeated the air.

Priscilla bunched her skirt so the squelching mud wouldn't splatter the hem, and she started toward the building Eli had entered. With each step, she tried not to notice that men were stopping their conversations and work to stare at her. With their scruffy, weather-wizened faces, rugged clothes, and hungry eyes, they weren't the sort of men she was accustomed to seeing.

When one of the men smiled at her and another whistled, she picked up her pace. Her heart sped forward with fear. Had she made a mistake in leaving the boat?

Out of the corner of her eye she saw one of the men start toward her. She hiked her skirt higher and started to run, panic slapping after her. She was glad Mother couldn't see her unlady-like behavior. It was downright scandalous.

When she came to the office door, she burst through it. With gasping breath, she slammed it shut and leaned back, lifting a hand to her forehead to smooth away loose tendrils.

Only then did she realize the office had grown completely silent and every man in the crowded room had turned to stare at her—more of the same grizzly men she'd hoped to escape outside. Some were sitting at tables smoking cigars; others were lounging against the wall. A few were leaning against a long counter and conducting business with the uniformed men on the other side.

"Well, well, well. What do we have here?"

Her rasping breath froze. Regret poured over her. She'd been rash to disobey her husband's orders. The danger of her predicament swarmed at her from all sides, and she could see no escape.

A towering bearlike man wearing a black patch over one eye lumbered toward her. "Ain't you the purtiest little thing."

She shrank against the wood.

"What cloud did you fall from?" The man's coarse hair curled in disarray down his neck and around his face, ending in an overgrown beard. His fringed buckskin breeches and tunic were stained dark. A leather belt surrounded his hefty waist, holding a sheathed knife and pistols. A bullet pouch hung from his neck, and a powder horn was strapped under his arm.

She didn't know whether or not he expected her to answer his question, and she wasn't sure she could get her voice working if he did.

"This ain't no place for a real lady like yourself." His one good eye took her in with a giant sweep. "But I can find you a nice place to stay if you need one."

"I'm just fine, thank you." She tried to keep her voice from trembling.

"I got a perfect place. . . ." He came a step closer, and the staleness of his body odor assaulted her. He tossed a grin over his shoulder at the spectators. "And there ain't no better place than here in Black Squire's arms. Right, fellas?"

Panic rustled over her skin, giving her chills. Her fingers went to the cameo pinned at her throat.

He held open his long, beefy arms. And the men hooted and encouraged him with words that burned Priscilla's ears.

"That's enough, Squire." Eli shoved the man aside and grabbed Priscilla. "Leave her alone."

Black Squire growled at Eli. "You got a wife now, Doc. So for tonight, this purty thing is mine." He lunged for her, and his enormous hand grazed her cheek.

She slapped his hand away. "I beg your pardon."

Squire's grin widened, and the other men called out encouragement to him.

Eli tugged her against his side and slipped his arm around her. "She's mine." His voice was low. "This *is* my wife."

At the fury of his hold and the possessiveness of his tone, relief drained away her fear. She sidled against him. The security of his embrace reassured her. Whatever else happened, now she was safe—completely and utterly safe—even if his eyes chastised her for her foolishness and warned her of the tongue-lashing he would give her later.

"Besides, you've got a woman already." Eli nodded toward the corner.

Priscilla peeked at the lone Indian woman standing by herself with a papoose strapped to her back.

Eyes as black as midnight met Priscilla's. For an instant she felt as though she were looking into a dark empty cave. There was nothing—no emotion—not even curiosity, almost as if the woman wasn't really there.

Her buckskin dress was splotched with stains and her skin darkened with dust and mire. But underneath the grime, the woman's features were soft and beautiful.

"This here's your wife?" Black Squire's voice boomed through the room.

"Yep." Eli's arms tightened. "Don't ever touch her again."

Priscilla shuddered to think of life with a man like Black Squire. No wonder the Indian woman was a walking tomb.

"Well, why didn't you say she was so purty?" The man rubbed his beard and tilted his head to center his eye upon her. "That changes everything."

Henry appeared from behind Eli. "Then you're willing to have the women come along?"

"How can I say no now?" the big man said. "What red-blooded man wouldn't want this little lady riding along?"

The tension in Henry's face eased.

Priscilla's heart sputtered with dread. Surely they wouldn't have to travel the rest of their trip with this bear of a man.

"It really doesn't make much difference if you've changed your mind." Eli's muscles tightened. "We already paid. Captain Fitzpatrick agreed to take us. Parker will be waiting for us at the Rendezvous. The deal's done."

A hard glint flashed in Squire's eye. But he shrugged. "You're right. You made your deal with a bunch of schoolboys back

East who wouldn't know the butt end of a buffalo if they saw one."

A chorus of guffaws erupted around them.

"But," he continued, "if you wanna jeopardize the whole trip by bringin' your women, then you just go ahead."

"You know it wasn't my plan," Eli said.

Squire shrugged. "Guess if something happens to you, Doc, then I'd have me another woman. A real purty one." He grinned. "And if I don't need her, I bet I could find plenty of young braves who'd pay me a fortune for her."

"You wouldn't dare," Priscilla said with breathless distress.

Squire threw back his head and roared with laughter.

"Don't listen to him," Eli said into her ear. "He blows a lot of hot air."

Squire drew himself up and shook his head. "You want to ride on the *Diana* with us, be ready to go first thing in the morning."

"But tomorrow's the Sabbath," Henry said, his brow creasing.

Squire nodded at the Indian woman, and she started toward him.

"We can't possibly travel on the Lord's Day," Henry insisted.

"It's fine, Henry." Eli glared, his eyes cautioning Henry against saying anything else. "We'll be ready in the morning."

"But we received explicit instructions from the Mission Board that we shouldn't fail to observe the Sabbath for any reason."

"We *will* observe it, Henry." Eli's voice was tight. "On board the *Diana*. Tomorrow."

Squire touched the cheek of the Indian woman with a gentleness that startled Priscilla. The woman didn't smile, but she said something to him in her language. His reply was soft, and he patted the head of the baby in the cradleboard.

"I'd feel much better if we obeyed the Lord," Henry insisted.

"If we trust Him, don't you think He'll get us where we need to go in His timing?"

Squire started toward the door. "If you're not there, we'll leave without you." He shoved open the door and stepped outside.

"We'll be ready," Eli called.

The Indian woman pattered after Squire. The small baby in the case on her back bounced with each step. Every part of his little body was swaddled except his chubby face. His wide black eyes peered out and somehow seemed to find Priscilla.

Her heart twisted with sudden longing. When his lips lifted into a tiny smile made especially for her, she couldn't resist giving him one in return.

And as he disappeared through the door, he took her smile with him. Longing fell into its place. Would it ever get easier to look at a baby without wishing she could have one for herself?

Chapter

11

MISSOURI RIVER

It seems to me now that we are on the very border of civilization. Priscilla read over the words she'd scrawled in the letter to her family and then glanced to the chaos of the St. Louis levee.

In the early morning, the waterfront was already awake. There were more natives than she'd ever seen and foreigners shouting to one another in languages she couldn't understand but guessed to be German and French. Her eyes widened at the sight of the black slaves and young Spanish Creoles from New Orleans. Mostly, however, the levee swarmed with too many of the hunters and backwoodsmen she'd already encountered.

After her brush with danger the previous evening, she'd taken Eli's rebuke as justly deserved and stayed locked in her stateroom until he'd come for her.

"I need to mail my letter." She folded it and pressed the seal. "Can we stop by the office?"

Eli knocked his hat back and peered up and down the waterfront. "First, we're finding the *Diana* and loading up."

She nodded and swallowed the lump that pushed its way up every time she thought about the fact that none of her dear family or friends had written to her. She was glad Mabel had received a letter. But there'd been nothing for her. Not one word.

Eli's eyes narrowed. "You see them, Henry?"

Henry stretched to see over the heads of those around them, and John and Richard joined in the search.

The fog had finally rolled away and left an unblemished blue sky in its place. The whistles blew clear, and no two boats sounded alike. Some made chords, others a succession of notes— long blasts, followed by short toots. The various whistles had become almost like music to her.

"I have a bad feeling about this," Eli said. "Wait here, and I'll see what's going on."

He jogged toward the office.

"Please take my letter," she called after him. But he didn't turn around.

"I take." Richard held out his hand.

She managed a smile. "Thank you, Richard. You and John are always so helpful. What would I do without the two of you?"

The boy took the letter and bolted after Eli.

Henry turned his back to her at the pretense of searching the boats again.

"The Indian boys like you." Mabel held a handkerchief to her nose. She took a gulp of air and then blanched.

The dampness of molding wood and the mustiness of rotten fish permeated the air. The stench in the clear morning was as overpowering as it had been the night before.

"Richard and John are eager students. I've already taught them to write their English names, and I've had them memorize the Ten Commandments." Priscilla watched the young lad and thought of the Indian baby that had smiled at her. "They'll be of great service to the mission."

"They won't return to their families?" Mabel's brows shifted up.

"After becoming civilized, I'm not sure they'll have any desire to return to their savage ways. What do you think?"

Mabel opened her mouth to speak but could only utter a cry of alarm. She doubled over and retched, nearly spilling the acrid stream onto Priscilla's boots.

The splatter against the muddy ground and the bitter odor sent a wave of nausea through Priscilla and made her stomach lurch.

The foul air of the waterfront was enough to make even the strongest stomach churn. It was even worse for poor Mabel, suffering the discomforts of pregnancy.

Priscilla took several deep breaths through her mouth, swallowing her bile. She fumbled at her pocket to retrieve her handkerchief for Mabel but then stopped. It was stained with Eli's blood.

Henry murmured to Mabel in a soft, soothing voice.

"They're gone!" Eli shouted from the doorway of the office. He trotted toward them, his eyes crackling with bursts of fire. "They snuck out of here in the middle of the night."

Henry didn't say anything, but Priscilla could see the relief in his face. She'd heard the two men exchange words several times already that morning about traveling on the Sabbath.

Eli stopped in front of them, yanked off his hat, and scanned the river as if he could make the American Fur Company trappers appear if he looked hard enough.

"I know you were determined to leave with them," Henry said slowly. "But perhaps God has a better plan for us."

Eli's jaw worked up and down. "You know as well as I do the reason they left without us is that Black Squire doesn't want us taking the women."

Very few of the people they'd met during their travels supported their undertaking. Too many had raised their eyebrows and questioned whether a woman could endure the grueling experience day after day. Some had even called it an "unheard-of journey for females."

And although she knew Eli agreed with them, he'd made every effort to stand up for her and Mabel, explaining that he was taking wagons, and whenever she and Mabel grew weary of riding horseback, they could ride in one of the wagons.

"Maybe there's someone else we could ride with," Priscilla offered. Since her encounter with Squire, she'd dreaded the thought of spending the next few months traveling with him. If they could locate another group to travel with . . .

Eli shook his head, his frustration pulling the scar on his face taut. "Believe me, I've already thought about it, and there isn't anyone else. The American Fur Company caravan is our only chance for safe escort."

They would need the guidance and protection of the trappers for most of the journey, at least until they crossed the Continental Divide and reached the annual Rendezvous on the Green River. From there, Eli was counting on Parker, his explorer friend, to guide them for the last distance of their journey and help them make it over the Blue Mountain Range before the mountainous weather turned too treacherous for travel.

Until then, they would have to rely upon the trappers.

"I don't understand why they're so opposed to us." Mabel wiped her handkerchief across her mouth. "We won't be a bother."

"They're just stubborn," Henry said. "Once they see that we'll take care of ourselves, they'll be fine."

Eli turned his attention to the line of steamboats. "It's more complicated than that. They don't want any of us going. They know if we make it to the West, others will be more willing to try it. And they don't want any interference with their hunting and trapping."

"They don't have to worry about that," Henry said. "Beaver hats are going out of fashion, and that will force down the price of beaver skins. The changing style will put them out of business long before any of us missionaries do."

Eli heaved a long breath. "I'll go see if we can find another steamboat, a fast one that can take us to Liberty." He spun and started back toward the office.

Priscilla stared after Eli. Tension radiated in each step he took, and it reflected her own heart. What would happen if they missed their chance to go west? What would become of her partnership with Eli then?

The earliest any other boat was leaving for Liberty was the next day. They boarded the *Chariton*, a much smaller steamboat. Priscilla's hopes for a safe and comfortable vessel were left behind in St. Louis. The *Chariton*, with its peeling paint and rotting boards, deserved to hit a snag and be put out of its dilapidated misery. But she prayed the boat would wait to die its long overdue death until they reached Liberty.

A crowd of rough frontiersmen had also boarded the boat, and they spent all their time gambling and passing around whiskey. As day turned into night, the burly men grew increasingly loud and crude, and Eli had ordered Priscilla and Mabel to stay in the boat's only private cabin, which was barely big enough for both of them.

At a burst of raucous laughter outside the door, Priscilla stiffened in the narrow bed she shared with Mabel.

Under the tattered and much-too-dirty blanket, Mabel's trembling fingers found hers.

"You're still awake?" Priscilla whispered.

"They've gotten louder with each passing hour, haven't they?"

Priscilla shivered. "Too loud."

"Thank the Lord for our brave husbands watching over us."

Eli and Henry had taken to bedding down on the other side of the flimsy door, on the open deck, with no shelter but their own thin blankets.

"They're good men." Priscilla's heart warmed at the picture of Eli's tired blue eyes holding fast to hers, silently questioning her, making sure she was all right, before he'd closed the door of the cabin for the night.

The shattering of glass on the other side of the thin wall made her jump.

Mabel's fingers tightened around hers.

"I do hope everyone is all right." Priscilla's insides quavered. "Do you think this trip is too dangerous for us?"

For a long moment, Mabel didn't say anything. The nausea and tiredness caused by the pregnancy were taking their toll upon her already travel-weary body.

The drunken laughter of the frontiersmen swelled around them, almost as if they were in the same room.

Mabel finally sighed. "I've never experienced anything this hard in my life."

"Surely it can't get much worse, can it?"

"I don't know." Mabel's hand squeezed hers. "But, my dear, is there ever anything safe about serving the Lord with one's whole heart?"

Priscilla stared through the blackness of the night, the question ricocheting around and through her.

Mabel shifted and the bed bumped against the wall. "I try to remind myself that without sacrifice and discomfort, I won't be following in the footsteps of my Lord."

"You're right." Priscilla closed her eyes and reminded herself that she was willing to sacrifice everything, even her own life, if necessary. Wasn't she?

By midweek, Eli was tempted to get behind the boat and push it along to make it go faster. Instead, he leaned against the rail and held in a breath of frustration. The rocky shore of the Missouri River drew closer, and the stacks of four-foot logs beckoned the hungry boat.

Even though the *Chariton* was smaller than the other steamboat they'd traveled on, he'd discovered it was also the laziest he'd ever ridden. The pilot stopped the boat every chance he could. Of course, all steamboats needed to restock the supply of wood that fueled the boilers, but the *Chariton* made a holiday out of every landing.

"I must go ashore," Priscilla murmured. Her face was pale, and dark circles under her eyes testified to the sleepless nights of late.

He had to give her credit. She hadn't complained about the less than desirable conditions.

"I'll have to go with you," he said, following her to the landing stage. She wouldn't be safe anywhere alone, not with a boatload of drunken men ogling her whenever she made an appearance.

She didn't offer any resistance. When their feet finally touched land, she stopped and gulped in a breath of the crisp spring air.

All along the river, the tangled branches were sprouting light green. The reflection of the sun on the buds colored them almost yellow.

He turned to the lanky farm boy sitting on top of the stacked wood. A rough sign dangled from one of the logs. Scrawled letters read: *Notice to all persons takin wood from this landin, please leave a ticket payable to the subscriber, for $1.75 a cord.*

The young boy was likely a son of the farmer selling the wood, sent to make sure the steamboats were paying their fair share.

"How long since the American Fur Company's boat, *Diana*, passed through?" Eli asked.

"The *Diana*? Ooo-wee!" The boy slapped his knee. "Ain't you heard? The *Diana*, she got herself into a heap o' trouble up a ways. Hit a snag."

Eli's heart lurched. "What happened?"

"She sunk."

For a long moment, he couldn't move. Even his thoughts came to a crashing halt.

"But don't worry none," the boy went on. "Heard the water was shallow. Ain't nobody lost their lives."

"You're sure about that?"

The boy nodded. "Every boat going east been talkin' about it."

"What else have you heard?"

"They been sayin' she'll have to lay up for repairs and dry her freight 'fore she can continue on."

Silently Eli offered a grateful prayer to the Almighty. Relief blew over him and knocked the weight of worry off his shoulders. If the *Diana* wasn't moving, maybe they'd have a chance of overtaking the trappers before they reached Liberty.

He nodded his thanks to the boy and trotted to catch up with Priscilla, who'd started up a grassy knoll. "Priscilla, wait," he called to her.

She stopped and twisted to look at him. The wind rippled her dress and tugged at her bonnet. She caught the brim and held it in place.

His breathing skipped ahead. The sun outlined every graceful curve of her body. No doubt about it—she was beautiful. And that was turning out to be a problem in more than one way. Not only was she attracting the attention of the other men, but he was having more difficulty with each passing day fighting his own attraction.

"Never expected that I'd have to spend half the trip escorting you," he said when he reached her, his frustration at himself edging his voice.

Her eyes widened. "You don't need to escort me."

"Oh, yes I do."

She started forward, lifting her face to the sun and letting it bathe her pale skin. "I didn't ask you to accompany me, Dr. Ernest."

"You wouldn't be safe if I didn't."

"I'm sure you're exaggerating."

"*I'm sure* you've learned by now that I never exaggerate."

Her footsteps faltered. She glanced around. "There's no one here right now. I'll be perfectly fine. I certainly don't want to inconvenience you any longer."

She turned abruptly and picked her way through the rocks. The wind rustled the long rushes and creaked through the branches of the few trees that hadn't been chopped down for steamboat fuel.

"I don't need you," she called over her shoulder. "Just go take care of your business."

Priscilla's steps were choppy, making her skirt swish. He was almost tempted to let her go, to let her try to fend for herself.

"I'd rather be alone anyway," she called.

Her words stung, especially when the truth was that he liked being with her. "Have it your way."

She had to learn to get along on her own, without him coming to her rescue every time she broke a fingernail.

He took a few steps back toward the shore and then stopped. But what would she do if one of the trappers saw her alone and came after her? How would she fight off a man used to wrestling grizzlies?

His heart gave a thud, and he tossed a glance over his shoulder. She'd already disappeared into the thick undergrowth. She'd said she didn't need him. And he most certainly did not need her.

Besides, most of the men were still sleeping off their liquor. He started toward the boat again and steeled his back.

A yelp, distinctively hers, sent his heart into a teetering spin. He turned around and raced in the direction he'd heard her voice. He tripped over rocks and twigs but stumbled forward, his heart banging louder with each step.

"Priscilla?" He had the sudden vision of her pinned underneath one of the filthy drunken frontiersmen, and rage surged through him. He was afraid of what he was capable of doing to anyone who hurt her.

"Priscilla!" he yelled again. He scrutinized the tangled brush along the riverfront. What if the assailant had covered her mouth and dragged her off somewhere?

His breath spurted with growing panic. "Priscilla!"

"Dr. Ernest." Her calm voice addressed him. "I'm right here."

There, only feet away, she peered up at him from her perch on the edge of a rock.

His gaze darted around. "You're alone?"

"Yes." Her glance followed his lead. "Or at least I was—until you made an appearance."

He heaved a breath. And then a wave of embarrassment rolled

over him. He wanted to slink away like the fool he was and force himself to quit worrying about her.

"Did you need something?" she asked, slipping her hands behind her back.

What could he say? He couldn't very well tell her the truth—that she was always on his mind.

"Dr. Ernest?"

He scrambled for an excuse. "For starters, I want you to stop calling me Dr. Ernest."

She tilted her head, and one dainty eyebrow shot up.

"It's way too formal. And I'm not your doctor. I'm your husband."

Her other eyebrow lifted.

"Look. I don't care if it's the proper thing to do where you come from, but I don't like it. From now on, I want you to call me Eli."

"*Where I come from*, such an address shows respect."

"That so? Well, you'll show me more respect if you use my given name."

Her gaze flickered. She winced and brought forward one of her hands. For a moment he didn't see anything, but when she lifted her palm and began to pick at it, he noticed it was covered with bristles.

One glance at the prickly pears on the ground surrounding the rock told him she'd had the misfortune of picking one up.

"Got yourself into a little trouble, I see."

"I'll be fine in just a minute." She glared at him, as if warning him against saying *I told you so*.

He bit back a grin. "I don't suppose you *need* me to help you get the bristles out."

She hesitated then shook her head. "Of course not."

"Guess I'll meet you at the boat." He turned and took a step

away. When she didn't stop him, the muscles in his back tightened. He took another step, and another. Finally he glanced
at her again. His gut swirled with conflict. Everything in his
nature wanted to kneel beside her and help her. But not if she
didn't want him to . . .

He shuffled forward.

"Wait, Dr. Ernest."

His first reaction was to spin and run to her side. Instead, he
forced himself to count to ten.

"I mean—Eli." Her voice was soft.

He could only get to three before he turned.

Her big eyes were glistening like glass jewels. "I do need
your help."

His heart did an involuntary flip.

"Please," she whispered.

His feet moved toward her as if she had some kind of magic
hold upon him. He knew he ought to crack himself over the
head for his weakness, but he couldn't stop himself.

"Those buggers are tough to dislodge," he said. "I know
from personal experience."

She held out her hand to him. "I didn't realize the pears had
needles on them."

He knelt next to her and cupped her hand in his. "On the
last trip, I bit into one."

She gasped.

He smiled. "Yep."

"Doesn't quite seem fair for God to make them so attractive
only to cover them with such painful spines."

"At least they're on your hand and not in your mouth."

"True." She touched the thin black scar near his thumb. "And
how's your wound?"

"It's on the mend. Looks like it'll stay together just fine."

"Then my sewing job didn't ruin you for life?"

He grinned. "I'm already ruined."

Her lips curved into a small smile. And the sight of it made him realize how rare her smiles were. Had she always been so serious?

He bent his head over her hand. The thin, clear needles had punctured the tender skin on her palm and fingers. He pinched one between his fingernails and tugged it loose.

She winced.

"I'm sorry." He worked faster. "It'll hurt for a few minutes."

He tried not to think about her pain. Over the years he'd accustomed himself to the fact that he would always cause his patients some pain and discomfort. It was just part of the job, part of the healing process.

But with each needle he pried loose, the sting in her flesh radiated into his. By the time he was done, he was sweating.

"How does your hand feel now?" He grazed his fingers across the swollen red spots on her hand.

She sucked in a breath.

His gaze lifted to hers.

Teardrops glistened in her eyelashes, but her eyes were wide with wonder. "You have the gentlest hands."

"Comes from years of practice." He sank into the feather softness of her eyes.

"And I think they came from the Lord, who's obviously given you the perfect skills for doctoring."

If not for the sincerity in her tone, he might have scoffed at her comment. Anyone could be a doctor. His stepfather had been right about that. It didn't take much book learning, not like it did to become a minister.

Even so, he'd had to work harder than most to make it. "At first I didn't think I'd be content with doctoring. I thought I wanted to be someone important like a minister. But it didn't take me long to realize God can use a doctor just as much as a minister."

She cocked her head, as if she might argue with him.

"I realize you probably have the same view as most of the population—that becoming a minister is better, more noble, than anything else. But I've learned God can use a clay pot just as much as a glass jar."

For a moment she studied him and then gave him the barest of smiles. "I'm grateful you're a doctor and not a minister. Otherwise, I'd still be picking prickles out of my palm."

He touched the tender skin of her palm and swiped a dot of blood off the tip of her finger. Without thinking, he lifted her hand to his lips and kissed her finger.

She drew in a sharp breath but didn't make an effort to pull away from him.

He met her gaze. The silkiness in the depths sent a tremor through his body. He pressed his lips against her smooth skin again, tasting the saltiness of her blood.

His lips brushed a path to her palm, and in the tender, moist middle he pressed another kiss.

Her chest rose and fell in rapid succession, but she still made no move. Instead, she watched him, almost as if she was remembering the kiss he'd given her on their wedding day, the same kiss that still haunted him.

Maybe it was past time for him to give her another. How could one little kiss hurt anything?

He raised his head and studied her lips.

Her fingers trembled against his.

A crunching in the rushes nearby shattered the stillness of the moment.

She peered over his shoulder and jerked away from him.

His body tensed, and he turned.

Henry stumbled to a stop with Mabel bumping him from behind. Henry's shirt was half buttoned, out of his trousers, and Mabel's skirt was rumpled.

Eli raised an eyebrow. "Henry."

Henry jabbed at his shirttails. Mabel cowered behind him and combed her fingers over her hair.

Priscilla scrambled to her feet, her cheeks flushed.

"We were just trying to talk—" Henry fumbled. His Adam's apple wobbled up and down. "I mean, we were taking a walk. . . ."

Red crept up Mabel's neck and cheeks.

Eli glanced at the ground and rubbed a hand over his mouth and scruffy chin, trying to hide his smile. It was obvious Henry had wanted a private moment with his wife. Something he'd wanted with his but had no right to.

"We're sorry for intruding upon you," Henry started.

Eli knew he ought to be relieved Henry had saved him from kissing Priscilla. He couldn't take the chance of making a mess of their arrangement. And yet, part of him was sorry their rare moment alone had ended.

Henry coughed.

"Just heard that the *Diana* sank," Eli said quickly, hoping he could spare all of them further embarrassment.

"The *Diana* sank?" Henry lifted his head in surprise.

"Doesn't sound like anyone was hurt."

"Praise the Lord," Mabel murmured.

"You know what this means, don't you?" Eli asked Henry. "We'll be able to catch up to Black Squire."

"I guess it also means you learned a lesson, doesn't it, Dr. Ernest?"

Eli straightened. There were moments when Henry irritated him, and he had a feeling this was going to be one of those times.

Henry smiled. "Didn't I say we only needed to trust the Lord? If He wants us to make it to Oregon Country, He'll provide the way."

Eli's jaw tightened, and he held in his retort. God would indeed be with them each step of the way, but that didn't mean He'd whisk them there on a magic carpet.

They'd have to do their part too, and Eli was determined to make sure he did all he possibly could to get them where they needed to go.

Chapter
12

LIBERTY, MISSOURI

$\mathcal{P}$riscilla leaned against the rickety rail of the general store and looked at the wagons with a sinking heart.

When they'd arrived in Liberty, Eli had purchased two wagons. A larger one and then a light Dearborn. After several days of packing, he'd managed to squeeze her trunk into one of the wagons, but how would there be room for her or Mabel when they needed a break from riding their horses?

The wagons were crammed with barrels and crates, their tent, blankets, cooking utensils, tools, and the many provisions they would need over the next months as they journeyed through the central uncharted and unorganized territory of the United States.

"Not much else is gonna fit." Eli shoved the pole for their tent into a small crack along the top of the covered wagon.

A group of Indians stopped to stare at her, and she offered them a smile. If she'd thought St. Louis was the border of civilization, Liberty was another planet altogether. As the starting point for many of the trappers heading west and the last place to buy substantial supplies, the town was overrun with hardened men and Indians.

Except for a tavern, a hotel, and the store, Main Street was nothing more than a dirt road that passed through a dozen or more log cabins. The public square showed signs of growth, with several larger homes surrounding it, but the town couldn't even boast of a church.

She and Mabel were among the few white women and turned heads wherever they went.

"Will we have enough food to last us the trip?" she asked.

"I hope so," Eli replied. "At least it will be enough to last until we reach buffalo country."

"No worry," Richard said, patting his newly purchased rifle. "I shoot buffalo for Mrs. Doc."

Eli had generously provided for the Indian boys, and he'd also purchased twelve horses, six mules, and seventeen head of cattle, including four milk cows.

John fidgeted with the stirrup length on his horse. "No need saddler."

"*Saddle*," Priscilla corrected. "It's called a *saddle*, and it will make your long ride safer and more comfortable."

The boy shook his head. "No need."

"If you want to ride without it, that's fine with me." Eli straightened and tipped his hat back. "You need to do whatever works best for you."

Eli had decided he would ride ahead with the Indian boys, the wagons, and the animals to Bellevue, north of the Missouri state line. The small trading post, owned by the American Fur

Company, was the last connection they'd have with the East before they turned west into the open prairies and began the long overland part of their journey.

While Eli traveled with all their supplies, he'd made arrangements for her and Mabel and Henry to ride on one of the Fur Company's boats that would take them up the Missouri River to Bellevue. Eli wanted to spare her and Mabel as much of the hard riding as possible. Even though the distance between Liberty and Bellevue was only three hundred miles, it was that much less they'd have to ride their horses, especially with the danger of swollen rivers and the unpredictability of the spring weather.

Priscilla didn't like the idea of being separated for so long. Eli had reassured her he would meet them in Bellevue, where the trapper caravan, under the command of Black Squire and another mountain man, Fitzpatrick, would leave for the Rendezvous. But Eli's words failed to reassure her.

He walked to the front of the wagon, inspecting every inch of the boards, wheels, and axles, along with the canvas frame supported by hickory bows. He'd hired two young men to drive the wagons. Several other Nez Perce Indians who had wintered in Liberty had asked to join their party.

The small group would leave on the morrow to get a head start on taking their supplies to Bellevue. But the steamboat for the women and Henry wasn't scheduled to leave until the end of the week. The Fur Company had guaranteed their passage this time, but Priscilla couldn't stop worrying.

They'd promised them a ride on the *Diana* too. Even though she was glad God had spared them the ordeal of hitting the snag and sinking, anxiety nagged her regardless.

She wasn't sure if her fear stemmed from the knowledge that she would have to ride on the same boat as Black Squire, which had finally limped into Liberty long after they'd arrived on the

Chariton. Thankfully, the delay had given them the time they needed to assemble their equipment.

The cold April breeze slapped at Priscilla. She shivered and wrapped her shawl tighter, clutching it against her cameo pin. Her fingers grazed the raised pattern of the elegant young lady— the kind of woman she needed to be, well-mannered and poised, just as Mother had trained her. No matter where she went in the wilderness, the cameo would connect her to family and the civilities of home.

Eli jumped onto the jockey box and pulled on the canvas covering.

If she was honest with herself, she knew part of her fear came from the thought of being away from him. She didn't want to admit her need for him—she wanted to prove she was strong.

"Maybe Richard or John could stay with us," she called to him.

"You'll be safe enough if you stay by Henry." He jumped down. "Besides, I need the boys to help drive the animals."

"Dr. Ernest?" A dirty, half-naked Indian child trotted toward them. "Message for Dr. Ernest."

Eli stepped forward. "I'm Dr. Ernest."

The child's breaths came in gasps, evidence of a hard run. "Black Squire. He said to come. His squaw sick and need doctor."

Eli nodded. "Tell Squire I'll be there as soon as I can."

Surprise rippled through Priscilla. Surely Eli wasn't serious?

When the child spun away, Eli dug in the back of the wagon and pulled out his doctor's case.

"You can't possibly be going to help that man." The words spilled from her mouth before she could stop them.

"Of course I'm going to help him."

"Not after what he did to us."

Eli stopped, and his brows lifted. "Listen to yourself, Priscilla."

She stared at the tip of her boot and twisted it against a thatch of new green grass with a dandelion pushing up, its bud still tightly closed. "I'm sorry. It's not the most charitable attitude, but—"

"I'm a doctor. I help those in need, whether they deserve it or not." He started after the Indian child. "Besides, isn't that what our mission is all about?"

She wanted to argue with him, but she knew he was right. As much as she disliked Squire, hadn't Christ commanded them to love their enemies?

"What if I came with you?"

He stopped and turned. His gaze probed her face, as if searching for her motivation.

"I know you usually work alone," she offered, "but I'd like to learn more about what you do." Surely as a doctor's wife, she should know some basics so she could assist him if he needed it. She could show him she was more capable than he thought.

Finally he nodded. "I suppose it wouldn't hurt anything."

Her heart quickened, relieved that he would include her, especially since he'd seemed so intent over the past weeks at keeping his distance. As they wound along a river path, he patiently answered all of her medical questions. When they reached a white log house with a piazza, an old black man opened the gate and ushered them inside.

Priscilla followed Eli in, but froze. The courtyard was alive with flapping hens, wild turkeys, tamed geese, mangy dogs, and people of all kinds—black girls running and giggling, Indian women and children.

A group of Indian men were standing around an open fire

pit in the middle of the courtyard roasting what she assumed to be a deer. Their chatter faded and their expressions turned stony.

She swallowed a lump and forced her feet to move, to catch up with Eli. She almost grabbed the edge of his vest to make sure she wasn't separated from him.

The old black man led them across the piazza, through an open hallway littered with Indians sitting or sleeping on the floor. The charred smoke of venison drifted into the hallway and mingled with the sour odor of urine and the staleness of unwashed bodies.

She lifted her hand to her nose and tried not to trip over outstretched legs.

Finally the old man led them to a small room. He nodded at the door before backing away.

Eli ducked and went in. Priscilla hesitated only a moment before entering.

There on the ground, covered by a thin blanket, lay the Indian woman she'd seen with Black Squire in St. Louis.

Her eyes were closed, and she was so silent and still that, except for the rise and fall of her chest, Priscilla might have counted her for dead.

Eli knelt next to the woman and slipped a hand over her forehead.

A quick glance around the room brought Priscilla a measure of relief. Black Squire wasn't there. A wrinkled Indian woman was sitting in the room's only chair with an infant on her lap.

Free of his cradleboard, he was bigger than she'd realized. She wasn't experienced in guessing ages of infants, but she decided the child must be close to a year, if not older.

The baby squirmed and held out his arms toward her.

Priscilla sucked in a quick breath. Did he want her?

The old woman unfolded herself from the chair and stood. "You take baby."

"Oh! No thank you." Priscilla shook her head. Part of her longed to reach out and hug him. And the other part of her was scared of being anywhere near an infant, of letting down her guard.

"You care for baby. I be back soon." She shuffled toward Priscilla and dangled the child in midair. The woman's arms wavered, almost as if she didn't have the strength to carry him.

Priscilla grabbed him before the woman dropped him. "No, I can't care for him. Take him back." She held the child at arm's length.

The woman just gave her a toothless smile.

"Really." Priscilla tried to shove the boy back into the woman's arms, but she maneuvered toward the door. "I came to help with the sick woman, not the baby."

"I come back later. Squire pay me." The woman slunk through the door, her moccasins thumping against the floor.

"Wait," Priscilla called after her.

But the old woman didn't stop.

Priscilla dangled the child in front of her. Whatever in the world would she do with him?

He clapped his hands and squealed.

In the deathly silence of the room, the sound echoed off the whitewashed walls. The woman's eyes fluttered open.

Eli murmured to her.

The woman lifted her head and strained to see beyond Eli to her child, as if getting a look at him could revive her will to live.

"Bring the baby over here," Eli said. "She needs to see him." Priscilla stared at the child.

He smiled and his big black eyes sparkled at her.

A tiny corner of her heart cracked open. It wasn't this boy's fault that she was a grown woman of twenty-six and had so little experience with babies. And it wasn't his fault that being around babies brought her a depressing sense of pain.

With stiff arms, she jostled him into a loose hold and walked over to Eli.

"Kneel down," he said, fingering the pulse in the mother's neck.

Priscilla lowered herself and situated the child on her knees.

The Indian woman reached for the baby's fingers. He gurgled, and she leaned back and closed her eyes, the lines in her face smoother, more peaceful.

"Do you know what's wrong?" Priscilla whispered.

"Not yet."

The woman's eyes opened again and this time focused on Priscilla. The cavern in their depths was as hollow as the last time she'd peered there.

The woman dislodged her son's fingers from around hers. Then she groped for Priscilla's hand.

To her surprise, the woman took the baby's hand and wrapped his tiny fingers around Priscilla's thumb. Then she folded her hand over theirs and squeezed.

The pressure was strong, and Priscilla stared with fascination at the contrast of the bronzed skin against the paleness of hers.

Priscilla met her gaze. Was the woman trying to tell her something?

The mother gave the barest nod before letting her hand drop back to her side and closing her eyes.

The baby babbled, and Priscilla stared at the tiny fingers surrounding hers.

"Running Feet is bestowing an honor upon you," Eli said softly. "She's handing the baby to your care and safekeeping during her illness."

Protest rose to Priscilla's lips, but a groan from the Indian woman stopped her. The woman's beautiful features contorted with obvious pain.

Priscilla stretched her hand to Running Feet's face. She hesitated only a moment before caressing the woman's forehead, brushing back loose tendrils of hair. She pressed the coolness of her palm against the burning skin.

Her throat squeezed. This woman was entrusting her child into the care of a complete stranger. What kind of mother would do such a thing, unless she was desperate?

Priscilla prayed the coolness of her hand would soothe the woman. How could she do anything less than help the baby? Or Running Feet?

Eli probed his fingers gently against Running Feet's abdomen, and she groaned again.

"What can I do?" Priscilla asked.

Eli's eyes crinkled at the corners with worry. "You'll comfort Running Feet most if you take care of her son."

The baby squirmed and gave a soft whimper. Then he stretched both arms toward Priscilla.

"You poor dear." She gathered the boy to her chest and fought the ache that gripped her heart.

He leaned into her and nuzzled his face into her chest.

"Oh, God. Help me," she whispered, fighting against the intense longing the baby awakened inside her. If her infertility was the cross she must bear, why couldn't Providence make the bearing easier?

She pressed a kiss against the feathery strands of the baby's hair, and swallowed her longing, pushing it back to the secret place inside her where it belonged.

This woman. This baby. She must think about them. Why, then, was it so hard to stop thinking so much about herself?

"We're leaving this morning," Squire called as they entered the piazza courtyard five days later.

"Then Running Feet is feeling better?" Eli asked, striding through the chaos of playing children and clucking hens.

Priscilla followed behind him. Even after the past few days of coming and going, she still hadn't shed her fear of walking through the piazza, especially whenever Black Squire was present. His patchless eye seemed to follow her every move in an altogether too intimate way.

She offered another prayer of thanksgiving that Eli had decided to stay behind to care for Running Feet and had instead sent Henry ahead with the wagons and livestock.

Eli hadn't wanted to leave the care of the wagons and supplies to Henry's inexperienced hands, but his desire to help the Indian woman had prevailed. He hadn't been able to decide exactly what was ailing her but had settled upon biliousness and had given her routine doses of calomel.

"We can't delay no longer," Squire said, leading the way down the long hallway. "She's sittin' up today. That's a heap better than she's been so far."

When they entered the room, Running Feet struggled to sit up. Eli rushed to help her.

The toothless Indian woman rose from her chair and hoisted the baby up with her.

Priscilla smiled at the boy and reached for him. "And how's David this morning?"

The baby clapped his hands and smiled back.

The old woman relinquished him with a tired sigh.

Priscilla settled him onto her hip and smoothed a hand over his cheek. She'd decided to name him David, after the minister who'd brought her to a confession of faith. No one seemed to mind that she'd given him an English name, and it seemed to suit him just right. And since she'd be traveling with Running Feet and David for a few months, she decided she might as well give him a name she could actually say.

"Have you fed him?" she asked the old woman.

"He eat, yes."

"Is he clean?"

The woman nodded and glanced sideways at Squire, who had knelt next to Running Feet and Eli.

"You can go," she told the old woman. "I'll care for him now."

The woman hesitated and looked again at Squire.

"Really," Priscilla persisted, surprised by how much she wanted to have the baby to herself. She'd spent most of her time over the past days holding and playing with him. And she'd almost begun to think of herself as his caretaker instead of the woman Squire had hired.

"Squire tell me help take boy to boat," the old woman finally said.

Running Feet's eyes were glazed, and her face drawn with pain. Black Squire was wrong. "She's certainly not a 'heap' better," Priscilla blurted. "If anything, she looks worse."

Eli nodded, his mouth set in a grim line. "Do you think we can spare another day or two?" he asked Squire.

"We'll do just fine, Doc," Squire boomed. "You know as well as me, we can't wait no longer."

Eli's brow furrowed. "I guess we'll just have to try to make her as comfortable as possible on the boat."

"I'll do all I can to help take care of David," Priscilla offered.

"Good. Running Feet will be grateful for your help." Eli didn't exactly smile at her, but a light brightened in his eyes and reached across the dank room to envelop her. After being by his side these past days, had she finally proven herself to him? Could he see that she wasn't a burden but might, in fact, be a helpmate?

The burly trapper murmured to Running Feet as Eli finished administering a dose of calomel. Then gently, as if she were a fragile leaf he could crush, Black Squire slipped his arms under her and lifted her up.

She bit back a moan and closed her eyes.

"You ain't so bad, Doc," Squire said. "In fact, I like you. Just too bad you got yourself saddled with everyone else."

Eli folded up his doctor's case, and Priscilla waited for him to concur with the trapper. But he stood and started toward the door. "We'll see you at the boat."

Priscilla reluctantly handed David back to the old Indian woman and returned to the inn with Eli to gather their few belongings. Mabel was still in bed, and Priscilla helped her dress and pack.

When they finally made it outside, Eli was pacing. "It's about time." He reached for the bag Priscilla was carrying.

"I'm sorry," Mabel said. Her face was pallid, the usual shade of late. "It was my fault."

Priscilla slipped her arm around the woman's waist.

"Let's hurry." Eli started forward.

Mabel took a step but stopped. She covered her mouth. "I think I'm going to be sick." But before she could bend over, the bile spilled out of her mouth and poured down the front of her dress.

Priscilla jumped back and turned her head. The stench never failed to make her own stomach revolt. She closed her eyes and breathed through her mouth.

Mabel's distressed cry mingled with the choking heaves, and shame burned through Priscilla. Why couldn't she be stronger? When someone was sick, why must she always think of her own discomfort first? Had she been so sheltered during her life that she was filled with more selfishness than the piety she'd always prided herself in having?

With a gulp, she spun to face her friend. She put a hand on Mabel's stooped back and rubbed it while she finished her retching.

Eli approached Mabel, and when she finally straightened, he took hold of her elbow and steadied her. "Okay now?" he asked gently.

She nodded but looked down at her dress, her eyes widening with dismay. "Oh no. I'll need to change."

"There's no time."

Tears pooled in Mabel's eyes. "Could I have a moment to wash off?"

Eli shook his head. "When we get on the boat." But they all knew how impossible personal cleanliness was once they left shore. The steamboat would have only a limited supply of water aboard.

Priscilla pressed her hand to her nose. "Surely she can take just a few minutes?"

"We're already running late."

Tears spilled onto Mabel's cheeks, and she wiped them away with her sleeve. "I'm sorry. I've been so nauseous and emotional lately."

"It's to be expected at this stage in your pregnancy, and it'll probably last a few more weeks."

"I want to trust God's timing and plans, but I can't help but wish I was in Sister Ernest's condition at the present."

The words jabbed painfully through Priscilla, and she ducked her head. If only Mabel knew the truth . . . that she was barren and had no hope of experiencing child-bearing, but she would gladly trade places, even for the worst pregnancy moments, if only she could. . . .

Eli was quiet, as if he'd sensed the heartache Mabel's words had brought her.

"Look," he finally said. "Take a few minutes to clean off, but hurry."

Priscilla swallowed her pain. Her problems weren't Mabel's fault. The woman had offered her nothing but kindness, and she could do no less in return.

Priscilla assisted Mabel to the well at the back of the inn, where they worked together to clean off Mabel's skirt as much as they could.

By the time they reached the waterfront, Eli's face was taut.

"They wouldn't dare leave us again, would they?" Priscilla asked, huffing to keep up with him. "After all you've done for Running Feet . . ."

"I'm not resting secure until we're on that boat."

"But Running Feet still needs your doctoring."

"They have the calomel."

Her heart pattered faster. What if they didn't make it? What would become of David without her there to take care of him?

Eli scanned the waterfront. "There it is." He pointed to one of the smallest steamboats lined up along the bank.

"Thank the Lord," she murmured, lifting a hand to her heart to slow its rhythm.

"I don't believe it." Eli dropped the bags. "They've got the landing pulled up."

Sure enough, the captain had already raised the landing platform at the front of the boat with a system of pulleys.

"Wait!" Eli whistled between his teeth and sprinted toward the boat.

Priscilla grabbed the bags. "Come on, Mabel."

They chased after Eli, and when they finally reached the edge of the river, Priscilla gasped for breath.

The boat was gliding away from the shore.

Eli stuck his fingers in his teeth and whistled and then cupped his hands around his mouth. "Stop!"

The captain stepped out of the pilothouse at the top of the steamboat near the stacks. From his high position, the captain had the best view of the river and any trouble that might lie ahead.

"We need to get on the boat," Eli shouted.

The captain shrugged. "We're at capacity."

"But we've already paid for passage."

"We can't take on any more. We're already overloaded."

"Three more won't sink you."

The murky water churned as the boat moved further away. The captain shook his head. "Sorry, mister."

"Come on!" Eli yelled. "You've got to let us on!"

Priscilla wanted to shout out too, but propriety stifled her voice. The humidness of the river stuck to her face, and the stench of waste along the levy stifled her breath.

Eli inched nearer the water, and he eyed the dark depths as if debating whether to jump in and try to swim for the boat. It was still muddy and the current fast enough to drag a grown man to his death.

"You've got to be kidding," he shouted. "What are we supposed to do now? Swim to Bellevue?"

The captain shrugged. "You'll have to catch the next boat."

Eli threw up his hands. "I don't have time to wait!"

Priscilla's mind screamed after the boat, and her heart thudded with a sudden and intense longing to be aboard. David would surely need her. For a long moment, all she could see was his sparkling black eyes looking for her and not finding her.

"When's the next boat leaving?" she asked.

"Not soon enough." The long white scar on Eli's face was smooth amidst the other wrinkles.

"What can we do?"

He watched the departing boat as if he could will it to turn around and return to them.

"Do you think Black Squire was behind this?" Priscilla asked.

"It doesn't really matter. Not anymore."

"Can we find a way to catch them?"

"There's not another steamboat leaving for Bellevue until next week—and even that isn't certain."

Despair settled across her shoulders, and her legs trembled under the weight. For the first time in years, she'd held a child, allowed a tiny piece of herself to care about a baby. Everything within her had tried to resist, but somehow during the hours with him, he'd pulled her into his life. Now she didn't know how she could stop worrying about him.

Priscilla pressed a hand against her chest to ward off the sudden pain. "Who will take care of Running Feet and David?"

"They're the least of our concerns now." Eli stepped away from the shore and finally looked at her. Worry turned the blue of his eyes as dark as the river water.

"This is all my fault," Mabel said through a sob. "If only I hadn't taken the time to clean off my dress."

"Oh, it's not your fault," Priscilla said quickly. "They don't have room for us. That's all. And it wouldn't have made any difference if we'd arrived earlier."

Eli didn't say anything.

Just then she caught a glimpse of Squire within the shadows of the pilothouse. Despair shot through her. Had the man double-crossed them again?

Eli only shook his head, as if to warn her from saying anything to Mabel. Then he turned and stared at the growing distance between them and their last chance to make it to Bellevue on time.

Did he want to say *I told you so*, that he'd known all along they would slow him down? Priscilla fought against the despondency winding throughout her body.

"Is there nothing more we can do?" she asked. "Is it too late to try to catch up with Brother Spalding?"

"He's way too far by now." The muscles in Eli's jaw worked up and down. "It might be too late. But you better believe I'm not giving up yet."

Chapter
13

Northern Missouri

*E*li had resorted to tying Mabel to her sidesaddle to keep her from sliding off in her exhaustion. Her head drooped and bobbed with each jarring motion of the horse.

Priscilla rode alongside the pregnant woman, a silent sentinel, her chin up, her shoulders as straight as they'd been since they'd left Liberty four days ago. She had surprised him with her endurance. Except for the fatigue that lined her face, she hadn't complained about the rigorous pace he'd set.

He could only guess how badly her backside pained her. If it was anything like his, she was suffering with each jolt and bump, even with blankets padded underneath for extra cushion.

"We'll stop for the night up by yonder grove of dogwoods," he called to the man he'd hired to drive the wagon with their supplies.

The man tipped his hat and flicked the reins at the double team of horses.

The trail to the trading post in Bellevue followed the Missouri River north. Eli had been told they'd be safe from Indians and thieves as long as they stayed on the rutted path as it wound through the tall grasses on the banks above the river. Even so, he and his hired man took turns watching at night.

The last rays of the sun wove through the brilliant green of the fully awakened oaks and cottonwoods. The white flowers of the dogwoods glistened almost silver against them.

With the passing of the first of May, they'd had warm enough temperatures at night that they hadn't needed the tent and their India rubber cloth Henry carried in the wagons.

Eli could only pray that if they traveled fast enough, and if they didn't encounter any problems crossing flooded rivers, they would catch up to Henry before he reached Bellevue. He had a five-day head start, but he wouldn't be able to travel as quickly with the animals and heavily loaded wagons.

Eli reined his horse and breathed in the fresh woodsy scent of the blossoms hovering over his head.

Priscilla halted next to him. She pressed her face into a low branch loaded with the white flowers, and her lips caressed the petals.

His gut looped into a knot. She was so beautiful. Her face surrounded by the flowers was a sight like none other in God's creation.

After working so hard the past few days, after all of the worry and frustration, he wanted to do nothing more than paint her picture in his mind and make an imprint that would last forever.

"I love the fragrance." Her long lashes lifted, and she caught him staring at her.

He didn't bother to look away. He was too thirsty for her

beauty to care if he made a fool of himself. Did it really matter if she knew she could captivate his heart with one bat of her eyelashes?

She plucked one of the dogwood flowers. "I think I shall press a blossom in the pages of my journal once we catch up with the wagons." She chanced another glance at him, and a soft pink tinged her cheeks.

Somehow Priscilla had managed to find room for her portable writing desk along with ink and quill pen within the confines of her trunk. Although he hadn't seen her using it much, he'd occasionally found her writing letters to her family.

"I'm discovering so much beauty, so many delightful specimens to preserve—now that we're free of the confines of the boat."

He wanted to tell her that she was the only delightful specimen he had eyes for, but the words stuck in his throat. "Enjoy it while you can. Once we cross the Platte River, we'll take a straight course west and won't have anything but dry grass and blue skies."

She twirled the blossom between her fingers.

Suddenly he felt like a bigger fool than ever. Why couldn't he have said something more suave—something more encouraging? He could have at least told her he was sorry he'd had to push them so hard the past few days.

Mabel's horse nickered nearby. The woman had leaned forward and was resting her head against the horse's mane.

Priscilla breathed out a long weary breath. "I think I should help Mabel."

He nodded and inwardly berated himself. He didn't have time to sit and stare at her anyway, not when he had so little time for all that needed to be done.

He urged his horse away from her. He couldn't forget for a

single moment the precariousness of the trip, the danger, the chance of failing if he made one wrong move.

But all the while he helped with the team and gathered and chopped wood for a fire, his gaze kept sliding back to Priscilla. She had helped Mabel from her horse and to a spot under one of the dogwoods. There she assisted the woman in eating a few bites of the cold salted pork and beans she'd cooked last night. Then she spread Mabel's blankets on the ground and covered her.

Over the past days of riding together, Mabel had been too sick and tired to converse. In some ways, Eli had almost felt like he'd had time alone with Priscilla. He'd grown to appreciate the sharpness of her mind, her inquisitiveness, and her obvious delight in the beauty around them.

If she'd been attractive before, she was only more so now.

By the time he'd finished his work, the last traces of sunlight had faded. The chill was all that separated them from the gnats and mosquitoes, which would soon be out in swarms. He hoped they'd be far away from the Big Muddy by the time the pesky insects came to life.

Priscilla rested her back against the dogwood, her eyes closed, her chest rising and falling with the even breathing of sleep. Mabel was curled on the ground next to her.

He stood in front of them and hesitated. He didn't want to wake Priscilla, but he could at least help her lie down more comfortably.

The fire behind him crackled.

Her eyes flew open and she gave a soft gasp. Her fingers fluttered toward her cameo, then to her shawl, pulling it tighter. Her eyes collided with his.

"You fell asleep."

"I didn't mean to." She sat forward and smoothed the edge

179

of her dress, which had crept over the tops of her boots. "I was waiting for you—I saved you a plate of food."

He glanced toward the fire and the tin plate, with a second plate forming a lid over his meal. His stomach gurgled.

"I found something for you." He ignored the pangs of hunger and lowered himself to one knee before her.

Her eyes widened.

He swung his hand around from behind his back and held out a lone orchid the same shade as the moon overhead. And once again, he wished he knew what to say, how to talk to her, how to be more sophisticated.

Instead, he thrust it before her.

She tentatively took it from him and lifted questioning eyes.

"For your collection of specimens," he offered.

Her fingers caressed the drooping petals. "I think it's a yellow lady's slipper."

He didn't know nor did he care. He only knew that he wanted one of her rare smiles. For a long intense moment, he held his breath.

Finally her lips curved into a smile. "Thank you."

His pulse jolted forward and he swallowed hard. "You're welcome."

What was happening to him? Why did he want to make her happy?

When she lifted the flower to her nose and took a deep breath, her smile moved to her eyes . . .

And to his heart.

He tried to ignore the warning that rang in the back of his mind, the warning that he was overstepping his well-laid plans, the business deal he'd made with her, and that absolutely no good would come of allowing himself the pleasure of her smiles and her company.

The longer he was with her, the more he loathed the idea that he might ever become like his friend Dr. Newell, who'd lost his wife within weeks of arriving on the mission field. How would he live with himself if he ever allowed any danger to come to this beautiful lady God had entrusted to his care?

"Look." Priscilla pointed to a sandbar in the middle of the Missouri River. "The small island is alive with white feathers."

"Pelicans." Eli slowed his horse. "Captain Lewis saw them here too and wrote about them in his journal. Believe it or not, he even took the time to dissect one of the birds and determined that the bird's pouch can hold five gallons of water."

She never tired of hearing him share about the travels of Lewis and Clark, which he'd studied in preparation for their own expedition.

On the cliffs above the river, they had a clear view of the water. Most of the time, the lush growth of new leaves on the sedge and seedlings prevented them from seeing the rushing river. But at that moment, the wide openness of the cliffs had given them a peek at more of the fascinating wildlife she loved seeing.

The plump long-billed birds were poking their beaks into their feathers to clean themselves, but in the process of preening, their feathers were falling out and covering the water almost like a feather blanket.

"It's simply amazing." Priscilla wished they could stop so she could watch to her heart's content. She understood Eli's drive to catch up to Henry, but after a week of nonstop travel, she was as weary as poor Mabel.

"If we were able to find a way down to the river's edge," Priscilla suggested, "I could collect feathers and make several pillows."

Eli stood in his stirrups and stretched his backside. "My hind end would be eternally grateful for a pillow."

"Mine too." Mabel gave a weak smile.

"Too bad we don't have the time." Priscilla couldn't prevent wistfulness from creeping into her tone.

"Wasn't too far from here that some of the trappers came down with cholera last year."

Priscilla shivered at the dreaded word.

"Three men died before they finally listened to me and moved their camp to a cleaner site above the river."

"Then they should be indebted to you that the disease didn't claim more lives," Priscilla said. "And they should be grateful and willing for your assistance again."

Eli didn't respond but instead sat back in his saddle and gave the flank of his horse a nudge with his heel, spurring the horse back to the usual pace.

She did the same with hers.

The more days they traveled, the more she couldn't help wondering if perhaps Eli had exaggerated the dangers of the trip. They'd been perfectly safe so far. And if someone did get sick or hurt, he was a doctor. Surely he'd be able to help.

"There's Henry!" Mabel called with a rush of excitement.

"Can't be." Eli tipped the brim of his hat higher. "We should still be a few days behind the wagons."

For the first time all week Mabel sat up straight. "Praise the Lord."

Ahead of them, passing under a grove of willow and cottonwoods, two wagons were lumbering along the trail, followed by cattle and Indian boys on horseback, including John and Richard.

"Apparently Henry hasn't been going fast enough." Frustration furrowed Eli's eyebrows, and he kicked his horse into a gallop.

Priscilla followed with growing unease. Would Eli and Henry have another of their disagreements? Even though the men were always polite to each other, there was a tension between them that hadn't gone away. At times she couldn't help thinking that *she* was part of the cause of the strained relationship between the two men.

By the time she and Mabel finally reined their horses next to the group, Eli and Henry had already dismounted and were facing each other.

Mabel slid from her horse and sank to the ground. "My dear husband," she cried, her plain face transformed with joy.

Henry rushed over and lifted her to her feet. "You've obviously pushed the women too hard," he said to Eli.

"And *obviously* you don't know the meaning of the word *hard*, or you'd be days ahead at this point."

"We've been going as fast as we possibly can."

"Not if we already caught up with you."

Mabel's knees wobbled, and Henry slipped his arms around her waist. "My wife can hardly stand. It's clear she's exhausted beyond what she can endure."

Priscilla dismounted and tried to keep her knees from buckling. She was beyond tired too. And dirty. And ready for a break from the endless riding.

"Mrs. Doc." Richard smiled at her from his mount.

John reined in next to his brother. "Why Mrs. Doc not on steamboat?"

"They said they didn't have enough room for us. But . . ." She had no doubt Squire had convinced the captain to leave without them.

Henry glared at Eli. "Did you even take into consideration the fact that such riding is completely improper for a woman in Mrs. Spalding's condition?"

"Come on, Henry," Eli growled. "You know as well as I do, she'll be doing a lot more riding over the next few months. We can't jeopardize the entire trip because of her condition."

Priscilla tried to muster a smile for the boys, but dizziness swept through her. She grabbed the stirrup to keep from toppling over.

Richard hopped off his horse and moved to her side. He took her elbow and steadied her.

Eli shook his head at Henry. "And look at you. You probably haven't broken a sweat in the past two weeks."

"Have you taken any days off?"

"We've traveled hard. But it doesn't look like you've done the same."

Mabel's knees buckled, and Henry hoisted her back up. He murmured into her ear before scowling at Eli. "Have you no compassion?"

"Of course I do. I'm just not willing to give up."

"We don't have to give up. Just slow down."

For the first time since they'd started their mad race to reach Bellevue in time to catch the caravan, Priscilla was ready for a break. She understood Eli's urgency. The nagging need to be near David and Running Feet had prodded her onward. But now . . . she was almost too tired to care anymore.

"The women can take turns riding in the wagon if they need to," Eli said.

"We're taking a day off tomorrow to rest."

"You're jesting, aren't you?" Eli's brows shot up. "We can't afford a day off. It's going to be hard enough to catch up as it is."

"We're not going." Henry pulled Mabel closer. "You can go on without us if you want, but I refuse to make my wife travel one more day without resting."

"I realize we're all tired," Eli said slowly, as if trying to rein in his frustration. "But if we miss meeting up with the fur trappers, we might as well forget about the mission."

Priscilla's body sagged, and weariness nearly pushed her to the ground. More than anything she wanted to show Eli how strong she was.

He'd worked hard to get them to that point, had gone without sleep, had pushed himself harder than anyone. But the idea of taking a break from the endless jostling in the saddle to wash clothes and write in her journal was too hard to resist.

"Do you think it will hurt that much if we take one day off?" she asked.

Eli blew out an exasperated sigh. "Don't tell me you're taking his side?"

She shook her head. "Of course not. It's just that we're all exhausted, and once we've had the chance to rest, maybe we'll be able to go even faster—"

"You *are* taking his side."

"This isn't about sides." She wiped a hand across her dusty brow. Grit had made its home in every crevice of her face. What she wouldn't give for a bath—a real, hot bath. "This is about running ourselves ragged. Even you. You haven't slept a full night since we left."

"I should have known you'd agree with him." Hurt flashed through his eyes.

"Brother Spalding is merely trying to make a wise decision and do what's best for all of us."

"And how would he know what's best? I'm the one who's traveled west before. Not him. If anyone knows best, it's me."

"We do trust you, Brother Ernest, and we appreciate all your efforts," Mabel chimed in. "If not for you, we would have had to stop long ago."

"Can't any of you see the urgency of our situation? The Fur Company steamboat is probably nearing Bellevue. And we have several more days of hard travel ahead of us."

"God will make a way," Mabel offered.

"We need to do our part too," Eli retorted.

Mabel shrank back at his biting comment.

"We need to keep going," Eli persisted, "or we won't catch up."

"That's enough," Henry said calmly. "I'll get Mabel situated, and we can discuss this later. Privately."

Henry assisted Mabel toward one of the wagons. Priscilla stared after them, and a new and sudden longing poured over her. What would it be like to have the kind of marriage Henry and Mabel had? A real one, where people cared about each other openly, without reservation?

"I can't believe this," Eli muttered, glowering at the couple. "If the Board hadn't insisted that I bring everyone, I'd be half-way there by now."

Although his complaint didn't surprise her, the comment reached out to sting her anyway. After how hard she'd ridden, how uncomfortable and grueling the constant traveling had been, how little she'd complained—surely he could see she wasn't the burden he'd thought she'd be.

He jerked off his hat, wiped his sleeve across his sweaty forehead, then slammed his hat back down, but not before his gaze connected with hers.

She was sure the hurt was written on her face—especially when his eyes flickered with remorse.

"Look. I'm sorry. I shouldn't have said that."

"We're all just tired," she offered softly.

He nodded. "Let's just get some rest, and hopefully we'll be able to think more clearly tomorrow."

"Mrs. Doc go sit?" Richard tugged her.

"Yes, Richard. Thank you."

She'd lift up prayers day and night that God would help them catch the trappers' caravan. If they didn't, she hated to think how much more Eli would come to regret marrying her.

Chapter
14

SOUTH OF BELLEVUE

Priscilla sang the last note of their morning hymn and lifted her eyes heavenward to the overcast sky. She tried to block out the picture of Mabel's hand resting on her expanding stomach and focus instead on the object of her worship.

The Lord didn't deserve her halfhearted praise, tainted with pangs of envy and constant worry about whether they would reach the fur trappers on time.

Although Eli and Henry had finally come to an agreement that they would rest for half a day, Eli had been tense during the two days since then. He'd been short with everyone and had pushed them hard in their race to reach Bellevue before the caravan left.

Across the campfire, Henry opened his Bible.

He started to read, but Mabel stopped him with a touch of her hand. "Maybe Dr. Ernest would like to take a turn reading the Scripture this morning."

The low-hanging clouds had brought dampness to the air that surrounded them and seemed to push at them, urging them to hurry, to break camp and make haste in their pursuit.

Yet no matter the urgency, they had all agreed—even Eli— that they must start each day seeking the Lord for his blessing and guidance.

"Don't you think that would be a good idea, Brother Spalding?" Mabel's voice was too cheerful. "Let's have Dr. Ernest read from God's Word this morning."

"No thank you," Eli said, drawing himself up.

"I think it would be lovely," Mabel continued. "I'm sure we would all enjoy hearing you read."

Henry frowned. "I don't know—"

"Come now, Brother Spalding." She patted his arm and flashed her crooked teeth at her husband in a wide smile. "God's Word has a way of cheering up the heart. It's just the antidote Dr. Ernest needs."

Henry sighed but leaned forward and handed Eli the Bible. Eli shook his head.

"We'd love to hear you today," Priscilla said.

He turned upon her with a look as dark as a sudden spring storm. "I said I don't want to read. Let Henry."

His words snapped at her and pushed her to the back of the log she'd used for a seat. "I just thought it might help—"

"I don't like reading aloud. I never have."

A gust of wind blew the smoke from their campfire toward her, stung her eyes, and burned a path to her heart. She blinked back tears.

"Look. I'm sorry. I'm better at praying." Eli pushed himself off the overturned crate he'd been sitting on. "It's time to go anyway."

Priscilla batted at the gray swirls blowing into her face. It was only the smoke making her eyes water—certainly not his shortness with her.

"We need to load up." He grabbed the crate and tossed inside the spoons and plates they'd already rinsed. The clank of the metal ricocheted through the camp.

Mabel's smile wobbled. She looked from Eli to Priscilla and then back.

What must Mabel think of their marriage? Priscilla ducked her head and reached for the kettle left from breakfast. She was sure the Spaldings had noticed by now that she and Eli didn't have the same kind of relationship they had.

Henry obviously took his vows to his wife seriously and was doing his best to be a God-fearing and considerate husband. And even though Mabel was plain, he was apparently looking past that to the woman's sweet spirit.

"White man on horse coming," one of the Indian boys called.

Eli straightened and pushed up the brim of his hat.

They watched the rider gallop nearer. "Howdy," the stranger called over the clomping of his horse's hooves.

As the man drew up next to them, Eli nodded a greeting. "Where you from?"

The man touched the brim of his hat. "From the Otoe Mission Agency near Bellevue." His clean clothes and trimmed hair and beard made it clear he wasn't a trapper. "I've been helping Moses Merrill build his school for the Otoe Indian children."

"Merrill, the Baptist missionary?" Eli asked.

"Yessir, the one and the same."

"We're headed toward Bellevue. How far do we have to go?"

"You got a hard day's ride ahead of you, if not more."

Eli exchanged a look with Henry. "Then if we push hard, there's the chance we could make it by nightfall?"

"Maybe." The man glanced at their wagons and then at the women. His brows lifted. "Maybe not."

Eli frowned. He didn't have to say anything for Priscilla to know what he was thinking. They were slowing him down.

The stranger tipped his hat at her and smiled. "Morning, ma'am. Aren't you a bright spot on a cloudy day."

Priscilla smiled back. "Thank you."

"What's a lovely lady like you doing out here in the middle of nowhere?" the stranger asked.

"We're heading to Oregon Country to set up a mission among the Nez Perce Indians."

"You don't say?" His eyes filled with doubt. "Never heard of women crossing that far."

His eyes canvassed her, and his brows arched higher. "Seems like a right foolish idea to me. That trail is hard enough for the toughest trapper. No woman is gonna make it."

"Well, we will." She lifted her chin, but discouragement slithered around her stomach and squeezed it hard.

Eli came and stood next to her.

She refused to look at him and see the stranger's words reflected in his eyes.

"We're hooking up with Captain Fitzpatrick and his caravan," Eli said. "You know if they've left Bellevue yet?"

"Yep. They left yesterday mornin'."

"Yesterday?" Eli groaned.

"Well, let's stop conversing and get going." Henry tossed a crate into the back of one of the wagons.

"Best of luck to you." The man on the horse gathered the reins and then slapped a hand against his horse. "You're gonna need to ride day and night to catch up with that caravan." He spurred his horse forward at a gallop.

"If we hadn't taken that half a day off, maybe we'd have a chance to catch them," Eli mumbled, watching the man ride away.

"Stop grumbling, and let's load up." Henry reached for a blanket. "And let's all try to remember Psalm 9:10. 'And they that know thy name will put their trust in thee: for thou, Lord, hast not forsaken them that seek thee.' The Lord's been with us and brought us this far. He won't desert us now."

A battle of emotions waged across Eli's face—frustration with Henry and determination to control himself.

"He's just trying to do what's best for Mabel," Priscilla offered softly.

"And I'm just trying to do what's best for all of us."

"It's not his fault the trappers keep leaving without us."

His lips formed a thin line. "I haven't worked this hard or come this far to lose out on the opportunity to make it west."

"But we certainly don't want anything to happen to Mabel or the baby at the expense of trying to reach the caravan, do we?"

A battle waged across his features. For a long moment, he held himself rigid. He glanced sideways to where Mabel stood at the back of one of the wagons, folding and putting away their blankets.

Finally he let out a long breath. "The only thing left for me to do is to ride ahead and see if I can convince Fitzpatrick to wait for us."

Priscilla's heartbeat pattered to a stop. "Ride ahead? Is that really necessary?"

But he was already stalking away. "I'm leaving," he announced.

"Where are you going?" Henry asked.

"I'm going to catch up with the caravan and beg them to stop," Eli replied, grabbing some jerky and leftover johnnycakes from a crate.

"Do you really think that will work?" Henry swung Mabel's sidesaddle in place over her horse and turned a frown upon Eli.

"Fitzpatrick is a reasonable man. If I explain the situation and remind him that we already paid for the escort, maybe he'll give us a break." Eli strode toward his horse, wrapping the food in his handkerchief. "Even if I can't get them to stop, at least I can ask them to slow down. Maybe then we'll actually have a slight chance of catching them."

With growing dread, Priscilla watched him stuff the food into his saddlebag. "Now that we're together again, I don't think it's a good idea to split up."

What if they got lost without him? Or what if they got into trouble? Eli was right—Henry didn't have the expertise. Or the strength.

"Anything could happen," she added weakly. But hadn't she been priding herself on how well she was doing and how little danger they'd encountered?

"You'll be fine." Eli glanced to the darkening sky. A strong gust of wind whipped at his hat, and he jammed it further down on his head. "If it storms, don't stop. Wrap up in your India rubbers and keep going."

The humid scent of rain enshrouded her.

He slung himself over his saddle. "Push yourselves hard, and God willing, you'll catch up to me and the caravan in a couple days."

She wanted to reach out, to stop him, to tell him not to leave them. But she stood rigid, trying to make herself into the strong woman he wanted.

He urged his horse forward, his body straining, ready to be

on his way. But at the last second he looked back at her and swerved, drawing the beast up beside her.

From underneath the brim of his hat, he peered down at her. The intensity in the blue depths dragged her in until she felt as if she were drowning.

"You've done good so far, Priscilla."

At the unexpected words of praise, she sucked in a breath.

His gaze dropped to her lips, lingered there for an instant before returning to her eyes, darker, bluer.

Her lungs stopped working, and she clutched a hand to her chest.

"I'll see your pretty face in a couple days."

She nodded, too breathless to respond.

He kicked his heels into his horse and left her standing, watching after him, wondering if he was taking her heart with him.

A fool's errand. That's what it had been.

Eli should have known the caravan wouldn't change their plans. He didn't know why he had even bothered trying to convince them to wait.

His eyelids drooped and his body sagged. Aching weariness had invaded every muscle. After two straight days and nights of riding, he had to rest or he would drop off his horse in fatigue.

But if he didn't keep going, he wouldn't be able to make it back to Priscilla and the others in time to lead them through the shortcut.

His chin bobbed against his chest. Dizziness swirled with the pounding in his temples.

All his pleading with Fitzpatrick hadn't done him a lick of good. The man had claimed he had no objections to the missionaries joining the caravan but had insisted he couldn't slow down for them.

Of course, Black Squire had been right there, double-talking as usual. Out of one side of his mouth, he claimed he had nothing to do with them missing the steamboat in Liberty and thanked Eli for saving Running Feet's life. But out of the other side of his mouth, he made sure to remind Captain Fitzpatrick they were already behind schedule.

It was only when Eli was getting ready to leave that Captain Fitzpatrick finally pulled him aside and told him about the cutoff that could shave some time off their travel.

A drop of rain splattered against Eli's hand. He lifted his face to the billowing clouds. Another drop hit his cheek.

His cold fingers fumbled behind his saddle for his India rubber cloak, and he dragged it around his body just as the rain began to pelt him in full force.

He could only hope the thrashing rain would help keep him awake.

"Lord Almighty," he prayed, "this trip is testing me beyond my endurance. I don't know how much longer I can keep going on. I'd appreciate an extra measure of your strength right about now. 'Cuz mine's running out."

The long hours in the saddle alone had given him plenty of time to think about the precariousness of their situation. Even though he'd been wrong to blame the others for missing the caravan, he decided that if he was going to see his plans for the mission succeed, he couldn't rely on Henry or anyone else. It would have to be himself and the Almighty. Just like it always had been.

Eli ducked his head, and the rain poured off the brim of his hat in streams onto his cloak. He cupped his hands and caught the water, then lowered his head and took a long drink.

When he lifted his head, the wind brought him the faint echoes of a scream.

His muscles tightened, and he tugged the reins, bringing his horse to a standstill. Through the patter of raindrops against the leaves, he strained his ear, every sense in his body on edge.

Another burst of wind carried the scream again, this time clearer.

Apprehension wormed through his pores and into his blood. Was it Priscilla?

From the thickening of the undergrowth and foliage, he'd guessed he was drawing near to the Elkhorn River. What if Henry was attempting the crossing?

Eli had made it through the muddy waters on his way toward the caravan. It hadn't been easy, but he'd managed. But the rain had been heavy at times during the past twenty-four hours, and the river was likely overflowing its banks now.

If Henry had pushed the group at a decent pace, they'd likely be nearing the river by now. What if something had gone wrong?

He kicked his horse. "Get up," he shouted, slapping the beast, spurring it to move as fast as it could.

The gelding was tired too and couldn't move at nearly the pace Eli needed it to. He kicked it again and again, dread flowing from his blood into his nerves.

"Come on, come on." Rain pelted his face. Branches whipped him.

The horse stumbled down the rocky descent toward the river. With each lurch, fear settled deeper into Eli's bones.

Through the growth, he caught sight of a wagon across the river. The men he'd hired to drive the wagons would know how to make the crossing, but he didn't trust Henry.

When Eli reached the bottom of the ravine, he broke through the brush, and the full view of the river lay before him.

"O Lord Almighty!" He breathed a prayer as his heart crashed into his ribs.

The rushing water had swept Priscilla from her saddle into the water. Her horse had continued without her, following Henry and Mabel, who were already safe in the shallower water.

Priscilla was clinging to the drag rope that went from one bank to the other, but the water swelled around her, threatening to wrest her from the rope and sweep her away.

John and Richard had tossed aside their shirts and were swimming toward her. But their hold on the line was causing her to sway even more.

"Stop!" Eli galloped toward the bank and splashed into the water. He kicked his horse forward, praying the beast would have the strength to withstand the swift current.

"Stop!" he shouted again. The Indian boys halted and shifted to look at him.

Priscilla's pale face turned toward him. The terror in her eyes reached out and clawed at his gut, slicing it open and releasing a cold fear of his own.

"Don't let go!" He dug his heels into his horse. The water swirled around its legs, rushing higher with every unsteady step.

Her fingers around the rope were white. The skirt of her dress billowed above the surface, tugging at her, tangling her legs, a deadly enemy working at tearing her away from her precarious hold.

The water crashed over his boots and legs, rising to the horse's belly, but he urged his horse harder.

"I can't hold on." She closed her eyes and a sob escaped from her lips.

The cold fear turned his blood to ice. He reached a hand out to her. "I'm almost there."

One of her hands slipped from the rope.

Mabel's scream echoed from a distance—as if she were miles away instead of yards.

"Hang on!" He lunged forward and caught Priscilla's wrist just as her fingers began to lose their grip.

Her weight threatened to pull him from his mount. He gripped his horse with his thighs and dug his boots deeper into the stirrups. He wrapped the reins around his arm then let go so he could grab her with both hands.

The reins dug deep, burning his skin, but the hold anchored him to his horse. With a groan, he hefted her with a strength borne of panic. He couldn't lose her. Not here. Not now.

"Grab on to me."

Her eyes were round with terror. The rushing water had ripped her bonnet from her head and unraveled her hair so that it swirled in a wet tangle about her face.

She gave a cry and wrapped both her hands around his arm.

He wrenched her upward, but the strong current and the weight of her drenched clothes fought against him.

His horse took a step back, and the motion lifted Priscilla out of the river's hold. He urged his gelding back another step, and she came sliding upward.

With a last heave, Eli dragged her up the side of the horse and lifted her sideways into the saddle in front of him.

Her arms snaked around him, and she clung to him, burying her face into his chest as sobs shook her body.

He unwound his arm from the reins and turned his horse toward the shore.

The horse wobbled, and he gripped the reins hard.

"Come on, boy." He urged the gelding forward. His hold around Priscilla turned fierce. Now that he had her, he wouldn't lose her. Not unless he died first.

The horse sloshed into shallower water and finally stumbled

up the bank. Eli slid from the horse, pulling Priscilla down with him.

Dazed relief weakened his knees, and he fell back into the long grass, taking Priscilla with him.

"Thank you, God," he murmured against her hair.

She clung to him, trembling.

Mabel rushed over and reached for Priscilla. "Praise the Lord."

Too tired to speak, he shook his head. But he wasn't too tired to tighten his hold so that Mabel had no choice but to back away.

He ran a hand over the wet tangles of Priscilla's hair and combed them off her face.

She shuddered, every inch of her body thoroughly soaked.

Intense relief poured over him, and he pressed his lips to her temple.

Her pulse throbbed against his touch.

Death had captured her within its grasp and almost swallowed her. If he'd been a few minutes later . . .

He wound his fingers into her thick wet strands and took a deep breath, trying to still the frantic pounding of his heartbeat. He brushed his lips against the soft wet skin of her forehead, tasting her saltiness.

"I'm sorry," she murmured through chattering teeth.

He could only picture the planks of a coffin and her lying within the dark box, her skin translucent, her lips colorless, eyes closed forever.

"No. I'm sorry," he said, choking on the words. "I'm sorry I left you. I won't do it again."

He wouldn't—couldn't—risk losing her to death.

The strength of his fear pulsed hard, demanding that he do whatever it took to keep her safe. *Whatever* it took.

Chapter
15

NEAR THE PLATTE RIVER

They spent the next two days traveling from early dawn until well after dusk. They left the Missouri River and headed in a northwest direction toward the Loup Fork. With each mile they traveled away from the lush river valley, they encountered fewer and fewer trees until eventually nothing but the wide open prairie spread before them like an endless ocean of waving grass.

If Priscilla thought she'd been weary before, she hadn't known the true meaning of the word.

The coldness of the dark night was all that kept her awake.

"We've got to stop now, Dr. Ernest." Henry's voice penetrated the weary fog that had settled over her.

"We're near the fork," Eli replied. "A few more miles maybe."

"Horses, cows—need rest," John called. The boys rarely

defied Eli's instruction. But the sun had set hours ago, and Eli had continued to push the group onward.

They'd begun to see signs of Pawnee Indians in the area. Time was running out. If they didn't catch up with the caravan by the time they reached the Pawnee villages on the other side of the Platte River, they would have to turn around. They would be foolish to attempt passing the villages without the protection of the trappers.

"No good for animals or Mrs. Doc," Richard added.

For a moment Eli didn't reply. "All right." His voice hinted at weariness. "We'll stop here for a few hours' rest."

Mabel had long since retired to one of the wagons. When Eli had talked of throwing some of their supplies overboard to help them move faster, Priscilla hadn't dared ask if she could ride in the wagon too.

Her body sagged. All she'd been able to think about the past two days since her near drowning was that she wanted to be warm and dry and clean. Even though she'd eventually changed into dry clothes, rain had been their constant companion of late. Their India rubbers could keep them dry only to a point.

Besides, she was tired of traveling, tired of eating cold food, tired of sleeping on the hard, damp ground. And it was growing harder to prevent herself from wondering if she'd really made the right choice coming west. Had she been too hasty? If she'd waited, would God have made a way for her to go to India?

Worse than those nagging questions was the bigger one, the one that mocked her whenever she faced adversity—was everyone right that the journey was too hard for a lady like her?

She wriggled out of her sidesaddle and slumped to wet ground. Through the blackness of the night by the faint light of the shrouded moon, she watched Eli untie a cup from his saddle.

His words of praise from before her near drowning still

warmed her heart every time she thought about them. He'd told her she was doing well. She was proving herself to him. She couldn't give up yet.

Through the jangle of harnesses and the soft chirping of crickets, she could hear the ping of cow's milk squirting against Eli's tin cup. Those hands against the cow's udder had saved her life.

She hadn't been able to stop thinking about how he'd charged into the river after her and braved the rushing current. He'd appeared almost out of nowhere, and his face had been chiseled with a determination that had given her renewed hope.

He'd risked his life to save hers.

What kind of man would do that for a woman?

And the way he'd held her on the banks of the river . . .

A sweet ache wound through her belly at the memory. He'd crushed her—the fierceness of his embrace was like nothing she'd ever known before. And inside the safety of his strong arms she'd savored the steady thump of his heartbeat against her ear, the solidness of his chest, the musky scent of his body.

Maybe his concern had been borne of the moment. Maybe he would have cared for anyone else the same way. Even so, whenever she glanced at his broad shoulders and thought about what a strong, good man he was, her insides quivered with strange longing, the desire to be special to him, to be cherished, to be more than just another missionary.

Richard approached her and held out his hand. "Mrs. Doc, get sleep."

She nodded, weariness washing back over her.

He helped her up and propelled her toward the covered wagon. "Thank you, Richard."

He steadied her climb inside the damp, musty wagon bed.

Mabel was still asleep on the makeshift bed Henry had assembled for her out of blankets on top of crates pushed together.

Priscilla sank onto her trunk and leaned her head back against the side of the canvas. She didn't care if she fell asleep sitting up. She was just glad to be off the horse and out of the rain.

"Priscilla," Eli whispered.

She started.

"I have a cup of milk for you."

"You do?" She searched the blackness of the canvas opening and could make out the outline of his body.

"Come drink this."

She crawled toward him. Her hand found his, and he gently folded her fingers around the tin cup. She brought it to her lips and took a long drink of the warm, creamy liquid.

"Do you want some?" she asked, holding the cup out to him.

"No, you finish it."

"Are you sure?"

"There's plenty more where that came from." His tone had the hint of a smile.

"True." She was grateful Eli had thought to bring the milk cows along.

She took another long drink and finished it off. The warmth trickled through her.

"Do you want any more?"

She could just imagine him in the dark, fumbling at the cow's udder, squirting milk into the cup. It was the last thing he needed to be doing when they were all so weary.

"I'm very satisfied." She pressed the cup back into his hands. "Thank you."

He shifted but didn't make a move to leave. The even rhythm of his breath sent a cascade of tingles over her skin and a rush of energy through her, waking every nerve.

"I'm sorry you had to keep riding," he finally whispered, "and couldn't take a break in the wagon with Mabel."

"She needs the rest more than I do," Priscilla whispered back. At least that's what she'd told herself and prayed God would give her the strength to believe it.

He was quiet for a moment, as if he wanted to say something more but didn't know quite what.

"You're holding up, then?" he finally said.

"I'm surviving." She wasn't sure how well, but she didn't want him to know that. What she did know was that each day God was showing her just how selfish and pampered a life she'd led up until the trip.

"I'm glad you're making it—that you're still alive."

The relief in his voice sent a tremor through her middle.

"Get some sleep." His warm breath fanned her forehead.

She wanted him to linger, wanted to lay her head against his chest and have him encircle her with his arms.

But he stepped back and pulled the canvas closed. Utter darkness fell upon her. She shuddered from a sudden damp chill and clutched her arms across her chest.

Loneliness crept through the blackness and slithered next to her.

Thoughts of her family who loved her flooded her mind. She'd always had companionship and attention, even when she'd wanted to be alone.

But now . . .

What would it be like to have a different kind of relationship with Eli, one where he didn't have to leave her at night, where he could hold her and they could whisper together about their dreams and plans?

Surely she had sensed some desire from him. But was he ready to put aside their partnership for something more? Would he ever want to? Would she?

With a shiver, she rubbed her arms, lay back among the

blankets, and closed her weary eyes. She must never forget that God had called her to love and save the lost heathen. That was the most important thing. And no matter what happened, God would be her constant companion.

Still, she couldn't help that her last thought was of Eli's arms surrounding her and pulling her close.

At the first hint of dawn, Eli roused them. After a cold breakfast of dried beef and pickles, they started forward again.

The recent rains had saturated the ground, and the hired men struggled to drive the wagons through the long, soggy grass.

Priscilla didn't have the energy to hold her head up. Even when the sun began to rise and show promise of making its appearance for the first time in days, she couldn't find the stamina for cheerfulness.

Only after John and Richard pulled their horses next to hers and began to point out the fascinating wildlife of the open prairies did she begin to feel alive again.

Richard stared into the sky, at the thin black line floating in the distance. *"Weptes."*

Priscilla peered at the bird. "Is it another falcon, like the ones we saw among the bluffs of the Missouri River?"

"No falcon." Richard shook his head, and his long braid swished against his back. *"We-ptes."*

Priscilla studied the long wingspan and the lighter—almost white—head that contrasted with its dark body. "Is it an eagle?"

"Ea-gle?" the boys both said at once.

She smiled at them and lifted her gaze to the majestic bird soaring with the wind currents. "I've never seen a bald eagle before."

"River ahead," John said. *"Weptes* hunt fish." Excitement

lit the boy's face, and he spurred his horse to a gallop toward the front of their group.

"Did you know," she said to Richard, who lingered beside her, "the bald eagle was picked as our national emblem because at one of the first battles of the Revolution, the noise of the battle woke the sleeping eagles? They flew from their nests and circled over the fighting men, shrieking for freedom."

"The eagles were probably just waiting for carnage to eat." Eli's voice next to her made her jump.

He reined his horse until he matched her pace, then he grinned.

Her heart sped to a gallop.

Even with the dark circles under his eyes and the shadows of scruff on his face, he was still as ruggedly handsome as the first day she'd seen him in the meetinghouse. Could she dare say he was even more appealing?

She peered at the gliding eagle, lest he see deep into her eyes to her wild thoughts. "The eagle is a strange mixture of strength and gentleness, isn't it?"

"Maybe." His gaze didn't waver from her, and the intensity of it sent a shiver through her.

"You're like an eagle, Dr. Ernest." She tried to infuse humor into her tone. "You're a mixture of strength and gentleness too."

Even though she'd hoped to jest and cover the attraction, she was sure he could see it in her face and eyes.

He didn't say anything.

She chanced a glance at him.

"We have another river crossing ahead." His eyes gently probed hers. "Loup Fork, the place where the Loup River meets the Platte River."

A rush of fear cascaded through her body and chilled her blood.

"I just wanted to let you know that you don't have anything to fear."

The water of the Elkhorn River had been frigid, had weighted down her skirt, had clawed at her, had wanted to swallow her.

"And I wanted you to know that this time, I'll be right there with you."

She gave him what she hoped was a confident nod, but as he spurred his horse ahead, she pulled back on hers. Her heart pounded with dread. She was the last to straggle to the sandy banks of the river.

"We've done it, Sister Ernest." Tears streamed down Mabel's face. She pointed across the wide river to the opposite shore. "The Fur Company caravan is over there."

"Indeed?" A thrill of excitement mingled through Priscilla's fear.

A circle of baggage, tents, wagons, mules, and men was coming to life. Drifts of smoke rose into the clear morning air, and the braying of the mules wafted across the river. It was like a village. How would so many animals ever move forward in an organized fashion?

She lowered herself from her horse, and relief seeped through her. "We did it!"

"Praise the Lord." Mabel lifted her face heavenward.

Priscilla searched the figures across the river. Where were Running Feet and David? Had they survived without her?

Eli trotted his horse into the water. "I'll take the drag rope across and let Captain Fitzpatrick know we're here." He plunged his gelding deeper and moved quickly but in an instant the horse stumbled and started to sink down.

A scream stuck in Priscilla's throat.

"I'm in a patch of quicksand!" Eli shouted. The gray swirling water sucked at his horse until Eli was hip deep.

Richard, John, and the other Nez Perce traveling with them shed their shirts and charged in after Eli.

Henry stepped to the edge of the water. "Pull him loose, boys."

The Indians swam toward Eli, yelling to each other in their native language.

"Faster," Henry called. He glanced from his shoes to the water and then took a step away from the shore.

"Don't just stand there." Priscilla turned to Henry, desperation churning through her. "Go in and help him."

"Now, Sister Ernest, calm down," he said, staring at the men. Henry rarely spoke or looked directly at her, as if he hoped to avoid the unspoken awkwardness that still existed between them. "I'm sure the horse will be out in no time."

Richard had reached the head of the horse and lifted its muzzle between his hands. The other men pushed from the rear.

After a few unsuccessful shoves, Eli let go of the beast and swam around to the front with Richard.

They tugged together, and Priscilla watched with growing horror as the horse sank deeper. Its shrill whinny echoed through the air.

Mabel's hand connected with hers, and she latched onto it, squeezing it hard.

One of the hired hands gave a shout and splashed into the water. The other stripped off his boots and followed. After moments of grunting and pulling, the horse reared up and stumbled forward. And the group gave a cheer.

"Thank you, Lord," Mabel murmured.

Priscilla's breath swooshed. But her heart pattered hard with each halting move Eli made toward the far shore. When he finally dragged himself out of the water, the horse staggering to land behind him, she clung to Mabel, her knees weak.

The trappers stared at Eli but made no move to greet him.

Instead, they appeared to be packing up and preparing for their departure.

Dripping, Eli wound through the packs and mules, until she lost sight of his sagging wet hat. For some time, she watched and waited with Mabel, until finally Eli reappeared and began to swim back across the river.

"Hurry!" Eli called, towing a narrow leather boat behind him. "The caravan isn't going to wait for us to cross before they leave. Start unloading the wagons now."

But Priscilla couldn't move, even though the others around her had begun the task of taking all the supplies out of the wagons. Her focus—and her very soul—riveted upon Eli as he swam, this time holding on to the dragline he'd attached to one of the few trees on the opposite shore.

When he sloshed to the shore, his shirt and trousers stuck to his body. Water ran like spring rivers down the length of his hard muscles.

He sagged to the ground. After sleepless nights, hard rides, and now fighting the river, exhaustion drew haggard lines across his face.

Who could ask for a better, stronger man than Eli Ernest? She'd never met a braver, more determined man. And he was her husband.

A flush of pride stole over her.

"I could strangle Squire." Eli sucked in a ragged breath. "He'd rather see us drown in this river than ride with them."

"Doc. Find safe place to cross," Richard said. "Too much soft sand here."

"We don't have time." Eli shoved himself off the ground. "We've got to cross *now*. The Pawnee villages are only a day's ride away. If we don't stay with the caravan, we might as well turn around right here."

Priscilla was of half a mind to shout out that she'd much rather turn around than cross another river. But she bit her lip and hoped to put off the inevitable as long as possible. She slunk to the end of the line of horses and wagons and tried to make herself invisible.

By the time the men had ferried most of the supplies over in the little boat, the Fur Company caravan was long gone. Their next challenge was to have the horses pull the wagons across. Even though they steered clear of the spot where Eli's horse had gotten stuck, the quicksand still gave them trouble.

"Time for the women to go," Eli said.

She didn't move from her partially hidden spot at the back of their caravan. Her fingers dug into the coarse hair of the cow she stood beside.

"Priscilla?" he called.

She was sure Mabel was already in the boat. And now they'd all be waiting on her.

"Time to go, Priscilla." His voice drew nearer. "We need to leave now!"

"Lord, help me," she whispered, cringing.

For a long moment, she cowered next to the cow, hoping, praying that somehow God would dry up the river, just as He had the Red Sea for the Israelites.

"What are you doing?" Eli's question came from behind her. She jumped.

"It's time to go." His wet clothes clung to his body, outlining the strength in his limbs. Water dripped from his hat into the tall grass.

She avoided his eyes. "I can't go back into a river."

"There's no other way to cross."

She stared at a creamy splotch in the cow's hair.

"I know you're frightened. But I told you I'd be right beside you this time."

210

She was trapped. She couldn't go forward, and she couldn't go back. There was nothing for her to do but dig a hole and bury herself.

He reached for her arm and gently spun her around. The blue in his eyes was as clear as a perfect summer sky. "Don't you trust me?"

"Of course I do. . . ."

"Then let's go." He tugged her.

She resisted.

"Oh, I understand." Sunlight danced in his eyes. "You're waiting for me to pick you up and carry you."

She sucked in a breath. "You wouldn't dare."

A hint of a grin snared the corner of his mouth. "Don't you know you should never dare me? It's a sure bet I'll do it."

Before she could protest, he grabbed her around the middle. With one motion he lifted her to his shoulder and hung her there like a sack of seed grain.

"Eli Ernest! This is entirely uncivilized." Her cheeks burned. But not entirely from embarrassment.

"No one ever said I was civilized."

She made a halfhearted protest by squirming. The cold wetness from his clothes seeped through the thin layers of her dress and linen chemise.

He clamped his arm across her backside.

She gasped and grew motionless. The solidness of his arm pushed against the roundness of her flesh. "Your hold is quite indecent."

"Suits me just fine." He stalked forward with an ease that belied her weight and his exhaustion.

"It's entirely inappropriate." She couldn't think past the pressure his arm exerted.

"Please, put me down. You'll cause a scene."

211

His arm only tightened. "You know how much I like causing scenes."

Her mind whirled, and the heat in her cheeks blazed hotter. "Then you'll force me to take extreme measures to stop you."

He chuckled. "I'd like to see what you can do."

She took a deep breath, and then, before she lost courage, she sank her fingers into the hair that stuck in wet clumps to the back of his neck.

His steps faltered.

She combed through the thick locks, letting her fingers brush against the soft skin. "Looks like you're in need of a haircut," she said softly, in what she hoped was a seductive voice.

He stumbled.

Her brazenness shocked even her own delicate ears. But she couldn't help smiling. Her ploy was working.

She brushed her fingers through his hair again, pulling the wet strands up, making sure to trail her fingers across his neck. "I can give you a haircut." She wrapped a strand around one of her fingers. "If you want."

With a jolt, he stopped. He shifted her and slid her down. When her feet touched the ground, he didn't let her go but instead pulled her against him. His eyes flashed with a heat she couldn't begin to understand.

"You won." His palm nestled into the rounded spot at the base of her back, and his gaze narrowed on her lips.

Would he kiss her? Here? Now? Her stomach turned to warm mush at the thought of him pressing his lips against hers.

When he leaned in, she caught her breath.

But instead of touching her lips, he grazed the tender spot next to her ear.

The scratchiness of his cheek and heaviness of his breath sent tight quivers through her belly.

She wanted to slide her arms around him, to hold him, to forget about everyone else but them.

He pressed his mouth against her ear and then gave a ragged groan. "We have to go," he said breathlessly, pushing her to arm's length, setting her away from him.

"I know." She fought to catch her breath and composure.

"Our very lives depend on us crossing the river and catching the caravan."

She nodded, suddenly chagrined. She didn't want to be the cause of their delay in reaching the caravan. And she most certainly didn't want to ruin Eli's goodwill toward her. Not now. Not after he'd almost . . .

"You'll be all right, then?" He started forward, as if he needed to put more distance between them.

"I'll try." She fumbled at her skirt, pressing the ruffled cotton, one of the plain dresses Mother had sewn for the trip, which was now dirty beyond recognition since they'd had no opportunity for washing clothes since they'd left Liberty.

Even though her legs had no strength, she tried to make her feet move forward as gracefully as she could, following Eli.

When she reached the bank of the river, her stomach rippled with unease. Mabel was sitting in the native-made boat, clutching her India rubber life preserver.

The water lapped against the leather sides and threatened to splash over the sides. Priscilla took a quick step back. "I can't—"

Eli swept her off her feet into his arms. "We don't have any more time."

The solidness of his arms enveloped her.

She closed her eyes, and warmth flared back to life in the pit of her stomach, chasing away the fear. For a long moment, she didn't worry about what the others thought of her unladylike predicament. Instead, she relished the solidness of his arms, the safety of his chest, and the thought that he desired her.

He sloshed through the water to the boat, and when he bent over to deposit her inside, his breath hovered against her cheek. "You'll be fine, Priscilla."

Her gaze collided with his.

"I'm swimming alongside. And I promise I won't let anything happen to you."

She took a deep breath.

When he lowered her into the boat, she reluctantly released her hold.

And suddenly she knew what was happening to her.

For the first time in her life she was falling in love. . . . More than that—she was falling in love with the man she'd married.

Only she wasn't supposed to. It hadn't been part of their bargain.

Whatever would she do now?

Chapter
16

PLATTE RIVER

*F*irelight. Ahead." Richard pointed to the glow on the horizon.

Relief seeped through Eli. "Thank the Lord Almighty." His shoulders slumped and fatigue rolled over him.

They'd made it. Finally.

The crossing at Loup Fork had taken longer than he'd planned. No matter how hard they'd worked, the quicksand had slowed them down. After pushing hard all day, he'd begun to wonder if they'd ever reach the tail end of the caravan. When midnight had come and gone, he'd grown desperate, knowing he couldn't keep them up all night, especially Priscilla, who'd sacrificed riding in the wagon again so that Mabel could.

He choked back the frustration that had been building over

the past hours, thinking how weary Priscilla was, how much she needed to rest.

Now she could.

"We're almost there," he called to the others behind him.

When they pulled up to the caravan's circle, the night guard motioned for them to make their own camp outside the circle. Even though Eli had been hoping to pen their cattle and horses within the inner encampment for safekeeping, he didn't argue. It was too late. Besides, now that they were finally together, they couldn't chance stirring up any more animosity.

He dismounted and headed for Priscilla. She was slumped in her saddle and made no effort to get off.

He reached for her, fitting his hands around her waist. "I've got you."

She didn't offer any resistance and instead fell into his arms.

He hefted her against his chest.

Her arms wrapped around his neck, and she breathed a long sigh that simmered against his chin.

"I'm so tired," she whispered.

"Let's get you to bed." He started toward the wagon.

Her fingers stretched into the hair curling over the collar of his coat. And in a flash his body heated with the memory of her fingers there earlier in the day. Even if she'd been playing with him then, he'd feasted upon her touch much more than he wanted to admit.

The softness of her body melded against him. "Oh, Eli."

Her breath caressed his neck. It drove out the exhaustion and sent life through his blood.

"I'm so glad we're with the caravan." Her fingers slipped through his hair and brushed against his head.

He leaned into her hand. He didn't care if her boldness stemmed from her tiredness or was a continuation of her playfulness from earlier in the day. The pleasure of her touch warmed him all the way to his soul.

"Look at all the stars tonight," she whispered.

The cloudless sky was as open and endless as he remembered from his last trip, and the darkness of the night made each star shine like a polished gem.

"Maybe if we look hard enough we'll see Mars," she said. The sparkle of the heavenly lights reflected in the depths of her eyes.

He took a breath of the sweet summer air and exhaled all the tension that had built up over the past weeks of travel.

"Or perhaps we'll see Ceres, the new planet," she added.

"While you're at it, why don't you discover another one?" Lightheartedness breezed through him. "Then you could name it something more practical, like . . . 'faraway blurry spot.'"

She gave a soft laugh.

"Or what about 'another rock in the asteroid belt'?" he suggested.

"I see you're a helpless romantic."

He grinned.

"I understand now why you've wanted to come back," she whispered. "The vastness of the sky is breathtaking."

He turned his eyes heavenward, something he hadn't done often enough over the past weeks. The wide open sky went on forever. It *was* breathtaking.

On the last trip he'd had more time to take in passing scenery and to pray. "I know it's been hard to appreciate the beauty of the prairies with all the hard riding we've had to do. But I hope now we'll be able to enjoy it more."

"I'd like that."

They'd crossed hundreds of miles of country so far to get where they were, and they still had hundreds to go. But somehow, reaching the trapper caravan put his plans and dreams within grasp. Fresh excitement pulsed from his heart through his arteries to his tired limbs.

He shoved aside the flap of the canvas covering the back of the wagon.

Her arms gripped him tighter. "Will you be able to lie down for a while?"

He shrugged. "I'll take a turn at watching the animals first."

"I hope you can rest."

Did he hear wistfulness in her tone? He bent his head toward hers and couldn't resist the urge to lay his lips against the creamy skin of her forehead. The softness that met his lips stirred the hunger she'd awakened in him earlier.

Her breathing quickened and came in short bursts against his collarbone.

His chest pumped faster.

What was she doing to him?

His mind told him to go, to ignore the swirling of longing to stay with her. He'd promised her they'd keep things business-like, and he wasn't a man to go back on a promise. Besides, he didn't need the distraction of getting involved with her. He needed to stay focused on his number one job—getting them to the West safely.

"Eli." She breathed his name with the hint of a question, almost as if she were asking him to stay.

He held himself rigid and swallowed a moan. It wouldn't hurt anything to give her a little kiss, would it? Especially not now, after they'd caught up with the caravan. They would be safe. Their travels would be easier—at least until after the Rendezvous. Couldn't he enjoy just a moment with this woman? His wife?

He nuzzled his nose against the softness of her hair above her ear. Then he let his lips get a taste of the creaminess of her cheek. The flavor of her skin only made him want more.

He let his lips graze the length of her cheekbone and then straight down to her lips.

She dragged in a quick breath.

He captured that breath with his mouth upon hers. The softness of her lips melded with his, and he took his time trying and savoring the delicacy of her mouth. He'd never tasted anything like her and knew for certain he never would again this side of heaven.

The problem was that now that he'd gotten a taste of her, how would he be able to live without coming back for more? What would happen to their agreement then?

With a groan, he tore away from her. Then before he could change his mind, he hefted her into the wagon bed.

The motion forced her to let go of him and balance herself on the array of blankets and overturned crates. Through the dark, the reflection of the stars in her eyes beckoned to him.

His heart thudded with something deep and powerful, something that drew him to her with an intensity he'd never experienced with any other woman.

He stepped back and drew in a breath of the cold night air, needing to clear his head before he did something he would regret or before he took advantage of her exhausted state.

"It's late." His voice was gruff with the effort to keep himself from climbing in after her, lying down next to her, and kissing her until neither of them could breathe.

He spun away. He hadn't wanted to bring a wife along. But since the Board had forced his hand into it, he'd resolved to do the best he possibly could to keep her safe. And now that he'd come to know this woman, after seeing just how deep her beauty went, he was more determined than ever to make sure she stayed safe.

He could admit, yes, that he'd grown to care about her.

And he could admit he wanted to forget all about their business arrangement and his promise to keep their relationship platonic—especially at that moment. He didn't imagine he'd have too much trouble persuading her to abandon the agreement. She hadn't turned him away yet.

But if he took down the barriers around his heart and allowed himself to get involved with her, would he be able to protect her well enough? Would he be able to think clearly to help her survive?

And would it be fair to her? Especially if he would have to send her back home at some point? He'd vowed he would give her an annulment. He wouldn't be able to do that if he kept kissing her.

He let out a long breath and turned his face to the expanse of the heavens and to the Almighty. Involvement with a woman had never been part of his plans. He'd kept his focus and energy on God's call, on the mission, on the natives.

But now . . .

Was God giving him the opportunity for both?

Priscilla awoke to the shouts of men and the off-key braying of mules.

With a start she sat up and looked around. Through the darkness, the shadows of their dwindling supplies greeted her.

Mabel was still curled up under a pile of blankets.

The faint light of dawn peeking through the slits of the canvas told Priscilla it was past time for her to arise and begin their early morning meal preparations.

Why hadn't Eli called to them, as he usually did?

She unraveled her hair and quickly combed her fingers through the tangles. Every time she fixed it, she shuddered at how dirty and lusterless it had become over the past month of traveling overland. And her once-perfect skin was coated with a layer of filth that made her shiver whenever she looked closely enough.

She didn't want to complain to Eli, but she was growing desperate to wash her clothes.

With a sigh, she swept her hair into a knot at the back of her head. She groped for her bonnet and fixed it in place.

Her heart pumped with the sudden longing to see Eli, to be near him.

She touched her fingers to her lips and relished the memory of his lips pressed there. Her stomach whirled with a strange mix of sensations, the same that she'd felt last night—almost as if she wanted him to keep kissing her and never stop.

She blushed at the thought.

There was no doubt she was falling in love with him. Even though it was a new emotion, it was strong and deep and sure.

Perhaps he wasn't the type of man she would have married under normal circumstances, but he was proving to be the bravest, kindest, strongest man she'd ever met.

Her heart ached with the longing for one of his smiles of pleasure. What could she possibly do to earn one?

With trembling fingers, she opened the canvas flap and poked her head out.

The smoky air of the campfires swirled through the coolness of dawn. The men were busy saddling the horses and rustling up the cattle.

Ahead of their group, the caravan was getting into formation, the mules in a straight line, one in front of another, all loaded with enormous packs. She could count at least seven fully packed wagons drawn by six mules each.

If the caravan was already lining up, they must be leaving soon. There was no more time for dawdling. She would need to attend to her duties.

She swept aside the flap and climbed down.

Her feet had no more than touched the ground when a body stepped around the wagon into her path.

She jumped back against the wagon with a gasp.

Before she could scream, a dirty hand with blackened fingernails clasped her mouth.

"I was wantin' the chance to see the women," a voice rasped against her ear.

She struggled against the suffocating grip, gagging on the sour odor of liquor on the man's breath.

In the hazy light, his eyes were big and dark against sunken cheeks, his beard long and scraggly.

"Ah, pretty little girlie, I been waitin' here for you to come out. I'm aimin' to get me a taste of real woman flesh." He yanked her against him with a grip that sent panic racing through her like a wild out-of-control horse. "Haven't had me a white woman in longer'n I can remember."

She screamed, but his fingers pressed against her mouth and nose, cutting off all air. His limbs were scrawny, but when he started to pull her away from the wagon into the long prairie grass, his strength was as unyielding as a chain.

The more she struggled, the harder he pinched, until the world began to swirl in front of her.

With each shuddering heartbeat, her brain hammered dread through her body. If he dragged her much farther, no one would see them. No one would even realize she'd left the confines of the wagon until too late.

Her mind screamed. But with each second, the world grew more distant, and all she knew was that he'd trapped and overpowered her, and she was helpless to escape him and the horrible fate he intended.

God have mercy.

Had she come this far and endured so much adversity only to suffer the most defiling torture the devil had invented?

He shoved her to the ground and released her mouth and nose.

She struggled, unable to fight for anything but a lungful of air.

Before she could move, he'd rolled her to her back and straddled her.

Her lungs burned, and she writhed, desperate to get away.

His thin, weathered face contorted with lust. He yanked at the layers of her skirt, and his fingers scraped against her delicate skin like an old piece of bark. She drew in a long breath and then exhaled it in a shrill scream.

"Ah, shee-ut up." His hand crashed against her cheek.

Pain pierced her sensitive flesh and radiated to her cheekbone. She cried out at the intensity.

His palm smacked against her face again—this time making contact with her nose.

Blood spurted against his hand, and a warm trickle flowed down her upper lip.

"Just hold still, and I won't hurt you none." He jerked at her bodice, and the material gave way with a sickening rip. "You might even like what Old Ephraim's gonna give you."

The blood trickled through her teeth onto her tongue. She swallowed the metallic warmth and forced rising bile back down.

Suddenly Old Ephraim froze.

The glint of a silver blade hovered against the hairless part of his cheek.

"Let Flower Blossom go," a soft, calm voice demanded.

Priscilla peered beyond the old trapper and met the steady eyes of Squire's woman, Running Feet.

"I slice your cheek." She dug the pointed tip into his flesh.

He cried out.

"Then next I cut off your ear."

223

Old Ephraim squealed like a hog at slaughter. A drop of blood slid off his cheek onto Priscilla. "Don't do it. Don't do it."

"I cut off Gut-rot Bill's ear. I cut yours too."

"No. No. Please no!"

With a swiftness that surprised Priscilla, Running Feet sliced the flesh of Old Ephraim's cheek, then brought the blade to the top of his ear.

Terror widened his sunken eyes.

"You hurt me. Now you hurt Flower Blossom." Running Feet severed the tip of the skin holding his ear to his head.

Old Ephraim screamed.

Priscilla wanted to tell the Indian woman to stop, but fear left her mute. Even though the man likely deserved the worst punishment possible, horror rolled over her at the thought of Running Feet slicing off the man's ear.

"What's going on?" Eli's voice called across the tall grass beyond the wagon.

"Eli!" she shouted, her need for him bringing sobs to her chest. "Eli, please help!"

When Running Feet's knife pierced Ephraim's flesh again, Priscilla screamed with him.

It took only a moment for Eli to stumble to a breathless halt next to her. He took one glance at the old trapper on top of her, and his face contorted and his eyes flashed with fury.

"What have you done?" Eli roared. He grabbed the man's shirt and hauled him off Priscilla. With another roar, he threw Old Ephraim to the ground.

"How dare you hurt my wife!" Eli half lifted the man and sent his fist into the trapper's face and then again into his gut. He shoved him back to the hard earth.

Old Ephraim groaned.

"I'll teach you a lesson." Eli's voice rose with each word. "By the time I'm through with you, you'll wish you'd never laid a finger on her."

He kicked Old Ephraim in the stomach.

The man rolled into a ball.

Priscilla struggled to sit up, wiping her nose with her sleeve, trying to stop the flow of the blood.

"You no good, lousy, filthy, stupid idiot." Eli's boot slammed against the man with each word.

Her heart thudded with new dread. "Eli, stop! You're going to kill him."

"This one. He needs to die." Running Feet watched Eli, her eyes cold and emotionless. The edge of her long knife glistened with Old Ephraim's blood.

Just then Black Squire burst upon them, followed by Richard, John, and other men from both camps.

"What happened?" Squire's voice boomed. His eyes roved over each person and came to rest on Running Feet's knife. Anger transformed his face into that of a grizzly bear. He nodded toward Old Ephraim and then gestured toward her knife, speaking to her in her native tongue.

She shook her head and then pointed at Priscilla.

The tension in Squire's face eased, and he spoke to Running Feet again.

"Good for Doc kill him," she said in English.

Black Squire watched Eli give the man another kick.

"Okay, Doc." Squire lumbered over to Eli and grabbed him by the shoulders. "That's enough."

Eli shrugged Squire's hands off. "I'm not done with this good-for-nothin'."

Squire wrestled Eli away. "Yep. Yer done. You done give him the whoopin' he deserved. Now you leave the rest to me and the cap'n."

Eli's shoulders sagged, and he stared at Old Ephraim with glazed eyes, as if he were in another time and another place.

Priscilla shuddered. What demons were chasing Eli? He'd beaten the man almost as if he were punishing someone else.

Eli wiped an arm across the sweat rolling down his forehead, then rubbed his eyes and started toward her. "Are you hurt?"

"He didn't . . . wasn't able to . . . Running Feet stopped him." Bile rolled through her stomach at the thought of what had almost happened to her.

He stared at the blood smeared across her bodice. The anger sparked in his eyes again, and he glanced back at the unmoving body of the trapper.

"Old Ephraim's scum of the worst kind." Squire shoved the man with his boot. "But he ain't worth no more of your energy."

Eli sucked in a ragged breath and glowered at the men who continued to gather around them. "Nobody better touch my wife again. Ever."

Old Ephraim gave a soft groan, and Priscilla breathed in a shuddering sigh, thankful Eli hadn't killed the man.

"Next time I won't stop," he said.

He yanked the brim of his hat and pulled it low. Then he stalked over and towered over her. His keen eyes assessed her bloody nose, mouth, and cheek, but he didn't make a move to touch her. He turned to Running Feet. "Would you help Priscilla wash up?"

The Indian woman nodded.

"I'll be by to check on her soon as I get my wits back."

⌒

Priscilla snuggled David against her bosom and kissed his silky hair. "Oh, I've missed you." The chubby flesh of his little body, the fresh wind-tossed scent of his skin, his soft gurgles of contentment—his very presence soothed her trembling. And for a brief moment she was able to forget about Old Ephraim ripping her bodice and about the frightening lust in his eyes.

Running Feet wiped a cloth against Priscilla's cheek.

She winced.

The Indian woman pulled the cloth away.

Priscilla leaned her head back against the wagon wheel to still the pounding in her temples.

David's chubby fingers tugged on her bonnet strings, pulling them loose. A cool breeze blew against the strands of hair that had come free during her struggle.

Even though the men around them were busy hitching teams and saddling horses, Priscilla couldn't muster the energy for her usual duties.

Running Feet swiped at Priscilla's nose, and she stifled a cry. "We make deal." The Indian woman sat back on her heels, letting the rag drop to the crushed strands of grass.

"Deal?"

Running Feet nodded, but then she clutched her abdomen and doubled over.

Priscilla sat forward. "You're still sick, aren't you?"

The woman rocked back and forth for a moment before lifting her face. Pain pinched her gentle features.

"I saved you," she said between clenched teeth.

"And I'm grateful."

"Then we make deal."

David reached for the cameo Priscilla always wore pinned to her neckline. His fingers fumbled over the raised relief, and his eyes sparkled.

"What kind of deal?" She gave him another kiss, this one against his forehead.

"I save you. Now you save my baby." Running Feet's hollow eyes lingered over David's face.

"I'm sure you'll be fine." Priscilla searched the milling of men for Eli's familiar strong shoulders. "We'll just ask Dr. Ernest to give you more medicine."

Running Feet shook her head. "I not get better."

"You don't know that—"

"When I return to the earth, you take my baby. You make him your son."

Priscilla's heartbeat came to a stuttering stop. Running Feet had entrusted David into her care during her last illness. But that didn't qualify her to become the baby's mother if Running Feet died.

"What about the baby's father? How will Squire feel about me taking him? Or the baby's other family? Surely they won't want a white woman raising him."

Eli cut into the camp circle and headed their way.

"Squire not take care of one so young." Running Feet tried to straighten her back, but she gasped and balled her fist into her abdomen. "He no want."

"What about your family? Won't they want your son?"

The entrance to the empty cavern of Running Feet's soul widened. Only murky darkness swirled there. "My family all dead."

Priscilla wanted to ask what had happened, to understand more about this sad woman. But Eli was almost upon them.

"You must promise," Running Feet said breathlessly.

Priscilla hugged David tighter, and he chattered with abandon. If she didn't take care of this baby, what would become of him?

"We make deal. Raise my son as your own."

Something hard pressed into Priscilla's thigh. She glanced down at the leather scabbard encasing Running Feet's knife and shuddered. "I couldn't—"

"Keep you safe next time." She shoved the knife under the flowing material of Priscilla's dress, hiding it.

"I couldn't possibly take it." The hard length of sheathed metal burned into her. Would there be a next time? *Please, God, no.* And if there were, how would she ever have the courage to use the knife?

Eli stopped beside them. He nodded at Running Feet and then knelt beside Priscilla. "How are you feeling? Does anything hurt?" His eyes were troubled.

"I'll be fine."

"You have a nasty bruise already." His fingers made a gentle trail across her cheekbone.

How could a man use his hands to bring healing one moment, but in the next use his strength to nearly kill another?

What had elicited such a reaction from him? Of course he'd wanted to defend her. He'd proven to be a good man, ready to protect her and keep her safe from the dangers of the trail. But his violent response to her attacker went beyond that.

"What about you?" she asked softly. "Are you all right?"

His fingers skimmed over a trail of blood on her skirt, the scars on his hands reminding her of the many things about his past she didn't know, the painful parts of his childhood he never talked about.

"I didn't mean to get carried away." Anguish tinged his voice. "But I couldn't keep from thinking of Walt and the first time he hurt my sisters . . . their cries . . ."

The pain in his voice reverberated through her heart. She placed her hand over his. "I can't even begin to imagine how hard that must have been for you."

"When I heard your cries . . ." He met her gaze and the night-mares from his past had turned the blue dark. "I didn't think. I only reacted. And I shouldn't have hurt Old Ephraim that way."

She squeezed his hand.

"He'll live. I'll make sure of it." Eli sighed. "Even though I have a feeling the earth would be a better place without him."

She wasn't sure if she should be relieved or terrified that the old trapper would live.

"Don't worry. He won't come near you again." He touched her nose.

She cringed.

"This will hurt, but I want to see if it is broken."

She braced herself.

He placed a hand on either side of her nose and pushed down. A cry slipped from her lips.

David sat up and stared first at her and then at Eli. The baby's eyes wrinkled at the edges, and his bottom lip quavered.

Priscilla smoothed her fingers across the boy's cheek and tried to muster a smile for him.

"I don't think it's broken." Eli sat back on his heels and rubbed his eyes.

"Will you check Running Feet?" Priscilla asked. The Indian woman's face was pale, the same as the dead grass that the new stems had yet to hide. "She's suffering discomfort."

"As long as you're sure you're not hurt anywhere else . . ."

She quickly shook her head. "No. He didn't have enough time to—" The awful words stuck in her throat.

"You're telling me the truth?"

"Yes."

He swallowed hard and didn't say anything for a long moment.

David chattered softly, and Priscilla pressed her thumb into his hand. His fingers clamped around it, squeezing both her flesh and her heart.

"I'm sorry, Priscilla." Eli's voice was a mere whisper.

"It's not your fault," she whispered back.

"I hold myself completely responsible," he said louder and with more urgency.

"I don't blame you." She wanted to reach out to him, but he

pulled back and looked toward the distant horizon—an endless sea of waving prairie grass. "You couldn't have done anything—"

"I should have known one of these men would go crazy at the sight of a beautiful woman. I should have stayed by you—watched out for you—"

"God protected me." The solidness of Running Feet's knife rubbed her leg. He'd brought the Indian woman to the rescue just in time.

"This is exactly the kind of danger I didn't want to expose you to." Frustration poured from his voice.

"It's done. And I'll be fine." But would she be? She shivered and prayed to God that she wouldn't have to go through an ordeal like that again.

There was one thing that was certain. She would never be able to use the knife. Not even if her life depended on it.

Chapter
17

A chorus of whoops and screams jarred Priscilla awake later that morning. She scrambled to sit up amidst the clutter of the wagon bed. The weariness from the past weeks of traveling had lulled her to sleep even though the jolting of the wagon was enough to bruise even the stoutest body.

In the shadows of the canvas she groped for David. Her fingers found the gentle rhythm of his breath and skimmed over his closed eyelids.

The warlike cries outside the wagon grew louder.

She shivered. Were the Pawnee attacking?

Her hand slipped to the hard length pressing against her hip. Blood pounded through her head. Did she dare unsheathe Running Feet's knife?

A whoop echoed too close to the wagon.

What if they saw her golden hair and decided to scalp her? With trembling fingers she fumbled for her discarded bonnet. She couldn't get her hands to work quickly enough.

"Oh, Lord," she whispered, finally tying the ribbons beneath her chin.

The wagon lurched to a stop, and the Indian whoops faded.

Silence surrounded her. Except for the rapid hammer of her heartbeat, she could hear nothing. Her muscles tightened until she was as taut as the bow holding the canvas in place.

David stirred.

"Oh please, God," she murmured, reaching a hand to the boy. "Keep him from crying."

Eli had insisted she travel in the wagon for the morning. Even though her body had ached and her limbs trembled, she hadn't wanted to admit to him her need for a break from the riding. At first she'd resisted, but when Running Feet asked her to hold David for a little while, she'd willingly taken him into the wagon.

The Indian woman was obviously still ailing, and Eli hadn't been able to diagnose what was wrong with her. Priscilla couldn't imagine how Running Feet had managed to ride this far with David on her back or how she could possibly continue.

Priscilla smoothed her fingers over the baby. He was good natured, but energetic and heavy.

He began to squirm and make sleepy half cries.

She slipped her arms around him and drew him into her embrace. Maybe if she could keep him quiet, the Pawnee wouldn't find her.

His eyes opened, and when he saw her, he gave a loud squeal of delight.

"Shh." She laid her fingers gently against his lips.

He puckered his lips and made a slur that imitated hers.

She shook her head and tried to give him a stern look.

He tossed his head back and forth several times and wrinkled his brow.

If the situation hadn't been so grave, she would have been tempted to smile. "This isn't a game, silly." She kissed his head.

The canvas opening rattled.

Fresh fear slithered around her, and she shrank back.

The flap lifted, and Eli poked his face in. "I think it would be safer for you to stay in the wagon for now."

"What's happening?"

A small Indian boy peeked in next to Eli. His eyes grew wide, and he called out in his native language.

"We've reached the edge of the first Pawnee village, and they've come out to greet us."

"Then we're not being attacked?"

The lines in his face were deep and serious, just as they had been since he'd rescued her from Old Ephraim. "Captain Fitzpatrick stopped to see if he could trade with the Pawnee for food. Seems the trappers are running short already."

"How is that possible?" The mules were carrying enormous packs on their backs, and there were more animals than she could possibly count—upwards of three hundred she guessed. How could their supplies be running out, especially when they still had several more weeks before they reached the Rendezvous? "What are the mules carrying?"

"The supplies are for the trappers coming down from the mountains," Eli explained. "They'll meet at the Rendezvous. There Fitzpatrick will pay the mountain men for all their beaver pelts, and the men will stock up on things like sugar, coffee, knives, tobacco, and gunpowder before they head out for another season of trapping."

"Why didn't the caravan bring more food for themselves?"

234

"No room. Besides, we'll reach buffalo country soon enough, and there'll be plenty to eat then."

Another Indian child appeared next to Eli, and then another, until a group was crowding against him.

"The whole village is swarming us," he called above the chattering of the children. "Wait in here until the commotion dies down."

They stared at her and pointed, almost as if they'd never seen a woman before.

She climbed over the tangle of blankets and clothes toward the children. One day soon, she would have her very own school filled with bright-eyed native children. With a smile she waved at them.

They giggled and hid their laughter by cupping their hands over their mouths.

"Surely I'll be safe enough with these children." She leaned forward, ready to stretch her legs and breathe fresh air.

Eli hesitated, then he motioned her forward. "You can come out, but you need to stay next to me." He helped her climb down.

The Indian children surrounded her, their half-naked bodies jostled her, and their black eyes gawked at her.

She adjusted David on her hip and took a deep breath of air thick with the unfamiliar scent of whatever the Indians were cooking in their nearby village. To the south of their caravan near the Platte River, she caught her first glimpse of the Pawnee dome lodges. From a distance they appeared to be nothing more than large mounds of grass and earth. Smoke wisped into the sky out of the center holes in the tops of the homes.

"Amazing," she murmured.

Several Pawnee women drew close to her. Their ears were pierced with ornate beaded earrings. They appeared similar to Running Feet in their deerskin skirts and poncho-like shirts.

The women stared at her the same way the children did, curiosity and amazement widening their eyes.

"I had a feeling this would happen." Eli glanced over the growing crowd. The lines in his face were tense. "Seems you are about to be the main attraction."

One of the women called out, and within seconds more natives surrounded her. An older woman reached toward Priscilla's face and grazed her cheek with fingers as coarse as the gritty soil along the river.

"I'm pleased to meet you," Priscilla said.

The woman grinned, revealing discolored teeth. She said something to the others and then grazed Priscilla's opposite cheek.

The other women came closer, grinning shyly.

"What do they want?" If only she could communicate with them.

"They're just curious. You and Mabel are the first white women they've ever seen."

Nearby, Mabel was standing next to Henry. Native women and children had surrounded her too. They were stroking her face and skin, and she was greeting them with her wide smile.

Priscilla attempted to make her lips curve into a smile. If Mabel could withstand the mob, she could too, couldn't she? After all, she'd come west to minister to the Indians. Pawnee or Nez Perce or any tribe—they all needed the saving love of the Lord.

More dirty hands touched her and bodies crowded against her. The musty leather of their clothes and the filth of unwashed flesh walled her in. One of the women clutched her cameo pin, and another yanked at the lace of her collar.

"I'm not sure what to do." Panic began to mount inside her. She clutched at her cameo, protecting it with one hand while trying to keep David on her hip with the other.

Somehow in the bumping and elbowing, the natives pushed her away from Eli and the wagon.

More hands groped at her. The women giggled.

Priscilla tried to step away from them, but they pressed in from all sides, boxing her into the center of their attention.

"Eli," she called.

Someone pulled at her bonnet, and before she could rescue it, her head was bare. She gasped and clutched her cameo tighter.

Fingers pawed at her hair, her skirt, her face. She yelped at the pressure against the tender bruises on her cheek and nose.

"Stop!" Panic rose and threatened to knock her to the ground. Her hair came loose and tumbled about her face. At once, fingers gripped it.

A swift jerk brought tears to her eyes.

Would they tear her apart piece by piece? In all her grandest plans, she'd never imagined she'd die the first time she encountered the natives in their land.

The stench, the pain, the press of bodies, the clutching fingers—everything surrounded her and threatened to suffocate her.

"Stand back." Eli broke through the circle. His strength and size forced the women away from her. He reached for her, his eyes flashing with worry—the same worry she'd seen earlier when he'd rescued her from Old Ephraim.

"They just want to touch you and see you." He wrapped his arm around her and sheltered her against his broad chest. "But there are too many of them right now."

She ducked into him and wished her heart wasn't quivering with fear of the Indian women.

He pushed through the crowd, protecting her and David in the shelter of his arm. When they reached the back of the wagon, he lifted her into the confines of the canvas.

"I want you to stay inside until the natives have a chance to get used to seeing you." He slipped off his hat, revealing his crinkled brow.

She lowered David onto a pile of blankets and gasped for breath. Tangled masses of hair fell across her face.

"That's twice today that you've been mauled and man-handled." His voice dripped with frustration. "I shudder to think what could have happened to you if you'd been by yourself."

"Thank the Lord for His constant protection." She shivered, not daring to think about it. "And I thank Him that He's given me you."

"But what if I'm not there next time? The threat of danger isn't going to get any better," he said, almost regretfully. "If anything, it'll get worse."

"Yes, I've encountered danger today, but once we get going again, I'm sure everything will work out."

Eli's gaze pierced into her. Something about the intensity sent a quiver of fear through her belly.

"I was right from the start. . . ."

She turned to David and tugged down his long leather tunic. "Please don't say anything."

"I know you don't want to hear it." Misery threaded his voice. "And believe me, I wish I didn't have to say this—"

"Then don't." The ache in her throat echoed in her voice.

He was silent a long moment.

She fingered the beads on the fringes of David's garment, and agony rolled through her insides.

Finally Eli gave a long sigh and jammed his hat onto his head. "You've known how I've felt since the beginning, that I thought this trip would be too dangerous for a woman like you. After Old Ephraim this morning . . . and now this mobbing . . ."

She wanted to cover her ears.

"I can't help thinking I made a mistake to marry you and bring you out here into the middle of constant danger."

Even though she'd known what was coming, his words pierced her anyway, and she sucked in a breath at the pain they brought.

"And especially now," he continued, lowering his voice into an anguished whisper. "Now after getting to know you and . . . and . . . seeing just how special you are . . ."

She blinked back the tears that were rapidly pooling in her eyes.

"I just want to keep you safe. That's all." He backed away. "And if I have to, I'll send you back to New York, but it won't be in a coffin."

With that, he pulled the canvas shut.

She stared at the blank space where he'd stood and let the tears spill onto her cheeks.

David whimpered, and she reached for him.

She caught the sob that rose in her chest.

The boy nestled into her, and the warmth of his little body was her only comfort in the coldness that settled around her.

"Oh, Lord." Her throat constricted painfully. "Surely he doesn't regret marrying me?" Especially not after the way he'd kissed her last night.

"He's just frustrated," she whispered, trying to ignore the pain pulsing through her heart. Once he had the chance to put the recent dangers into perspective, he'd surely remember how well she'd endured the rigors of the journey thus far. And if she'd made it this far, she'd certainly be able to travel the rest of the distance and survive the rigors of the West.

She would show him he hadn't made a mistake—that he hadn't been foolish to marry her.

Priscilla ran a hand over Eli's bedroll next to hers, and she stared through the dark at the top pointed center of their tent.

She and Mabel had sewn the tent in conical form, similar to the ones the Pawnee used during their buffalo hunts. It was raised with a center pole and fastened down with pegs, and it was big enough for both couples plus John and Richard.

They hadn't had the opportunity to use it before because of the hectic pace of their travel. But now that they'd joined the caravan, their first day of travel had been much slower, even leisurely. After the first frightening encounter with the Pawnee, they'd passed several more villages, until finally the caravan had stopped for the night.

The Pawnee had followed them and hadn't stopped peeking into the tent at her and Mabel until darkness had blessedly given them the privacy they'd lacked all day. Eli had taken turns with Henry watching over them, attempting to keep the natives from overwhelming them.

Priscilla took a deep breath and settled herself against the blankets she'd rolled out on top of the India rubber cloth.

In the silence of the night, the chirp of the crickets was a loud chorus, broken only by the occasional nicker of one of the horses penned into the large circle they'd made with their wagons and tents.

Even though they'd passed safely by most of the Pawnee villages, they still faced the ever-present danger of horse theft. At least now that they were traveling with the caravan, the men of their party would share guard duty with the trappers.

She hoped their group would rest easier. John and Richard had fallen asleep the moment their tired young bodies had fallen to the ground. Mabel, too, had already closed her eyes in exhausted slumber. But their even breathing hadn't been able to lull Priscilla to sleep.

Her heart flipped in anticipation and nervousness, and she fingered the edge of Eli's blankets next to hers. After the difficult words they'd exchanged earlier in the day, she wanted a chance to try to make things right between them, to somehow convey the depth of her feelings for him. Yes, they'd made an arrangement, but now, couldn't she explain to him she was ready for more than a business partnership?

He'd said she was special. And if she could just tell him how much she cared about him, then surely they could have a real marriage. She wanted to continue with him every step of the journey, and to serve by his side and nowhere else for as long as God gave her life.

At the stirring outside the tent, she held her breath. They hadn't had the chance to lie side by side since the night at the inn, which seemed like years ago after all they'd been through.

The tent flap lifted. First Henry crawled through, and then Eli slipped in after him.

Her breath hitched deep in her lungs and every nerve in her body sprang to life.

Henry stumbled through the dark to his bedroll, and Eli worked at fastening the flap shut.

When he turned and began to make his way toward her, her heart pattered faster.

He tossed aside his hat but didn't bother taking off his boots before he flopped onto the blankets she'd spread close to hers.

Her body froze and she could hardly breathe.

He crossed his arms behind his head and blew out a weary sigh.

From the other side of the tent, Henry's snore was instant, almost as if he'd fallen asleep before laying his head down.

Priscilla squeezed her eyes shut. She had to talk to Eli before he fell asleep.

Eli's breathing was deep and steady, and she had no doubt after the exhaustion of the past weeks, he wouldn't be awake long either.

She rolled to her side and stretched out her hand. Her trembling fingers made contact with his.

His breathing quickened, but he didn't move.

She wrapped her fingers around his, letting the mixture of softness and solidness caress her hand.

"Eli?" she whispered.

"Hmm?"

"I wanted to talk." She leaned closer into the crook of his neck, and the scruff of his cheeks scraped against the flesh of her nose, still tender from earlier. Suddenly, more than anything, she wanted him to hold her and tell her they would be fine, that everything would work out between them the way it should.

She nuzzled her lips into the soft, smooth place below his ear, tasting the smokiness of his flesh against the tip of her tongue.

His body tightened. "What do you think you're doing?" His breath came fast and ragged, as if he'd just swum across a river.

What was she doing? How could she explain what she wanted from him? Maybe if he kissed her again. Maybe then he'd feel her desire to be more than just his partner.

She tipped back her head and gave him access to her lips.

The heat of his breath bathed her cheek, then her mouth. His lips hovered above hers.

For a long aching moment, she waited for him to give her what she longed for: his heart.

But in one shattering instant, he gripped her upper arms and wrenched her away. "No." His whisper against her ear was hoarse.

She sucked in a sharp, painful breath.

"We had an agreement."

242

"With all the danger, I realize you probably think it's wise for us to guard ourselves against getting too close, but—"

"You're right. There's no sense in complicating things. Not now."

"But after these many weeks, after getting to know each other. Surely you aren't holding on to your prejudices toward me. . . ." Frustration pulsed to life inside her.

He hesitated. "You're still a beautiful, fine lady. And the West is still just as harsh and demanding."

"If I must suffer, then I shall do so gladly."

"I won't stand back and watch you suffer." His voice tightened. "I've had to watch those I care about suffer too many times in my life. And I won't do it again."

Was he thinking of his sisters? Of the torment they'd endured at the hands of Walt? "But I chose to come, to suffer of my own free will."

"No." His whisper was low and taut, and it crushed the delicate bloom inside her. "I won't go back on my word. If living in the West is too dangerous for you, then I'll send you back home. With an annulment."

Her heart grew silent. An annulment?

"Then you'll be free to marry someone else and go serve the Lord in India, like you wanted."

At that moment, she couldn't imagine ever wanting to marry someone else or go to India. Not when she wanted to be with Eli more than she'd ever wanted anything else.

"It'll be best for both of us if we keep to our business arrangement," he continued hoarsely. "Easier—less complicated—less painful."

She wanted to argue with him more, to convince him that he was wrong, that it would be infinitely more painful to live with the knowledge that he didn't want her love.

But she was a fine lady, after all. Hadn't he just said so? And ladies didn't throw themselves at men, hoping for their love. And ladies most certainly didn't plead and beg for affection, especially after a man refused them.

Humiliation blew from her heart to her face, and she was glad for the cover of darkness to hide her embarrassment.

"Besides, we both need to remember why we're doing this—why we're here." He pushed himself up. "We're missionaries, and our top priority is starting the mission and ministering to the natives. We can't let other things distract us."

His reprimand was like a cold slap against her hot cheeks.

"I have to clear my head." He grabbed his bedroll and crawled toward the door.

She sat up and wanted to call after him. But through the faint moonlight that illuminated the tent, Henry's snoring ceased, and he pushed himself up on one elbow, glancing from her to Eli and back.

Horror pummeled her down to her mat. She closed her eyes and wished she could disappear. Of all people, did Henry have to witness Eli's rejection? Now Henry would know that her marriage to Eli was nothing . . . truly was nothing at all but a business deal.

She listened to the flap of canvas and knew Eli was gone.

Pain ripped through her heart with the sharpness of Running Feet's knife. It sliced up her throat with an intense burning that brought tears to her eyes.

He'd left her. . . .

She shuddered and wrapped her arms across her chest. Hot tears spilled down her cheeks, and the pain in her throat swelled to an unbearable lump. The awful truth fell across her.

He didn't want her.

She'd only wanted to tell him how much she cared about him—about them—but he'd pushed her away. . . .

Chapter
18

ABOVE THE FORKS
OF THE PLATTE RIVER

*T*he ground vibrated with the pounding hooves of buffalo. Eli took aim down the barrel of his rifle. He stood in his stirrups and squeezed his horse with his thighs, trying to steady himself.

"Hold on, boy," he urged his gelding. Eli was sure the tremor of excitement that pulsed through his own blood radiated into his horse, making it shimmy and snort as it galloped at top speed across the hard-packed prairie.

Shots from the other hunters had already stirred the herd, and Eli had little time left to make the kill before the buffalo within his aim escaped to safer ground.

His muscles tightened and his finger was taut against the trigger.

Squire's whoops carried over the snorting and stomping of the beasts.

In the past week since leaving the Pawnee villages, the fur company's food supplies had dwindled to nothing. Of course Squire hadn't thought twice about asking the missionaries to share some of their extra calves. Eli had obliged the double-crosser, and the passage about forgiving seventy times seven had taken on new meaning.

Squire was pushing them hard to get to the Rendezvous on time, not allowing them a day's rest, even on the Sabbath. They'd traveled along the Platte River close to two hundred miles and earlier that day had finally moved beyond the fork and entered buffalo country. For once, Squire had allowed them to stop early. After they finished their hunt, they would butcher their kills and feast on steaks.

Eli closed one eye and tried to focus on the nearest bull through the rising swirls of dust. A shot broadside into the lungs would bring the beast down the quickest. Even though their group still had cattle to eat, they would need to dry some of the buffalo meat for later, when they moved far beyond the plentiful prairies into the dry hills and deserts that lay northwest of the fertile valley of the Rendezvous meeting spot.

He steadied his arm and waited a second longer before pulling the trigger.

The crack was followed by a puff of smoke and a jerk to the pit of his arm where the gun kicked back. An instant later the buffalo gave a pained bellow and crumpled to the ground with a thump that sent puffs of dust into the air.

Satisfaction settled across Eli's shoulders, and he lowered himself into his saddle. Hunger gurgled through his stomach. He could almost smell the smoky meat and hear the fat sizzle against the cast-iron skillet.

He wiped his sleeve across the sweat making trails down his temple, and glanced toward the flat bluff rising out of the prairie, where Priscilla stood with Henry, Mabel, and Running Feet. From their position, they could watch the buffalo in safety.

For an instant, envy gnawed him—envy at Henry for getting to be the one to take the women to the bluff and witness the amazement that was sure to have transformed their faces at the sight of so many enormous, wild creatures. He didn't doubt Priscilla was feeling the same awe he'd experienced last year at his first encounter.

At least he could console himself that she cared about *him* more than Henry. He never liked thinking about what had transpired between the two in the past, but certainly Henry didn't hold her affection anymore—not after the way she'd responded to his kiss, not after the way she'd reached for him in the tent.

Eli's stomach tightened. She was his now, wasn't she?

The breeze rippled her skirt, and against the blue evening sky she looked like one of the delicate white flowers that grew in the long waving grass all around them. She was as poised and graceful and beautiful as always, holding her chin high and her shoulders straight.

With a mental shake, he ripped his gaze away from her. Like any flower, all it would take was one misstep, and she would be flattened into the ground and crushed. He had only to remind himself of how close Old Ephraim had come to raping her, and frustration wrapped around his gut with a hard squeeze.

The deep places in his soul ached with the echoes of his sisters' helpless whimpers in the dark. Priscilla's voice had held the same terrified note when she'd screamed for him.

Even if she was holding up to the rigors of the trip, the attack by Old Ephraim had only confirmed the foolishness of bringing a lady like her. It could easily happen again. Anything could happen to her.

And what if he wasn't able to keep her safe next time? He hadn't been able to keep his sisters safe, no matter how hard he'd tried.

He stared at the lines of scars on his hands. They appeared whiter since his skin had grown more weathered over the past weeks. They were a constant reminder of mistakes he'd made in his past and that he couldn't fail again.

The West was no place for a lady.

"Eli!" Priscilla's call was faint, but the urgency in it grabbed him. He swiveled toward her, his heart thudding.

Near the edge of the bluff, she was kneeling next to Running Feet, who was doubled over.

"Hurry!" Priscilla's voice was laced with panic.

For an instant, relief seized him, but then also the realization of how tense he'd been lately, wondering and waiting for something else to happen to Priscilla. It was just a matter of time. Wasn't it?

He shouted instructions to John and Richard to take care of the buffalo he'd shot. Then he steered his horse away from the stampede and kicked it into a gallop toward the bluff. He crossed the distance with a sense of dread pooling in his gut.

"What happened?" Eli jumped off his mount and scrambled up the ledge toward Running Feet. Small rocks and clods of dirt crumbled away behind him with each step.

Priscilla turned her wide eyes upon him, the space between her brows wrinkled. "I don't know. Running Feet just fell to the ground. And when I came over to her, I noticed the puddle of blood at her feet."

Eli knelt beside the woman and set to work untying the cradleboard from her back.

"What is it, Doc?" Squire climbed up next to them, his breathing heavy. "What's wrong with her?"

Blood ran down her legs and seeped into the leather of her moccasins, staining them dark brown.

She clutched her abdomen and groaned.

"Take the baby." Eli handed the papoose to Priscilla.

She started unraveling the rope that bound the baby in place.

"Let's get her back to the wagon, and I'll check her there." Running Feet was obviously hemorrhaging. But how badly? And why?

Squire bent over and murmured to her. She didn't respond. His forehead furrowed, and he swooped her up into his arms.

She gave a pained cry.

"Come on, Doc." Squire started back down the bluff, slipping and sliding in the loose dirt. "Let's see what you can do. You saved her once. I know you can do it again."

Eli straightened and blew out a shaky breath. His gut told him Running Feet was beyond his help. But he would do all he could to help her—just as he always did.

Priscilla loosened David from the confines of the pack and pulled him into her arms. Her lips brushed against the baby's forehead before her gaze collided with his over David's head. The confusion and hurt in her eyes reached out to him as it had done since the night he'd left her in the tent. And whenever he looked into her eyes and saw down into her heart, he couldn't keep from doubting himself. Had he made the right decision in making sure nothing changed in their business arrangement?

Or had he made the biggest mistake yet?

FORT WILLIAM

*T*he high June sun baked Priscilla like the slabs of buffalo steak Eli was an expert at frying. She dabbed the sweat on her forehead with her handkerchief.

The water in the wash bucket was as murky as the Missouri River had been back during the weeks when they'd traveled aboard the steamboats. What she wouldn't give to be riding on the river now, instead of on the dusty open grasslands for endless days.

She shielded her eyes from the sun and glanced at Fort William, standing tall like a lone sentinel in the empty wilderness. Near the banks where the North Platte and Laramie Rivers met, the fort was crudely built—nothing more than a stockade with several small log cabins built into the wooden palisade—but it was still the first sight of civilization in the nearly seven hundred miles they'd traversed since leaving Liberty, and for that, Priscilla was grateful.

The cabins, along with the blacksmith's quarters and storehouse, had been built with the fort only two years prior by the fur trader William Sublette in an effort to trade with the local tribes.

She and Mabel were the first white women to ever set foot inside the walls of the fort, and the fort manager had extended them as much hospitality as the barrenness of the place allowed. The furnishings in their small room inside the fort were Spartan—thin feather mattresses, a chair with a buffalo-skin seat, an old pewter washbasin. And yet the fort reminded her of what she'd left behind, what she'd missed all these long weeks of travel—the simple comforts of a home.

"We absolutely cannot wait this long again between washings," she said to Mabel, lifting the last shirt from the scrub board and twisting it. It was the first time in over a month that they'd had a break of any kind and the opportunity to attend to their personal needs.

Mabel plucked a pair of Henry's trousers off the thicket where they'd draped some of the clothing and the linens. She ran a hand over it and then shook it hard. "Praise the Lord. At least they're drying quickly."

They'd arrived at Fort William several days earlier, but Priscilla had been too busy helping Eli care for Running Feet and David to have time for much else. The woman had languished over the two weeks since she'd started hemorrhaging, having to ride in the wagon most of the time. When they'd finally reached the fort, Eli had insisted they give her a few days' rest.

Every day, Squire had exchanged heated words with Eli about the need to move on, to get the supplies to the Rendezvous. Yet, in spite of Squire's grumbling, he hadn't forced them on. Finally, after Running Feet had sat up earlier in the day, Squire had bellowed that they would leave on the morrow without further delay.

Priscilla stole a glance at Eli, who was standing nearby speaking with a group of Sioux Indians, his rifle tucked under his arm as a warning to leave the white women alone.

A twinge of pain radiated from Priscilla's battered heart, and she stared at her hands, now red from the lye soap. She needed his protection. The grounds swarmed with Sioux who'd come to Fort William to trade buffalo robes for alcohol and tobacco. Every night in their beds, she and Mabel could hear the wild dancing and singing and revelry of the Indians and trappers camped outside the stockade.

Yes, she was grateful Eli stood guard over her. But . . .

She squeezed the wet shirt tighter, and the last gray drops of water dripped onto the grass.

He'd made it clear he wanted to keep his distance from her, that his calling to serve the natives and his desire to start his mission were more important than she was. She was nothing more than a way for him to get to the West. He needed her to fulfill his dreams but didn't really want her.

After all they'd been through together, after how much she'd endured, she'd hoped he was beginning to see that she could handle a hard life. But obviously he was still intent on sending her home at the least problem, and now was planning to give her an annulment too.

Each beat of her heart pumped the pain into her blood. How had she allowed herself to fall in love with him?

She shook the shirt and flapped it open, trying to muster anger toward herself. After all, it was her fault she was in the predicament of loving a man who didn't want to love her in return. They'd made an agreement to have a business partnership. Nothing more. She was the one who wanted to change their status. Not he.

If she should be angry at anyone, it should be herself.

A waft of warm wind blew from the direction of the Platte River and soothed her face, giving her a break from the stench of manure that arose in the hot air both inside and outside the walls of the fort.

She laid the wet shirt on top of the low branches in the warm sunshine. With a deep breath she squeezed her eyes shut and forced herself to remember why she'd come west. It wasn't to fall in love with a man. Eli was right. They'd come to share God's love with the heathen, to help them, to teach them, to give them a better way of living.

"Lord, help me not to forget your call," she whispered.

"Mrs. Doc!" Richard shouted from the front entrance underneath the large blockhouse. There was an urgency in his voice that snapped her body to attention. "Running Feet need you."

Eli rubbed a hand across his eyes and nodded. "Tell Squire I'll be right there."

"She call for Mrs. Doc."

Priscilla wiped her hands on her apron and started toward the palisade gate. Her heartbeat faltered with sudden dread.

Upon examination earlier, Eli had discovered that Running Feet was bleeding because she was having a miscarriage. However, he hadn't been able to find the cause of her abdominal pain or the fever that had developed.

He'd attended her night and day, fighting for her life. Even though the bleeding had finally stopped, she'd grown continually weaker.

Priscilla raced through the open gate. "How is she, Richard?" Her voice was breathless.

The Indian boy jogged alongside her. "She leave this world very soon."

"No. She certainly won't." Priscilla crossed the open interior courtyard, dodging piles of manure with flies buzzing around them. "She was doing fine just a short while ago."

She passed the stables and the well and headed to the cabin Squire had commandeered for Running Feet. The door was already wide open. Squire was pacing back and forth beside the bed.

"Where's Doc?" he roared.

"I'm sure he's not far behind me." She dodged the bear of a man and rushed to Running Feet's side. Squire didn't make her tremble with fear the way he used to. But she still wasn't used to the way he looked at her with his one eye, and she hadn't quite forgiven him for leaving them behind.

She knelt next to the bed and swept her fingers through David's tousled hair. He was sleeping tucked under Running

Feet's arm and against her bosom, just the way Priscilla had left him when she'd gone to do the washing.

The pained lines in Running Feet's face had disappeared. With her eyes closed and her breathing calmer than it had been in days, Priscilla wanted to believe the woman was merely asleep.

But when Running Feet's eyes opened and fixed on her, a shiver of fear prickled Priscilla's skin. She grasped the cloth in the washbasin, wrung it out, and pressed it against Running Feet's forehead.

Eli burst into the room, crossed to the bed, and knelt next to her. He reached for Running Feet's wrist, his fingers ready to check her pulse.

The woman pulled away from Eli and instead grabbed Priscilla's hand. "I go now."

Priscilla shook her head. "No. You're getting better."

The woman's grip tightened. "I go." Running Feet's words were softer. "You keep promise."

She took Priscilla's hand and placed it on David's head. Then she moved her own hand on top of Priscilla's.

The silkiness of David's hair and the warmth of his baby skin roused the longing deep inside of her. Did she dare think— hope—this sweet baby could be hers?

"Promise." The breathless word out of Running Feet's mouth was not a question.

Priscilla met the woman's gaze.

The dark hollowness was fading. Her grip was weakening.

"Promise," she whispered again.

Sudden tears burned in Priscilla's eyes. "I promise."

Running Feet gave an imperceptible nod and then closed her eyes.

Eli reached for his medical kit and began unraveling it. "This isn't looking good," he mumbled.

"Can you save her, Doc?" Squire stopped his pacing to stare at Running Feet.

"I'll try bleeding her again."

Running Feet's hand on top of hers grew heavy.

David squirmed.

At the slight movement, Running Feet's hand fell off of hers and slid into an awkward angle against the mattress.

Priscilla's body tensed.

David's eyes flashed open, and he gave a loud whimper.

Eli rummaged through his case. "I can't think of anything more to do to help her. We've already tried everything."

Priscilla tried to speak but couldn't get words past the ache in her throat. Instead she laid her hand on Eli's arm.

His gaze jerked to the Indian woman. In an instant his shoulders drooped, and he let the scalpel slip from his fingers. "I'm sorry, Squire."

The big man stared at Running Feet's face. He ran a hand down the length of his long beard.

She waited for a flicker of emotion to cross his features, for sorrow to pool in his eyes. But he spun toward the door and stalked from the room without a word.

As much as she disliked Squire, she couldn't prevent an ache from rolling down her throat into her chest. Had he loved Running Feet? Surely he would grieve her loss in his heart, even if he didn't express it.

David's whimper changed into a wail. He pushed himself up and held his arms toward Priscilla.

She reached for him and he leaned into her embrace, eager for her—almost as if he'd heard the promise she'd just made to his mother. "Oh, you poor, sweet motherless baby." He'd lost the most important person in his life, the woman who'd loved him more than anyone else.

Priscilla swallowed past the tightness in her throat. Could she really take this child as her own? What hope did David have to survive now, unless she kept her word to Running Feet?

She wrapped her arms around him in a fierce embrace.

His cries faded, and he curled against her.

She kissed the top of his head and rested her chin there. Would her heart and arms ever widen enough to make a home for this child?

Chapter
19

JULY 4, 1836
CONTINENTAL DIVIDE

*M*rs. Doc! Mrs. Doc!" The excitement in Richard's voice roused her.

Even with both ends of the covered wagon open, the faint breeze could not find its way under the canvas dome. The heat, along with the bumping and rocking, had lulled her to a drowsy half sleep.

Richard's voice propelled her up, and she realized they'd stopped.

Her fingers grazed the rounded cheek of the baby next to her. He stirred, his skin hot to her touch. His hair stuck to his forehead, and she combed it back.

His lips puckered in his sleep, and he sighed softly.

Her heart squeezed with a new protectiveness, a realization that she'd do anything to keep David safe and content.

She turned to peer out the back of the wagon to the same landscape they'd had for days—broad, gently sloping hills covered with dry sage and yellowed weeds growing from the hard-packed earth.

The blue sky against the eastern horizon was broken only by the gentle puffs of a scattering of clouds.

It was hard to believe it had been only four months since she'd left home—it felt like four years. And in the scorching heat of July, the frigidness of the early part of their trip was like a distant dream.

"Mrs. Doc!" Richard bounded up the end of the wagon. His wide smile greeted her, and his ebony eyes glowed. "Come see."

"Why have we stopped?" She reached for David, ready to wake him to take advantage of any opportunity to get out of the wagon. After they'd buried Running Feet and left Fort William a week ago, she'd had no choice but to travel in the confines of the wagon with the baby. She wasn't adept in wearing the cradleboard and riding a horse the way Running Feet had been.

Even though Mabel had offered to share in the care of the infant, Priscilla hadn't wanted to relinquish him. She kept him with her all the time, and thankfully no one had questioned her, not even Black Squire. From what she could tell, he'd lost all interest in the baby the day Running Feet had died. At least she hoped so.

David's eyes opened. At the sight of Priscilla's face, he gave her a slow, sleepy smile.

Her heart dipped, and she smiled back. "There he is. My little sunshine."

His smile widened, and he held out his arms to her.

She lifted him and breathed in the sweetness of his baby

skin. The breath she exhaled left her with a new and strange contentment.

Richard helped her down from the wagon and steadied her as her feet touched the ground. "Mrs. Doc make good mother." He tousled David's hair.

The baby giggled.

"Thank you, Richard." She tickled the baby's belly and earned another giggle. The soft sound bubbled through her heart, making it float.

"David like you."

"He's a sweet baby."

Richard's eyes were round with admiration. "Mrs. Doc mother to many children—some day."

Her heart rolled over and then toppled to a crashing fall inside her stomach. "No. Actually, I won't be a mother to many."

She dropped her chin to stare at the brittle sagebrush, which had become their staple fuel on the barren plains in their endless travel to reach the Rendezvous.

Richard was silent for a moment. "Doc no give Mrs. Doc children?"

She gasped, and mortification spilled over her. Had he figured out that Eli wasn't her husband in the truest sense of the word? Eli had taken to sleeping outside the tent at night, telling everyone that he liked sleeping in the open under the stars.

But Priscilla knew differently, and she had the feeling Henry did too. But she'd prayed no one else would suspect the true nature of her relationship with Eli.

"Hurry, Sister Ernest, hurry." Mabel's call came from the front of the wagon.

"What is it?"

Priscilla hefted David onto her hip and started toward the others who had congregated at the front of the wagons.

"Come celebrate with us, Sister Ernest." Mabel rushed toward her, her pale face alight with a smile. Even though the dried buffalo meat made Mabel weak and sick, her stomach continued to swell with her growing child. "We've officially crossed the Continental Divide through South Pass."

"We have?" Priscilla peered over the rolling hills. Nothing had changed. The same dry brush and dusty earth stretched before them. This was it? The history-making moment? The event Mother had believed would make her the most important woman of her generation? Had she and Mabel truly now become the first white women to travel overland this far west?

Mabel threw her arms around Priscilla and squeezed her in a hug. "Congratulations, my dear."

David squealed with delight.

Priscilla pulled back. "This is it? Really? I thought the Continental Divide would be high in the Rocky Mountains, in some narrow, snowy pass."

Mabel chuckled. "Believe it or not, this is it. When the trappers discovered this low valley through the Rockies, it was a miracle crossing compared to the dangerous passes they'd had to travel previously."

Priscilla took a deep breath of the hot, dry air and let her gaze drift with growing satisfaction. Far in the distance to the north and the south, the hills of the Rocky Mountains rose up. "We're indeed getting the adventure of a lifetime, aren't we, Sister Spalding?"

For a long moment they stood shoulder to shoulder, gazing to the west. Priscilla slipped her arm through Mabel's. "I couldn't have asked the Lord for a better woman to share these adventures with."

Mabel patted her hand. "Me either, dear."

Henry motioned to them. "Let's gather together for a prayer.

On this fourth day of July, we have much for which to give thanks."

Priscilla joined the circle and found herself jostled next to Eli. He grinned like the others, and for the first time, his forehead was void of the anxious grooves that had cut deeper with each step of their journey.

Every day brought them nearer to the Green River and the Rendezvous. They were close enough that two days ago Captain Fitzpatrick had sent out a man to ride ahead of them and alert the camp that they were almost there.

Of course, the Green River Valley was only their halfway point in the overland part of the journey. There they would meet Samuel Parker, who would lead them the rest of the way, with the hope of guiding them into Oregon Country by September, before the mountain passes in eastern Oregon became impass-able with the first snowfall.

Even so, with all the obstacles they'd overcome so far, she didn't begrudge Eli his joy. If not for his hard work and deter-mination, they wouldn't have made it nearly as far as they had.

Mabel intertwined her hand with Henry's and gave him a wide smile. Henry returned the smile.

Priscilla's heart pinched with a shard of jealousy. It wasn't that she wished she was married to Henry. Compared to the rugged, vibrant Eli, Henry was only a shadow. Rather, she was envious of Henry's relationship with Mabel—the way he showered her with affection. She wished that Eli might do the same with her.

She glanced sideways at Eli, to the excitement sparkling in his eyes, knowing he was thinking of the mission and the plans he had for it. If only she could share the excitement of the moment with him, hold his hand, and have him direct one of his smiles at her.

"Let's bow our heads," Henry said, taking off his hat.

Eli and the other men followed suit.

And she swallowed her longings, reprimanding herself. She would only get hurt again if she didn't guard her heart more carefully.

⌒

Eli sank his teeth into the juicy flesh of the roasted prairie hen and savored the sweet tenderness, a fine change from the endless days of buffalo meat.

The first shadows of twilight had settled over their camp, and he rested his back against a crate.

They'd made good progress out of South Pass after crossing over the Continental Divide. Only twenty miles later they'd found a fertile camp along the Pacific Springs. From now on, all the rivers would flow west, leading them to their new home and eventually to the Pacific Ocean.

He let his gaze linger upon the wide open sky and the peaks of the Wind River Mountain Range on the horizon. The majesty of it was a feast to his hungry soul. Anticipation burned through him. Each day brought them one step closer to the West and the Nez Perce. If they continued to make good timing, he'd be able to get a home built before winter and make a room for a clinic.

Of course he planned to visit the Nez Perce at their winter camps too. But he already had sketched a diagram of the house in his mind. Nothing fancy. But still a place where he could meet with the Indians.

He took a deep breath of the warm, smoky air. The chatter of the others around the campfire was soft, almost as if everyone was overcome with the same awe.

Priscilla spoke in hushed tones with Mabel, drinking in the view of the mountains in the distance. The sparkle in her eyes reflected the exhilaration rushing through his blood.

As much as he wanted to deny his longing, he couldn't. He wanted to sit next to her and share the thrilling moment together. He'd worked to keep his distance, but he missed hearing her curious questions and seeing the wonder in her face at each new stretch of their journey.

He tore another chunk of meat from the bone.

Suddenly the distant whoop of Indian cries and the crack of gunfire echoed in the evening air.

Eli scrambled to his feet and grabbed his rifle. His heart slammed into his ribs. Were the Blackfeet attacking? They were a vicious, warring tribe that inhabited the area to the north. Trappers captured by the Blackfeet were lucky to escape alive. Once, they'd set trapper John Colter free, but only because they'd wanted to hunt him down like an animal. They'd stripped him naked, took all his possessions and weapons, and then chased after him in a human hunt. Colter had survived the deadly game. But barely.

Eli didn't want to begin to think about what the Blackfeet would do to the women if they captured them. The pounding of horses' hooves drew nearer, and the gunshots grew louder. The Indian calls were shrill and sent chills over his hot skin.

He started toward Black Squire's campfire. "Stay here and protect the women," he called to Henry.

"Where are you going?" Henry shouldered his rifle.

"Just watch over the women," Eli shouted.

He trotted toward Squire, who wielded a long knife in one hand and his gun in the other. "Take aim!" he roared to the others who'd gathered around him.

Eli lifted his rifle and stared down the long barrel.

The horses were galloping full speed at them, kicking up the dust into swirling clouds.

He cocked his head and closed one eye, getting an Indian

into his line of vision. Setting his jaw with cold determination, he fingered the trigger. He was a doctor and wanted to save lives. And he'd wanted to befriend the natives, to be God's voice of hope and peace. But at that moment he wanted nothing more than to take down anyone who dared to threaten his camp.

"Wait!" one of the trappers shouted. "One of 'em has a white flag on his gun."

"Hold your fire!" Squire yelled.

Eli kept his gun trained on the Indian at whom he'd taken aim.

When they reared their horses in front of the caravan, Squire spat on the ground and swore. Then he grinned. "Tackensuatis."

The lead Indian jumped off his horse.

He spoke to Squire in the Nez Perce language.

Squire replied in the brave's native tongue, but they spoke too fast for Eli to understand.

John and Richard lowered their guns and smiled.

Another Indian dismounted and started toward Eli. The smooth face of the brave was a familiar one. "Kentuc?" Eli relaxed his hold on his gun.

The tall Nez Perce brave grinned.

The tension eased from Eli's shoulders, and he chanced a smile.

"It's good to see you." He nodded at Kentuc, the strong, stealthy young man he'd met on the journey west last summer. "Where's Parker?"

Kentuc shot off a stream of words in his native language.

Eli glanced beyond the Indian to the others, more braves and a few women. "John." Eli nodded at the boy. "Come translate for me."

The young Indian boy trotted over to him.

"Ask him about Parker," Eli said.

John nodded and then conversed with Kentuc. The brave shrugged his shoulders and pointed toward the west.

Eli watched the exchange, picking up only a few words of their conversation. His body tensed. "What happened?"

"Kentuc at Rendezvous," John explained. "Come to meet us here. Excited to see white women."

"But where is Parker? Ask him to tell us where Parker is."

Kentuc stared beyond the trappers to the missionary camp. John spoke to him again.

Kentuc finally spoke in English. "Parker go home."

Eli's heart skidded to a halt. "When? Why?" He looked to John for the translation.

"He left after thaw for Fort Vancouver," John said. "He sail home by sea."

Eli's mind reeled, and for a moment he couldn't comprehend the news.

Kentuc dug into a leather pouch at his hip and pulled out a wrinkled letter. "From Parker."

Eli took the sheet and scrambled to make sense of what had happened. Parker had left and was returning to the States by sailing around the continent.

"But why?" When Eli had returned east last fall, he'd left so many of the final details of the mission in Parker's hands. The explorer had planned to speak with the native Nez Perce, purchase the land, map it out. And most importantly, lead them there from the Rendezvous.

"You're sure Parker isn't meeting us at the Rendezvous?" he asked.

"Parker gone." Kentuc tapped the letter. "You read."

"He tell in letter," John said.

Eli straightened his back. He unfolded the smudged sheet with Parker's scrawled handwriting. He smoothed it out, and his heart plummeted. The letters bled together, and he knew he'd never be able to read it. He had trouble enough when writing was legible. How could he ever make his way through line after line of scribbles?

He folded the sheet and stuffed it inside his vest. Frustration crackled through his veins. He would need help reading the letter if he was ever going to find out what instructions, if any, Parker had left for him.

But he loathed the thought of having to rely on anyone else. He could picture the pity and condescension in their eyes. He'd had enough of that in his life already and didn't need any more.

Kentuc grinned and nodded in the direction of the missionary camp. The brave said something to John and laughed.

Eli rubbed a hand over his scruffy chin, fighting back disappointment.

The Indian women had already dismounted and made their way to the covered wagon. Mabel stood and greeted them with a wide smile. Priscilla hefted David onto her hip and sidled next to Mabel, offering the natives a kind but hesitant smile. He didn't doubt she was remembering her experience with the Pawnee women.

His muscles contracted. Would he need to rush to her aid again?

Mabel hugged first one Indian woman and then another, and she attempted a few words in Nez Perce.

The native women giggled but hugged her again.

Priscilla shifted David higher on her hip, and when the Indian women turned to her, she attempted loose embraces with each of the women.

Kentuc, Tackensuatis, and the other men from the newly arrived party joined the women. Some of them just stared at Mabel and Priscilla, while others grinned and laughed among themselves.

Mabel smiled and greeted them with her usual cheerfulness, and Priscilla imitated the woman.

Tackensuatis stretched out his hand and touched Priscilla's cheek.

Her face paled, and she stepped away from him. But the men drew closer.

Eli's pulse spurted forward. Of course, Tackensuatis would have to touch Priscilla and not Mabel. He closed his fingers around his rifle and started forward.

Squire's hand on his shoulder stopped him. "You gotta toughen her up, or she ain't gonna survive out here."

Tackensuatis reached for Priscilla again.

Eli's nerves crackled with the need to rush to her defense and keep anyone else from handling her.

"You been coddlin' her like a baby." Squire ogled Priscilla with the all-too-familiar desire Eli had seen in the trapper. But the man's one eye shone with something more than desire. Since Running Feet's death, Squire had started staring at Priscilla in a way that was too calculated, and it never failed to spark Eli's nerves.

"You can't be jumpin' to her rescue anytime a fly buzzes around her," Squire said.

"I'm not."

"You got to let her fend for herself, or she ain't never gonna learn how."

Squire had a point. Priscilla needed to toughen up. Maybe she'd have a better chance at surviving if he didn't step in every time she needed something.

Priscilla slapped at Tackensuatis's hand, and he laughed.

Squire grinned. "I done figured she had some spit in her."

"She's got spit all right." He strained against the current that threatened to propel him toward her.

Squire socked Eli's arm and guffawed. "Can't you leave her be for even a minute?"

Every sinew ached to go to her side. He hadn't wanted to bring a woman along, but the day he'd married her, he'd made it his duty to protect her. And he was determined to keep her safe during this journey. No matter what.

"They ain't gonna hurt her." Squire's scrutiny of Priscilla was too hard, the carnality too raw. "'Sides, maybe it's time to give the rest of us a chance with her."

Eli bristled. What was Squire thinking? Was the trapper forgetting what he'd done to Old Ephraim? "Nobody better even think about touching her."

"Well, if you ain't gonna have your way with her, then let someone else. We ain't got enough women to go around, 'specially one as purty as her."

Eli turned on the man and grabbed a fistful of his shirt. Anger spurted through him. "Don't you even think about it!"

Squire straightened to his full height and spread his broad shoulders. "Whoa, boy! Back off now."

"Stay away from her." Eli took a step back and drew in a deep breath. "She's my wife."

Squire's lips curved into a mocking smile. "Don't take an idiot to see you been keeping your distance from the woman."

He had to get away from Squire before he did something he'd regret. He couldn't afford to put their trip in jeopardy. Not now. Not after coming so far.

The laughter of the Indian braves drew him forward. Forget Squire's advice. He was bound to keep Priscilla safe or die trying. He made his way through the Indians until he reached her. Then he slipped his arm around her and drew her to his side.

"My wife," he said to the Indians, trying hard not to scowl at them. For emphasis, he squeezed her harder.

The men stepped back.

"Don't touch her again."

Priscilla's elbow dug into his side. "Let go."

"I'm just trying to keep you safe," he said between clenched teeth.

"I *was* safe." She wriggled from his grasp, and with her chin high, crossed to the tent.

David gave a gurgle, and she kissed his head before she lifted the flap and ducked inside.

He had to give her credit. She did have spark. And she was doing a good job of caring for the baby. But was she getting too close?

Kentuc grinned at Eli. "Doc's wife? She don't like Doc."

Eli just shook his head. How could he ever explain to the natives the differences between Priscilla and him, the mountain that separated them? They were two different people from two different worlds.

She didn't belong out there. She belonged in her safe home in New York, planning prayer meetings.

And yet, he'd brought her anyway. He'd put her in danger so he could have his mission.

His heartbeat crashed to a halt at the thought. Had he been selfish? Had he used her? Since the start, he'd told himself they were both called to missions, that she'd wanted to come, that if he hadn't proposed, she wouldn't have been able to fulfill her dream of being a missionary.

But . . . if he hadn't asked her, hadn't convinced her to agree to the arrangement . . . she likely would have lived at home in safety the rest of her life.

A shudder crept up his spine. If anything happened to her, he would be solely to blame. He would be no better than a murderer.

Across the heads in the growing dusk, Squire's dark look dug

269

into him. The man nodded and gave him the kind of gloating smirk that said he'd seen Priscilla's jab and their exchange.

For the first time since he'd met Squire, a surge of dislike jolted through Eli. He'd been able to excuse the man's shiftiness before—had known he only had the best interest of the trappers in mind when he'd tried to leave their missionary party behind. He hadn't wanted to jeopardize the lives of others because their women could slow them down.

Eli could understand that. And he respected it.

But now, Squire had crossed the boundary when it came to Priscilla. For a reason Eli couldn't explain, that made him worry more than ever.

Chapter
20

GREEN RIVER VALLEY

*T*wo days later, on July 6, they descended into the Green River Valley.

Priscilla surveyed the vast flat prairie, watered by the Green River on one side and Horse Creek on another. The Wind River mountain range, with its snow-covered peaks, formed an imposing wall in the distance, and the beauty of it took her breath away.

In the middle of a wide open valley, the annual Rendezvous gathering spread out mile after mile—horses, mules, tepees, and the smoke of campfires—as far as the eye could see. All gathered to sell their furs and buy supplies for the coming year.

"Is there no end to it?" Her body trembled from fear and excitement.

"Think of all the opportunities we'll have to share the gospel." Mabel clasped her hands and smiled.

"So many opportunities." Priscilla tried to muster the same enthusiasm as Mabel. After all, this was why she'd come, to meet the natives, to live among them, and to love them. Why, then, was she nervous at the thought of being in the center of so many of them?

Even as they stood on the hill above the outskirts of the camp, the trappers and Indians in their party began to shoot their guns, signaling their arrival.

The Indians in the valley below began to run toward them, whooping and calling out with a shrillness that sent chills up Priscilla's backbone. Holding rifles in the air, the young Indian men drew nearer, their brown faces fierce. Most of them wore only breechcloths that revealed far too much of their firm legs.

Trappers abandoned their whiskey and card games to stare at the caravan. Even from this distance she could see that the camps were dotted with hard-earned beaver pelts compressed into packs and encased in wrappers of deerskin. The mountain men had gathered to trade the sixty-pound stacks to Fitzpatrick and Black Squire for enough money to buy supplies for the next beaver-trapping season. Apparently the Rendezvous had become an excuse for the area Indian tribes to congregate too.

She clutched David against her.

Eli's horse whinnied near her, but she refused to turn toward him. She grabbed on to the back of the wagon. She wouldn't impose on him again. More than ever, she wanted to prove to him that she could take care of herself.

She hefted herself onto the wagon bed.

"This isn't the time to hide," he called.

"I'm not hiding." She scrambled to smooth her skirt, stained and dirty again.

"I want you to ride with me." His voice behind her left no room for argument.

"I'm not able to ride and hold David."

At the mention of his name, the boy gurgled.

"You're riding *with* me. On my horse."

She turned and met Eli's unflinching gaze. "I couldn't possibly—"

"Now."

"You don't have the proper saddle."

He held out his gloved hand.

The shrill Indian cries grew closer.

She hesitated. She'd told herself she wouldn't be afraid the next time she encountered the natives, that she wouldn't look to Eli to protect her.

"Get on, Priscilla, before you get mobbed." The command held the hint of a plea.

She placed her hand into his, and in an instant he'd hoisted her and David onto his saddle in front of him.

Heat rose up her neck. She was practically sitting in Eli's lap.

"You'll be more comfortable if you straddle."

"That wouldn't be the least bit proper."

His breath fanned the skin beneath her ear. The hard muscles of his thighs pressed against her softness. Was anything about her predicament proper?

"Then hang on." He kicked the horse forward.

The jolt propelled her against his torso and forced her to slip an arm around his waist to keep her balance. David gave a whimper and clutched the bodice of her dress. She tightened her grip on the baby.

She leaned her head against the solidness of Eli's chest, knowing she shouldn't relish the security of being in his arms. . . .

But she couldn't stop herself. She breathed a long sigh and

nestled against him. Now, within the circle of his arms, she couldn't pretend she didn't care. He was a good man, and she loved so many things about him—she loved his dreams about the mission, his determination to make it to the West, his steadiness in leading them, his bravery against the elements, his willingness to sacrifice for everyone, the tenderness of his skilled hands.

His breath warmed her temple, and the scruff on his chin scraped at her tender skin.

The Indians closed in around them, their wild cries sending shivers through her. Everything about them was frightening—the strange hairstyles, the half-naked bodies, the harshness of their language, the dark eyes staring at her with curiosity.

"When we get to Oregon Country, will the Indians get used to us eventually? Or will we always be a fascination to them?"

"They'll settle down." Eli slid a hand around her waist, and his fingers spanned her hip.

She knew he meant nothing by the hold except to keep her from sliding off the horse. But the intimacy sparked a flame in her middle.

"Now you can imagine how John and Richard felt when they were visiting the East—attracting attention wherever they went."

"I hadn't thought of that." Her mind flashed back to the first time she'd seen the boys, when they'd walked into the meeting-house that fateful Sabbath in February, the day that had changed the course of her life. Eli was right—they had attracted attention, fascination, even fear.

She glanced over the faces surrounding them, women and children joining the men.

"John and Richard had to adapt while they were living among us," Eli said. "And we'd be wise to follow their example while we're among the natives—do what we can to learn from them."

"But I thought we were going so we can teach them *our* ways."

"You mean our *superior* ways?"

"Yes, of course."

He snorted.

"Don't we want to save them from their heathen practices and help them have a better way of living?"

"Their way of life might be different from ours, but that doesn't mean it's inferior."

Ahead, John and Richard were riding straight and proud like returning heroes. She had to admit that the more she got to know the boys, the less savage they became.

"What of their pagan practices?" she asked. "Surely you don't condone those?"

"They still need the saving grace of the gospel. But they'll accept the message much better if we share it with love. Not with prideful superiority."

His reasoning was strange, especially when all she'd ever heard in revival gatherings and Home Missionary Society meetings was how the heathen needed the benefits of a civilized culture.

He pulled on the reins to keep the horse from rearing amidst the overwhelming commotion surrounding them. He nodded a greeting to the natives who'd left their camps to come out to meet them.

She forced her lips into a smile and followed Eli's example in nodding a greeting. She clutched David tighter as Eli paraded her through the Indians and trappers. Once again, she and Mabel were the first white women the Indians had ever encountered.

Even though she longed for the safety and seclusion of the back of the wagon, she began to see the wisdom in Eli's plan to give the Indians their first look at her from a safe distance.

The trappers whistled and shouted calls that burned Priscilla's ears.

"Better watch her good, Doc," Squire shouted from his mount. "Some of these here fellas been out in the mountains for years and ain't seen a purty woman in all that time."

Eli stiffened.

"They gonna be downright starvin' for a taste of a real lady."

Priscilla shuddered, and Running Feet's knife weighed against her leg. Would she have need of it?

"Better keep her hidden in your wagon." Squire's grin mocked Eli.

"And you and every other lustful idiot better keep away."

David bounced on her knee, and she buried her burning face into the soft strands of his hair.

Squire didn't say anything else. But when she peeked at him over David's head, his dark eye was fixed on the baby.

She shivered and hugged David closer.

Squire gave her the hint of a smile.

A chill crept through her heart.

Eli muttered under his breath. "Once I make sure every one of them knows what I did to Old Ephraim, they won't dare touch you."

She prayed he was right.

~

They found a spot for their camp close to the Snake River, east of Fort Bonneville, which was nothing more than a square log pen covered with poles and brush. There Squire and his men unloaded the caravan and stored the freight they'd brought from St. Louis, preparing to sell the goods to the trappers in exchange for the furs.

Priscilla soon learned that close to one hundred fifty trappers had made camp in the valley and the number of Indians who had joined the Rendezvous reached upward of two, maybe three, thousand. Snake, Bannock, Flatheads, Nez Perce—the various tribes had separate camps clustered with their buffalo-skin tepees.

The first night as she lay on her sleeping mat inside their tepee, the drums, dancing, and shouting kept her awake—the same drunken revelry between the trappers and Indians that she'd heard at Fort William, only then she'd been inside the palisades in the safety of her room.

Now, all that separated her from the wild partying was a flimsy canvas cover.

Of course, Eli was sleeping outside the flap door of the tent, but that didn't stop her from shivering in the stale heat of the darkness and wondering if she'd been wrong about God calling her to the West instead of to India.

~

For two days she didn't venture outside their camp and was content to visit with the Indian women and children who wandered over to get a glimpse of the white women. After hearing Priscilla sing during the morning devotions, the Indian women were continually asking her to sing for them. She'd tried to teach them a line of one of the hymns, but they seemed content to listen rather than to join in.

"Are you sure you don't want to go with us?" Mabel asked one morning, holding a basket of Bibles and tracts she carried with her whenever she went visiting.

Priscilla wrung the river water from David's miniature leather tunic. "You go ahead. I've plenty more to wash. And I promised John and Richard another English lesson."

On a nearby blanket David babbled as he played with the stones Richard had gathered for him from the river. Washing clothes and listening to David's baby talk could almost make her believe she was a real mother.

"Maybe tomorrow, then?" Mabel smoothed a hand over her growing stomach.

"I'm sure I'll be ready by then." Priscilla flapped the cloth to shake out the wrinkles. She waited for the usual sting that came whenever someone reminded her of her empty womb, but lately, the pain had diminished to a dull prick.

"Let's go," Henry said, swatting the dust from his trousers.

Mabel opened her mouth but then closed it.

"Go on. I'll be fine." Priscilla glanced at John and Richard perched on the open end of the wagon, swinging their feet, their rifles across their laps. They'd been content to swim and wrestle and play together the way any brothers would. But she could also tell from the anxious questions they'd asked Eli that they were ready to continue on to Oregon Country, back to their home.

They were worried about making it over the Blue Mountains before the first snow fell. And although it was only July, their small group still had six to eight weeks of hard travel before they would reach the last imposing ridge that separated them from the valley where they would build their mission. No one talked about what would happen to them if they couldn't make it over, but the worry on the boys' faces was a constant reminder of the danger.

And now that Samuel Parker had deserted them, they couldn't leave without finding someone else to guide them through the wilderness.

"Come along, dear." Henry finished polishing the tip of his boot with a handkerchief. "I'm to meet Dr. Ernest at the Nez Perce camp to talk with the elders."

Mabel smiled at him, and when she reached his side, she wrapped her hand around his.

Priscilla's gaze lingered on their intertwined hands swinging between them as they walked toward the Indian camps. She wouldn't want to follow them around anyway. She'd only get in the way. And she'd have to deal with the uncomfortable tension that surfaced whenever she and Henry were near each other. Even though he'd remained polite about her situation with Eli and the rejection he'd witnessed in the tent, she couldn't shake the feeling he was secretly gloating over her misfortune.

At David's squeal of delight, she tore her attention away from Mabel and smiled at the baby. His chubby fingers piled one rock on top of another until they toppled and earned his giggles.

She might not have a marriage like Mabel or a baby growing inside her, but at least she had David. When they reached Fort Vancouver in Oregon Country, the first thing she'd buy would be material to make him new clothes.

He clapped his hands and chirped a babbling of words. He held out his arms toward her. "Ma-ma-ma-ma."

Priscilla's breath caught in her throat. "Ma-ma?" She often referred to Running Feet as his *mother*. Did David now think *she* was his mother?

"Oh, my sweet, sweet baby." She crossed to him and knelt on the blanket, scooping him into her arms.

He laid his head against her chest, and his eyes drooped.

He'd called her *mama*. She squeezed back tears and tried to swallow the painful lump in her throat. She'd given up her dream of having a baby. But maybe God was giving her the chance to be a mother after all.

A lump in her throat ached but in a tenuously joyful way.

The warmth of the early morning sun poured over her head and sent rays all the way to her heart. She lined David's breeches with fresh moss and rocked him until he fell asleep. With a prayer of thanksgiving in her heart, she laid him in the shade inside the tepee.

"I think I shall join Mabel in the Indian camp today." She

tied her bonnet in place. Why should she cower any longer? She'd told herself that she'd just been busy with long-neglected chores and with taking care of David, but the fact was, she was more nervous about meeting the natives than she cared to admit.

And it was past time to put aside her fears and do what she'd come west to do.

Richard and John jumped off the wagon bed.

"Would you tend to David if he awakes while I'm gone?"

"Mrs. Doc cannot go alone." Richard crossed toward her.

She hesitated. The memory of Old Ephraim's filthy hands strangling her wasn't something she could forget. Ever.

"Doc tell me not to let Mrs. Doc go anywhere alone."

"I'm not worried about what Dr. Ernest wants." She'd managed well enough while he'd been visiting the sick and injured among the trappers and Indians.

"Where is the Nez Perce camp?" She started past the tent and wagons and then stopped, trying to ignore the trembling in her legs. "If you could just point me in the right direction, I'll be fine."

"I go with," Richard said. "I take you to camp. John stay with David."

Even though she didn't want to admit it, she was glad to have him accompany her. They made their way along the river, past several other tribes, until they reached the edge of the Nez Perce camp.

Through the haze of campfires, she spotted Mabel amidst a group of women and waved.

Mabel stood. "Sister Ernest!"

Beyond Mabel, Eli and Henry were in a deep discussion with a party of Indian men. At Mabel's call, they looked to Mabel and then to her.

Worry flashed across Eli's face before he could hide it. For a moment, he started, almost as if contemplating coming toward her. But then something Henry said brought his attention back to the circle of men.

She smiled at the cluster of children that followed each step she took. Their greasy fingers clutched at her skirt. She couldn't look at their mostly naked bodies without flushing with embarrassment.

Half-clad dirty children. She couldn't understand Eli's reasoning. Surely these children would benefit from learning a more civilized manner of living—proper clothes, good hygiene, healthy foods. Wasn't that what God had called her to do—to teach them how to better themselves?

As she reached Mabel and the native women, she bent over and patted the heads of several children, earning giggles.

"They're teaching me to make pemmican," Mabel explained.

The stench of stale buffalo meat assaulted Priscilla, and she pressed a hand to her nose.

The Indian women greeted her with shy smiles and their gibberish speech. One of them passed her a grinding stone and another a thin dried strip of buffalo meat.

It was similar to the strips they'd hung to dry from their wagon. Theirs had attracted more dust and maggots than she could stomach, and she couldn't imagine how she would ever be able to eat it.

"Grind the meat into powder," Mabel instructed. "Then once it's fine enough, we add chopped huckleberries and melted buffalo fat."

Priscilla tried to hold back a shudder.

One of the Indian women broke off a piece—the same muddy brown and crumbly texture as dried dung. She held it out to Priscilla and motioned for her to eat it.

"Try it," Mabel said. "I know it doesn't look appetizing, but it's actually quite sweet."

The Indian woman grunted at her and motioned again for her to eat it.

Priscilla said a silent prayer and then stuffed the piece of pemmican into her mouth, trying to breathe through her nose. The rotten stench was enough to drive out the fruity flavor.

She chewed, forced herself to swallow, and resisted the urge to think about how much dirt and how many insects she was eating. Instead, she smiled at the women who'd stopped their work to watch her.

Had she made a mistake coming? She certainly didn't want to spend the morning grinding dirty buffalo meat and trying not to get sick from the odor.

"I thought you were passing out Bibles and tracts," Priscilla said, pressing her fingers against her nose again.

Mabel laughed. "Oh no, dear. Not here. The Bibles are for the trappers. You know the natives can't read yet."

"Of course." Heat fanned into her face.

"I'm just trying to befriend the women," Mabel explained, "and learn more of their language and customs."

Out of the corner of her eye, she could see Eli and Henry making their way toward them. Mabel's words echoed those Eli had spoken recently. "But shouldn't we be attempting to teach *them* something useful, like sewing clothes for their children?"

"Perhaps, eventually. But I'm sure they'll have just as many things to teach us as we will them," Mabel said. "Don't you think?"

Priscilla tried to smile at the Indian women who were watching her while they worked. Could she really learn from them? If so, what?

Eli stopped beside her. A light sparked in his eyes. "I'm glad you finally decided to join Mabel today."

Priscilla hesitated. Did she detect sincerity in his voice?

"I see you got your first taste of pemmican." He nodded toward the heap of the dried mixture in one of the baskets. "Wasn't it delicious?"

"It was—" Could she find anything even remotely positive to say about the moldy meat mixture? "I'd say it had a rather unique flavor."

The glimmer in his eyes grew brighter, and the hint of a grin teased his lips. "It's my favorite."

"Is that so?"

"I don't know how I've survived these past months without it."

A tiny smile worked its way into her heart. "Then I shall have to be a good wife and learn to make it for you, so you can eat it for every meal."

"Only if you promise to add as many maggots as you possibly can."

The smile inside finally made it to her lips. "And I'll be sure to add spider legs for good measure." Why couldn't they enjoy each other's company like this more often?

Mabel's face had grown pale during their banter and her eyes wide. "Maybe I should refrain from involving Sister Ernest in any more of the pemmican making."

Laughter danced in Eli's eyes.

When had she heard him laugh? Had she ever? They'd had so little to laugh about during the trip.

"Oh, but Sister Spalding." She tried to keep her tone serious. "I was hoping I could take over the duty for the rest of the trip."

Eli coughed back a laugh, and Priscilla's heart warmed.

"I hate to be the one to cast a shadow over your jesting." Henry looked at Priscilla's forehead instead of her eyes. Even after all the weeks of traveling together, he never sought her out or spoke to her unless he had to. "But we have much more important matters that need our immediate attention—the first being whether we should take the Nez Perce up on their offer to travel with them to Fort Walla Walla."

The smile faded from Eli's face, replaced by the anxious crinkles at the corner of his eyes. "I already told you we can't ride with the tribe. Their route is too long. If we head northward over the mountains into the Bitterroot Valley, we'd lose the time we'll need to get supplies and build lodges before winter sets in."

"But who else can safely guide us the other way? It's much too risky."

"We'll hire Kentuc."

"He's immature and unreliable. The chiefs even said as much themselves."

"He traveled with Parker, and hopefully, he'll know where to take us."

Henry smoothed down his mustache. Somehow he managed to keep his mustache impeccably trimmed and his wearing apparel nearly spotless while the rest of the group looked like they rolled around on the dusty earth several times a day.

"When the chiefs are practically begging us to travel with them, how can we say no?" Henry tossed the Indian men a glance, and his Adam's apple rose up and down.

They watched from a distance, their expressions stoic and their arms crossed.

Eli sighed. "It won't work. As much as I'd like to ride with them and strengthen our bonds, we just don't have the time to take their route."

"What if we anger them by refusing their offer?"

"They'll understand that we must move faster than they will."

"I don't know why I'm standing here arguing with you."

Henry's voice sparked with irritation. "You haven't valued my advice during this trip."

"I'm the one who's done this before. Don't you think you should trust me?"

Henry was silent for a long moment.

The Indian women around them worked quietly, watching with wide eyes. Priscilla gave them a reassuring smile, but they lowered their eyes back to their grinding.

"The hard reality is that we don't have much time either way we go." Eli gazed west, his face tight with anxiety. "We've gotta make it to Fort Walla Walla by the beginning of September, or we'll be in trouble."

"You're two very fine leaders," Mabel rushed in. "And both of your plans have merit. Perhaps if we took them before the Lord in prayer—"

"I already have—" Eli started.

"Good idea," Henry said at the same time.

Mabel's cheerful smile withered. "It's just a shame that Mr. Parker isn't here to guide us."

"He should have left us with some instructions," Henry mumbled. "It's the least he could have done."

Eli kept his gaze fixed on the distance.

"If we can't all pray," Mabel said, "then Sister Ernest and I certainly can. Right, Sister Ernest?" Mabel's kind eyes reached out to her.

Before Priscilla could respond, Henry slipped his arm around Mabel and pulled her against his side. "God has surely blessed me with the perfect wife." He beamed down at her, careful to avoid looking at Priscilla.

A sliver of pain pierced Priscilla. She was sure he hadn't meant his comment to hurt her, but it had nevertheless. She wasn't able to be the perfect wife to any man—not even to Eli, who'd claimed her infertility didn't matter. "You're right. Mabel is the perfect wife. You're blessed. You both are."

For once, Henry met her gaze, and she caught a glimpse of something in his eyes—gratefulness?

She nodded. It was true. Henry and Mabel were blessed. They had a real, loving marriage. All she had was the empty shell of an arrangement.

No, that wasn't true. It wasn't all she had. She had David. God had given her the opportunity to experience motherhood, albeit in an unusual way and under odd circumstances. It was a joy she'd never thought she'd have, a delight that went beyond her greatest expectations.

Maybe she'd failed in securing Eli's love. But she certainly wouldn't fail at mothering the baby entrusted to her care. She wouldn't fail David or her promise to Running Feet to make him her son.

Chapter
21

They couldn't delay leaving another day.

Eli had traded one of their wagons for more coffee beans and gunpowder. It was robbery—not nearly an equal exchange. But they needed only one wagon for the remainder of their journey. He had planned to take it all the way to Fort Walla Walla, but none of the trappers believed the wagon could go that far—especially through the Blue Mountains.

Priscilla didn't know how she'd manage David without it.

She stood on her tiptoes and reached into the wagon, packing the last of the blankets into the back with the few remaining food stores. Her fingers lingered over her trunk, her only connection to her family and the life she'd once had.

Her sister, Mary Ann, would have had her baby by now. Did she have a girl or boy? And what name had she given the child?

An intense longing for home shot through Priscilla—so swift and sharp it took her breath away.

She brushed her hand over the brass dots that scrolled into an intricate design on the lid of the trunk. Who knew when she'd see her family again. If ever—

"Heard tell you're leavin' early." Squire's voice boomed through their camp.

Priscilla blinked hard and swiped at her cheeks to make sure they were dry. "Come on, big boy." She stretched after David, who was crawling among the crates, having grown more daring over the past days.

She didn't know what she'd do with him once he gained full mobility.

He came to her with a half giggle, half squeal, and her heart melted into a smile. She hoisted him onto her hip, wishing she could avoid another encounter with Squire but grateful it would be her last.

"You tryin' to sneak outta here without any of us knowin'?" Squire asked. "We still got several more days of gamblin' and drinkin' before we call an end to the Rendezvous."

Eli wrapped the tie strap through the cinch and tightened it until it fit snugly around his horse's belly before turning to face the burly man and several other trappers who stood behind him.

"That means you still got time here to try and convert all us wayward souls." There was something hard in Squire's expression that was reflected in the faces of the men with him.

"We're hoping to get an early start," Eli said calmly. "You know as well as I do that we have to get over the Blue Mountains before the first snowfall."

Squire's glance passed over the smoldering fire pit and the yellow matted grass where the tent had stood before coming to rest on Priscilla. His one eye narrowed.

She lifted her chin and hefted David against her chest. His arms and legs wrapped around her just as if he belonged there.

"I'm thinkin' you didn't want me to know you was leaving."

Henry stepped around the horse he was saddling. "We surely wouldn't leave without giving you our thanks for getting us this far in our journey."

"I doubt that." Squire's voice was laced with accusation. "Everyone thought you was gonna go with the Nez Perce when they break camp. Then I got word this mornin' you hired Kentuc to lead you on out."

"That's right," Eli said. "We decided to take the more direct, easier route."

Squire stared at Priscilla, then flicked his gaze to David and back to her.

This time she couldn't suppress a shudder.

"I hope you wasn't plannin' to kidnap my son."

She started. "Kidnap?"

"Yep. I get the feelin' you was planning on takin' him without asking."

A thunderclap reverberated through her heart. "Running Feet gave him to my care."

"He's my son."

"But Running Feet—she made me promise—she wanted me to raise David as my child. She said you wouldn't want the baby."

"Then seems we got a problem here. 'Cuz he's my son, and I aim to raise him."

The raging storm in Priscilla's chest pounded hard enough to break her ribs. She clutched David and took a step back. She bumped into the hard edge of the wagon bed.

"Come on, Squire," Eli said. "You know as well as I do that Running Feet wanted Priscilla to have the baby. She'll be able to give him a better life and home than you ever could. Running Feet knew that, and so do you."

"He's my son. No one can blame me for wanting to keep my own flesh and blood." He shot a glance at the men behind him. Their hands slipped to their guns.

"You can't take the baby from her after all these weeks she's cared for him. That's downright cruel. And I never took you for a cruel man."

"Oh, I ain't cruel."

Desperate panic charged through her. She wouldn't let Squire take David from her. She pressed the baby's head against her bosom. "But what about Running Feet's wishes? Surely you wouldn't have me break my promise to her?"

One side of Squire's mouth turned up in a grin. "Naw. Don't want you to break your promise. What kinda fella do you take me for?"

Mabel had edged over to her and slipped a hand around her back.

Priscilla leaned into the woman, suddenly weak.

"You can keep the baby"—Squire looked directly at her—"if you come back to St. Louis with me."

Her gasp echoed Mabel's and was followed by a chorus of protests from Henry and Eli.

Squire's grin spread. "I'll build you a purty house, and you can live there and take care of the baby."

"Don't say any more!" Eli shouted and started toward Squire.

One of the men behind Squire raised his gun and cocked the trigger.

Eli stopped. "I can't believe this! Priscilla's not going back with you. Don't even think about it."

"I'm asking *her*. Not *you*." Squire's voice turned low and dangerous.

Eli's hand dropped to his knife, sheathed at his hip. "She's my wife. So no, you're not asking her."

Priscilla's flesh crawled, and she buried her face against David's head.

"She ain't your wife."

"You don't know what you're talking about—"

"You ain't been sleepin' with her. So I figure she ain't your wife."

Her heart pinched with mortification. She couldn't breathe, couldn't think, couldn't move.

"It's not your concern what goes on between me and Priscilla."

"It's my concern now. 'Cuz if she ain't your wife, then she's free to come to St. Louis with me."

She sucked in a deep breath of David's soft downy scent and hid her face.

"We're legally married. And it doesn't matter what has or hasn't happened between us."

"It'll matter to a judge—especially if you ain't never taken her to bed."

Humiliation dumped over her like dirty bath water. She wanted to shrivel up and disappear. But instead, every eye was fixed upon her, upon her naked shame.

"The truth is—" Eli hesitated and tossed her a look of apology. "The truth is, we made a deal. Neither one of us wanted to get married, so we decided on a business partnership."

Oh, Lord. Oh, Lord. Priscilla closed her eyes. But the prayer stuck in her throat. Now everyone knew about her shell of a marriage. How would she be able to face any of them again without burning with embarrassment?

"We made a deal. And I aim to keep my part of the bargain to get her to the West safely. If it's too dangerous there, I'll put her on the first ship back to the East, back to her home. That's the only place she's going."

Mabel's arm tightened around her.

"I'm thinkin' we should let her decide," Squire said. "Does she want to come with me and keep David or stay with you and keep your empty *deal*."

"'Course she's going to stay with me," Eli said, but the hesitancy in his voice made her lift her head.

Would she even dare consider leaving Eli and staying with David? Her heart knocked hard against her chest. How much was she willing to sacrifice to keep the baby?

She squeezed David hard, her chest constricting until she could hardly breathe.

Could she even consider the possibility of being around Squire? Was David worth the discomfort of having to be near that devious man every day?

"Ma-ma-ma." His chubby fingers patted her cheek.

She leaned into his palm and kissed it. A sob caught in her throat. Was she willing to endure Squire for the rest of her life for the sake of this baby—the child she thought she'd never have?

"You're not seriously considering his offer, are you?" Eli's voice rose with a ring of surprise.

She lifted her chin. He'd just embarrassed her in front of everyone by telling them about their business arrangement—when he'd known how much she wanted to keep the matter private. Why wouldn't she consider it? Especially since he might end up sending her back home anyway?

Maybe she'd do them both a favor by accepting Squire's offer. Why should she continue with a man who hadn't wanted her in the first place? He'd made it clear he wasn't interested in her love. He didn't need her anymore—not for himself or for the mission.

And David desperately needed her.

"I been stashing away a heap of money on this here beaver trading," Squire said. "I could afford to give you a real nice home, fancy clothes, and everything a real lady like you could ever want."

"Why?" Eli asked. "What's in it for you?"

The trapper's grin turned lopsided. "My son gets a real fine mother. That's all."

"I'll bet that isn't all you want."

"And she gets to keep the baby." Squire's eye swept over her with a look that stopped the thumping of her heart and sent it pattering with unease.

"You can't take Priscilla." Eli's voice rang with finality.

"If she wants to do what's best for the baby, she'll accept my offer."

How could this be happening? The trembling in her knees radiated to her belly.

"What do you say, sweetheart? You want to keep the baby?" Squire leveled his one eye upon her.

For an instant, gentleness softened the lines of his face—the same tenderness he'd bestowed upon Running Feet.

Yes, her heart screamed. She wanted to keep the baby. She'd ached for one for so long, though she'd tried not to. And now God was finally giving her the chance to be a mother when she'd thought the joy of motherhood would never be hers.

David's happy chirp carried through the silence of the camp. Everyone was staring at her, waiting for her answer.

"Oh, God," she whispered. Agony roiled through her stomach.

Next to her Mabel whispered a prayer.

Could she give up her dreams and plans for missions—the very calling God had placed upon her life so long ago? Could she give it up now on a whim? For the desire to experience motherhood? For the very thing she'd come to believe God had called her to sacrifice?

Despair pushed down on her. She knew what she must do. But how could she possibly let go of David?

"*Please*," she pleaded, "don't take him from me."

Squire barked something in Nez Perce.

Out of the shadows behind him, an old squaw stepped forward and started toward her.

"No!" Priscilla clutched David tighter.

David strained back. "Ma-ma?"

The word ripped her heart.

The Indian woman shuffled to Priscilla.

"Put an end to this, Squire." Eli took a step toward the burly man, but the cocking of another rifle stopped him.

At the sight of two loaded barrels aimed at Eli's heart, fear pounded through Priscilla. He might have hurt her and he might not need her, but she didn't want him to die.

"Give the squaw my son," Squire commanded.

The Indian woman reached for David. Her dark eyes crinkled with apology.

Priscilla clung to the baby. Tears rolled down her cheeks and dripped from her chin onto his head. "He wants me—needs me—"

"Stop all this now, Squire," Eli called. "The game is over. Let Priscilla have the child."

The squaw's hands closed around David.

Priscilla couldn't let go. "No, you can't do this. Who else will love him like I do?"

"You got two choices," Squire said. "You can give the squaw the baby. Or you can walk over here and stand by my side."

Eli strained forward, but Henry grabbed him and wrestled him back. "You tried; you lost," Eli yelled. "Let her have the baby."

Mabel's sobs wafted over Priscilla.

The old woman mumbled something in Nez Perce. Squire folded his arms across his chest.

"I can't believe you're doing this," Eli said, his voice cracking. "If you take that baby from her, you'll lose the little respect I still have for you."

Squire didn't move.

David whimpered again.

Priscilla lifted David until her cheek was pressing against his soft one. With fierce love clawing at her heart, she laid her lips against the warm flesh of his cheek and tasted the saltiness of her own tears there.

With a sob, she released her hold.

The squaw stumbled backward and gripped the baby to her chest.

David squirmed around and held out his arms toward Priscilla. "Ma-ma . . ."

His wail caught her heart and shredded it.

The squaw tried to turn him away, but he craned his neck. "Ma-ma?"

The confusion and desperation in his cry threatened to tear her apart. Another sob escaped.

When Mabel's outstretched arms pulled her into an embrace, Priscilla was helpless to do anything but fall against her.

Chapter

22

NORTHWEST OF GREEN RIVER VALLEY

*E*li tried to swallow the lump in his throat—the one that had been lodged there all day. He plucked another handful of half-ripe gooseberries and added them to the pile in his hat.

His gaze strayed again to Priscilla. With her back propped against the wagon wheel, she sat unmoving in the same spot to which she'd dropped when they'd stopped to make camp for the evening.

They'd only made ten miles, not as far as they needed. But with each step away from the Rendezvous, his heart had urged him to go back and fight Squire for the baby.

He stood and brushed a sleeve against his dripping forehead.

Had he given up too easily? Could he have done more to fight against Squire? The questions had haunted him all day.

Eli's intestines still twisted into a clump every time he thought about Squire's underhanded attempt to lure Priscilla away from him. He had no doubt the man had wanted Priscilla and not the baby.

Even if they hadn't been on a race against time and had the luxury of going back, he'd only have gotten himself shot, maybe even killed if he'd tried to go after the boy.

Squire was right. The baby was his. He could do whatever he wanted, and no one could find fault in that. No one could make the trapper give the child to Priscilla, even if that's what Running Feet had wanted, even if Squire knew that the boy belonged with Priscilla and she'd provide a much better home and life for the boy than he ever could.

The trapper had gambled . . . and lost. Unfortunately, his gamble had cost Priscilla the most.

Eli should have paid attention to that place deep inside him that had warned him Priscilla had gotten too close to the baby. He should have cautioned her against getting attached.

He sighed. It was too late now for that.

With hesitant steps, he crossed toward her. He stopped in front of her, but she didn't look up.

"You've got to eat something."

Her shoulders had lost their usual poise, and she stared at the impending mountain range as though in a daze.

He knelt and held the hat out to her. "I've picked some gooseberries for you."

She didn't answer.

"They're a little sour but still mighty good."

Something sparked in her eyes, but she still didn't look at him.

"I'm really sorry about the baby. I know it was hard to give him up. And I wish there was more I could have done to keep Squire from taking him."

She pressed her lips together.

"I trusted Squire—maybe more than I should have."

"And I trusted you more than I should have." She spat the words.

He sat back on his heels and rubbed a hand across the scruff on his chin. "I said I'm sorry—"

"I made it abundantly clear that I wanted to keep the conditions of our marriage partnership private." Her flashing eyes turned toward him.

"I didn't need to say a word. He figured it out on his own."

"You didn't have to acknowledge his crudeness."

"Don't you think everyone would have found out about us eventually? Besides, don't you get tired of pretending all the time? What's wrong with being open about the way things really are?"

"Don't talk to me about living openly." Her voice was hot. "You've wanted to keep your past private."

His gaze dropped to his hands, to the skeletal pattern of white scars. "Some things aren't anybody else's business."

"Exactly."

The thin lines gave way to memories . . . of peering into the dirty window, of struggling to see through the thick layer of swirling smoke, of finally seeing his pa on the bed. . . . The flames had danced higher. But the door had been locked, and no amount of pounding or slamming against it had awakened the man from his drunken stupor. In his panic, Eli had done the only thing he'd known to do—he'd smashed his hands through the window.

"This is crazy." He pushed his hat with the gooseberries onto her lap and then stood. "You need to eat."

She looked away.

He straightened to his full height and blew out a breath. For a long awful moment that morning, he'd almost believed she would accept Squire's offer. And it had frightened him more than he wanted to acknowledge.

He was surprised to admit how relieved he was that she was still with him, that she'd chosen to continue. Of course, he hadn't wanted her to go with Squire—he *wouldn't* have let her go with the weasel. He'd vowed to keep her safe—and he'd have fought Squire to keep Priscilla from going.

But it wasn't just for her safety that he was glad she was still with them. Could it be that he had wanted her along—truly desired for her to be there? After all his resistance to the idea of bringing a wife, what was happening to him?

And when it came right down to it, would he really be able to give her an annulment and put her on a ship back home?

Over the next two days, the terrain grew steadily steeper and rockier as they left the fertile river valley and started on a northwest course through the desert toward Fort Hall. They made twelve miles one day and fifteen the following. But they couldn't travel fast enough or far enough to suit Kentuc.

And Eli couldn't stop worrying either. He didn't want to blame the women for slowing them down. Instead, he kicked the wagon.

"Maybe we should just leave the wagon behind," he said to Richard and John as they shoved the tent into the wagon bed. In the light of the early morning, everyone was working quickly to pack so they could get a head start on the day's travel.

The boys shrugged. It was another one of those times when he had the feeling the Indian boys thought he was a fool. And maybe he was.

He was more than ready for an excuse to give up the wagon seat for good and have a break from the constant jostling. The hired hands had ridden only as far as the Rendezvous and were returning east with the caravan. Now Eli had to drive the wagon himself. He certainly didn't trust Henry to manage it. The paths winding up some of the steep hillsides had been narrow the day before, and the wagon had skidded too close to the edge more than once.

"Eat up, boys." Mabel handed John and Richard their carefully rationed slices of dried buffalo meat. Priscilla followed behind, giving them both a dipper of their diminishing water supply.

Eli glanced to the pink-tinged cloudless sky. Dust had settled in the cracks of his lips and textured his tongue with grainy grit. They'd need rain soon. The longer they went without fresh water, the more they'd have to resort to using the murky pools and creeks that sufficed for their cattle but would only bring trouble to the rest of them.

"Dr. Ernest." Mabel offered him a thin slab of the meat. The stale odor was enough to dampen any appetite, but he reached for his portion.

Just then Richard handed his slice to John. The younger brother protested, but Richard grunted his insistence before turning to grab another crate.

Eli pushed his piece back into Mabel's hands. "Give mine to Richard."

Mabel's eyebrows lifted in surprise.

"I'll be fine." His stomach growled with the pangs of hunger. "I can wait until nooning."

He turned away and reached for his bedroll. He'd have to convince Kentuc to let them stop early to hunt that evening. What good would it do them to travel hard only to grow weak from hunger and exhaustion?

"Eli?" Priscilla's voice was soft behind him.

Was she finally forgiving him? He spun so fast he nearly tripped over his boots. She'd hardly spoken with him since they'd left the Rendezvous, and he was more than ready to see something in her eyes besides anger.

She held out the dipper. "Your turn."

He searched her face for something, for anything that would give him the slightest hope that she didn't hate him.

She pushed the dipper at him. Her eyes were clouded but void of the flashes of lightning.

He took the ladle and lifted it to his lips for a drink that was altogether too short. Then he handed the dipper back to her. "Thank you."

She lowered it back into the pail. "You were kind to give Richard your portion."

"I was holding out for pemmican."

Her lips twitched with the beginning of a smile.

A grin of his own pushed for release, but the concern for her that had been weighing him down made its way to the surface first. "How are you—I mean—are you doing all right—without the baby?"

The clouds in her eyes darkened and any hint of a smile disappeared. "I'll survive." She turned and rushed to catch up with Mabel.

He watched the frayed edges of her dress swish in the dust and wanted to pound himself over the head. Why had he expected that she'd want to talk about the baby with him?

"Has anyone seen Kentuc?" Henry called.

Eli tipped up the brim of his hat and peered around the camp, noticing for the first time that Kentuc and his horse were gone. Dread pinched the back of his neck and raised the hairs there.

After only a matter of minutes, it was clear that Kentuc was nowhere in sight and had likely snuck off sometime during the dark of night.

Kentuc gone? What would they do now?

With growing despair, Eli stared ahead at the rocky hills spotted with sage and gnarled yellowed brush. The ground was riddled with cracks like a maze of dry capillaries.

How could they possibly navigate through the wilderness without a guide? As much as he wanted to manage without help, he knew he'd be a fool to risk it. They'd get lost, run out of food, and chance danger at the hands of the elements and hostile Blackfeet.

"Guess we'll need to turn around, head back to the Rendezvous," he said, "and look for another guide." That meant he'd have to take the wagon back along the treacherous paths they'd already crossed. And worse than that, they'd lose precious time.

"What if everyone is gone by the time we get back to Green River?" Henry asked.

"We'll have to push hard to make it and pray there are a few stragglers left who can help us."

"And waste days of travel time." Accusation laced Henry's voice.

Eli could only shake his head. "I'm just as upset as you."

"But you're the one who insisted we hire Kentuc and travel this way. We should have taken the offer of the Nez Perce chiefs to travel with them as I'd suggested."

"How was I to know that something would happen to Kentuc?"

"We knew it was the riskier option." Henry brushed the dust off his trousers.

Eli pressed his hand against his chest, against Parker's crinkled letter tucked in the pocket inside his vest. He'd tried to decipher it several times without any luck. At medical school he'd had a hard enough time keeping the printed words in his textbooks from getting twisted around. Dr. Baldwin had assisted him, but mostly he'd had to rely upon his own hard-earned efforts.

And the scrawled, messy handwriting in the letter made reading—already difficult—impossible.

He'd taken the letter out on several occasions, ready to hand it over to Henry, but he'd only had to imagine the humiliation he'd suffer, and he'd tucked it back into his pocket.

But what if he'd made a life-threatening mistake? What if in all his efforts to shoulder everything on his own, he'd put Priscilla's life—all of their lives—in the greatest danger yet?

He glanced to where she stood next to Mabel. She trusted him to keep her safe. His heart constricted with new fear. After keeping her alive this long, he couldn't let his pride be the cause of her demise.

He pulled out the letter. "Here." He held it out.

Henry arched his brow.

"Take it." He needed Henry to grab it before he lost his resolve.

"What is it?"

"Just read it."

Henry took the paper and unfolded it. "It's from Parker."

Mabel gasped.

"Why didn't you tell me you'd gotten a letter from him?" Henry asked.

"Kentuc gave it to me."

"You've had this all along and you didn't share it with me?"

Eli nodded.

"I thought we were a team, working together. I thought I could trust you." Henry's voice was laced with disappointment. "Now I find out you've been holding back information?"

"I'm sorry, Henry. I only did it because—because I couldn't read the letter."

"You couldn't read the letter?"

Eli stiffened and prepared himself for the humiliation that was sure to come.

Henry flapped open the sheet and began to read. "'Dr. Ernest, I regret to inform you that after nearly two years away from home, I am inclined to return . . .'" Henry paused and slanted a gaze at Eli. "It appears perfectly legible to me. What about the letter couldn't you read?"

"Reading is sometimes difficult for me." He had to choke the words out and was more than ready for the conversation to be over.

"Do you need spectacles, Doctor?"

"No."

Henry stared at him for a long moment.

"Just read the letter," Eli growled, "and tell us what it says." He swallowed the bitterness of having to rely upon someone else. But at this point, he had no other choice.

Henry bent his head over the letter for a few minutes and read silently. The camp grew so quiet that they could've heard Eli's stammering heartbeat if they'd listened closely enough.

Finally Henry lifted his head and shook it. "The letter does us absolutely no good now." Frustration drew lines across his forehead. "You should have given me the letter at the Rendezvous when we were trying to decide which way to go."

"What did Parker say?"

"That Kentuc is entirely unreliable. Not to use him. To leave with the tribe and go the long way. That they'll take us directly where we need to go."

Each word socked him in the gut and drove the air from his lungs. How could he have been so foolish? He'd quite possibly made a mistake that had put the entire trip in jeopardy, a misjudgment that could cost them their lives.

Lord Almighty, help us all.

Priscilla glanced over her shoulder to the mountains of dark clouds that stretched up into the heavens. From all appearances, they were in for a storm.

She sagged in her saddle. The heat of the sun burned her back until her chemise and dress stuck to her sweaty skin. If it finally rained, she would lie down in the rain and soak it up to her heart's content. Then she would drink long and hard of the cool, clean water.

After that, she would find something to eat besides the dirty, dried buffalo meat they had for every meal—perhaps Mother's hot bread with a dollop of sweet, creamy butter melting on top.

The thought made her want to groan.

Had Eli been right about her all along? Yes, she'd survived the journey so far, but how could she withstand living in the West if it only brought more of the same unending hardships they'd faced during their travels? Had she lived too sheltered a life to ever adjust to the wilderness?

The heartache of leaving her family, the discomforts of the long ride, the privations of the past weeks wrestled within her chest and bumped against her already battered heart. And now David was gone. Her baby . . .

Ready tears sprang to her eyes. Who would hold him when he cried? Who would kiss his round cheeks? Who would hold his tiny fingers?

A strangled cry rose in her throat. And who would he call mama now?

The confusion in his dark eyes, his outstretched arms when

the Indian woman had taken him away haunted her. His cries echoed in the hollow chambers of her chest. She gripped her middle as a spasm tightened and took her breath away.

"Sister Ernest?" Mabel rode next to her, and her gently rounding abdomen mocked Priscilla. "Is something ailing you?"

She shook her head, unable to speak past the pain that racked her body. Suddenly, more than anything, she wanted to lie down on her girlhood bed and bury her face against the wind-dried sheets.

The travel over the mountainous paths had been difficult the first time, and now they had to retrace their steps back to the Rendezvous. If they didn't make it back by the time the last stragglers left the Green River Valley, they'd be stuck in the wilderness alone.

She'd overheard Eli and Henry arguing. They'd debated their options. Henry insisted they try to catch up with the American Fur Company caravan that would be traveling back to St. Louis with the furs. But Eli wanted to chase after the Nez Perce who had gone the long route back to their winter quarters near the Walla Walla River.

Maybe Eli would send them all home and continue on without them. It was what he wanted, wasn't it?

She would return as a great disappointment to Mother, who'd had such high hopes and grand plans. But at least she'd be home, and at that moment, nothing sounded better.

Another painful spasm clenched her abdomen and twisted it. She bent over and fought off a dizzying wave.

Tears sprang to her eyes. She was doing it again. At the least hardship she was whining and complaining—like the spoiled young lady she was. Would she ever learn to endure discomfort with the bravery and grace that a true missionary should exhibit?

"Sister Ernest?" Mabel's voice came as from a distance.

"It's just a bit of indigestion," she managed. "I'll be all right."

It had to be the dried buffalo meat. If only she could have a taste of Mother's fried potatoes and a slice of ham baked in honey.

She tried to straighten, but a sudden swell of nausea rose, and she swayed.

"You're looking very ill." Mabel put out a hand to steady her.

Priscilla took a deep breath and tried to swallow the rising bile. But pain tore through her stomach, and she cried out from the intensity of it.

"Something is ailing Sister Ernest," Mabel called out.

Priscilla clutched her stomach and moaned with the agony of the tightening cramp. The world swayed, and she felt herself slipping from the sidesaddle.

Mabel screamed and grabbed onto her sleeve. But the young woman was too weak to manage Priscilla's weight.

The pain in her abdomen was too intense, and the nausea too overwhelming. She couldn't hang on and found herself falling. She hit the ground with a jolt that took her breath away.

Eli called her name.

But the world spun around her. She heard the sound of retching, tasted the acidity. Another spasm attacked her stomach.

Surely she was going to die.

Chapter
23

*C*holera.

Priscilla could hear whispers of the dreaded word around her. Somehow she found herself in the tent. Hour after hour she vomited with painful heaves that left her so weak she was trembling with fatigue.

At one point Henry carried in another person. "John," said the hushed voices around her.

Priscilla's heart wrenched, and she tried to pray. *Not one of the Indian boys. Please, Lord.* But she was too violently sick to pray anything more.

Through a haze of pain, she could only watch helplessly as Eli scrambled back and forth between her and John, making them sip water and cleaning up their vomit. At times she thought she saw Richard hovering over his brother, and at other times Mabel was at her side, spooning water through her cracked lips.

And every time Eli leaned over her, his gentle hands were cool upon her hot skin.

"You're working too hard, Dr. Ernest," Mabel said. "Why don't I take over for a while so you can sleep? You won't be able to help anyone if you wear yourself out."

"No." His whisper was fierce. "I have to keep them both from getting dehydrated. It's their only chance of surviving."

"Not their *only* chance," Mabel said softly. "We have prayer too."

"You're right." He sighed. "I've been praying all night, and the Almighty has spared them so far."

"That he has, Doctor."

"Did anyone else drink the contaminated water?" he asked.

"We dumped the rest, and nobody else is complaining of stomach cramps yet."

Their whispers continued above Priscilla. If she and John did indeed have cholera, their chances of survival were slim. She'd been at the bedside of her younger brother when he'd died of cholera a few years earlier during the epidemic that had swept through New York. In the morning he'd been climbing trees in the backyard. By bedtime he'd been dead.

She groped for Eli's hand. "Help John." Her voice was so hoarse she wasn't sure it truly belonged to her, except that they both turned to her.

"Don't worry about me," she gasped. "Save the boy."

Eli's blue eyes clouded with worry. "Shh." He placed a finger against her lips. "Save your energy."

Her lids drooped.

Blessedly, she lost track of time. She faded in and out of sleep, waking only when Eli prodded her to drink more water.

She finally stopped vomiting, but the spasms in her abdomen continued.

A wretched cry finally prodded her to wakefulness. She struggled to sit up but was too weak to do anything but turn her head.

Across from her, Richard had thrown himself across John's body. Tormented sobs filled the stale air of the tent, and it took a moment for her to realize the cries were coming from Richard, that they were shaking his thin torso.

Eli knelt next to him, his head bowed in defeat. Anguish grooved deep crevices into his face. He rubbed a hand across his eyes, pushing his thumb and forefinger into the sockets as if he were trying to stop the flow of his own tears.

Distress twisted through her, and she cried, "No!"

Eli lifted his head and looked at her. His eyes were bloodshot, and the sorrow in them reached across the distance and told her the awful truth.

The boy was dead.

She shook her head. Every weary inch of her body cried out in protest. Not John. Not now. *Oh, Lord. Why not me instead?*

Tears trickled down her cheek, but she was too weak to lift her hand to wipe them away. She was sure of her eternal destiny. She was prepared to give up her life for the natives. If she had ten thousand lives, she would gladly give them all to the Lord. But John—what had become of his soul? Had he been ready for eternity?

Eli buried his face in his hands, and his shoulders shook.

She tried to push herself up again. Now more than ever, she wanted to crawl to Eli, wrap her arms around him, and let him pour out his sorrows in the comfort of her embrace. But she only managed to raise herself to one elbow before she fell back in exhaustion.

The next time Priscilla awoke, John was gone—every trace of him, even his bedroll. Eli was gone too.

Tears burned her eyes and throat.

Mabel's grave gaze met hers. "They buried the boy."

Priscilla swallowed a lump that threatened to choke her. "And how's Richard?"

"He's been very quiet."

If only she weren't so weak, she would have been able to go to the boy and hold him the way his mother would. Her chest ached at the thought of how heartbroken his parents would be when they arrived without John.

Mabel lifted a tin cup to Priscilla's mouth. "Even though we're grieving this tragedy, there is good news."

Priscilla took a sip. The sweet flavor of sugar mingled with the coolness of the water. Had Eli added some of their precious sugar supply to her water?

"While you were ill, Mr. McLeod of the Hudson Bay Company and his party of trappers coming from the Rendezvous came by here. They're on their way back to Fort Walla Walla, and Dr. Ernest is trying to make arrangements for us to join them."

Priscilla sucked in a hopeful breath. "Are they agreeable?"

"Dr. Ernest has asked them to wait one more day—to make sure you're able to travel."

"And?" Her heart lurched.

"He is still working out the details. But it appears that Mr. McLeod is a reasonable man."

Relief wafted through her, only for a burst of anxiety to rapidly chase it away. How long had she already delayed them with her cholera? And how could they spare another day? They needed every possible day in their effort to reach the Blue Mountains.

She lay back and groaned as another spasm attacked her abdomen. If she had slowed down the travels before when she'd been healthy, she hated to think of how much she would delay their progress now—and how much she would frustrate Eli.

"Dr. Ernest wants you to try to sit up and eat a little."

Priscilla shook her head. "I don't want to eat."

"I have a few gooseberries."

The thought of food made her nauseous.

"You're blessed," Mabel said. "Your husband is a very good doctor. I've seen other doctors try to treat cholera, but none have been as confident and competent as he's been."

Priscilla agreed. Eli had proven himself to be an excellent doctor, not only with his skill but also his compassion. He deserved to make it to the West and start his mission. The natives would be blessed to have a man of his caliber.

"I expected him to bleed you. But he seemed to think that would only make you weaker. Instead, he insisted you keep drinking water until I thought you would drown in it."

"I don't think I kept much of it down."

Mabel stuffed a couple of berries into Priscilla's mouth. "But the Lord be praised. Look at you. You're still alive."

Priscilla leaned back, overwhelmingly tired. She tried to make herself chew but wasn't so sure she could be glad she was still alive.

Mabel tugged on her blanket and tucked it under her chin. "Dr. Ernest is working tirelessly to save your life." She peered down at her with sympathy. "I think he cares about you more than you realize."

Priscilla closed her eyes.

"He may not know it yet, but he needs you." Mabel's words were as gentle as her hands caressing Priscilla's cheek.

She wanted so badly to believe Mabel. But she knew Eli didn't need anyone, least of all a lady like her.

She had slept fitfully, and whenever she awoke, Eli or Mabel was there to give her more water and urge her to eat.

"We have to leave this morning." Eli's brow pinched with worry as he worked to spread more blankets underneath her. "McLeod waited for us yesterday, but he's anxious to get going."

"I understand."

"You'll have to ride in the wagon." He rolled a blanket and tucked it next to her.

She didn't say anything. She was too weak to ride her horse. Her stomach still cramped with unbearable spasms. What choice did she have? Unless they left her behind . . .

Eli knelt beside her. "You need to eat a little before we go."

"I'm not hungry."

He slipped his arm behind her and lifted her to a sitting position. She didn't have the strength to resist him. He tipped the cup to her lips, and she tasted the creamy warmth of the cow's milk.

His gaze probed her with a liberty that only doctors could have. She might have blushed at his scrutiny in the past, but she was now as listless on the inside as she was on the outside.

"Our cattle are enduring the journey remarkably well." He helped her finish the last drop. "With the strain of travel and the lack of fertile grass, I'm amazed we're still getting milk."

He held out a plate before her. "Roasted antelope. McLeod's men shot one and shared their meal with us."

Eli put a piece between her lips. The thick juicy bite was a pleasant change from the dried buffalo meat.

"I'm surprised McLeod is letting us ride with him," Eli said, continuing the one-sided conversation. She made no effort to join in. She was too weary to care that she was being impolite.

"Considering the fact that they're from the British Hudson Bay Company, I would've guessed they'd feel threatened by us—Americans—moving into Oregon and making a permanent settlement there."

She'd learned from Eli earlier in their trip that Oregon was occupied jointly by Great Britain and the United States. No one had claimed it as their own—yet.

"But I'm not complaining." Eli fed her another piece of the meat. "After the mistake I made with Parker's letter . . ."

She longed to reach for his hand, to trace a pattern through the scars there. But even if she'd had the strength—and even if she didn't fear him pushing her away—an ache deep in her heart told her she'd be wise to keep her distance.

"Seems that God is trying to teach me a lesson or two these days. . . ."

The discouragement in his voice reflected the despair that had been growing inside her—the nagging question of whether she was truly strong enough to be a missionary, not just physically, but more importantly, spiritually.

"Perhaps God is trying to teach us both something," she whispered. Was He trying to show her it was time to let go of her plans and dreams so that Eli could reach for his?

⌒

The trail through the desert toward the Blue Mountain Range was worse than Eli remembered. And all he could think about was Priscilla in the back of the wagon and whether she would be able to survive the strain of the jolting and jostling.

He wanted to plead with McLeod to slow down the pace, but

he knew they'd already lost too much time and they couldn't waste any more.

There were long stretches without water over dry parched earth, spotted with native sage that grew in stiff bunches as high as a man's head and often got in the way of the wagon and cattle.

They had to pass through Canyon Hill, a wall of perpendicular rocks several hundred feet high, but even though the canyon was more majestic than anything he'd seen yet, Eli was too worried to appreciate it.

McLeod sent some of his men to hunt in the nearby mountains, and when they returned they were loaded with three elk and two antelope. The supply of fresh meat lasted until they reached the salmon fishery at Snake Falls.

Finally, they spotted the log stockade of Snake Fort in the distance on the northern side of the Snake River, not far from the mouth of the Boise River.

The weary travelers gave a cheerful cry, but Eli stared ahead and forced back the sudden swell of grateful relief that stung his eyes.

With each passing day in the hot wagon, Priscilla had wilted into a drooping flower. She didn't eat enough and continued to have recurring stomach pain.

To make the situation worse, one of the axles had cracked. Thankfully, for the past day their route had been more level, over sandy plains. But he knew it was just a matter of time before the axle gave way altogether.

He glanced over his shoulder to the wagon bed, where Priscilla was reclining in the shade of the canvas covering.

He'd hoped that once they reached the fort, she would have a few days to recuperate and that he'd be able to fix the wagon. McLeod had been more considerate than Squire had ever been. Eli prayed the man's goodwill would hold out awhile longer.

He nodded to Richard, riding silently behind the wagon. But

the boy glanced into the distance and refused to meet his gaze. Richard hadn't talked to him since the day they'd dug the hole in the ground and put John into it.

Pain sat with guilt on Eli's shoulder and whispered into his ear. Why had he let John die? Could he have done more to save the boy's life? Could he have tried harder?

"Welcome, welcome." A short, well-dressed man with a British accent called to them.

"Got a spare room for a couple of ladies?" McLeod asked as he swung down from his mount and shook the man's hand.

"*Ladies?*" The man's eyes combed eagerly over the weary travelers. "You have real ladies?"

Eli jumped from the wagon seat and made his way to the back. Priscilla was already attempting to climb out. "Hang on. I'll get you." He reached for her, and she batted his hands away.

"I can do this myself." But he could see she hardly had the strength to stand, let alone climb out of the wagon. He steadied her as her feet touched the ground.

She'd forgotten to pull up her bonnet, and the heat had plastered strands of damp hair to her forehead.

"Looks like the owner of this fort is a fancy English gentleman," Eli said, tapping her bonnet.

She fumbled for it and situated it over her hair, tucking loose strands out of sight. Then she brushed at the helplessly dusty folds of her skirt. "I'm a mess. Completely and utterly filthy. I'm in no condition to meet someone who's civilized."

He usually didn't care a whole lot about his own appearance, but he had to admit he was more than ready for a dip in the nearby Big Wood River. "We're all filthy."

She gave a huff. "You're not supposed to agree with me."

He couldn't hold back his grin. "I guess I should have said you look like a queen about to enter her castle?"

She wiped her sleeve over her face as if she could somehow free it from the grime. But she only managed to add to the streaks smudged on her cheeks.

"The truth is, no matter how dirty you get, nothing can hide how pretty you are." He rubbed his thumb against one of the smudges.

At his touch, she sucked in her breath and took a step back. She swayed and reached out to grab the wagon.

He didn't bother asking for permission to help her. Instead, he scooped her into his arms like a baby.

"Put me down." Her voice was weak. "You know how much I dislike causing a scene."

"And you know how much I like making them."

He was relieved when she didn't fight him. Instead, she gave a soft, almost contented sigh.

When Mr. Kay introduced himself and fawned over her, she could only manage a weak smile. Eli carried her and followed Mr. Kay upstairs, where he settled her on the bed in one of the cool windowless rooms.

The buildings were made of hewed logs, and the roofs and chimneys were covered with mud bricks. The fort wasn't anything fancy, but it was a break from the blazing desert heat and the constant motion of the wagon. If he could convince McLeod to let them stay for a few days, Priscilla would have a chance to get stronger before they moved on.

Mr. Kay brought the ladies bread, stewed serviceberries, and tea. "I hope you don't mind if I watch them enjoy the luxury," he said, settling himself beside Priscilla's bed on one of the stools.

Mabel sat on the other stool, and Eli leaned against the wall near the door. The bright sunshine spilling in the doorway provided the room's only light, enough that he could see the way Mr. Kay was eyeing Priscilla. He wished the man would just go about his business. But flour was a rare commodity and had likely been brought in from Fort Vancouver. How could he refuse Mr. Kay when he was sacrificing of his provisions and providing such important sustenance to the women?

"Thank you, Mr. Kay." Eli pushed aside his pride. "You're kind to share this food."

"If only I could teach the staff to make the bread right." Mr. Kay smiled at Priscilla. "They're mixing it with water and frying it in buffalo grease."

"It's the best bread I can remember ever eating." Mabel took another bite.

Eli's stomach growled. It had been too long since all of them had enjoyed a decent meal.

"I'm sorry I can't offer you anything from our vegetable garden," Mr. Kay continued. "When I built the fort two years ago, I hired Hawaiians from the western coast to help me. We finally attempted the garden and cornfield this spring. But there was not a man among us who knew what we were doing. The corn did well until a frost in early June completely prostrated it."

Mabel and Priscilla gave appropriate murmurs.

"So you see, that's why I need to get married." His voice was playful. "We men are good for nothing without wives to order us around."

Soft laughter followed his statement.

Jealousy pricked Eli's spine, and he straightened. How had Mr. Kay managed to tease a laugh from Priscilla? And why? Was he planning to try to steal her away from him the same way Squire had?

"Not only are we men completely inept without women, we're also absolute bores." Mr. Kay winked at Priscilla. "I do believe we have quite forgotten how to have any fun."

Eli's muscles tightened with the urge to pick Mr. Kay up by

his trousers and boot him out of the room. The man was flirting with his wife, in broad view of him, likely knowing that there was no way Eli would chastise him and chance losing the food he was sharing.

"I know just the thing for you," Mabel chimed in. "We shall have Sister Ernest sing for us. She has the most beautiful singing voice you've ever heard."

Priscilla gave a soft gasp of protest.

Mr. Kay smiled. "How absolutely delightful. I can't imagine anything I'd like to hear more."

"I'm not sure—"

"Please indulge me." Mr. Kay reached for one of her hands and took it between his. "It's been such a long time since I've enjoyed the company of two lovely ladies."

Eli started forward. How dare the man touch his wife?

She quickly pulled her hand away, but a pink blush blossomed in her thin, pale cheeks.

"She's too weak," Eli said in a hard voice, holding himself back. "She needs her rest—"

"Actually"—Priscilla's eyes flashed with a sudden spark—"I would love to sing for you, Mr. Kay."

Eli settled his shoulder back against the doorframe.

She sat quietly for a moment and then began singing "O God Our Help in Ages Past."

Her voice was soft at first. But by the second stanza, it rose until the sweet song filtered into every pore of his skin, seeped into his blood, and pulsed through his body.

As with her smile, he couldn't remember the last time he'd heard her sing. He watched her lips form the words and had the deep overwhelming need to see her smile again—but this time at him.

When was the last time she'd given one to him?

Now, watching her with Mr. Kay, he realized he loathed the thought of her smiling at any other man but him. The very thought of her in any other man's arms stirred him to something akin to fear.

He couldn't deny that he wanted her for himself.

And he couldn't deny that during the days and nights of trying to save her life, the panic that had driven him had been unlike anything he'd ever experienced before—especially after he'd lost John. In all his years of tending to patients, he'd been able to distance himself, to know that death was just an inevitable part of the process of doctoring.

But with her, a quiet desperation had plagued him, and still did.

"Beautiful," Mr. Kay murmured at the last strains of her song.

Eli clamped his mouth shut to keep from saying something he'd regret.

"Will you sing another?" Mr. Kay asked. "Please?"

"Hate to break up the lovely singing," McLeod said from behind Eli, "but I'm thinking we all have some serious talking to do."

Eli stepped aside. As McLeod strode into the small room, dread coiled in the pit of Eli's stomach.

"Two days," Eli started quickly. "Give us two days to rest here at the fort. And we'll be ready." But even as he said the words, deep inside he knew they couldn't afford two days.

"I'm sorry, Doc." McLeod leaned against the wall. "We can't delay. Not even one day. We're behind where we need to be, and the wagon has slowed us down even more."

"I'm gonna need a little time to fix the axle—"

"Probably isn't worth fixing at this point. Once we cross into the Blue Mountains, you'd have to leave the wagon behind anyhow. The trail would be impassable for it."

"And what will we do with our supplies?"

"You'll have to pack what you absolutely need onto your mules and leave the rest."

The women gasped.

What would they be able to do without? Clothes? Blankets? The tent? The cooking utensils? Priscilla's trunk?

"And you may want to consider leaving behind your weakest cattle," McLeod continued. "Trade for them now while you have the chance."

Eli's shoulders slumped. "But what about Priscilla? We need the wagon for her. She's not strong enough to travel by horse yet."

A shadow fell across McLeod's face. "Mr. Kay told me she could stay at the fort until she recovers."

Mr. Kay's head bobbed up and down. "It would be my pleasure to shelter Mrs. Ernest until she's sufficiently recuperated."

McLeod leveled Eli an honest look. "You know as well as I do, she'd have to spend the winter here. Then late spring or early summer, once the trails in the Blue Mountains are passable, you could come get her."

Eli couldn't get a breath past the constriction of his chest. How could he leave Priscilla here that long? But how could he transport her without the wagon? She wasn't strong enough to ride alone. He could have her ride in front of him, but how long would his horse be able to withstand the extra weight before growing too weary?

"I'm sorry, Doc." McLeod's eyes radiated regret. "We've got about two hundred fifty miles to go to Fort Walla Walla. We can't jeopardize the safety of the whole group for one person."

Eli didn't dare look at Priscilla. Even if he figured out a way to take her, she'd still slow them down, and he'd end up putting everyone in danger, including her. He rubbed a hand across his mouth and chin. "I'm gonna need some time to think on all this—"

"I don't need time." Priscilla's voice rang clear and decisive in the small room. "I've already made up my mind. I'm going to stay at Snake Fort."

Chapter
24

I'm staying." Priscilla folded her hands in her lap.

"Let's not rush into a decision." Eli shoved away from the wall. "Listen, everybody. Give me and Priscilla a few minutes to talk this through."

She leaned her head back against the cool adobe wall and closed her eyes. She'd made up her mind. And now her heart ached as much as her tired head.

Within a few moments, everyone left the room. It grew so quiet she began to wonder if Eli had departed with them. But then his boots clunked across the floor, the stool scraped next to the bed, and he gave a long sigh as he lowered himself.

She waited for him to say something—anything. But he sat silently.

When she opened her eyes, she saw that he'd taken off his

hat, rested his elbows on his knees, and buried his face in his hands.

Her heart pinched. Was this decision hard for him? She would have guessed that he'd rejoice over the opportunity to be rid of her, especially now that she was slowing him down so much.

His scraggly hair fell across his forehead, and she wanted to smooth it back, to tell him she finally understood, and that everything would be all right. God's call upon him was strong. She'd witnessed his love for the natives, his heartbreak over losing John, his skill in doctoring people, and his determination in leading them. He wasn't perfect, but he was *the perfect man* for the job of starting the mission in the West.

"You must go on without me," she said softly. "You have to make it all the way. The Indians need you. Need your doctoring. Need the gospel. Besides, you can build the house you told me about. And then in the spring, everything will be ready for my coming."

He lifted his head, revealing the turbulent storm raging inside him.

"I don't want to be the cause of your failure to fulfill your dreams and plans. I want you to make it and to do all that God has called you to do."

He held her gaze for a long moment, as if trying to peer into her soul and test the truth of her words.

"I can wait here." She tentatively reached her fingers toward the hair hanging above his eyes. "This mission was your dream. You've worked so hard to accomplish it. And I want you to succeed." She brushed her fingers through his strands and tried to push aside her doubts—doubts about her own calling and purpose.

When she eventually made it over the Blue Mountains in the

spring, if Eli decided to send her home, God could still use her *anywhere*. Wasn't that what she'd told herself so many months ago when she'd made the decision to come?

"I swore to protect you, and if I leave you here . . ." He groaned and reached for her hand with both of his. He cupped her fingers against his cheek and buried his face again, this time against her hand.

The scruff of his unshaven skin tickled her palm, and the warmth of his breath caressed the pulse in her wrist. Her heart squeezed with the sudden knowledge of how much she would miss him, how much she wanted to be with him.

"Oh, Priscilla," he whispered, sliding her hand to his mouth and pressing his lips into the soft spot in the middle of her palm.

The heat of his touch shimmied over her skin, making her suddenly hot with the longing for him to press his lips somewhere else instead.

But with a growl, he let go of her and pushed away from the bed. He stood and the stool hit the floor with a clatter. "You're coming with me." He towered over her.

Her heart stopped beating.

"I won't leave you behind." His expression hardened. "We've come this far, and we're not giving up now."

She couldn't breathe.

He spun away and stalked to the door. "I don't care what anyone else says. You're coming with me. And that's all I'm going to say about it."

⟡

"Time to march!" McLeod's voice came from the head of the caravan the next morning.

Against the outer stockade wall, Priscilla leaned against Mabel, hardly able to hold herself upright.

325

The early morning air had only a hint of coolness that would evaporate once the scorching August sun rose higher.

Eli strapped a bundle to the back of one of the mules.

She glanced to the other animals and the mounds piled upon each of them, and her heart lurched. How would she travel without the wagon? And where was her trunk?

Mr. Kay strode through the stockade gate and approached them. "You don't mean to leave without saying good-bye, do you?"

"Oh, Mr. Kay," Mabel said, "we can't thank you enough for your gracious hospitality."

"It's been my great pleasure."

Out of the corner of her eye, she could see Eli crossing toward them.

"If you change your mind, you are always welcome here," Mr. Kay said. "It would be an absolute delight to have you stay with us as long as you need."

"Thank you," Priscilla murmured. "You're too kind." Should she insist on staying? Eli had said he'd wanted her to go. But how could she go, knowing she would slow the group down and quite possibly put them in danger?

"Are you ready?" Eli asked as he reached her side.

She hesitated.

Mr. Kay straightened the brim of his hat. "I was just urging Mrs. Ernest to stay here at the fort until she is stronger."

"Perhaps it's for the best. . . ." Priscilla said weakly.

"I was thinking you could try riding your horse for a while. Until you get tired." Eli reached for her hand and tucked it into the crook of his arm. "We'll get along all right."

Did he mean it?

She looked deep into his eyes. The blue was clear and true all the way to the bottom of his heart.

"When you get tired, you can ride with me."

"We'll all help you, Sister Ernest," Mabel added.

The braying of the animals and the calls of McLeod's trappers floated around her.

She swallowed the protest she knew she should utter and allowed Eli to lead her toward her horse.

"And where is my trunk?" she asked as he assisted her into her saddle.

For a long moment he didn't move. Then finally he shifted his gaze to their abandoned wagon, perched at an angle in the dry grass. Her trunk sat next to it, open and empty.

"Then we must leave my trunk here?" she asked, her voice wobbling.

"I packed your wearing apparel, writing desk, and other personal items in a bundle—"

"I had hoped we could find a way to transport it."

"We can't carry it any further."

"But it belonged to my sister." Her chest constricted. "I hate to discard something I treasure like it's a piece of garbage."

"At this point, there are other things that are more critical to our survival—like food." His shoulders slumped. "I'm sorry, Priscilla. This is as far as it's coming."

Quick tears pooled in her eyes, and she shifted in her saddle so she didn't have to look at him. He cleared his throat as if he would say something more. But then he gave a soft sigh and left her alone.

Through blurry eyes, she glanced to the deserted chest. The spiraling pattern of brass dots stared back at her, dull from the dust of their travel.

It was silly, she knew, to get so sad over a trunk. But she hadn't been able to bring much from home in the first place. And now she was losing the little she had, the last connection to her family and home.

Losing David had been hard enough. And then John. And now this too?

Ahead of her, Henry helped Mabel onto her horse. He situated her carefully, as if she would break, his attention fixed upon her rounded belly.

If only Priscilla had the hope of having a family of her own, maybe it wouldn't hurt so much to sever the last ties to the family she'd left behind.

Priscilla shifted to face the Indian tepees scattered around the stockade and willed her eyes to hold back the tears that threatened to spill. All the while she reminded herself that following God's calling wasn't supposed to be easy. In fact, it was turning out to be excruciatingly difficult.

She tried to hold her head high, but by midmorning she could hardly keep from sliding off her horse in exhaustion. When they stopped beside the Snake River to prepare for the crossing, she was beyond ready for a break.

Among the rushes, they discovered a canoe made of sticks and willows that the local Indians used for fishing. She squeezed into it next to Mabel. Richard, on horseback, towed them over with ropes attached to the canoe. With his somber face and stooped shoulders, she could only guess how much he was missing his brother.

After all the river crossings they'd made, Priscilla had shed her fear of the water. But relief overwhelmed her when they made it to the other side and she was finally able to lower herself into the shade of a boulder and lean her head back.

Mabel plopped down next to her. "Our bundles will all be wet after this crossing."

Priscilla couldn't find the strength to care or the ability to offer a word of comfort to Richard before he plunged into the river to collect the cows to drive them across next. Henry and

Eli had finished tying their goods to the tallest horses and had waded in.

"I suppose it was a good thing I had to leave most of my books behind at the fort," Mabel said, her voice wistful. "They've been wet one too many times. I'm sure this crossing would have been their ruination."

Priscilla closed her eyes against the thought of her trunk, discarded and alone, left for the ravaging of the Indians.

"Dr. Ernest tried to secure your trunk on the back of one of the mules," Mabel said, as if reading her mind.

Priscilla sat up and stared at Eli. "He did?" With his battered hat pulled low, he drove his horse and the mules into the rushing water.

"I've never seen him so frustrated," Mabel continued. "He was determined to bring it along, but he couldn't get it strapped tightly enough, and Mr. McLeod insisted he leave it with the wagon."

The angry snorting and braying of the mules rose above the rushing of the water. Eli rode behind them, driving them with the flick of his whip. Priscilla's heart gave a funny dip.

"You're blessed," Mabel said. "Dr. Ernest made arrangements with Mr. Kay to keep the trunk until he could come back for it."

"He never made mention of it to me."

"I heard him speaking to Mr. Kay about it before we left."

Her heart dipped again, this time deeper. She couldn't fault him for his kindness to her.

Priscilla watched Eli's shirt strain across his shoulders and noticed the gaping hole at one of the shoulder seams. Perhaps she should offer to mend it for him after they made camp.

At the tickle upon the back of her neck, she scratched her skin, only to find two fleas on her hand. A shiver of disgust shimmied up her back.

"Ouch!" Mabel slapped at her ear.

Priscilla glanced at her lap and recoiled. Thousands of black dots were swarming over her skirt. They skittered into the folds of the linen and made haste for the bare flesh of her hands and wrists.

She jumped to her feet and screamed. Frantic, she brushed at the fleas. They clung to her and laid siege to her neck and ears.

Mabel was on her feet beating her dress and stomping like an Indian woman doing a war dance.

Priscilla screamed again and this time couldn't stop. She slapped at her neck and her face, but the creatures swarmed over her.

She fought them off her skin, her screams growing shriller. This was it. She was going to die, devoured by fleas.

"What's wrong?" Dripping and breathless, Eli stumbled before her.

She couldn't speak.

"Oh! You sat in a colony of fleas." He wiped the water out of his eyes and swatted at the biting insects teeming over her.

He brushed at her skirt and arms and neck.

Eli dragged her toward the river away from the fleas, and Henry did the same with Mabel.

"It's okay," Eli said, trying to soothe her.

Everything around her spun in a dizzying haze. "I'm not suitable for the West." Tears streamed down her cheeks. "Please, just take me back to Snake Fort. I don't want to go on."

She was so tired, and her heart couldn't hold another disappointment. It was too full of pain for one more thing. Why would God allow her to suffer more, after everything she'd already borne?

Eli brushed as fast as he could. "We'll make it, Priscilla. Just wait and see." His breath was ragged.

She shook her head. Surely she'd been mistaken to think God had wanted her to make the trip. And Eli had warned her, tried to tell her a lady like her wouldn't survive. "You were right all along. I'm too weak. I'm not made for this."

"No. Don't say that." His hands smoothed over her neck and ears.

"I shouldn't have come." She beat against her skirt. "And now I just want to go home. If I ever make it to Oregon Country, you can put me on the first ship. You can give me an annulment. And I won't care."

Her world unraveled before her, and she couldn't stop herself from spinning out of control. She knew she was making a scene in front of everyone, especially in front of Henry and Mabel. She wasn't the gracious, proper lady she was supposed to be. But at that moment, she couldn't find the reserves to care.

Even after the men rushed to set up the tent so that Mabel and she could change out of their infested clothes, her broken sobs shook her.

"Oh, my dear Sister Ernest." Inside the privacy of the tent, Mabel reached for her, and Priscilla sagged against her.

"I've made a mistake. I don't know why I ever thought God was calling me to be a missionary," she cried softly against Mabel's shoulder. "I've been so foolish to think that I could ever withstand the rigors. I'm too weak. Too spoiled. Too selfish."

Mabel patted her back. "Hush. Don't say such things."

"If only I were more like you."

"And here I've been wishing I were more like you."

"You have?" Priscilla pulled back and wiped at the tears on her cheek.

"I was jealous of how strong you were during those early days of our travel when I was so weak and sick."

"But look at me now. . . ."

"You're beautiful and charming, and everyone loves you—"

"Not everyone."

"Yes, everyone." Mabel's smile faltered. "Even my own husband can't help it, though I know he tries."

Priscilla flushed.

"None of us are perfect missionaries, Sister Ernest," Mabel continued softly. "We will all falter at one time or another. Fortunately, perfection is not one of God's requirements."

Priscilla was ashamed to think she'd once believed she'd been the perfect missionary candidate. She'd thought so highly of her piety, commitment, youth, and education. But out here in the harsh wilderness, none of that mattered. The harshness of the trip had stripped away the façade and let her see the true condition of her heart—the selfishness, the self-pity, and the pride that had made a home there.

"If we're all flawed," she said, "then that must mean there are so few of us that God can truly use for service to Him."

"On the contrary," Mabel replied, slapping at another flea on her clean dress. "God often chooses the weak in the eyes of this world."

Priscilla rubbed her fingers over the red swollen bites on her hand. "I was wrong to think He would choose me."

"But, Sister Ernest," Mabel protested, "He's given you a compassionate heart for the Indian children. From early on you loved John and Richard—and David."

"But John's dead." The ache in Priscilla's heart pushed fresh tears into her eyes. "And David—" Her voice cracked. "Who knows where he is and whether he's safe and loved. . . ."

"God will surely have many more children for you to love. And yes, you'll have your own someday too. Eli will come around eventually. I'm sure of it."

"No. We won't ever have any children." The words poured

out before she could stop them, flowing hard and fast like her tears. "He made it clear that he didn't want to change the nature of our relationship. Besides—" She choked.

Mabel rubbed a hand over Priscilla's tangled hair.

"I can't—I won't ever be able to have my own baby."

The kind woman's eyebrows furrowed, as if she were trying to make sense of Priscilla's heartache. It took a moment before understanding dawned in Mabel's eyes. "Oh, my dear, dear friend."

"The doctors all said the same thing." Priscilla's throat squeezed closed.

Mabel grabbed Priscilla into a fierce embrace. "Oh, my sweet, dear Priscilla. I'm so sorry" came the agonized whisper.

At that, Priscilla fell against Mabel, buried her face into the woman's shoulder, and sobbed out all the pain that had lingered in her heart. She was surprised to hear Mabel's sobs as heartbroken as her own. And she was surprised at how good it felt to cry with someone, to finally give voice to the secret she'd kept bottled up for so many years.

Finally, their sobs turned to sniffling. Mabel pulled back to wipe her eyes on her sleeve. "Let's not forget the words of that wonderful hymn 'O God Our Help in Ages Past.'"

Priscilla nodded and wiped at her own wet cheeks.

"God doesn't expect us to be perfect women or perfect missionaries. Rather, He wants us to learn to lean upon Him more, to let Him be our help during those stormy blasts."

Priscilla whispered the last lines of the song. "'Be thou our guard while troubles last.'"

"Yes, dear. I'm sure we'll have many more troubles in the days to come. And we'll question whether we have the strength to endure." There was no pity in Mabel's eyes, only hope and friendship. "But we can't give up. Please don't give up."

"Okay, let's have a look at your hands first." Eli knelt in front of her with the smoke of the campfire wafting around them. They'd had to travel a distance from the river before they were out of the flea-infested area. All of them had been bitten, but the women had suffered the worst.

"I'll be fine." She folded her hands in her lap and stared past him at the low flames of the fire, where he'd set the water to boil for coffee.

Her eyes glazed with exhaustion, and the paleness of her skin made the dark crescents under her eyes shimmer like bruises.

He sat back on his heels. Helplessness weighed heavy upon his heart. "Please. Let me treat your bites."

"I don't want to be any more of a burden to you than I already am."

"You're not a burden to me."

Her gaze flickered to him and demanded the truth. "You know I've been nothing but an inconvenience to you this entire trip."

Had she really been more of an inconvenience than any other woman would've been, or had he just been unfair to her? "I know I've said things—that I haven't given you the chance you deserved. . . ."

"Well, you were right—"

"No, I wasn't. You've held up just as well, if not better, than Mabel."

She started to speak but then stopped and cocked her head.

He sat forward again and took her hands. "You're a strong woman, Priscilla. Much stronger than I thought you'd be."

She studied his face.

And when he turned her hand over and examined the swollen red lumps where the fleas had bitten her, she didn't resist.

"They must have liked your blood." The spots covered her wrists and the backs of her hands, and she had several on her face and neck.

He dipped a strip of clean rag into the pail of icy water he'd collected from the nearby stream. "I'm going to wash the bites with cold soapy water. Then I'll apply lavender oil."

She sucked in a sharp breath when he dabbed her wrist with the frigid water.

"The coldness will help reduce the swelling."

He washed carefully, trying not to irritate the skin any further. Frustration nagged him. Her cries had pierced his heart again and again. When she'd told him she wanted him to take her back to Snake Fort and that she wanted to go home, he'd been surprised by the vehemence that had swelled in his chest against the idea.

What if she really did decide to leave? He'd always said he wouldn't hesitate to send her home and give her an annulment. But when he'd heard *her* say the words—when *she'd* been the one to tell him to put her on the first ship and give her the annulment, every organ inside his body had stopped working in protest.

How could he ever let her go?

"The bites will be extremely itchy, but try not to scratch them."

"They already itch."

He slipped open the button at the wrist of her sleeve and pushed up the material, gliding his fingers along the inside of her arm.

She gasped.

"I'm checking for further bites."

"But this isn't modest." She glanced around the camp.

Richard was the only one watching them. His dark eyes narrowed on him, almost as if the boy were angry with him.

335

"Here's another bite." Eli dabbed at one in the crook of her arm. Then he pushed the sleeve higher.

"Please, Eli," she whispered. "If you must unclothe me in this manner, I would prefer privacy." Her cheeks were flushed, and her eyes had taken on a renewed spark—the kind of spark he liked there but thought he'd extinguished.

With the tips of his fingers he traced the path of a vein down to her wrist. "If you'd like me to unclothe you in private, I can oblige."

She gave a soft gasp. "I didn't say I wanted you to—"

"But you're right. It would be more helpful in my examination."

"You've misunderstood me." Her fingers trembled. "I only meant to say that if you must touch me—"

"You mean like this?" He glided his fingers back up her arm.

"Yes—I mean no—"

"What about like this?" He lowered his mouth to the delicate spot just below her wrist. He took a deep breath of her soft sweet skin, then exhaled, letting his breath fan over her. He followed with his lips, pressing them against her thudding pulse.

Longing swelled within his chest—the desire to start over with Priscilla and try to get things right between them. He kissed a path to the ring on her finger—the ring he'd given, one that should have symbolized his devotion to her but hadn't.

Could he change that? Did he dare?

Her arm quivered. Then she jerked her hand away and pushed her sleeve back into place.

"Please don't toy with me." Her eyes sparkled with unshed tears, but beneath them was something akin to desire.

"I'm not toying with you," he said softly. He reached for her hand again, and this time she hid it in the folds of her skirt.

The look in her eyes said she didn't believe him.

"I know I've been an idiot, and I haven't always treated you the way you deserve. But I want to try to do better."

Her eyes widened, but she didn't say anything. An unspoken question filled the space between them. Did he want her *in plenty and in want, in joy and in sorrow, in sickness and in health, as long as they both shall live?* Or did he still plan to turn his back on their marriage if the danger became too threatening?

Old fears lingered in the corners of his mind and whispered that he couldn't promise her anything. But something in his heart shouted at him, forcing him to face the truth: He couldn't begin to imagine his life without her in it.

Chapter
25

POWDER RIVER VALLEY

Priscilla refused to utter one word of complaint, but inwardly she didn't know how she could possibly make it another day.

Even though it was entirely unladylike, she pulled her knees up to her chest and rested her head against them. Why worry about etiquette when she no longer looked or felt like a lady? Gone were her smooth, unblemished skin and her soft complexion. Her hands were stained with grime and her fingernails crusted with grit. And her once lovely clothes were tattered and threadbare.

With the lingering effects of the cholera, weariness was her constant companion. And even though she was pushing herself beyond endurance every day, she was still slowing the group down.

Although neither Eli nor McLeod said anything, she could see the lines that furrowed their foreheads every time they looked into the distance to the barely visible tips of the Blue Mountains.

A shadow fell across her.

"I've made a shelter for you," Eli said, holding out his hand to her.

They'd made their noonday break in the open plain, and there weren't any trees—not even a single low willow like they occasionally found.

She looked up at him from her ungracious heap on the ground, the place she'd dropped after dismounting. She didn't care that the high burning sun beat down on her and was instead grateful for a break from the constant jarring.

"Come."

Shielding her eyes from the glare of the sun, she searched his face for the irritation, for the regret she was sure he couldn't hide. But instead his eyes only radiated gentle concern.

She allowed him to pull her to her feet and lead her to a strange makeshift shelter.

"What do you think?" He stood back and watched her reaction.

He'd draped their saddle blankets over sticks he'd driven into the earth like tent poles. Underneath, he'd spread a buffalo calfskin blanket. It covered the ground and their saddles.

He crawled into the shelter and leaned his back against one of the saddles, crossing his arms behind his head. "Care to join me?" He grinned up at her.

She hesitated.

"I promise I won't ravish you."

She wasn't worried about *his* ravishing. She was worried about *herself.* After already failing once to keep their relationship businesslike, she couldn't fail again. And it was altogether too hard to keep her distance under the ordinary circumstances, much less sitting right next to him.

He patted the spot next to him. "You need to get out of the sun and rest."

Her legs trembled with the effort to stand.

He reached for her hand and tugged her, leaving her little choice but to duck under the blanket—at least that's what she told herself. She situated herself against her saddle, making sure she left plenty of space between her and Eli. Running Feet's knife lay hard against her thigh, more of a nuisance than necessity.

"Now, isn't this nice?" Eli asked.

"Yes," she admitted, letting the coolness of the shade soothe her.

"I know it's always nice to sit next to me, but I was asking about the shade." His voice hinted at playfulness. "Isn't that nice too?"

She couldn't keep from smiling, grateful he wasn't angry with her, as he very well should have been for slowing them down so much.

"I love seeing you smile," he said softly.

Her heartbeat sputtered to life.

"I want to make you smile more." He hesitated. "And I know I haven't given you much reason to do so, but I'd like to change that."

She stared at her wrists, at the fleabites that had turned into small blisters. "I've had a hard time wanting to smile lately." She missed David more than she'd ever imagined she would. Sometimes his "mama" echoed through her heart and made her arms ache to hold him.

"I'm not an expert at smiling," he said. "I didn't grow up in a home with much of anything but angry words."

"I can't remember much smiling or laughter in my home either."

"At least you had parents who loved you."

"And yours didn't?" She held her breath and waited for him to get angry at her probing question and stomp away.

He didn't say anything.

She peeked at him. He was staring off in the distance.

"There was once a time when I think my ma might have loved me. . . ."

His ma. Priscilla had met her only once, and she'd been colder than a New York winter. Priscilla couldn't imagine him receiving love from such a woman.

"But everything changed . . . the day my pa . . ." The muscles in Eli's jaw flexed.

Priscilla had the urge to reach for his hand, to take it between hers and offer him the love he'd missed growing up.

"My pa had a hankering for strong drink." Eli's voice was forced. "He had his own distillery, and when he wasn't drinking or passed out on the bed from too much whiskey, he was out back making more."

He stopped. The nightmare in the depths of his eyes darkened them to midnight blue.

"My ma hired herself out to some of the rich folk as a laundress. I was supposed to stay home and help Pa in the distillery. But whenever she left for work, I snuck away to the swimming hole or any other place I could find. I hated helping Pa make the drink that only served to take him away from us."

He blew out a deep sigh and continued. "I always returned home before Ma could catch me. But the last time—when I rounded the bend, I smelled the smoke before I saw it curling up from the roof. At first I didn't understand what was happening. But when I got to the house and looked in, I realized Pa had passed out on the bed, and he'd left his pipe burning. The house was on fire."

Priscilla sucked in a breath, unable to imagine the torment Eli must have experienced at that moment.

"Somehow in his drunkenness he'd let the latch of the door fall, and I couldn't get to him. I stood outside the window and screamed and banged on the glass. Finally, I smashed my fists through it, crawled through the shards, cut up my face, hands, and legs. . . . By the time I got to him, the smoke had already killed him."

"Oh, Eli." An ache formed in her throat. She reached for his scarred hands.

For an instant he pulled away, but then he stopped.

She laced her fingers through his. When she met his gaze, the sharp pain there radiated through her chest and brought tears to her eyes.

"My ma never stopped blaming me for his death," he whispered hoarsely.

"But it wasn't your fault. If he hadn't gotten drunk . . . If he had been more responsible with his pipe . . ."

"But I wasn't there. And I should have been."

She grazed her fingers across the raised skin of his scars, shuddering at the picture of his lacerated bloody flesh. "Your mother has no right to hold you responsible for your father's foolishness."

"I hold myself responsible."

She shifted to face him, lifted one of his hands, and grazed her lips along the long white lines.

His breath hitched.

"I can't imagine the pain and fear you must have experienced." She released his hand and traced the scar along his cheek. "But you cannot take responsibility for everyone and everything."

He raised his fingers to her cheek and touched the tears she hadn't realized had spilled over.

"You aren't God," she whispered. "You're human. And humans fail."

In the shadows of their makeshift shelter, his face was only inches from hers. "I vowed that I wouldn't fail like that again."

She swept his hair away from his neck, the tenderness of his vulnerability giving her boldness. "We all make mistakes."

"I'm realizing that I'm pretty good at making them." His gaze hung on to hers and wouldn't let go. "I've made plenty of mistakes with us, haven't I?"

The hurt of the past weeks rushed over her, but so did all of the memories of the ways Eli had cared for her—how he'd labored day and night to save her, how he'd tried to strap her trunk onto the mule, how he'd wanted to bring her anyway, even though he'd had the perfect chance to leave her behind. She swallowed the sudden lump and dipped her head, afraid to say what was in her heart and aching for him to reveal what was in his.

His fingers went to her chin, and he forced her head back up. "I'm sorry, Priscilla. Sorry for hurting you." His voice cracked. "I wish I could take back the things I said, especially for embarrassing you in front of everybody. Squire baited me, and I fell into his trap. I shouldn't have said anything."

As mortified as she'd been at the time, deep inside she knew the others would have discovered their predicament eventually, the same way Henry had. She would have spared herself the heartache had she just lived openly and honestly from the start—as Eli had suggested.

Why had it been so important to keep everything private? Now that she'd shared her infertility with Mabel, she found herself wealthier for having done so. She drank in Mabel's encouragement and understanding. She couldn't help but wonder what it would have been like if she and her family had chosen to share the burden with others right from the start—how different things might have been.

"And I'm sorry for not standing up to Squire and fighting for David."

The ache in her chest swelled.

"I don't know if it would have made any difference, but I could have tried harder. I know how important the baby was to you."

If she spoke she knew she'd sob.

"Do you think you can ever forgive me?"

Could she? She hesitated. What more could Eli have done to stop Squire? He would have only gotten himself killed.

Suddenly, the blanket of their shelter caved in upon their heads.

The scratchy wool fell against her face, and she gave a startled cry.

Eli scrambled to untangle them from the smothering cover. It took him only an instant to pull the blanket off, leaving them blinking in the bright sunshine.

He sat up and glanced around.

The only one nearby was Richard, and he was leaning against his horse, brushing it with long, smooth strokes.

When Eli raised his brow at the boy, Richard only glared back at them, his face sullen.

"I don't understand what's gotten into him lately," Eli murmured.

The gleam in Richard's eyes told her he'd purposefully kicked the shelter in on them.

"I've tried talking with him," Eli said, "but he won't say much."

"He's still grieving over John. Maybe I should talk with him."

"Maybe you should," Eli joked, "before he decides to kill me."

McLeod had left them earlier in the morning to hunt. They'd expected him to return during their nooning. Eli paced, his anxiety escalating with each wasted minute.

When McLeod and a few of his trappers finally rode into camp at three o'clock, loaded with over twenty ducks they'd shot, Eli took one look at the men and the resigned looks on their faces, and his heart sank with dread.

"Ma'am." McLeod dismounted in front of Priscilla and dropped half of the fowl at her feet. "For you."

"Thank you, Mr. McLeod. You're too kind," she said. Then she turned her wide kitten eyes upon Eli. "Roasted duck. It will be a taste of home, won't it?"

He tried to hide the anxiousness from his face and voice. "After the maggoty pemmican, I'd say it'll be more like a taste of heaven."

She gave a mock gasp and her eyes danced with laughter. "Why, Dr. Ernest, I thought pemmican was your favorite food."

With a slow grin, he let his gaze linger on her lips. "I think you'll find that I'm a man with a very big appetite."

"In that case, I'll have Mabel help me find some camas to cook with the duck." She turned away, but not before he caught sight of a rosy blush blooming in her cheeks.

They'd begun to find the camas root in abundance. It was a staple food of the Nez Perce. Even though it resembled an onion in shape and color, when cooked it was sweet, like a fig.

"Doc, my men are getting anxious to reach Walla Walla," McLeod said after Priscilla went to find Mabel. His eyes took on a seriousness that sent a shiver of trepidation through Eli.

"We're all tired of the trail."

McLeod nodded to his horses and mules. "Your animals are worn out. And they're slowing us down."

Two of his mules and one of the horses had almost entirely given out. The terrain was rough on them and the packs on their backs heavy. "Maybe I can lighten their loads."

McLeod glanced at Priscilla and Mabel. "It's not just the animals."

Eli swallowed hard. They'd gone slower for the women too. Both tired easily, Mabel from her ever-growing pregnancy and Priscilla still weak from the cholera. "Maybe we can cut back on the breaks we take."

McLeod met his gaze head on. "I've already made my decision. We're splitting up."

Eli's heart fell to the bottom of his ribcage.

"I'm leaving my most trustworthy man to guide you the rest of the way. Then you can go as slowly as you need."

"But what about our safety? Wouldn't we be safer with the large group?"

"The Indians hereabout are friendly enough—mostly Cayuse and Nez Perce. You shouldn't have any trouble with them."

Eli's gut roiled. "I don't like it, McLeod. We've come this far. What's a few more days?"

"My men and I could have been there by now, and they're grumbling about it."

Eli poked the tip of his boot into one of the lifeless fowl. He didn't have a right to demand anything more of McLeod. The man had already done more for them than he could ever repay.

Pressing his lips together, Eli stared into the distance to the Blue Mountains. With each passing day, they didn't seem to move any closer.

And with each passing day, the dangers grew more significant. September would soon be upon them, along with cooler temperatures, especially once they started ascending to the higher elevations. They needed to make the pass through the mountains soon, before the temperatures dropped too low and the first significant snow fell.

Discouragement twisted through Eli. They had so little time left to make it to Walla Walla.

"Be honest with me, McLeod. If I keep going with the women, will we make it?"

"I've already pushed you as fast as you can go." McLeod's voice was laced with regret. "If you try to go any faster, you'll chance them dropping from exhaustion or illness."

Eli nodded. Even though Priscilla had grown stronger, she was still much too weak to push harder.

"But if you continue at your current pace, barring no further problems—and if the snow holds off—you'll be on track to reach Fort Walla Walla in less than two weeks."

"Two weeks?" Eli almost groaned. Two weeks was too long. How would they ever make it in time?

"You might be safer heading back to Snake Fort." McLeod's overgrown eyebrows framed grave eyes. "Mr. Kay might not have enough supplies to feed you through the winter, but at least you'd have a better chance of surviving there than if you got stuck in the mountains."

Eli blew out a long breath.

He glanced at Priscilla, to the graceful outline of her body as she bent over a nearby camas plant. She was thinner than when they'd started months ago but was just as beautiful. And if he'd thought she was beautiful on the outside, he'd learned she was even more so on the inside.

She'd come thousands of miles, had survived river crossings, treacherous trappers, poor food rations, and even cholera. And she'd borne it better than any lady ever could. If she could survive the dangerous trip, wouldn't she be able to survive life in the West?

And now that they'd made it this far together, how could he ever make her go home?

Agony pounded through his head.

All he knew was that he didn't want to go one step forward without her, even if it meant that he'd have to go back to Snake Fort and wait out the winter there. With her.

They'd be together, and suddenly that was more important than anything else.

He nodded at McLeod. "We'll go as far and do as much as we can. And we'll have to trust the Almighty for the rest."

They rode with McLeod and his men to the Lone Tree in the valley of the Powder River, where they dismounted to make their evening camp. Then with slumped shoulders, they watched the trappers ride on without them.

A breeze lifted the damp strands of hair from Eli's neck. He took off his hat and let the wind cool his forehead too.

Priscilla edged next to him. For a long moment she didn't say anything as the horses and men disappeared over the dusty horizon with the thin sinews of the sunset bleeding across the sky.

"This is my fault, isn't it?" Her voice was quiet and resigned.

Keen disappointment rammed through every blood cell. Everything he'd worked so hard to accomplish over the past year was riding away into the distance.

She sighed and stepped away from him. "I'm sorry, Eli. I should have stayed at Snake Fort—"

"No." He grabbed her arm and dragged her against his chest.

She fell against him with a gasp, her body stiff.

His arms circled her waist and pinned her in place so that even if she'd tried to escape from him she couldn't.

"We're staying together." His whisper was harsh.

The silky loose strands of her hair blew against his lips. He released a long breath and softened his voice. "Wherever that might be, I want us to be together."

Her body melted against him. Then her arms snaked around his middle, and she rested her cheek against his chest.

His heart filled with something strange and new. Boldly, he tugged her bonnet off and let it hang down her back.

He let his lips caress the soft gold of her hair. Then with a sigh, he rested his chin on her head, tightened his hold, and stared at the horizon, praying he would have enough courage to do the right thing when the time came.

Chapter
26

Eli didn't have to say anything for Priscilla to understand the gravity of their situation. His silence spoke loudly enough.

For days they'd been traveling gradually higher, always trying to go faster, but she knew it wasn't fast enough.

Finally the Blue Mountain Range loomed before them, rising up out of the earth like a wall they had to climb—the last barrier between them and their new home.

"Stay close together," Eli shouted as they began their ascent. He glanced around at the dark shadows of the forest warily.

But Priscilla eyed the range with budding hope.

The slopes were covered with spruce and ponderosa pine. The coolness of their shade was a pleasant change from the days traveling through the dry, desertlike terrain they'd traversed for the past week. The chattering songs of the familiar chickadees and jays echoed through the woods and reminded her of the hills around Allegany County.

Surely the mountain wouldn't give them trouble, not when it beckoned them with its beauty.

She longed to linger and gather a handful of the wild flowers, especially the bright bluish purple lupines. But Eli urged them steadily upward. And she was determined she wouldn't slow them down any more than she already had.

Eli hadn't complained, not even one grumble. But the tenseness of his shoulders testified to the load of responsibility he'd placed upon himself.

It took them most of the day to reach the summit of the first peak. Priscilla wanted to cheer as her horse stumbled to the narrow level table.

But the victory was short-lived. A length of mountain sloped downward before them—the steepest she'd ever seen. The air had grown noticeably cooler, and she shivered, pulling her shawl tighter. The sun had disappeared behind clouds that seemed altogether too close.

"I don't think I can do this," she said when Eli patted the head of her horse. Even the beast was balking, snorting in fright at the sight of the rocky climb down.

"I'll be leading the horses and mules right ahead of you." Eli held out a handful of lupines. "Maybe these will help."

The sudden smile in her heart made its way to her lips. "How did you know I'd been longing for a breath of them?"

"Don't you know I have eyes in the back of my head?"

She reached for the flowers, letting her fingers linger against his. The gentleness of his touch always went straight to her heart and stole her breath away. She lifted the bright bouquet to her face and buried her nose in the fresh wild beauty, drawing in the sweet aroma.

"Thank you," she murmured.

When she lifted her gaze to his, the window to his soul was open wide, and his desire for her was as clear as the water of the nearby mountain creek.

"You know I'll expect a proper thank-you later."

Her cheeks flushed. His eyes sent her a message, the kind of message that said he would lift her off her horse and crush her in his arms and kiss her if he could.

She nibbled her lip. And bittersweet longing welled up within her. She'd tasted his kisses and couldn't deny her hunger for more of them. But what could possibly come of it?

He might have told her he wanted them to stay together, but that didn't mean he was ready to change their agreement. He'd continued to keep their relationship platonic, just as he'd always done.

Was she delusional to think he could want to change their arrangement now, after all the months of his resistance?

"Tonight, when we make camp, you can thank me." He tossed her a grin and left her reeling with confusion and desire.

They made their way down the cliff with painstakingly slow steps, zigzagging all the way. The men went by foot and led the animals, while she and Mabel clung to their saddles with dread.

By the time they made it to the bottom, darkness had settled in. They could hardly see to make camp. The temperature had dropped, and after Priscilla slid from her horse in exhaustion, all she could do was snuggle next to Mabel for warmth. She knew Eli wouldn't be able to come for his thank-you—if he'd even been serious about it in the first place.

Priscilla slept fitfully, the calls of wild animals somewhere in the distance echoing through the thin air.

When they awoke in the morning, a light dusting of snow covered the ground. She could hardly make her stiff limbs work to climb back onto her horse. She only needed one look at Eli's ragged expression to know he hadn't slept at all.

An icy mixture of rain and snow began to fall as they started up a steeper and more dreadful climb. If McLeod's man hadn't been leading them, she would have guessed that somewhere, somehow, they had made a wrong turn. The rocky route was covered in places with black, broken basalt, and she couldn't imagine God had ever intended it for man or beast.

But they climbed onward, slipping and sliding over the treacherous trail. By evening they reached the highest elevation of the pass. After yet another dinner of cold duck, they traveled along the main divide, searching for water for the animals and a safe camping place.

When the sun dipped beyond the horizon, she gazed with awe at the sunset gloriously displayed between the two distant conical peaks of Mount Hood and Mount St. Helens. Lying before them was the grandeur of the Columbia River Valley, and somewhere in the middle of it all, their new home waited for them—if they could make it out of the mountains alive.

Big flakes of snow began to fall, and she huddled against Mabel. The woman had slipped into a weary slumber the moment they'd laid their bedrolls on the damp ground. But Priscilla couldn't stop from shuddering as she listened to Henry and Eli and their guide argue in hushed tones.

"But what about the snow?" Eli said in hushed tones. "Will we be able to make it down through the snow?"

"We'll have to try," Henry said, "because we can't continue tonight."

"You're sure?" Eli's voice held resignation.

"The descent is too steep to attempt in the darkness. One

misstep would send a mule to the bottom," the guide said. "Even with the snowfall, we'd be safer to wait until first light."

"We must pray," Henry said.

The snow continued to come down, and later through the light of their fire she saw Eli huddled on a boulder at the edge of their camp, his rifle pointed at the shadows of the surrounding cliffs. At the distant shrill cry of a cougar, he readjusted the barrel of his gun.

She wanted to go to him, sit with him, and keep him company through the long hours of his watch. But what if he turned her away? What if she'd only dreamed she'd seen desire in his eyes the other day?

With a sigh, she forced herself to close her eyes and get the sleep she would need to face the daunting descent the next day.

At the first traces of light, they brushed a thick layer of snow from their blankets, packed their mules, and tried to soothe the jitters of their horses.

She longed for Eli to give her a special look, to toss her even the smallest of grins, to assure her they'd be all right. But he'd pulled his hat low and stood with the travel guide, speaking in low, urgent tones.

The snow slowed their steps, and the mules brayed at each slip they made. Ahead of her, Mabel called over her shoulder, "Come on, Sister Ernest."

Priscilla's horse limped through the snow, leaving bloody footprints. The climb had been rough on their animals too. And now, with each jarring step down the mountain, Priscilla sucked in her breath and prayed her horse wouldn't slide off one of the dangerous outcroppings.

Behind her, Henry mumbled to his pack of mules and slapped their hindquarters whenever they started to slide too close to the edge of the trail. Near the front of their caravan, Eli kept his rifle under one arm, continually scanning the rocks.

Suddenly her horse whinnied and jerked to a halt.

She loosened her grip on the reins and flexed her stiff fingers.

A sharp scream, like that of an injured girl, penetrated the morning air.

Before she could regain her hold, the horse reared with a frightened snort. She lost hold of the reins, fell, and hit the ground with a thud that knocked the breath from her. She slid down the snowy slope for several feet before landing in a clump of brush.

For a long moment she sat in stunned silence. Above her, the horse whinnied and tried to gallop. But it stumbled against a rock, and its legs buckled, forcing it to the ground.

Only then did she get a view of the ledge ahead, to the yellow slanted eyes of the cougar fixed upon her. They glowed like hungry flames.

A chill crawled over her skin.

The cougar gave another shrill cry. It laid its ears back and crouched, ready to spring.

She couldn't move, couldn't scream, couldn't breathe. Her eyes locked with the cougar's, and the fire there burned into her.

In the distance, she heard shouts, the roar of Eli's cry from the trail further down the mountainside, the desperation in his voice.

But it was too late. He was too far away to help. The cougar would be upon her long before Eli could climb to the slope where she'd fallen. For once, he wouldn't be able to come to her rescue.

Her fingers fumbled to unsheathe her knife. Even if she could get it out, how would she fend off a wildcat with a weapon she didn't know how to use?

"Oh, God," she whispered past dry lips, "be thou my help during the stormy blast."

The cougar hissed, baring its long sharp incisors.

Where would the beast rip into her first? If she must die at the fangs of a hungry animal, please, God, let her faint before she felt the pain of tearing flesh.

The black-rimmed eyes wouldn't let go of her. The cat gave a flick of its tail and lurched forward.

Only then did she scream. Her body tensed harder than the rocky cliffs. She pinched her eyes closed and waited for the claws and teeth to sink into her.

A gunshot cracked in the air.

For an eternal moment she cowered.

"Priscilla!" Eli's shout rang closer.

She chanced a peek.

The cougar was sprawled near her horse, bright blood spurting from a hole in its chest, leaving a crimson puddle in the snow. Its golden eyes stared lifelessly at her.

A relieved sob pressed into her throat.

Eli scrambled through the snow up the mountainside, fear drawing tight lines across his face. "Are you hurt?"

She shook her head.

"I didn't know the cougar was so close." He finally reached her, and his ragged breath made white puffs in the morning air. "We sighted it last night, but this morning it was gone."

Her body began to tremble uncontrollably.

With one arm, he grabbed her and drew her against his chest. His other hand had a shaky grip on his rifle. "Thank the Almighty," he murmured hoarsely against her cheek.

She wrapped her arms around him and clung to him.

"I thought for sure I'd lost you this time."

"If not for your shot, I'd be dead."

"I didn't shoot. I didn't have time." Frustration punctuated every syllable. "I was too far away."

She pulled back. "Then who—"

He looked over her shoulder.

She craned her neck and caught sight of Henry. He was standing with his feet slightly apart, his rifle still pointed at the cougar, smoke drifting from the barrel.

His gaze met hers, and for the first time since they'd begun the journey, she saw something she hadn't known she craved—his acceptance. The look said he had put their past behind him and had given her the greatest gift he could possibly offer—the chance at having a loving relationship with someone else . . . her husband.

Gratitude swelled through her. Henry could see it in her eyes. He lowered his gun and nodded.

Eli touched the brim of his hat to Henry and looked back at her. "I've been so busy trying to shoulder everything myself, I ignored the possibility that maybe God wants me to share the load."

"It's possible," she said softly.

"I've been working to keep you alive and safe, thinking it was all up to me. It figures the Almighty would use Henry to snatch you out of death's claws."

She laid her head against Eli's chest, wound her arms around him tighter, and squeezed.

He heaved a sigh and pressed a kiss against her forehead.

Priscilla didn't know how they made it down the rest of the slippery slope without injury, but by midafternoon the snow had melted and the air began to warm. When they reached the edge of the forest line, they finally stopped.

Once her feet touched the level ground, she dropped to it and wanted to weep in gratefulness at being off the awful slope.

After the cougar attack, Eli had been forced to shoot her horse. It hadn't been able to get back up—he guessed it had broken its leg, and she'd had to ride his horse. Two of their mules had also fallen during the descent.

What would they do with all their supplies now, and where would she ride once Eli needed his horse?

Mabel groped for her hand. "Remember, God will give us the strength we need. When we are weak, then He is strong."

Oh, that she had Mabel's faith. She squeezed the hand of her friend. "He's given me you. You have been His gift of strength to me."

They shared a smile, and Priscilla whispered a prayer of thankfulness in her heart. Her own strength had faltered many times during the trip. But Mabel was right. In experiencing her weaknesses, she was learning just how much she needed the One who could truly sustain her.

"We're going to make camp for the night here," Eli said from above her.

At the hint of happiness in his voice, Priscilla looked up.

"We did it." His eyes were alight with excitement.

She sat up. "What did we do?"

"We made it through. The worst is behind us."

"Then we're safe?"

"McLeod's man says we can probably make it to Fort Walla Walla in three, maybe four, days."

Relief expanded through her chest. "We're that close?"

He nodded.

"Praise the Lord," Mabel said.

Priscilla smiled. She reached out her hand to him. She knew how important this accomplishment was to him. He'd succeeded in doing something no other man had ever done in the history of their country—he'd brought two women over the long, difficult trail to the West.

"You're an amazing man, Eli Ernest."

"Guess I was wrong from the start," he said softly. "The Almighty's shown me loud and clear that wherever a wagon could go, a woman could go. And even beyond." His eyes filled with an apology that made her heart hum.

"It hasn't been easy, and if not for you—"

"You persevered bravely. You both did." He offered a smile to Mabel too.

Then his fingers gripped Priscilla's, and he tugged. "Come with me." The invitation in his eyes swept over her like warm maple syrup, its sweetness flowing right to her heart.

"I saw some cherries downstream." He hefted her up. "Let's go pick some."

Her heart sped with anticipation.

"You two run along." Mabel gave her a knowing smile. "If anyone asks where you've gone, I'll point them upstream in the opposite direction."

Heat rushed into Priscilla's cheeks.

Eli grinned and pulled her along.

Her weariness evaporated. A surge of energy spread through her limbs, and she strolled beside him, her heart pounding at the thought of being alone with him.

What would he do? What would he say?

He pushed back branches and stepped over logs. Their footsteps crunched among the twigs.

Richard stepped out of the brush and intersected their path. He spread his feet apart and crossed his arms over his chest. Anger turned his boyish face into that of a fierce warrior.

Eli frowned. "What's wrong, Richard?"

The boy's ebony eyes narrowed to slits. "You kill my brother. Now I kill you."

Priscilla shuddered at the venom in his words.

"I didn't kill him. You were there." Anguish transformed

Eli's voice. "You saw that I did everything I possibly could to save John's life."

"You save Mrs. Doc. Why you not save my brother?" Richard shoved Eli's chest.

"I tried to save him."

"You no good medicine man." Richard pushed him again.

"I don't want to fight you, Richard." Eli maneuvered Priscilla until she was well behind him.

"Bad medicine man must die." The boy doubled his fists and threw one at Eli's chin. It connected with a thud.

Priscilla screamed, and Eli stumbled.

He rubbed his chin. "Come on. Don't do this. Don't you think I hated to lose John too? That it tore me up inside? That I wished I could have done more for him?"

The boy jumped at Eli, his fists swinging.

Eli pushed him away. "I refuse to fight you."

But Richard pummeled Eli in the stomach and wouldn't stop. Eli grunted but didn't lift a hand against the boy. His only move was to raise his arms to deflect the blows to his head.

Priscilla screamed again. "Stop, Richard! Please stop!"

Eli stumbled back until he fell into the sharp brush. Richard pounced on top of him.

Why wouldn't Eli fight back? The boy seemed determined to kill Eli, and with the strength of his anger, she didn't want to find out if he was capable of murder or not.

Her hand dropped to her hip, to Running Feet's knife hidden beneath her dress. With trembling fingers, she inched up her skirt, turning her side away from Richard. "Let him go now, Richard!" She'd never wanted to use the knife, never thought she could.

Her fingers groped for the scabbard. "You don't know how much I prayed that God would spare John and take me instead."

"Go back to the camp, Priscilla." Eli's voice was haggard. Blood trickled from a gash on his chin.

"Why won't you defend yourself?" she asked.

"I came to help the Nez Perce." He gasped for a breath. "I know my strength. I refuse to use it to hurt this boy or any of the natives. Not here. Not ever."

Desperation poured over her like the cold water from the nearby stream.

She inched the knife out of its scabbard and hid it in the folds of fabric. If Eli wouldn't help himself, then he left her with no choice but to save him.

"Richard, please, I'm begging you to release Eli," she said, her voice cracking on a sob. "He's not perfect—he can't save everyone, although he tries."

Richard's fist slammed into Eli's mouth, and he fell back against the brush with a grunt. "He let my brother die," the boy shouted.

He pounded again and again. Then the boy slipped his hands around Eli's neck and squeezed.

"Stop." Desperation propelled Priscilla's steps toward the boy. "You know you'll always regret it if you hurt him."

The boy glanced over his shoulder at her, and his eyes wavered with doubt.

The strength of her fear pushed her closer until she swung the knife from behind her back and pointed it at Richard. "Please don't make me use this against you."

His dark eyes widened, and he loosened his hold on Eli's neck.

With a wheezing cough, Eli scrambled to sit up and catch his breath.

Richard's focus flickered to Eli and back to her.

"Eli is a good man. Your people need him." She reached a

hand toward Richard, and her knife wobbled. "And though he won't be able to save every life, he will be able to save many."

Richard shifted.

"Don't you want to give your family, your people, hope?"

He let go of Eli and sat back on his heels.

"I would have died for John if I could have," Eli said hoarsely. "As hard as it is for me to admit this—I can't do everything. I can't save everyone. Only God has that kind of power."

A tear trickled down Richard's cheek.

"And someday," Eli continued, his voice broken, "maybe I'll die in my efforts to save your people. I'm willing to do that. To sacrifice my very life if need be."

Eli's eyes connected with hers, and for the first time, she knew he understood—understood that she was willing to sacrifice her life too. And if they must die for the people they'd come to love, then they would do it together.

She tossed her knife to the ground, reached both arms toward Richard, and gathered him into an embrace.

For a long moment he sobbed against her, releasing the tears he'd held back during the past weeks, venting his grief and anger.

Finally Richard wrenched away from her. "I go to my people now. Tell them my brother dead."

"You cannot go by yourself." Priscilla reached after him. "It's too dangerous."

But Richard was already slipping through the trees away from them.

"Will we see you again?" she called, starting after him.

Eli wrapped his fingers around her wrist and stopped her. "Let him go."

The boy wound through the woods and, without a backward glance, was gone.

Heaviness weighed on Priscilla's heart, and she turned to Eli.

He'd already ripped off part of his sleeve and was pressing it against the slash on his chin. "We still have many things to learn about the natives, their emotions, their customs, their way of life. I'm sure it won't be the last time I get beat up by one of them."

She gingerly touched the rag. The blood was already seeping through the thin linen. "Will I need to give you stitches again?"

His eyes took on a sparkle. "Are you looking for a reason to torture me?"

She gave him a shaky smile. "If I had to sew you back together, I'm not sure who would hurt more, me or you."

He tried to grin but winced. He reached for her hand, lifted it to his lips, and brushed a kiss against her palm. "My brave and beautiful wife."

The softness of his lips and the tenderness of his words sent a ripple of warmth to her belly. And when he tugged her forward, his eyes wide with invitation, she stumbled along behind him, her heartbeat tripping with anticipation.

He led her beside the river until they were well out of sight of the camp.

"I see the cherries," she said. The crimson clusters were like jewels after the past days of eating nothing but cold duck.

She plucked a handful and savored each one slowly. They weren't as sweet as the ones she'd grown up eating, but the juicy tartness was a bite of heaven.

"Welcome to Oregon Country." His eyes shone. "Isn't it beautiful?"

She took a deep breath of the crisp air laden with the scent of pine. In some ways, the woodland was very much the same as any wooded hill she'd explored around Angelica. If only it weren't seven months of wearisome, perilous travel away.

"Do you think you would have been happier going to India?" He picked a cherry and popped it into his mouth.

She stopped. "From all I've learned about myself during this trip, I'm fairly certain I would have ended up being a terrible missionary there too."

"You're not terrible, Priscilla." He took her hands into his. "I'm sorry I led you to believe that you wouldn't make a good missionary—"

"Well, you were right." She slipped her hands out of his and busied herself picking cherries and dropping them into the basket she'd made with her apron. "I'm not really sure what I thought missionary life would be like, but I certainly wasn't prepared for anything I've experienced."

"Maybe you were naïve and unaware of the realities of the calling. But you have a willing heart." He turned her until she had no choice but to face him. "If you could survive the long hard trip here, then I think from hereafter you can handle anything that might come your way."

She couldn't meet his gaze and stared instead at the top button of his shirt.

"What I'm trying to say is that I don't want you to leave—to go home." His fingers caressed her chin and then forced it up so she was helpless to do anything but look into his eyes. "I almost lost you again today, and I don't want to lose you. I want you to stay here in Oregon Country—with me. Always and forever."

Her breath hitched. "What about giving me an annulment and sending me back ho—"

He put a finger on her lips, stopping her words. "The day I married you, I made a covenant to you and to God to be a loving husband in plenty and in want, in joy and in sorrow, in sickness and in health, as long as we both lived. I'm realizing I can't desert you or send you away when things get hard. After making vows to you, you've become just as much a part of God's plan for my life as the mission is."

He moved his fingers from her chin to her cheek and made a soft trail down to her neck.

Her pulse thrummed.

His fingers stilled at the base of her throat. His eyes darkened with something that took her breath away. It was desire, but surely so much more than that. . . .

He untied her bonnet and pushed it back, letting it fall into the brush. Then, before she could protest, he unpinned the tight knot of her hair at the back of her neck.

The heavy strands cascaded down her shoulders and across her chest.

He stepped back, and his gaze swept over her.

Heat rippled through her stomach.

"I've dreamed about doing that—ever since our wedding night."

The heat swirled into her cheeks.

His fingers tentatively touched the curls floating by her ear.

She leaned her head against his hand.

He dug into the thickness, intertwining his fingers as if he couldn't get enough of her. His chest rose up and down. And when he spoke, his voice was hoarse. "I haven't forgotten about the thank-you that you owe me."

"And I haven't forgotten either."

The hand that was buried in her thick hair tipped her head back so her lips were exposed, open, and parted with readiness.

He dipped his head, and she closed her eyes, her body singing with desire for him.

His lips teased hers before moving to the pulse in her throat and tasting her there.

She gasped and abandoned her apronful of cherries.

"I love you," he whispered.

"You do?" Hope sprang anew in her heart.

"I've just been an idiot and too proud to let myself admit it." His declaration reflected in the clear blue of his eyes. "I can't delude myself any longer. I have to confess. I'm madly and passionately in love with my wife."

She traced the scar on his cheek, savoring the thrill of his words.

"I don't expect you to return my love. I know I need to earn it still—"

She moved her fingers to his lips and silenced him. "Oh, Eli. I think I fell in love with you that first day when you walked into my church and put me in my place."

He chuckled. "Well, if putting you in your place is what did it, I'll have to make sure I humble you more often."

"You'd better not." She smiled. "Once a lady, always a lady."

"Only now you're *my* lady."

"I'll always be yours."

His fingers combed her hair back. "Does this mean you've forgiven me?"

"Why don't I show you my answer?" She stood on her toes until her lips touched his. With the softness of a flower petal, she caressed him.

His breath caught.

She tilted her head back and smiled.

"I guess that means yes." His voice was low, and the charge in it sparked her nerves in anticipation.

"So what about our business arrangement?"

He cocked one of his brows. "And just what are you asking, Mrs. Ernest?"

She flushed. "I was thinking maybe we don't need to be business partners anymore."

He gave her a slow grin and his eyes sparkled. "Why don't I show you *my* answer?"

His lips fell upon hers, and he claimed them with a strength that left her breathless.

She'd traveled thousands of miles away from everything she'd ever known and loved. But she was finally home—would always be home—in his arms.

Chapter
27

*K*eep your eyes closed," Eli murmured against Priscilla's ear.

"I thought you said we were almost there." She snuggled against him on his horse, where she had gladly ridden the last several miles. A cold December wind had battered them for most of the twenty-five miles from Fort Walla Walla to Waiilatpu.

She'd been chilled through her flesh into her bones when Eli had finally insisted she ride with him the remainder of the distance to their new mission and the home he'd spent the past weeks building.

"Be patient." His voice hinted at excitement—the same excitement that was bubbling in her now that they were so close.

"Maybe you're riding around in circles just so you can have a few more minutes with me on your lap."

"And a few more kisses." His warm breath in her ear sent a shiver of delight to the deepest place in her belly.

His lips moved to the tender spot beneath her ear, and his warm kiss stirred an ache for more of him.

She'd had so little time with him recently. First, they'd traveled to Fort Vancouver to buy supplies. After that, she'd lived at Fort Walla Walla while he'd traveled ahead with two Hawaiian laborers he'd hired to help him build the mission.

Eli and Henry couldn't agree on the location of the mission, so after numerous discussions, the two men had decided to part ways. Henry had settled upon a location a hundred miles east of them. Eli had helped deliver Mabel's baby girl. Then the dear woman had ridden away with Henry, carrying her newborn baby in a sling. And she'd gone, knowing they would have to live in an Indian lodge until their log cabin was completed.

Priscilla's admiration of her friend had only grown.

"Have I told you how much I love you?" Eli whispered.

Priscilla leaned her head back and opened her eyes to meet his. "And have I told you how much I love you?"

He captured her lips in a sweet kiss that held the promise of many more to come.

"Look over there." He nodded his head.

She sat forward and surveyed the wide open plain. The Walla Walla River cut through the land, and there, situated close to the river, stood a lean-to and a small house with a newly built chimney. The smoke rising from it beckoned them.

In the distance, the formidable Blue Mountains stood along the horizon, covered with snow and completely impassable now.

Against the pink-tinted twilight sky, the beauty of the valley took her breath away. "It's absolutely perfect, Eli."

"We'll have almost three hundred acres." He pointed to the land surrounding the mission. "I'll be able to enclose most of it with a fence—eventually."

"Then we'll have plenty of space and water for the cattle and the crops."

"And room to add on to the mission."

"Perhaps we could plant peach and apple trees," she suggested.

"Plum and pear too."

Sweet contentment wafted through her. She was with Eli, and anything was possible.

"We aren't far from the winter dwelling of the natives." Eli pointed upriver, and she could distinguish several lodges.

"Many of the men have come to help with the building—as best they are able." Next to the mission were the two tents Eli and his laborers had used while they built the house.

"We've laid the floor, but we don't have windows or a door yet."

Blankets hung in the frames. "Then you shall have to keep me warm at night until we are able to get them."

He grinned. "I'll be keeping you warm at night even after we get them."

Heat infused the cold skin of her cheeks.

He urged the horse forward, and the young men he'd hired to pack supplies from Fort Walla Walla followed them down the hill until they reined their mounts before the cabin.

"I must warn you," he said, a crinkle of worry forming in his brow, "it won't be fancy. We won't have furnishings—no bed-stead, no chairs or table. I haven't had time to make them yet."

"I've made do all these months without them," she reassured him. "And I'll be fine now too."

His gaze met hers, and the intensity in his depths made her shiver with pleasure. "I was so wrong about you, Priscilla. You've proven to be one of the strongest women I've ever met. You've endured this journey like a heroine."

His words wrapped around her heart. She had failed more times than she could count, had wanted to give up, had lost hope. But through it all, God had given her the strength she'd needed to survive.

The blanket over the door lifted, and Richard stepped outside.

"Richard!" She smiled at the young man.

His eyes lit, and he strode toward the horse. "Mrs. Doc." He reached for her and helped her to the ground.

"I've missed you." She pulled him into a fierce hug and lifted her eyes to heaven in thanksgiving. On one of his trips back to Fort Walla Walla, Eli had told her that Richard had finally shown up on the new mission site. While his parents had mourned John's death, they hadn't blamed Richard or Eli for the boy's death. And with the blessing of his parents, Richard had made peace with Eli. He'd even asked Eli to teach him about the white man's medicine.

"Do you like house?" Richard asked, breaking away from her in his excitement. "I help Doc with all the work."

"It's lovely. I couldn't have asked for a better home." And truly she couldn't imagine anything finer than this home that had been crafted with such love by her husband and the natives.

"How is *everything*?" Eli asked, lifting his brow at the boy.

Richard grinned. "*Everything* is still here and waiting."

"Then let's get Mrs. Doc inside and get her warmed up." Eli jumped from his saddle.

Richard took her by the arm. "Come."

Even though the cabin wouldn't have furnishings, they'd purchased many other supplies during their trip down the Columbia River to the British-owned Fort Vancouver. Since the fort was stocked with goods from ships that came from as far away as

London, they were able to acquire products of the best quality—milk pails, coffeepots and teapots, candlesticks and molds, farming utensils, and other necessities.

She'd been disappointed in the lack of books and school supplies. But she'd posted a letter home, asking for their supporters to send teaching supplies, religious books, papers, and the like by sea. She'd even made a special request for her science books.

In the meantime, she was grateful for all the comforts they were able to acquire, more than she had expected in the strange land.

Richard tugged her to the door. He pushed aside the blanket—one of the India rubbers they'd used on their overland trip.

"Here." He helped her through the doorframe.

She glanced around the large room, not yet partitioned into the smaller rooms that would form bedrooms, a pantry, and a kitchen. A fire blazed in the fireplace, and the warmth was a welcoming embrace.

On the floor in front of the fire sat an Indian woman with a long braid that touched the newly laid floorboards. At the sound of their footsteps, she stood and turned.

There was something about her face that looked familiar. But it was the child in her arms that took Priscilla's breath away.

Could it really be? "David?" Her heart thudded in a frantic crescendo.

At the sound of her voice, David craned his neck until his big eyes found hers.

She flew across the room, and a sob drummed against her chest. "David."

The Indian woman smiled and loosened her hold.

Priscilla smoothed a hand over David's head, over his cheeks, over his arms.

He smiled and reached out a hand to her.

The woman said something in her native tongue, something soft and obviously encouraging. She nodded and held David out.

Priscilla's mind couldn't begin to comprehend what was happening, but she was helpless to do anything other than what her heart demanded. She took the boy into her arms and held him against her chest—knowing she could never let him go again.

She kissed his hair, letting its familiar silkiness brush her lips. "Oh, my baby," she whispered. Her throat squeezed with all of the weeks of missing him and worrying about whether he was being cared for and loved.

And now he was here.

She pulled back and rubbed his cheek. He was thinner and his clothes were dirty, but he was alive, and his eyes were as bright as she remembered.

His fingers groped for the cameo at her throat and her bonnet strings. Then his eyes regarded hers for a long moment. "Ma-ma."

Tears welled in her eyes. "Yes. Mama."

Eli slipped his arm around her waist. "I think he remembers you."

"Oh, Eli, where—how—" She couldn't get the words past the tightness of her throat.

"Apparently Squire had a change of heart. Either that or he realized what a great responsibility he'd taken on in caring for a baby."

"But how did David get here?"

He nodded at the Indian woman—the same woman who had taken the baby from her that awful day at the Rendezvous. "She traveled with the Nez Perce group that had been at the Rendezvous. They arrived about a week ago, after they finished their hunting."

The woman smiled at Priscilla with kind eyes.

Her return smile was wobbly. How could she have ever been so proud as to think of the natives as savages?

"Thank you," she whispered.

The woman nodded.

David tugged on the cameo again.

And suddenly Priscilla knew what she had to do.

With one hand, she fumbled at the pin that held the cameo in place. She unhooked it and slipped it off her collar.

She looked at the delicate pattern, kissed it, and then held it out to the Indian woman. It was time to say good-bye to her past, to forge ahead with her new life, and to fully embrace a different kind of plan for having children. Maybe she would always feel the sting of having a barren womb. But that didn't mean she couldn't fill her heart and home with the children that God brought into her life.

"I want you to have this—a thank-you for taking such good care of my baby."

The woman hesitated.

Priscilla pushed it into her palm and closed her fingers around it.

Eli's arm tightened around her, and his lips brushed her temple.

She hugged David to her chest, overwhelmed with gratefulness. She'd given up everything to leave her home and to head into the wild unknown. But in doing so, she'd gained more than she could have ever imagined possible.

Author's Note

$\mathcal{T}$his book was inspired by the true story of Marcus and Narcissa Whitman, a young missionary couple who traveled overland to Oregon in 1836 for the purpose of starting a mission among the Nez Perce natives. Narcissa Whitman is lauded as the first white woman to cross the Continental Divide and travel to the far West (along with her traveling companion Eliza Spalding). Today, if you traveled to South Pass, Wyoming, you would find a monument that reads *Narcissa Prentiss Whitman, Eliza Hart Spalding, First White Women to Cross This Pass, July 4, 1836.*

It was my hope in this story to bring Narcissa Whitman to life. This heroic woman has often been ignored and at times even disparaged. In reality, she exuded incredible courage to attempt a trip many proclaimed foolishly dangerous. It was called an "unheard-of journey for females." Because of her willingness to brave the unknown, she led the way for the many women who would follow in her footsteps on what would later become known as the Oregon Trail.

As with any story of historical fiction, the large majority of what I've written was truly from the depths of my imagination and my creative meanderings of "what could have happened."

However, as you sift through the fiction versus fact, you may be wondering what really happened. In my research of the Whitmans, I drew from numerous biographies. While I wasn't able to stick to every historical detail in complete accuracy, most of the story outline is taken directly from Narcissa's diary.

The spiritual revivals of the early 1800s led to the early missionary movement, in which thousands of young people desired to spread the gospel to the so-called uncivilized people of the world. Many of them, like Narcissa, had the appropriate zeal, piety, and education that were considered important by the Mission Board, but the candidates were largely unprepared for the harshness of missionary life. And many more women died than survived the hardships and cultural challenges missionary life brought.

The Mission Board really did require their potential candidates to get married before going to the mission field. Marcus and Narcissa didn't know each other very well when they made the decision to get married for the purpose of starting the mission in the West. But both of them desired to go and were willing to engage in a marriage of convenience for the sake of their missionary dreams.

Henry Spalding really was an old beau of the beautiful Narcissa and had at one time proposed to her. Henry and his wife Eliza traveled with the Whitmans. There was continual tension between the couples, and when they reached Oregon Country, they did in fact settle in two different places.

I tried to follow the trail they took west as closely as possible. While I was unable to include every stop and incident of their travel for the sake of brevity, I did try to capture the essence of their journey. I included their travel first by sleigh, then steamboat, and lastly by wagon and horse. The American Fur Company steamboat left without them on two separate occasions. Marcus had to travel with the women to catch up to Henry and the wagons. They also had to chase after the Fur Company caravan, finally reaching them at one o'clock in the morning. The next day they passed the Pawnee villages.

They traveled with the caravan to the Rendezvous meeting spot at Green River and discovered that Parker had left them without any instructions except one letter. McLeod of the Hudson Bay Company led them the rest of the distance to Fort Walla Walla, although they did split into two parties before crossing the Blue Mountains.

Many of the incidents of the trip—Narcissa picking up the prickly pears, Marcus offering her the cup of milk, Marcus building the shelter out of their saddle blankets, eating the stale buffalo meat, sitting in the fleas, leaving Narcissa's trunk behind—are all historic facts and are penned in fascinating detail by Narcissa herself in her diaries.

Richard and John, the Nez Perce Indians, were real people who traveled east with Marcus from his first exploration trip. And they were a great help to the missionaries during their seven long months of traveling to Oregon Country. Because cholera was often a significant problem for those who traveled west, I added it to this story, along with John's death.

Was Narcissa infertile? Probably to a degree, but not to the extent to which I've portrayed. We do know that she went on to have one daughter, Alice, who tragically died in a drowning accident outside their mission home when she was only two years old. Narcissa never had any more children of her own. But she did open her arms and home to many orphan children, possibly one very much like David, whom I placed in her life for the purposes of this story. She adopted Indian children as well as immigrant children whose parents died in the overland journey. God filled her heart and life to overflowing with children.

Both Narcissa and Marcus were willing to give their lives for the people they'd come to love. When he said these words to Richard, "Maybe I'll die in my efforts to save your people. I'm willing to do that. To sacrifice my very life if need be," little did he know that eleven years after starting the mission, a band of disgruntled Nez Perce would murder him and Narcissa in their home.

Narcissa and Marcus's marriage may have started out as one of convenience, but in a letter to her mother Narcissa says this about Marcus: "If I had looked the world over, I could not have found one more careful and better qualified to transport a female such a distance."

Most inspiring are these words she wrote: "I have not one feeling of regret at the step which I have taken but count it a privilege to go forth in the name of my Master, cheerfully bearing the toil and privation that we expect to encounter."

May you be encouraged and inspired by her bravery to know that in whatever path you are traversing, no matter how difficult, the Master will walk alongside you, helping you each step of the way.

Acknowledgments

*W*hile the writing of a book may be a solitary endeavor, getting a book ready for publication is a team effort. There were many, many people who worked on *The Doctor's Lady*, and I am deeply grateful for each person who helped at one stage or another.

I must give special recognition to my Bethany House editors Dave Long and Sharon Asmus for their dedication to me and this story. They believed in me, went above and beyond the call of duty, and pushed me hard (sometimes painfully so) to make this story the best it could be.

I'd also like to thank my critique partner and talented historical romance novelist, Keli Gwyn. She deserves a medal of honor for thoroughly critiquing my book not once but twice (and in some places even three times). Her attention to detail and her suggestions were an enormous blessing, not to mention her faithful and loving encouragement in everything I do.

Last but not least, I'd like to thank my husband. Without his daily support and help, I would not be able to accomplish nearly as much as I do. He's willing to pitch in and do *anything* that needs to be done so that I have time to fulfill my dream of writing amidst the very busy life of mothering and homeschooling our five children.

Thank you, Readers, for taking the time to join me in this adventure west with Priscilla and Eli. I would love to hear from you! In fact, hearing from readers is one of the best things about being an author. Here are several ways you can connect with me:

Mail: Jody Hedlund
P.O. Box 1230
Midland, MI 48641

Website: JodyHedlund.com
Email: *jodyhedlund@jodyhedlund.com*
Facebook: *http://www.facebook.com/AuthorJodyHedlund*
Twitter: @JodyHedlund

JODY HEDLUND is a historical romance novelist and author of the bestselling book *The Preacher's Bride*, which won the 2011 Award of Excellence from Colorado Romance Writers. She received a bachelor's degree from Taylor University and a master's from the University of Wisconsin, both in social work. Currently she makes her home in Michigan with her husband and five busy children.